Woman Soldier

by

Linda Penninga

1663 Liberty Drive, Suite 200
Bloomington, Indiana 47403
(800) 839-8640
www.AuthorHouse.com

First published by AuthorHouse 11/22/05

ISBN: 1-4208-8814-5 (sc)

Printed in the United States of America
Bloomington, Indiana

This book is printed on acid-free paper.

CHAPTER ONE
—Summer 1860

The vast plantation lane stretched out to the main road for more than half a mile, but Colleen strained to see down its length. Guests were always a welcome diversion, but more so when the guest was the handsome young man, Steven Covington.

Finally the carriage with its four regal horses was visible coming down the wide drive to the vast three storied, pillared mansion of the McBride main house.

Once the darkie servant had stopped the carriage, Steven glanced over at Colleen as he helped his mother and father from the open carriage.

His mother was a slight woman, frail with jet-black hair, making her pale skin seem even whiter beneath its darkness. His father was just the opposite, burly, tall with a flashing smile beneath a large bushy mustache.

Steven patiently waited while their Negro slave Renny, led the horses away to the stables behind the house before he moved to stand next to Colleen and give her a dazzling smile.

Colleen felt lightheaded and her heart was pounding madly. She felt her face flush and she wondered if it was noticeable to Steven, but then she always felt that way when she was around him. She thought him the most handsome man she had ever seen, tall, with dark hair like his mothers. He had a habit of running his fingers through it when he was nervous. He had the most piercing blue eyes that could dazzle her with a glance. His physique was solid and muscular, he was tall like his father, nineteen and the son of her parents' friends, but best of all, he was in love with her.

She had taken great care in preparing herself for Steven's visit today. She had washed and lavished her skin with perfumed oil. Her personal servant, Dora, had brushed and curled her waist length, auburn hair, putting the sides up at the crown of her head with beautiful combs, while allowing the rest to cascade down her back. Steven had once said he liked her hair down. Then she had put on her tightest corset to make her waist look as thin as possible, followed by layers of petticoats and of course her pantaloons underneath. The dress she chose was a pale green with white ribbons and lace at the sleeves and neckline. Her father always said green made her amber eyes stand out even more. Her ruddy skin stood out in contrast to the white lace at her neck. Her mother would berate her for going out in the sun without a parasol, but she didn't care. She always thought the pasty white belles looked rather sickly anyway.

Her mother hadn't allowed her to make up her face, but she pinched her cheeks until they glowed. Lastly, she put on pair of white, soft kid leather shoes on her feet. Now at least she felt prepared to greet Steven.

Of course, their relationship hadn't started out with mutual attraction. Colleen and Steven's parents had been friends for many years, their plantations being adjacent to each other and not far from Savannah in Georgia. Anna Bell Covington first gave birth to Steven and not long afterward, Mary McBride gave birth to her first son Gerritt, Colleen's brother and two years later Colleen made her appearance. Anna Bell however, was never able to have more children and Steven became their pride and joy. They lavished every extravagance they could afford on him. He had gone to the best schools, visited Europe several times and had all the material possessions he desired.

Now in the summer of 1860 when Steven was nineteen and she seventeen, she was happier than she had ever been in her entire life. She was in love, in love with Steven Covington.

Colleen's parents James and Mary had come out on the veranda to greet their guests. Colleen thought her mother looked beautiful as usual in her long floral dress with the long bow draped down the back. Her blonde hair hung down her back in ringlets, pulled demurely from her face with just a hint of ringlets at her temples. She was only forty years old and had maintained her tiny waist after the birth of her children. She knew her father was proud of her mother and as much in love with her as he had been when they were first married. Colleen could tell by the way he encircled her waist and looked into her eyes with complete adoration. She imagined they must have some wonderful private secrets and hoped that someday she and Steven might share those intimate times.

She knew her mother was just as adoring of him, also. She had met him at a Cotillion in Atlanta, dancing the night away and falling helplessly in love with the tall, auburn haired man with the green eyes and dazzling smile.

They all adjourned into the house, the men going into the library to talk politics and the women to the parlor to discuss who would wear what to the next ball, who was seeing whom and problems with servants.

Colleen looked longingly after Steven as his back disappeared into the mahogany lined library. He looked back at her also and shrugged his shoulders as if to say, what am I to do?

She followed her mother and Anna Bell into the parlor. Why couldn't she join the men in talking politics? Granted, she didn't know much about it, especially now that the talk all seemed to be about secession and war. She didn't know what the ruckus was about anyway. Would Georgia and some the other southern states leave the Union? She had heard her father say it was over slavery. Why would they go to war over slaves? They were only part of the system, the workers who maintained their plantation. She had heard of abuses of slaves, but she felt that must be rare. They owned over a hundred and so did the Covingtons and neither had made a practice of abusing their slaves .It was beyond her and she decided to think only of Steven.

Rose, one of the house servants knocked quietly and brought them tea and scones, her starched skirts rustling as she walked. She was young, perhaps only seventeen or eighteen and the daughter of their cook. She had been born here and helped her mother in the house since a child.

Colleen sipped her tea and tried to think of a way she could gracefully excuse herself. For what seemed an hour, she listened to her mother and Anna Bell talk of the new dresses and hats that would be coming in from Paris. Across her mother's lap lay her tatting, her fingers working nimbly at the tiny stitches. She watched her mother's hands almost hypnotically. Her long slender fingers worked deftly with the tatting hook, creating the beautiful lace doilies that graced their furniture and tables.

"Colleen, dear" she heard her mother say, "Mrs. Covington was speaking to you."

"I'm sorry, ma'am, you were saying?" Colleen said looking up at their guest.

"I asked you, dear, what colors you prefer for the gown you will wear to the Christmas Ball?"

"Oh, green is always nice, it goes well with my eyes. Papa says I look good in green but then, I have a lot of it." She rose from her chair and went to the window over looking the orchards to the west of the house. "But, then, perhaps rose would be nice, too." Her voice drifted off as she watched a group of slaves cutting the weeds from around the trees.

Anna Bell gave a knowing smile to Colleen's mother. "It's alright dear, why don't you run along. I think your mother and I will manage on our own."

"What was that?" Colleen asked turning back to the ladies.

"We said you could run along now," her mother answered.

Her smile flashed a little too quickly, but she recovered politely and excused herself from the room. She walked across the expansive hallway with its marble floor, passing in front of the wide, red carpeted stairway to the library on the other side. She pressed her ear to the door to see if she could hear Steven's voice.

Instead, she heard Mr. Covington's loud booming voice speaking out about secession, something about how the south had had enough of those aristocratic snobs from the north trying to tell them what they should do with their darkies.

She heard the clinking of glasses as they poured another glass of their port. Then her father's softer voice saying how secession could hurt the south, how they had all fought together in the Revolution against the British.

It was then Rose appeared around the corner of the banister causing Colleen to jump at her appearance. "Miss Colleen?" she said quietly. "Mr. Steven says to tell youse he gwine to meet youse out by the gazebo."

"Thank-you, Rose," she whispered back lifting her skirts and hurrying out the front door. She ran across the wide front yard towards the willow trees that lined the banks of the Canoochee River. Nestled among the long flowing fronds of the trees, stood the gazebo. It was an open Victorian structure painted white to match the big house.

She arrived under the cool shade panting from her run. She clung to one of the support posts, searching the area for any glimpse of Steven. The river flowed lazily along its banks; the willows dipping their long branches like thirsty tongues into its cool depths. Sunlight filtered and danced on the long grasses at the river's edge. Several swans floated down the current, stretching their long necks into the water. On the other side of the river were the vast cotton fields and wooden cabins of their field darkies. The fields and cabins were accessible by an arched wooden bridge across a narrow portion of the river. Colleen could see many of the darkies toiling in the field while others worked around the cabins. She could hear many of them singing as they worked, as was their habit. Small children played games while their mothers tended gardens and worked near the barns. Everything seemed so peaceful, so tranquil. She could picture her life as being no different as it was now.

She was so engrossed in watching the workers, her back to the house that she did not see Steven approach. When he spoke her name she was so startled she turned suddenly, her face glowing crimson.

Steven smiled at her embarrassment. She was so beautiful he could barely resist taking her into his arms then and there. Her auburn hair was pulled back from her face with ornate hand carved combs and then hung to her waist in the back. The green dress she wore accentuated her amber eyes with the incredibly long lashes fanning out over her creamy complexion. His eyes drifted down to her ample bosom showing above the dress and narrowing down to her trim waist.

The top of her head only came to his shoulder and she had to tilt her head to look into his eyes. "Rose told me you would meet me here," she said breathlessly. "I ran all the way." She smiled and then he could resist no longer. He grasped her arms and when she turned her face to his, he placed his mouth on hers, tenderly, sensuously. When their lips parted Colleen rested her head on his shoulder and inhaled deeply. She loved the smell of him, the musky masculine aroma filling her with the scent of him.

Steven's kisses always made her feel tingly and weak. She could feel his hands on her back, trembling and knew he felt the same.

He began to kiss her again, but she stopped him. "Steven, we mustn't. We're alone."

"That's the way I prefer it," he said smiling at her.

"You know what I mean," she said moving away from him. "Our mothers would be scandalized if they knew we were out here kissing unchaperoned."

"We wouldn't be kissing if we had a chaperone," he told her, moving to stand behind her. He began to stroke her hair and his desire for her intensified.

"My beautiful Colleen," he whispered. "Do you know how much I love you?"

She turned to face him again, lifting her eyes to look boldly into his. "As much as I love you, Steven Covington." And this time she kissed him, moving her mouth sensuously, passionately on his.

This time it was he who pulled away. "My god girl, do you know what you're doing to me? That kind of thing could drive a man crazy!"

She smiled at him, at the power she had to invoke such feelings in him, this tall muscular man who trembled and grew weak with her kisses.

He caressed her cheek with the back of his hand. "When can we be married, my darling Colleen? When will you at last consent to be Mrs. Steven Covington?"

"As soon as you properly ask my father for my hand. You know I would adore to be your wife."

"I have tried my darling, and he only puts me off, telling me you are too young."

A frown crossed her face. "I'm no younger than Mama was when he took her for a bride. It's not fair!" she pouted.

Steven lifted her chin to look into her eyes. "It may not be what we'd prefer right now, but just know this my Colleen, we will be together. We were meant to be. You are my heart and come hell or high water, you will be my bride." He made this last statement with such conviction and determination; she knew it would be true.

They sat together on the bench encircling the interior of the gazebo and Steven took her hand in his own, caressing her fingers, feeling the softness of her skin.

"You know they're talkin' war, Colleen," Steven said softly.

She had no response and so sat silently, her head down. She had no notions of what war might mean. She knew only what she had heard from the adults and even then she hadn't really paid close attention. She felt it didn't involve her. It seemed to be all about slavery and how those Yankee northerners wanted to take them away. Why, she didn't know. She wondered how the Yankees thought they could possibly manage without them. Who would tend the grounds and care for their animals? Who would cook their food and do the laundry. It was preposterous.

"What does that mean?" she asked Steven.

"It means I might have to go fight," he said quietly, "if there is a war."

Colleen was startled at his words and stood up. "Fight! No! That can't be so!"

"I'm afraid it is, my darling," Steven replied rising to stand beside her. "If it comes to war, I will go."

"But you could be killed," she interrupted. Thoughts of bloodshed, missing body parts and death filled her mind.

"In war there's always that chance, but I must do what I must do to protect our rights."

"To keep our slaves?" she asked. "Is that all this means?" She had heard the resolve that had come into his voice and the passion that showed on his face was unmistakable.

"That's part of it, but there's so much more involved. If the northern states had their way, they would completely change our way of life. Things are different in the north. They live a different lifestyle. They don't rely on the slaves for their livelihood. Without them, our entire economy would change.

Things are more relaxed in the south, more genteel. Northerners are a crude bunch and always in a hurry. They don't appreciate the finer things of life.

You know the south is decidin' whether or not we should secede from the Union, have our own government, to be able to live the life we choose, without the damn officials in Washington tellin' us what we can or can't do."

Just then they heard the voice of Colleen's father James, calling them to come back to the house for dinner. They walked slowly, a cloud now hovering over their exuberance for each other and that cloud was war.

Joining them for dinner was Colleen's older brother Gerritt, a tall rapscallion who loved to tease and always seemed to be able to lighten any dark mood. Just the presence of her tall sandy haired brother caused Colleen to smile. She adored him as he did her.

They entered the large formal dining room and noticed the long table was elegant and formally set, as it always was when they had guests. The brightly colored walls were covered with expensive paintings, the gold frames decorated with damask tassels. On the highly polished wood floors were coverings of imported oriental rugs. A large, ornately carved sideboard covered the entirety of one wall and at the moment contained steaming dishes of food.

Against the adjoining wall was the massive fireplace used to heat the room in cold weather. On each side were tall windows flooding the room with orange light.

The elaborate table with its high backed chairs was covered with a hand stitched lace tablecloth and on it was laid out some of their best china from England with goblets from Italy and silver from France.

Three of the house slaves were standing quietly near the sideboard waiting to serve them. As they took their seats, Carlton the butler, wearing a starched white shirt and black suit, began pouring the delicate wine from their vast cellars, the wine being obtained from all over the world.

The kitchen maids Bess and Naomi began ladling and serving the soup, the first course of the evening. After that came the roast lamb with basil and small red potatoes sliced and sautéed in butter. There were green beans and baby carrots, fresh breads and creamy butter.

The men apparently were not willing to give up their earlier conversations from the library and continued over dinner, something they usually did not do, declaring things of politics to be strictly for men's ears. But things being what they were, felt it necessary to get off their chests some of the concerns they were now facing.

"The problem with Washington," Clifford was saying, "is that the legislature could very well pass a stiff high tariff law. If that happens, we shall surely be ruined." He pushed another fork full of lamb into his mouth, chewed a moment and then went on, gesturing with his now empty fork.

"Why those northern abolitionist are already disruptin' the thinkin' of people against those of us who own slaves. That…that William Garrison, denouncing all of us as sinners. What kind of rubbish is that?"

"'Course in my opinion, it was the Fugitive Slave Act that aroused more antislave sentiment in the north than anything else," James replied. "Imagine, encouragin' slaves to run north and then when those that own them go after them, not being able to recover their property."

"They cause their own troubles in these matters." Clifford continued. "If it hadn't been for that Senator Douglas and his Kansas Nebraska Act, there wouldn't have been the situation with John Brown last year in '59.

"The trouble with the John Brown situation," James said, "was that when he seized the Federal arsenal at Harper's Ferry and even though Robert Lee snuffed out his conspiracy and he was hanged, he started the Yankee sympathizers into beginnin' this servile insurrection. Now evera'one's havin' troubles with their darkies getting' uppity. No one knows whether or not they might turn on you."

Clifford wiped the rest of his plate with a last bite of bread and chewed his mouthful before speaking. "I think the only solution is succession," he said emphatically. "It's really goin' come down to that what with this bein' an election year. If Lincoln wins the election, you can be sure the southern states won't tolerate it and they'll vote to secede and we'll have our own union.

James rose from his chair with a nod to the ladies. "I think you could be right about that, Cliff," he said. "But why don't we retire to the library? I think we are borin' our ladies with all this talk of politics."

Mary rolled her eyes at Anna Bell as if to agree with James. None of the rest of them had spoken a word. She really was getting weary of all this talk of secession and war.

"Come, ladies, let's go to the parlor for our tea," she said as she waved her hand at Bess and Naomi to begin clearing the table.

"Gerritt sweetheart, would you escort us to the parlor?" she asked her son.

He smiled and went to her, hooking her hand in the crook of his arm. "I'd be delighted to, Mother," he told her.

"You sure you wouldn't rather be with the men in the library?" she said looking up at him.

"Oh no, that talk has me bored as well. Besides, I'd like to take Steven out to the stables and show him my new roan stallion," Gerritt said inclining his head Steven's way. "Would you care to accompany me there?" he asked.

"I should very much like to see him," Steven answered. "I understand he is an impressive piece of horse flesh."

Once the ladies had been deposited in the parlor, Gerritt and Steven excused themselves to go to the stables. Colleen looked longingly after Steven. She would have rather gone with the boys than stay in the hot stuffy parlor with her mother and Mrs. Covington.

The August heat in Georgia was nearly unbearable. Even though it was now nine P.M. in the evening, the air still felt oppressive. Her undergarments were sticking to her and her stays on her corset were poking her mercilessly in the ribs.

But as polite society dictated, she sat down with the ladies and sipped her lemonade that had been handed to her by Rose. Two small boy child slaves held large ornate fans and waved them back and forth over them to try and move about some of the air in the room, but mostly, it was for naught. She could still feel the small trickle of perspiration running down her back like small ants tickling her spine. The large floor to ceiling windows at the front of the house were open wide to bring in any errant breeze that might happen to filter by.

"I called on Mrs. Spencer the other day," Anna Bell was saying.

"Is she still planning on helping with our ball in December?" Mary asked.

"Oh yes, but you know how she does like to complain. Here it is still four months away and she doesn't know how she's going to accomplish her share of the tasks," Anna Bell said setting her delicate crystal glass on the French table near her chair, "which of course, isn't nearly as complicated as what you and I have to tend with."

"Not to mention all the other daily tasks we attend to, overseeing the food buying, meal planning, harvesting the garden, making the candles and soap, dairy products, making sure the preserves are done properly, cleaning the house, rugs, linens, clothing.... Why, it wears me out just talking about it." Mary said fanning herself as if the effort of her long list had raised her temperature considerably.

Colleen knew her mother held great responsibility in overseeing the great many tasks of the plantation, but she also knew the slaves themselves performed most of the chores.

"And if it weren't enough," Anna Bell said, her voice lowered as if the slaves in the room couldn't hear her, "I've been havin' trouble with some of my darkies. Some of them have gotten real uppity with all this talk of war, doing their chores poorly or not at all. Why, we had to have Mr. Jenkins our overseer, whip one of the field hands for trying to run away."

Colleen pictured the scene in her mind of their overseer Mr. Jenkins, whipping the errant slave. She had only witnessed a couple of whippings in her life, as her father did not really believe in them. He thought it to be cruel and unusual punishment. But she had witnessed them on other plantations, the Covingtons being one of them as Clifford Covington had no compunctions against it himself.

It still made her rather ill whenever she thought about it. The black man, a field hand she thought, was brought to the yard in the center of the various barns, stripped of his shirt and bound by his wrists to a pole set in the ground. Many of the other slaves were made to watch as a deterrent for further misconduct.

The overseer brought out a long whip with as many as half a dozen tails; each tipped with metal cones to invoke the maximum damage.

When he first began the lashing, the man cried out, the metal tips of the whip ripping the flesh from the man's back. Soon however, with the blood flowing freely down unto the darkie's pants, he had passed out; his head slumped between his bound arms.

Colleen had stopped watching long before the man had been rendered unconscious. The sight of it had sickened her and she had focused instead on the group of slaves who had been made to watch the lashing. Many of them were crying silently, tears flowing freely down their faces. Others tried to shield the children's eyes from the spectacle before them, while the men stood stoically, grim faced and silent.

That was the first time she had thought about the prospect of owning other human beings, that possibly these people were capable of more emotion than she had ever admitted to herself in the past. At least she was glad her father did not make a practice of whipping his slaves.

"In the last month," Anna Bell continued, "I've had six of our darkies down sick in the hospital cabin with one ailment or another. Personally, I think many of them were fakin' just to get out of work. But it still takes my time away goin' down there to nurse them."

"I know just what you mean." Mary sympathized. "I had more'n usual sick myself this month."

Colleen's mind drifted off from the ladies' conversation. Their talk of plantation responsibilities bored her and her mind wandered to Steven.

She thought of his tall frame and dark hair and blue eyes, how his lips felt on hers when he kissed her and how his body was hard and firm against hers when he held her. What was he doing right now? Was he thinking of her? Was he wishing he could be with her as she wished to be with him?

It was so difficult for her to be apart from him. When would her father give his consent for her to marry him? It wasn't as if Steven hadn't proved himself a worthy candidate for her hand. After all, he came from one of societies most prestigious families, his plantation being second only to theirs with land equaling nearly 2500 acres. The Covingtons, as well as their own, had hundreds of acres of fields in cotton, many slaves to work them, as well as the cabins to house them. Surrounding the grand antebellum house were the many added buildings, including two stables, one for the work horses and one for riding horses, a carriage house adjacent to the stables, the weaving house, a workshop, the dairy, fodder house, cotton barn, corn barn, smoke house and hospital. Not to mention the kitchen house, overseer's house, and more cabins for the house slaves. And all of this would someday be Steven's, he being the sole heir. So it wasn't that he wouldn't be able to support her in her customary manner nor was it because they didn't like Steven.

Her parents had known the Covingtons as long as she could remember, often hearing the story of how her great grandparents, the McBrides, had made the perilous journey across the ocean from Ireland, escaping war, oppression, and famine to settle here in the new world. Her great grandfather, a thrifty man, who felt land the most valuable of all assets, began buying up all he could afford. After acquiring his land holdings he began the task of building his home. The three-story structure with its massive columns and porches with ornate wrought iron railings, took three years to build. He named the plantation Shannon, after the great river in Ireland.

In the meantime he went to the docks in port Savannah and began acquiring slaves from the action block to begin working his fields. He saw the great demand for cotton and knew his rich soil near the riverbank would be fertile for cotton. He built a small log home for himself and his new bride and cabins for the slaves and went into the business of cotton. As soon as his grand home was finished, he turned the log house over to his overseer.

His investments proved extremely profitable and his holdings and wealth grew and grew, acquiring more land and more slaves as he went along.

Likewise, the story of the Covingtons was similar; Steven's grandparents having come from England, acquired the land adjacent to the McBrides. The rest was history, friendships blossomed, children were born, fortunes were made and inherited and so now today

Colleen could see herself married to no one else but Steven.

Meanwhile, Steven had followed Gerritt down to the stables behind the main house. Large oak and ash trees hung over the large corral connected to the riding stable. They could hear the darkies in their cabins talking together and preparing their evening meals. Crickets and tree frogs sang along the riverbank.

When they entered the stable the air was noticeably cooler and the faint smell of hay and manure filled their nostrils. The sounds of stomping hooves and soft nickers could be heard from the horses. A lantern light bobbed toward them in the dark and soon in the glow, Steven saw one of the McBride stable slaves Henry, holding the light for them.

"Massa Gerrittt, you gwine ridin'? he asked.

"No Henry, but I will take the lantern. I want to show Mr. Covington my new roan stallion."

"Yas suh," Henry said handing over the lantern.

"And go light the lantern on the post next to his stall," Gerritt directed.

"Yas suh, massa suh," Henry obliged as he went off to light the lantern. Henry was their head groom for the riding stable and saw to it the horses were well cared for and the stables clean. If any one of them wanted to go riding, Henry saw to it the particular horse was saddled and ready.

Once the stall lantern was lit, the two men proceeded down the corridor of the stable, the boards under their feet creaking as they moved along its length. As soon as they reached the stall the large head of the roan colored stallion poked over the half door.

Gerritt held the lantern high so that Steven might see the beautiful animal. He stroked his head and muzzle and the creature gave appreciative sounds of pleasure.

"He's a beauty alright," Steven told him raising his hand to stroke the animal's head as well. "Have you named him yet?"

"Not yet," Gerritt told him. "I rather wanted to see what kind of spirit he had before namin' him. I think he'll be strong as well as in body. In that case he'll need a strong name."

"Have you run him?" Steven asked as he peered into the stall at the large roan. He was at least seventeen hands high with muscular hindquarters and a broad chest. His legs showed the strength of a powerful runner.

"I had him out yesterday," Gerritt answered. "He was fast as the wind. I'll not doubt he could beat any horse in the county."

Steven smiled. "He'd have to go some to beat my Travis," he said speaking of his large black stallion.

"Would you like to wager a bet on that?" Gerritt countered.

"I'll take that bet," Steven said looking the horse over once more. "You name the time and place."

Gerritt nodded his affirmation. "As soon as he's settled," he told Steven. He closed the lower door and went to a bin at the other side of the stable to get some oats for his roan. After he had filled the small trough inside the stall, he leaned against the door and fidgeted with the bridle hanging from the post next to the door.

"So what'll you do if war comes, Steven?" he asked finally.

"Why, I'll go fight, of course," he answered without hesitation. "We need to do something to protect our rights. If the north had their way, we would lose all our slaves, our plantations, our way of life and then where would we be?"

"If we go to war, we might lose them anyhow" Gerritt said quietly still fingering the bridle. "Already the talk is of abolishing slavery altogether. There are prohibitions and British and American slave squadrons who patrol the Atlantic stoppin' the slave ships from crossin' the ocean." He knew Steven's policies on the matter differed from his own, but he wanted to try and make Steven see another side to it.

"I don't see it that way at all," Steven said a little agitated. "If we fight for our rights, for our freedom to live our lives the way we see fit, even if it means creating our own union, then we gain the goals we have striven to attain. The slave trade will have to go on."

"And I believe secession is perfect madness and if it leads to war, it will lead to emancipation for the slaves." Gerritt let drop the bridle and moved closer to Steven. He could see his face furrowed from his anger in the light of the lantern. "Think of where the balance of power lies," he continued. "Most of the manufacturing is in the north, they have the greater numbers….."

"The Yankees are just a bunch of mudsills and ignorant immigrants ruled by money mad men who'll not fight a war to free a bunch of darkies," Steven interrupted. His voice had risen and was now clearly agitated at his friend's Unionist talk.

"We have the agriculture, we are rich with our cotton and our people are loyal to the cause. These issues are the same as our forefathers fought for in the Revolution, liberty and freedom against this conspiratorial and tyrannical government."

"That's all well and good," Gerritt said blowing out the stall lantern and beginning to walk towards the stable door, "but even if the north does not free the slaves, there may be insurrection by the slaves themselves. Your father has said another one of your darkies tried to run away just the other day. War won't just endanger all of us losing our slaves, but all of our property and prosperity as well. I am just afraid if it comes to that we shall see the Yankees treading over our cotton fields, freeing our slaves and striking us to the dust." Gerritt handed the lantern he carried to Henry who had appeared at the stable entrance.

They continued on to the house in silence for a bit before Steven spoke again. "It just grieves me to think you have these opinions about our Southern states and their abilities to protect their rights. I truly believe the Northerners may never fight and even if they do, Southern men will make short work of those Yankees."

Gerritt argued with him no further. He apparently carried many of the same opinions of his father and nothing would do to sway his outlook.

When they arrived back at the house, the Covingtons were preparing to leave. Renny had brought their carriage around to the front of the house.

When Colleen saw Steven she could tell he was upset by something and distracted. He was not paying her the attention he usually did and his warm smile for her was absent. What had Gerritt done to upset him, she wondered. She shot daggerous looks her brother's way, but he merely shrugged his shoulders.

As the Covingtons were all saying their good-byes, she knew she would not be spending anymore time this evening with Steven. She was furious with Gerritt for keeping him so long at the stables and for apparently invoking his displeasure.

Steven took her hand and led her out onto the veranda where he touched her face and gave her a discreet kiss on the cheek. He dared not do more with the adults looking on. Then he said good-bye and he was gone.

Colleen had desperately wanted to be held in his strong arms, to feel his body next to hers and to taste his sensuous kisses. And because she had felt cheated of those, she felt angry and frustrated, most of which was directed at her brother, Gerritt. For it was he, she reasoned who had kept him from her. Yes, even denying her the pleasure of his company.

When the carriage had reached the end of the lane, they all went back into the house and closed the door. Carlton, Bess and Rose were closing up the house for the night, shutting drapes and snuffing candles.

"The bedchambers is ready, Massa," Bess told James.

"Thank-you, Bess," he said as he and Mary climbed the wide, curving staircase to the second floor.

Colleen and Gerritt remained behind in the dim foyer. "Well, sist'a," Gerritt said in his best drawl. "It appe'ars ta me, that you have a bee in your bonnet. You care to tell me what it's all about?"

"You know what it's about," she hissed quietly. "You kept Steven down at the stables so long, I barely got to see him!"

"Well, can I help it if the man has an eye for good horseflesh? Then he just got to talkin' politics. You know how it is."

"No, I don't know how it is. You know he's my beau and he came here to see me!" She was so angry and frustrated she was nearly crying. "I am so sick to death of all this talk of secession and Yankees and war," she continued encouraged by his silence. "Can you men talk of nothin' else?"

Gerrit went to her and put his arm around her shoulders. "I know dear, it is difficult to listen to and we do seem to go on incessantly, but we certainly are in the midst of difficult times. I only hope you can be patient with all of us boors and I promise you, the next time Steven comes to call, you can have him all to yourself."

"Oh alright," she said demurely, "but you'd best not let it happen again."

Bess appeared at their side with a candle for them to carry to their rooms and they ascended the stairway together, Gerritt's arm still around her shoulder.

Carlton was lowering the massive chandelier in the foyer to snuff out the candles, throwing the house into darkness.

At the top of the stairs there was a large open area that faced the front of the house. Large French doors opened out unto the second story balcony with its white wrought iron railings. Behind this and down the entire length of the house were bedrooms along each side of a wide hallway. The pale blue walls were furnished with exquisite oil paintings rendered by a famous artist in France. The polished floors had long runners of floral tapestry rugs. Sconces along the walls lit their way. At the furthest end of the house was another staircase leading to the third floor. The third floor bedrooms were nurseries and playroom where Colleen and Gerritt resided when they were small. A black nursemaid stayed in their room with them and tended to their needs whenever they were warranted. Now that they were older and had bedrooms on the second floor, the nurseries went unused, although many of their childhood clothing and possessions were still packed away in trunks up there.

There was also a down staircase that would afford access to the back pantry area of the house. Many a time Colleen and Gerritt had sneaked down those stairs for a glass of warm buttermilk from cook.

Colleen retreated into her room where Dora was waiting to prepare her for bed. Several lamps were lit on each side of the large four poster bed and Colleen could see the covers had been drawn back. Along one wall was her massive armoire where her many dresses were kept. Next to it, was the large dressing table with equally large mirror with its satin covered bench. On the inside wall was the large fireplace which was kept burning in the winter months. The opposite wall was covered with large windows, which were open to the night air. White lace curtains fluttered in the breeze.

She turned to allow Dora to unfasten the small buttons at the back of her dress. Once this was accomplished, she let it fall to the floor as well as the petticoats underneath. Dora then unfastened the stays on her corset and removed it. Colleen emitted an audible sigh and went to sit at her dressing table, clad only in her bloomers and chemise.

Dora began taking the combs and pins out of her hair and brushing it until it shone. "You'se sad tonight, Miss Colleen?" Dora ventured to ask. She was Colleen's personal maid and had also been with her as an infant, acting at that time as her nanny, being only eighteen herself. She had slept on a pallet at the foot of her crib, had fed her, changed her, bathed her and clothed her. She had played games with her as a toddler and taken her to the slave cabins to play with the darkie children there. Dora was like a second mother to her.

"Oh, I'm just put out some at Gerritt," she said answering her question. "He took up way too much of Steven's time and I didn't get to spend much time with him myself."

"You'se get to spend lots o' time together when you'se gets married," Dora tried to reassure her.

"If that ever happens," Colleen said making a face in the mirror. "Papa keeps draggin' his feet, we'll neve'a get married." Having finished brushing her hair, Dora helped her off with her pantaloons and chemise and into her nightgown.

Colleen slipped under the cool sheets beneath the folds of netting surrounding the bed.

Dora blew out the lamps, taking a candle with her as she went out the door. "Good-night, Miss Colleen," she said quietly as she turned to go.

"Good-night, Dora," she yawned in response. It wasn't long before she was sound asleep.

The following morning, Dora woke her early to help her dress. “You Mama wants you to gets ready to go to town,” she told Colleen.

“But, I don’t want to,” Colleen wailed, snuggling down further into the bed.

Dora stripped the sheet from her and began laying out her clothes for the day. “You Mama says you needs to start buyin’ new clothes fo the holidays.”

“But it’s only August,” Colleen protested. “There are still three months before the holidays.”

“Nev’a too soon, you Mama says,” Dora said pulling her feet off the bed. “They’se fabrics to order from Europe and decorations for the house, foods to order, quests lists to makes, the bigs ball to plans, not to mentions de work here. Why, they’se gardens to harvest, cannin’ to does, herbs to dry, hog butcherin’s…..”

“Alright, alright, I get the point. I can tell you’ve been listening to my mother,” Colleen said standing up. “It just seems like so much fuss when we should be planning my wedding’.”

“It’ll happens soons ‘nough,” Dora said slipping a yellow dress over her head. She steered her to the dressing table where she brushed her hair, braided it and piled it unto the top of her head, securing it with combs. “Now you’se better gets downstairs for breakfast.”

Colleen did as she was told. After breakfast the open carriage with its matching gray horses, was brought to the house by their driver Matthew. Mary was helped into the buggy with Colleen following.

Gerritt stood on the steps of the wide porch to see them off. “Are you sure you don’t want me to go along with you, Mama?" he asked. "I don't like the idea of you ladies going into Savannah alone."

"We have Matthew to watch over us," Mary told him reassuredly, referring to the large, burly driver. "And besides, you would be bored silly escorting us around the dress shops and milliners."

"Well, you're probably right about that, but I do worry about you all," he told her.

Mary looked up at her tall handsome son and her heart filled with pride. She did love him so and he had always been a joy to her. He had always been considerate and kind even when he was a small child. He thought about others, putting their feelings before his own. She smiled at his concern for them.

"We'll be fine, dear," she told him. "Now run along and help your father out at the mill."

He returned her smile. "Yes mother," he replied and waved to them as they drove off.

On the ride into Savannah, Colleen and her mother discussed the Covington's visit the previous night, the upcoming holidays, and the Christmas ball they would give.

As usual, Colleen's mind wandered to Steven. She fantasized of the day they would wed. In her mind she envisioned the lawn at their plantation bedecked in bouquets of flowers, honeysuckle and roses. There would be linen covered tables laden with drink and food. Hundreds of guests would be in attendance with many of their slaves serving them. She would have the most beautiful gown that any designer could create with yards of lace from Italy and a jeweled tiara on her head. She would walk down the grand staircase on her father's arm and out to the floral decked arbor where her handsome Steven would be waiting for her.

She was jolted back to reality when her mother tugged at her sleeve. "Colleen, are you listening to me?"

"Oh yes, of course," she answered, but she didn't know if her mother had just asked her a question or not.

"So what do you think, roast beef or suckling pig for the main course?" she asked, saving Colleen from belying her inattentiveness.

"Oh I don't know mother. You know best how to decide these matters."

"Colleen, it's important for you to be involved in these kinds of decisions. Someday you'll be the mistress of a plantation and you will have many tasks to perform for your home, your husband and your children; believe me it's not an easy job."

"Yes, mother," she answered respectfully, but inside she was thinking how she would certainly like to try being the mistress of Covington plantation and Steven's wife sooner than later.

They finally arrived in the burgeoning city of Savannah. They passed large stately homes on the outskirts and along the elegant avenues of town. Slaves worked out in the massive gardens while house darkies served lemonade to their masters and mistresses on the wide verandas.

Mary yoohoo'd and waved at those she recognized. "There's Cynthia Wilkins," Mary whispered to Colleen as if the woman they just past could hear them. "You know it has been said by some that she takes whiskey in her tea, even in the morning."

Colleen turned her head away from her mother's gaze and rolled her eyes. What was it about all this gossip her mother and her friends were always sharing with each other? Who cared who was imbibing with their tea or that someone wore the wrong dress to the Cotillion? Is this all they had to do for entertainment?

They arrived on the main street with its many shops and businesses. Carriages, horses, carts and people thronged the thoroughfare. Well dressed ladies and gentlemen made their way to the theater and restaurants. Off from the main section of town, the train depot held passengers and freight waiting for the steaming, hissing locomotives to take them to other destinations. Further on were the large docks in the port of Savannah, where they traveled down the wide channel to the Atlantic, bringing out the rich resources of Georgia; tobacco, sugarcane, rice and of course, cotton. They also brought in the riches and luxuries from Europe. Nearby the docks were the sawmills, bringing in the logs to cut into boards for lumber.

Colleen and her mother went from shop to shop, ordering foodstuffs, wine from France, truffles, dates and figs, flour, sugar and spices from the West Indies.

At the clothing stores they tried on and bought dresses, hats and shoes. They ordered yards of fabric and lace that would come over the ocean to be made into gowns for the holidays

By the time they were finished, Matthew was laden down with packages.

"Come Colleen," her mother directed, "we'll get a bite to eat and then we'll head home." They took the parcel-laden carriage to one of the elite hotels downtown, where they left Matthew to watch over their purchases while they went inside to eat.

The large plush foyer was elaborate with massive pillars, a wide staircase, and gold gilt sconces. Romanesque statues stood behind broad palm plants and beautiful floral displays graced marble topped tables. Beautiful tapestry rugs covered the marbled floors while damask curtains hung on the long windows. Delicate French furniture was scattered about in groupings around the reception area and various members of the aristocracy could be seen talking together, reading or sipping tea.

Colleen and Mary walked to the rear of the front desk where the large and elegant restaurant was located. The Matre'd greeted them and seated them at the white linen covered table and handed them a menu. It wasn't long before they were dining on escargot and delicate white fish from New England.

When they finally left Savannah and started down the road for home, it had already turned to dusk, the waning sunlight throwing shadows across the road and streaking the sky with gold and red hues.

Colleen felt exhausted from her day in the big city. Her head reclined back on the seat and she was nearly dozing, when suddenly the carriage jolted and she heard the horses scream. Matthew was yelling and cracking his whip. She bolted forward to look out and see what the commotion was about. Her mother had looked out an instant before she had and heard her sharp intake of breath.

What she saw frightened her. A large muscular black man had grabbed the reins on the front of the horses' heads. He was muddy and his clothes were torn. The shirt was actually in shreds and his muscular arms could be seen straining against the terrified horses. His round face was twisted in fear and showed many cuts and bruises. His wide nostrils flared and the sweat poured off his body in rivulets.

What was he trying to do? Was he going to rob them, beat them, rape them? Her fear grew and she clung to her mother's arm.

"Mama, what's he doing? Who is he?" she cried.

But her mother did not answer and called out to Matthew. "Matthew, what's happening? Stop him! Stop that man!" She was screaming and clutching the sides of the carriage and Colleen realized she was just as terrified as she.

The large black man began yelling, calling out to Matthew.

"Brother! Helps me! Please, brother," he pleaded. "Helps me gets away!"

Matthew had stood at his seat and was pulling on the reins, trying to regain control of the horses. "Gets away from dem hosses," he told the man and flung his whip out at him.

The man flinched but did not move away or release his hold on the horses. He seemed to grow even more agitated and the horses reacted by trying to rear away from him in their traces.

From behind them they could hear the pounding of many horse hooves and suddenly, many riders in dark clothing and broad hats surrounded them. Dust swirled around them as the horses were reined in and men jumped to the ground. They grabbed the man holding the reins and threw him to the ground. Several of them began striking him with sticks and clubs.

The scene before Colleen was jumbled and confused. The man on the ground was screaming and writhing about. The others kept repeatedly hitting him about his body and head. One tall man in a long black coat drew out a whip and began striking the man on the ground with it. The horses continued to whinny and prance about with excitement. It seemed to go on and on, but probably only lasted a few minutes. Colleen glanced over at her mother and noticed she had gone very pale and she wondered if she were about to pass out.

Finally they bound the man's hands behind his back and jerked him to his feet. The sight of him caused Colleen to gasp and cover her mouth with her hand. The man's face was barely recognizable, the cheeks torn open. Blood flowed freely down his face and neck, running unto what remained of his shirt and chest. His lips were swollen and bleeding. His nose was crooked and spewing blood, obviously broken. But his eyes were dark and piercing and he looked directly at her. She had never seen such a look of hatred and loathing in her entire life and it hit her with a force she had never known before. She had never been faced with such raw emotion and none such directed at her.

He was finally led away and Colleen sank back in her seat, her heart pounding wildly in her chest. The tall man with the long coat approached her mother's side of the carriage. She could smell his rancid body odor before she could even see him. He tipped his hat to her and rested one arm on the side of the carriage. Mary drew back slightly at the familiarity of his action. His face was deeply pitted and a large scar tore through his upper lip, giving him the semblance of a permanent sneer.

"Sorry, if you all was frightened ma'am," he said to them and Colleen saw he had several teeth missing and the foul odor of his breath could be smelled from her side of the carriage. "We been huntin' this here nigger for a week now," he continued. "I'm overseer at the Oaks Plantation near Atlanta and this here nigger escaped near a week back."

"Oh, I see," Mary said in response.

"Yes'm. There's a bounty on this'ns head and I'm bound to fetch it. It took awhile, but we finally gots 'im."

"I see," Mary said again, not really knowing what her response should be.

"Anyways, we'll be on to it and I'm sorry if'n he frightened you ladies at all."

"Well, we're quite all right now, Mr……."

"Mr. Atkins," he said tipping his hat again.

"Mr. Atkins, yes," Mary said, "thank-you sir."

The man walked away and mounted his horse. Colleen looked back to see they had put the man in chains and were nearly dragging him down the road behind one of the horses. She wondered if he would even survive to get back to the Oaks Plantation. Atlanta was a long way off.

She turned back to see her mother directing Matthew to drive on. By now it had grown quite dark and they had no lantern for their carriage. Colleen could hear Matthew mumbling to himself. Her mother had her hand over her heart and she could see she was trembling.

"How perfectly awful," she told Colleen. "The whole incident was just terrible, that run away slave grabbing our horses that way and then that horrible overseer.... Oh, I just hate to think what could have happened."

Colleen said nothing, but she couldn't help but remember those eyes, the hate she had seen there. But, why would he hate her so? Was it because they had done nothing to help him?

They finally arrived at their own drive and Mary closed her eyes in relief. The tall magnolias lining the drive seemed to wave them along its length, whispering to them, calling them home. Perhaps it was her imagination, but to Colleen, even the air seemed fresher here, cooler on her sweat beaded brow.

Just before they arrived at the house, Gerritt came riding out to meet them. "Mother," he called out to them, "I was just comin' to look for you. We were worried something had happened." He rode along side them until they pulled up in front of the wide stairs. James was waiting for them, holding out a lantern. He helped his wife from the carriage and put a protective arm around her.

"My god Mary, what happened? You're trembling. You should never have been gone this long," he said to her a little angrily.

"Oh James, it was horrible, just horrible," she told him beginning to cry. "We were attacked on the road by a large black man, a run away slave."

"Did he hurt you?" James asked looking her over.

"No no, but it was awful just the same and there was that awful overseer, Mr. Atkins…." And she proceeded to tell him all the details as they walked up the staircase together.

Gerritt and Colleen stood together in the drive as Matthew led away the carriage and Gerritt's roan. "I knew I should have gone with you," he said quietly to Colleen.

"You couldn't have known," she said wearily. The long day and the incident on the road had totally exhausted her.

"Things are different now, Colleen," he told her. "With all this talk of secession and war, it has emboldened more of the slaves and more'n more of 'em are runnin' away. They can be desperate and dangerous. You should never have been alone out on that road this late. Why, when I think what could have happened….."

"Well it didn't and we're safe at home now." She began climbing the stairs to the front door where Rose waited for them with a lamp. Gerritt took her arm and helped her up.

"Gerritt," she began hesitatingly.

"Yes, punkin'," he answered using his pet name for her.

"What will they do to that man, the run away slave, I mean?"

"Don't know for sure. He was obviously valuable to his owner or they wouldn't have gone to all the trouble of goin' that far to catch him. So they won't kill him, but they may beat him to within an inch of his life. Darkies are like children, they don't have a lot of intelligence and if they disobey the rules, they need to be taught a lesson. Hopefully, they learn and don't do it again. Why do you ask?"

"Oh, no reason. I was just wonderin'. Do you think any of our slaves will ever run away?"

"Can't say," he answered "but we do treat our darkies well. You treat 'em good and they should have no reason to run. After all, what's out there for them? We take care of them here, give 'em everythin' they need. It's their home."

At his last words, Colleen saw Rose turn and as she did so, she saw an expression on her face she had never seen before. What was it, sadness, pain? It was indescribable to her and only caused to confuse her all the more.

As tired as she was, when she lay down in her bed that night, she could not sleep. She kept thinking of their experience on the road, the black man's face, the desperation, the panic. Why would someone subject themselves to the possibility of capture and then a beating? If what Gerritt said was true and the slaves were happy, then why would they run? She had never thought much about them before. They had always been here since before she was born. And if they didn't have them, how could they possibly run their plantation? How would the acres and acres of crops be planted, tended and picked? Who would take care of all their livestock and the hundreds of chores it took to run the house? After all, slavery was Biblical. She guessed if it was in the Bible, it must be okay.

She knew there were those who mistreated their slaves. Maybe they were the only ones who ran. Perhaps Gerritt was right. Perhaps theirs wouldn't run. After all, as far as she knew, her father seldom had one of their darkies whipped that way.

CHAPTER TWO

It was two weeks later, after the incident on the road, that Gerritt announced to the family one morning at breakfast, that he had organized a horse race between himself and Steven Covington.

Everyone became very excited, for a horserace was an excuse for a grand social event. Mary began planning who they would invite, what foods they would bring and what to wear. James began talking to Gerritt about what bets he would place and which ones of his contemporaries would lose theirs shirts.

But all Colleen could think about was Steven. She would finally be able to see her love again. They had not been together since that last time when he and his parents had come to dinner. He had sent her a note asking about their encounter with the run away slave. He had also expressed regret about not being able to see her and then had told her how much he missed and loved her.

Colleen had clutched the note to her heart and tears had come to her eyes. When would she and Steven ever be able to share a life together? It was nearly all she could think about. She loved him so much!

Now there was to be a race and she would be able to be with him again. Of course lots of other people would be there and he would be in the race, but surely they would be able to find a time when they could be together. She would try to think of a place where they could be alone. Somehow, somewhere she just had to see him again, touch him and kiss him.

Plans went forward for the big race. It would be held at a small lake nearby. It was a beautiful setting with blue shimmering waters surrounded by long grasses and stately cattails. Large willows graced the grounds offering shade to those who picnicked on the grass. And nearby was the large open field where many a race had been run and where Gerritt and Steven would see whose stallion would best the other.

Mary had contacted their friends and neighbors and a large crowd was expected on the day of the race. Food was prepared and picnic linens were packed.

Colleen laid out nearly all of her day dresses, trying to decide which to wear to the race, which would make her look her prettiest for Steven. As she went about trying on one after the other, Dora went behind her, picking them up off the floor.

"Oh, I just can't decide," Colleen sighed. "I can't wear the dark green in the middle of the afternoon, even though it looks wonderful with my eyes. And the blue I just wore the last time Steven saw me."

"You looks nice in whats ever you wants," Dora told her as she picked up yet another dress from the floor.

"Yes, but it has to be just right, perfect; so when Steven looks at me, he'll melt and want to marry me on the spot." She finally decided on the white organza with the pale roses and wide skirt. Ruffles surrounded the neckline with just a hint of her bare shoulder exposed.

When the day finally arrived, Colleen spent the entire morning dressing and attending to her toilet

Three carriages were laden with supplies and family members to be transported to the race area, along with a horse drawn cart to carry their darkies who would serve them.

Gerritt rode his stallion that had been bathed and groomed just for the race. He was a magnificent animal and had been properly named King.

Once there, tables were set up under the large willow trees and covered with linen tablecloths. China place settings were arranged and bountiful amounts of food, hams, potatoes, yams, corn bread and jars of cold lemonade covered in netting to keep out flies.

More and more people began arriving, the ladies in their taffeta dresses, wide hats, carting their parasols to keep off the sun and the men in their light colored day suits with wide brimmed straw hats.

The day had turned bright and sunny after an overcast morning. The breeze across the lake stirred the branches of the trees, fanning those who stood beneath their shade. Colleen could smell the clean freshness of the blue water and the lilies that graced the shallows.

She saw the men gathering around Gerritt admiring his new roan, but she had yet to spot Steven. Finally in the distance, down the winding dirt road, she saw the Covington carriage with Steven riding next to it. As usual when she saw him, her heart beat faster and her breathing became more rapid. She thought him to be the most handsome man there, although several other young men her age were present, she only had eyes for Steven.

He sat tall in his saddle, wearing black riding pants and shinny black riding boots, with a full white shirt open at the neck. His raven black hair was combed back accentuating his eyes and full lips.

She noticed several young ladies crowding up to speak to him, laughing and giggling as he dismounted from his horse, but his eyes sought her out and he smiled his wonderful smile. She smiled back, but did not go to him as he was already leading his horse to the race area.

Bets were made and everyone lined up along the racecourse. They were to race along the straightaway to the far end of the lake, circle around and come back. One of the men stood in front of the horses, making sure they lined up nose to nose.

The air filled with anticipated excitement, men shouted and women called out to their favorite rider. The horses sensed the excitement and began to snort and stomp their hooves. Gerritt held his big roan at bay, speaking quietly to him, stroking his neck to calm him. Steven too, pulled back on the reins of his black stallion, the horse moving sideways, nearly crashing into the crowd. Steven pressed his knees into the horse's sides, bending over to stroke his neck and getting him back in line.

The man in front of the horses raised his arms and in a loud voice called out, "Ready!"

To Colleen it seemed as if everything suddenly were taking place in slow motion, Gerritt's horse suddenly rearing up, the crowd yelling, the man's arms coming down along his sides with the shout, "Go!" the horses leaping forward, their powerful hindquarters bulging with effort. Their long strides carried them across the field; the crowds surged forward to be able to see the riders.

Colleen's hand had gone to her throat and she could feel her pulse pounding beneath her fingers. Who would win the race? Who should she be cheering for? Her brother or the man she adored?

They were nearly neck and neck, the horse's long slender legs stretched out to their full length. The men were leaned far over their necks, slapping at the horse's hindquarters, urging them to go faster. Steven's white shirt billowed out behind him as they neared the lake.

Another man stood at the other end to mark the spot they were to turn back. Steven's horse was on the inside of the turn and made it more quickly than Gerritt's roan, but as they came back into the straight away, the big horse again came along side the black stallion.

Now she could see them more closely, the horse's wide nostrils flaring, their sides shiny with sweat. Gerritt and Steven were calling out to their studs, urging them to go just a little faster, just a little harder.

Closer and closer they came, the crowd yelling their encouragement. They were neck and neck, nose to nose, the finish line nearer and nearer. Then, just a few yards to go and Steven pulled ahead and his stallion crossed the line just ahead of Gerritt.

Those who had bet on Steven cheered loudly, the young ladies jumping up and down. They pulled their horses up and climbed down out of the saddles. Slave groomsmen took the bridles to walk them and cool them down. Gerritt and Steven shook hands with backslapping and good humor all around.

Colleen wanted to go to Steven, but so many people surrounded him, she couldn't get near him. Finally the crowd dissipated, the men paying off their bets, the women going off to prepare to serve the food.

Colleen walked the short distance to the lake, hoping Steven would follow her. She was not disappointed, for he was by her side in just a few moments. He took her hand in his and kissed her fingers, smiling as he did so.

"Congratulations on winning the race," she told him.

"Thank-you," he said still holding her hand, "but I had great inspiration. All I had to do as I was coming down the home stretch was look at you and I couldn't fail."

"I think perhaps the horse had something to do with it," she said looking up into his blue eyes. Sometimes she felt as though she could get lost in those eyes, if she could just stare into them for hours.

"Travis is a great runner, but you always inspire me, my darling." He took her other hand in both of his and held them to his chest.

"Do you feel my heart, dear Colleen? It's beating so hard because of you. I love you so much. I can barely resist taking you into my arms and kissing you properly and I don't mean like a lady."

Colleen's imagination made her feel flushed with excitement. She wanted more than anything for Steven to take her in his arms and shower her with passionate kisses.

He had moved even closer and his nose was only inches from hers. "I want to touch you, Colleen," he whispered to her. "I want to feel your soft velvety skin against mine. I want to press my body against you until you feel my hardness."

"Steven!" she gasped. He was arousing her to the point that she was sure everyone would notice. "How can you talk that way" she said embarrassed.

"Because it's the truth, because I love you so much, I can barely restrain my passion for you. I swear Colleen, if we don't marry soon, I'll go mad."

She could see in his eyes, what he said was true. His mouth was slightly opened and was so close to hers that she thought she would surely die if he didn't kiss her.

"Oh Steven, it's what I want too." she told him.

"Please, won't you speak to my father again?"

"Today, I promise. I'll speak to him this very day. I can't wait for you to be my wife." He slipped her hand into the crook of his arm and began walking her back to the trees where the picnic had begun.

"I need to see you alone, Colleen," he said quietly so as not to be overheard by anyone. "To hell with proper etiquette; I need to kiss you and touch you without worrying whether or not anyone is looking over our shoulders. You trust me, don't you, Colleen?" he asked glancing over at her.

"With my life," she answered. "I'll find a place and let you know."

He nodded and smiled as they the reached the others. Steven was immediately surrounded by admiring girls, all of them exclaiming over his win in the horse race.

Another group of ladies was seated and talking over the latest fashions from Paris while they ate barbecue chicken and cornbread. Children ran about playing games, rolling the hoop, hide and seek and frozen tag.

The men had gathered near the buggies and of course, were discussing politics.

Colleen wandered to one of the tables where several young men were standing about talking over who was the prettiest girl at the picnic and who would be taking whom to the Christmas Ball. When they saw Colleen approach, they suddenly stopped their conversation and rushed to be the one whom she would notice first.

A tall lanky boy with curly blond hair, his name was Andrew, brought her a plate filled with chicken, biscuits, yams and other assorted delicacies. His blue eyes were wide as he smiled at her.

"This is for you, Colleen," he told her. "I was hopin' you'd do me the pleasure of sittin' with me at the picnic."

"Why, I don't know," she said glancing over at Steven who still seemed to be occupied with his many admirers.

"I was hopin' you'd sit with me," a voice said behind her and when she turned she saw Robert Banyon, a muscular, dark haired young man whose parents owned a plantation near the many islands off Georgia's coast. They grew sugar cane and exported most of their crop.

"Well, I'll tell you what," she said noticing that Steven had still failed to extricate himself from the throngs. "I'll have picnic with both of you, Robert and Andrew, if that's alright with the two of you," she added quickly. She thought perhaps if Steven saw her with two other good looking young men, then he might be a little quicker to ask her father for her hand.

They walked to the shade of a large spreading oak, the breeze swaying its branches ever so slightly. They sat on a quilt that had been spread out on the ground. Colleen arranged her skirts around her so as not to muss them.

Andrew handed her the plate of food, but she only took a few bites. She didn't feel hungry. She just wanted to be with Steven. If only she could think of a way to be alone with him.

"I think you are the most beautiful girl at the picnic," Andrew told her.

"What….? Oh thank-you, Andrew," she said rather distracted.

"It would be an honor if you would accompany me to the Christmas Ball," Andrew said reaching out to take her hand.

Before she could answer, Robert had knocked his hand away and glared at Andrew. "I was just about to ask her myself," he said a little too loudly.

"Now boys," she said taking both their hands. "I can't be thinkin' about that right now." Her southern drawl had thickened considerably trying to calm them. "Ya'll know how scary it is thinkin' on this here war that might be comin'"? Why, just what would I do if ya'll went to war?"

"Well Miss Colleen, we would have to do our duty," Andrew told her. "If war broke out, I would surely go."

"Yes, and so would I, "Robert told her pushing back a lock of hair that fallen across his forehead.

A deep sadness suddenly filled her heart; all these young men only a little older than herself, so willing to go fight a war. If it did come, how many of them would die?

"I declare, I don't understand why ya'll are so anxious to leave your homes and go to war," she said looking at them more closely than she ever had before.

"We would have to, don't you see?" Andrew said empathetically. "The Yankees want to take away our slaves, to ruin our plantations so they can take our land and change the way we live. They want us to be like them."

"That's true," Robert told her, "secession is the only way to preserve our way of life, to be able to live our lives the way we always have."

"Oh, pish tosh," Colleen said getting to her feet. "Do you know how many times I've heard that? People been sayin' secession for years and so far nothin's happened."

"But, Colleen….."

"I just don't think I can stand hearin' it one more time, is all," she said stepping gingerly around them and began walking towards Steven who was by now, by himself, leaning against a tree, watching her. As she drew closer she noticed his eyes looked dark and he wasn't smiling. She decided to ignore that observation.

"I thought of a place we could be alone," she told him when she stood in front of him. It had come to her as she walked across the grass to where he stood.

Since he hadn't responded, she continued. "Do you know that old storage barn at the edge of our property? The one we don't use any more?"

"Yes," he answered.

"You go there first. Make some excuse. I'll wait a bit so it won't look suspicious and then I'll come in awhile with the buggy."

He nodded and then touched her face. "I'll be waitin,'" he said his voice husky. He left her then and walked to where the group of men stood talking and smoking, his father amongst them. She saw him saying something to Clifford and gesturing toward his horse. Then he walked off, mounted Travis and rode off in the opposite direction of the old barn.

Now all she had to do was wait a bit, make her excuses and go to meet her love.

Steven took the road away from the lake, then when he thought no one would be following him, he doubled back and circled around the other side and took the road to the McBride Plantation.

He arrived at the small abandoned barn and tied Travis in back where he wouldn't be spotted from the road. Then he entered the darkened barn. The smell of dried oats and hay filled his nostrils. At one time it had been used as storage for these items and some of it still remained, blanketing the floor and sifting down from the crumbling loft.

Several boards were missing from the roof, presumably blown off in strong winds, allowing shafts of sunlight to slice through the darkness of the barn. Consequently, there were also many slat boards that had shifted on the walls, making space where he could look out to the road.

So far he could not see Colleen. It was probably too soon. They didn't want anyone to have cause for suspicion. It was just that he was so anxious to be with her. He had been in love with her as long as he could remember. When they were children he had loved playing with her, had delighted at her laugh and had considered her his best friend. When he had waded into the river against strict orders, Colleen had been there, holding his hand. They had both gotten drenched and a stern lecture from their mothers.

When he had gone exploring in the woods, pretending to be Indians, Colleen had been there with him, helping to build a twig wigwam. Then in their early teens when they had both learned to ride, she would race him and invariably would win, turning in her saddle to laugh at him.

He could still remember the exact day his heart had melted forever. She had bested him again and had turned to taunt him. Her long auburn hair swirled about her shoulders, the sun turning the highlights into gold. Her face was flushed from the race and her eyes were shinning. Her full lips were slightly parted and he suddenly caught his breath at her beauty.

When had she grown so lovely? It seemed she had become a woman overnight. From then on his love for her had grown stronger and stronger until he knew he never wanted to be without her, that he wanted her to be his wife.

Not only had his love for her grown, but so had his desire. Each time he was with her, he desperately wanted to kiss her, to touch her, even to make love to her. But, they were seldom alone and the short periods of time they had been, he had felt fearful of hurting her, of scaring her and he would do anything not to hurt her.

Now he waited for her to come to him, for them to be alone together. What would happen, he wasn't sure, but his imagination was doing a good job of filling in the blanks.

He paced the floor, the old boards creaking under his feet. He thought about how she had looked at the picnic, her beautiful hair braided up and surrounding her head like a crown. Her bare shoulders had looked soft and invited him to touch her. Her lips were moist and sensuous and he had had all he could do to keep from kissing her right there in front of everyone.

When he had been preoccupied with those girls who had merely been congratulating him for his win at the race, she had gone off to eat with Andrew and Robert. He had felt angry, the ugly dragon of jealousy had risen its breast. She was his and he wanted no other man to be near her. He had seen how those two had looked at her, the adoration in their eyes. He would put off no longer asking her father again for her hand. And if he would not consent then well, he would just have to elope with her. He would not be denied.

Just then he heard the sound of a carriage and horses hooves on the road outside. He glanced through the gaps in the boards and saw Colleen driving her buggy around to the back of the barn.

When Colleen first entered the barn, she could not see Steven. Sunlight filtered through gaps in the roof and she could see shards of hay floating through the air.

"Steven?" she called quietly and suddenly he was beside her, taking her into his arms, pressing his lips on hers. His mouth moved sensuously on hers, tasting, feeling. Then his tongue probed her mouth and she drew back surprised, not only at his actions, but also at the response her body had made to his overtures.

"I love you so much, Colleen," he told her, his voice husky with passion. And then he kissed her again, deeply, hard and fierce.

She kissed him back, loving the way he made her feel. She was almost light headed and her body tingled as she had never felt it before. Steven's mouth moved from her lips to her shoulders. He pulled the neckline of her dress further down, exposing more of the tops of her breasts. His mouth moved to her cleavage, kissing, licking.

She put her neck back, savoring the incredible feelings flooding through her body. She had never felt so alive. She could feel her heart pulsing in her neck, her breasts, and in that place between her thighs.

Suddenly Steven picked her up and carried her to a pile of straw, laying her down gently and then lying next to her. He continued his kissing and now his hands had moved to her breasts, caressing, touching. He was trembling and he moved to half lay over her. She could feel the hardness of his manhood and it excited her even more.

Then he was pulling on her skirts, reaching his hand up underneath her petticoats until he had found the tops of her pantaloons and bare skin. He began pulling them down.

She suddenly felt afraid, as if things were getting out of hand, as if she were out of control. "Steven," she said pushing at him. "Steven, please don't!" she turned her head trying to avoid his kisses.

"Please, Colleen," he pleaded. "I love you. I need you so much."

"No!" she told him. "Steven, stop!" This time she yelled his name and pushed him off of her. "This is wrong. We can't do this!" She was nearly crying now and she wasn't really sure why, except that she had never felt so out of control before, so afraid they would not have been able to stop.

Steven sat up and put his head in his hands. Colleen could see he was still trembling. "I'm sorry," he said so quietly she could barely hear him.

She sat up next to him and touched his arm. "I'm so sorry," he said again and when he took his hands away from his face, she saw he had tears in his eyes. "I would never do anything to hurt you and now I have."

"No Steven, you didn't hurt me. I was only afraid, that's all."

"There's no excuse for me, except to say I love you so much that it's almost painful to look at you and not touch you. It drives me crazy. Oh God, Colleen, what have I done? Can you ever trust me again?"

"I was just as much to blame," she said touching his face. "There is no harm done." The tears still shimmered in his eyes. Somehow she needed to make him feel better, to let him know she felt the same. "You made me feel things I've never felt before," she told him, "and I loved it. I never wanted you to stop. But when I felt you touching my pantaloons, I became afraid. As much as I wanted you, we need to wait until we marry."

"You're right. I know you are, but I can't wait much longer," he said standing up. He reached out and took her hand, helping her to her feet. He went behind her and meticulously began to remove pieces of straw stuck in her hair.

"I've been thinking a lot about us, darling," he said placing his hands on her shoulders. "If your father won't let you marry yet, then I want you to run away with me."

She turned to face him, surprise clearing showing in hr eyes. "Elope?" she asked.

"I know it isn't what you would wish. It isn't for me either. I know you want a big wedding with all the trimmings, but I can't wait any longer. All I can think about is having you with me, for you to be my wife."

"Yes Steven, yes," she said excitedly. "I would run away with you."

"Oh god, Colleen, I love you so much," he said embracing her. "My beautiful Colleen, I promise you, I will ask your father first, but if he refuses, we will be together."

She pulled back and looked up into his face. "I want to be your wife, Steven. Nothing could make me happier and then we can love each other completely."

He kissed her then, tenderly, lovingly. "We'd better go before they begin lookin' for us."

"Oh, and I have to go all the way to the house first," Colleen said turning to leave.

"Why must you go there?" he asked.

"That was my excuse to come here. I told Mama I had to go to the house to get a book I promised Cynthia," she said referring to her best friend. "She was insisting I had to have Matthew drive me, but I finally persuaded her into letting me come alone. You know she's been real jittery since that experience with the slave on the road. If I'm gone too long, she'll send an armada after me."

"I don't blame her," he said touching her face. They were standing in the door of the barn, the sun shinning full on her hair making the gold highlights shimmer. Her face was slightly flushed and her lips were parted. He thought he had never seen anyone so beautiful.

"I must go," she told him. She left then and his heart ached for her.

Colleen got into the buggy and continued on down the road to the large house. All the way there she kept thinking of what had just happened.

They had been alone before, briefly, but had never been in a place where they had had the opportunity to do what they had done today. It excited her to think of the way he had touched her, kissed her, the passion he had shown. She closed her eyes at the way he had made her feel, the way her body had throbbed and pulsed with the beat of her heart. She could still feel how he had trembled, the hardness of his manhood. "Oh god," she whispered aloud, "I love you so much, Steven."

Steven had arrived back at the lake, trying to swing around the backside, the way he had left. Once he had gotten within sight of the picnic area, he dismounted and walked Travis to the picket line where the other horses and buggies were tethered.

He searched out and finally found Mr. McBride talking passionately with the other men. The breeze blew the smoke from their cigars and bits of their conversation his way. He stood nervously on the outside of the group waiting for an opportunity to speak with him. Finally he glanced Steven's way and he motioned to him. James excused himself and began walking with Steven.

He inhaled deeply on the cigar he held before speaking. He knew Steven was in love with his daughter and he had a pretty good idea what it was he wanted to talk with him about. He had approached him once before and at the time, he had rejected Steven's request. Colleen was his baby, his little girl and the concept of her getting married and leaving with another man had been inconceivable to him. Since that time however, he had had more of an opportunity to think it over. She was definitely of marriageable age and watching the two of them together, he knew they loved each other deeply. Steven was a good man and he knew he would be a good husband to Colleen.

"So what is it you wanted to discuss with me, Steven?" he asked exhaling the cigar smoke.

"Well sir," Steven began nervously, "you know I've expressed to you before, my desire to marry Colleen. I would like to approach you again sir, to stress how very much I love her and my great desire to make her my wife."

"So you think you could take good care of my little girl, do you?"

"Yes, sir," Steven answered quickly. "You know my family, that we are good people and have the means to give Colleen a good life. I've already discussed with my father what my future would be and he has said when I marry, he will give us the south forty acres of land to build a home and slaves to serve us. Later on, when my father is unable to take care of the plantation, I will inherit all of it. And I know I will do my best to take care of the estate the way my father has."

"That's all well and good for the financial stability for Colleen's future, but how do you intend to make her happy, son?" They had walked as far as the shore of the lake where they stood looking out over the rippling water.

Steven thought about James's question a moment before answering. He watched small water bugs dancing across the surface and the fast darting of minnows beneath the opaque water.

He turned to look James in the eyes. "I love Colleen with all my heart," he said quietly. "She's my soul, my life. I would do anything to make her happy. I want to shower her with attention. I will always be kind to her and give her all the respect she desires. I would always be faithful to her and care for her until the day I die." His voice caught in his throat from the emotion he was feeling and he had to look away. "Mr. McBride, she is my life. I can't imagine it without her."

James put his hand on Steven's shoulder. "You remind me of myself at your age," he told him. "I too, had someone I was deeply in love with and now here I am twenty-four years later, still passionately in love with the same woman." He stopped to say his words carefully. His next sentences would not only affect Steven's life, but his own.

"I think you are an honorable man Steven," he told him "and I believe you truly love my daughter with all your heart and saying all that, I would be honored to have you for my son-in-law."

Steven knew he suddenly had the biggest grin on his face, but he didn't care. He was so elated he wanted to shout and whoop for joy. Instead he grasped James's hand and shook it. "Thank-you sir, thank-you, I promise to take good care of your daughter."

"I know you will son, but I'd like you to slow down a little."

"What do you mean, sir?"

"I just mean that perhaps it would be best to wait until the holidays to announce your engagement. By then the elections will be over and we'll know better which way the country is going. Then the two of you could plan a spring wedding."

Steven's joy dampened quickly. "I see what you mean. It is a very volatile time and we still don't know if there will be war."

"I'm glad you understand, Steven. And I'm sure if the situation is explained to Colleen, she will understand also. And after all, spring really isn't that far away, especially when you consider you two will have the rest of your lives to be together."

"Yes sir," Steven answered. They both turned and began walking back towards the picnic.

"I think Mrs. McBride will still think it not a proper length of time for an engagement and will be frantic trying to plan the wedding by spring."

Steven only nodded his head. He couldn't help but feel disappointed it couldn't be sooner. But he also understood Mr. McBride's point. The South was in turmoil. They were on the verge of secession. And if that happened, who knew, there might be war. If it came to that, he knew he would go.

As they drew closer to the group of people under the trees, Steven saw that Colleen had returned and was talking to Cynthia. As soon as Mr. McBride had returned to the group of men, Steven went to her. Colleen looked up at him expectantly, anxious.

Cynthia was looking at them curiously, wondering what was going on between the two of them. "Cynthia, could you excuse us, please?" Steven asked of her, although he still hadn't taken his eyes from Colleen. "We have something we need to talk about."

"Well, I declare," Cynthia said as if she were offended. "You all are rather rude. Afta' all, Colleen and I were havin' a conversation."

"Please Cynthia, it's important," Colleen said turning to her friend.

"Alright, but only for you sweetie," Cynthia said turning to go. She flounced off, her blonde curls bouncing as she walked.

Colleen turned back to Steven, an anxious look on her face. "Well, did you talk to my father?" she asked, knowing full well he had as she had seen them together.

Steven took both her hands in his and looked lovingly into her eyes. "Yes, I talked to your father and yes, I asked for your hand."

"And, and...?" she said excitedly. "What did he say?"

He was very gracious….and he said he would be delighted to have me for a son-in-law."

Colleen squealed and threw her arms around his neck, kissing his cheek over and over. "I knew it! I just knew it!" she said.

Suddenly she was aware of others watching them and she dropped her arms and stepped back. "Oh, Steven, it's wonderful," she whispered. "When, when? Did he say when we could marry? Will it be this Christmas?"

He was grinning at her enthusiasm. "Slow down sweetheart; Christmas? Yes, at Christmas we can announce our engagement and then be married in the spring."

"Spring, but that seems so far away and I feel as if I've been waiting so long already." Her smile had faded and her lower lip stuck out in a pout.

Steven put his arm around her shoulder. "It's not so bad and in only seven months, you will be my wife."

"But just a little while ago you were so anxious to marry me, you wanted to elope," she pointed out to him.

He thought about their encounter in the barn and how physically stimulated he had been, how intensely his feelings had been for her and how much he loved her. That certainly hadn't changed. He wanted her just as much as ever, but he also knew her father had been right about waiting until after the elections.

"Your father pointed out the votility of the state of the nation right now……"

"Oh no, not that again," she interrupted.

"It just makes sense, darling," he said, his arm still around her shoulder. "Besides, I think your mother will probably faint dead away when she realizes she only has seven months to prepare for the biggest event of the year."

Colleen smiled, "Well, at least you're right about that."

"It looks as though the picnic is breaking up," Steven said observing the servants gathering up the food and dishes and loading them onto the buggies. "I'll walk you to your carriage."

The next few months were filled with such frenzy, the likes of which Colleen had seldom seen before. Many more trips into town had been made, this time under escort, to purchase more goods and order supplies. Mary poured over pattern books looking for the perfect bridesmaid's dresses. She and Colleen worked with a designer to create the most beautiful wedding gown that had never before been seen in the entire county. Extra linens were ordered and decisions made about which floral arrangements would be used. Invitations were discussed and guest lists were begun. Cousins and relatives from all over the state would be invited.

In addition to the plans being made for Colleen and Steven's wedding, the arrangements were still going forward to hold the Christmas Ball at their plantation. Foodstuffs ordered earlier were beginning to come in and stored in the cold cellar and over burgeoning pantry. The menu was finalized and seamstresses went to work on the ball gowns.

James and Gerritt were kept busy with the fall harvest. The slaves were hard at work in the fields, picking the cotton. One field hand was expected to pick ninety pounds of cotton boils a day with an overseer making sure their quota was met. So much cotton had been planted that even the blacksmiths, carpenters and anyone else they could round up were required to work the fields. After the cotton was picked, it was brought to the largest barn on the plantation where the cotton gin and cotton press were located.

The gin was raised up off the floor to a height of eight feet and supported by wooden pillars. The slaves hitched draft horses to the vertical axle, which turned in a circular path rotating the large gears, which in turn furnished power to the wheels and belts of the gin itself. As the canvas bags of cotton were brought in from the fields, they were put into the gin to have the seeds separated from the cotton.

From the cotton gin it then went to the gin press, which took the seeded cotton and pressed it into bales. It was a massive structure, reaching thirty feet to the very top of the huge barn. The press's frame supported a threaded screw more than a foot in diameter, positioned over a box which held the loose cotton lint. At the top of the screw two long beams stretched out horizontal to the floor and then down, resembling arms. Onto these arms, mules were harnessed and made to walk in a circular pattern turning the screw and compacting the cotton.

After being pressed into large bales, they were loaded onto massive flatbeds and taken downriver to the large auction and warehouse near the docks. There, they were sold and most were put on ships to be taken overseas to Europe. Others were shipped up north.

James and Gerritt were responsible to make sure all steps of the operation went smoothly and the highest dollar was gotten for prime cotton.

While the men were busy with the cotton harvest, many chores were required to ready the plantation for the coming winter months. These duties fell on the shoulders of the mistress of the house.

Mary saw it her duty to instruct Colleen as to the vast undertakings of a plantation owner's wife. She took Colleen to the weaving house where slaves were busy weaving and spinning their cotton into cloth for clothing, most of which was used for the slaves.

From the weaving house they went to the cattle barns where an extensive dairy operation was in progress, the milking of cows, and making of cheese and butter.

In addition to the cattle for milking and eating, in the livestock barns there were also chickens, hogs and geese and next door to the livestock barn was the slaughter and smoke house where the livestock was butchered and then smoked. The bristles from the hogs were used for making brushes, the intestines for sausage and the fat for lard. While they were at the barn, several geese were being killed and plucked. Mary walked among the women slaves, overseeing their progress.

"You there," she said pointing at one young negress, "mind how you sort those feathers. The large ones are to be for beds and the smaller for pillows. And be sure you save the quills." She turned to Colleen. "Good quills can be used for pens, you know," she told her.

On their way back to the main house, they passed the vast gardens, where other slaves were harvesting vegetables and fruits. The vegetables were cleaned, prepared and canned, to be used throughout the winter months. Others were weeding the last of the summer flowers, roses, dalalias, that were used in bouquets to grace the house.

Mary looked toward the river, shading her eyes from the sun. "See down there near the river," she pointed out to Colleen using her other hand, "those darkies down there are gathering milkweed pods. They spin the down into wicks for candle making." She turned from the garden, continuing to instruct Colleen as they went. "We have several good women who perform the soap and candle making. It's very time consuming and takes a great deal of skill. It's very important to have people who know what they're doing…..Colleen! Are you listening to me?" she reprimanded her daughter who seemed to be lost in her own thoughts.

"Um, of course Mother," Colleen responded appropriately.

"As I was saying," Mary continued, "you must have skilled crafts women or the candles will be shoddy and not burn properly, smoke and all that. Why, the darkies we have can make thirty dozen candles in a day, each and that's enough for a months supply. I'm not sure who does the soap and candle making at Briarwood, but when Steven gets his own slaves, you be sure they are schooled properly."

"Yes Mother," Colleen answered dutifully, but her mind was not on the semantics of soap and candle making nor of how many goose feathers it took to stuff a bed. All she could think of was how it would be to walk down the aisle with Steven, what it would be like to be his wife, and to share his bed. She could see herself wearing fabulous gowns and entertaining at lavious balls. She would be well known in society and Steven would build her a beautiful mansion on their vast holdings at Briarwood. Then someday he would inherit all of it.

As they passed the kitchen house which was disconnected from the main house, Colleen barely took notice of the slave women who were washing clothes on the battlin' blocks, sudsing them in hot water over a fire, then pounding them with a paddle on the battlin' block, a large post of wood smoothed slick by many washings. The clothes were then hung to dry on racks.

Colleen and Mary walked into the kitchen where the cooks were preparing the evening meal. Wonderful scents filled their nostrils, warmth and goodness seemed to permeate the room. The kitchen had always been one of Colleen's favorite places to go when she was a young child.

One large woman named Ellen, her head wrapped in a bandana, was stirring a bubbling liquid in one of the numerous pots hung over the enormous fireplace that stretched along one entire wall. On the brick were racks containing numerous pots and pans and other cooking utensils. Large meat hooks protruded down from the chimney, which could hold an entire pig or lamb. The logs for the fire were twelve feet long in order to also heat the ovens enclosed in the brick. Opposite the fireplace wall were racks and racks of cooking pots and utensils and in front of these, a long work table where all the fine foods stuffs were prepared.

"How's that lamb stew coming for dinner?" Mary asked as they passed through, glancing over at the kettle.

"Comin' jes fine," Ellen answered turning to face her mistress. She had a round pleasant face that matched her round body. Colleen thought she must taste a great deal of her own cooking. She remembered coming to Ellen as a child for goodies between meals without her mother knowing.

They continued on through the kitchen and under the porch that connected it to the house. "Colleen," Mary said in a quieter tone. "there are other things a woman should know before her marriage. Things other than what it takes to run a plantation."

"Like what, Mother?" Colleen asked.

"Like, what is expected of a wife in the marriage bed." Mary appeared clearly embarrassed by the subject she had broached.

"Mother, this really isn't necessary," Colleen tried interrupting. She couldn't imagine what it was her mother would tell her about the subject of sex, but she was sure she didn't want to hear it.

"Yes it is necessary," her mother responded. "There are certain……duties a wife must perform in order to please her husband. Do you understand?" she asked turning to face Colleen. They had stopped before entering the house.

"I understand Mother," she told her, although she felt certain it wouldn't be a duty. She couldn't imagine anything more wonderful than being in Steven's arms. Just remembering their time in the barn brought shivers to her body.

"However," her mother continued, "men have greater needs than women and may from time to time desire to seek out a way to……relieve those needs."

"What are you saying?" Colleen asked.

Mary sighed. She only wished there were an easy way to tell her what she needed to hear. "Sometimes a man will go to another woman……."

"No, that can't be right," Colleen interrupted. "An honorable man would not do what you are suggesting."

"Even honorable men, Colleen. It's as I said, men have greater needs……"

"Where do they go to find these women?" Colleen asked, clearly shocked by what she was hearing.

"For some men there are certain women who make their living at such things. For plantation men, the slave quarters offer their release," Mary said quietly. She knew it was something Colleen didn't want to hear, but she also knew it was something she needed to hear.

Colleen was silent at first, absorbing what she had just heard. "Not Daddy, surely not Daddy?" she asked quietly.

Mary nodded, "yes, even your Daddy and I'm grateful for it."

"How can you say that?" Colleen said turning to face her mother tears shinning in her eyes. "How could Daddy or any married man going and…..going to another woman, be a good thing?"

Mary hooked her arm into Colleen's and walked her into the back entrance of the house. "Because my dear, then the wife is relieved from being continually burdened by the constant sexual advances of her husband."

Colleen said no more, but her mind whirled with the thoughts her mother had invoked by her discussion. She imagined her father sneaking out of his bed in the middle of the night and making his way stealthily down to the servants quarters and crawling in bed with one of the negresses and then……. No, it was just unthinkable. And what about Steven, would he make ritual visits to relieve his needs? Or had he already been participating in such fruits of the flesh? It made her ill to her stomach to think of such things.

That evening she had a difficult time looking at her father in the same way. He didn't look any different, but just knowing now what she did, somehow made him different in her eyes. In some way, she had lost some measure of respect for him. And likewise, she wondered about Gerritt. Did he too, participate in these activities? After all, he was a normal young man with desires like anyone else.

After retiring, lying in her bed, she thought again about the day she and Steven had been together in the barn, how he had kissed her, how he had touched her. It brought tears to her eyes to think of Steven doing those things with some darkie woman. But, when she thought about it and searched her memories, she realized that on some level, she had known that plantation men had been doing this all along and the evidence was to be seen in the occasional mulatto child born to slave women. Needless to say, Colleen did not sleep very well.

Sometime in the middle of the night, Colleen felt she had only just gotten to sleep, when her mother was shaking her awake. "Colleen, wake up," she said for the third time. "I need you to help me."

"What is it? What's happened?" she said sleepily, slowly sitting up.

"I need you to go down to the slave cabins with me. One of the darkie women is havin' her baby. You might as well learn this part of plantation life as well."

Colleen felt groggy with sleep. She wasn't quite sure she understood what her mother was asking of her. She could see Dora standing at the foot of her bed holding a lamp. Her mother stood before her, a simple dress on, her hair uncombed and pulled back by a ribbon. A shawl was flung around her shoulders. It was still dark. What was it she had said, go down to the slave quarters?

"Colleen!" her mother said more sharply, "get up now and get dressed."

"Why, Mother? Why are you getting' me up in the middle of the night to go to the slave quarters?" she asked as she swung her legs over the side of the bed. The room was cool and she shivered as she climbed out from under her warm quilts. The fireplaces had not yet been lite in the house.

"I told you why, one of the slaves is havin' her baby." Mary told her daughter as she flung a housedress at her. "We've got to down there and help her. Put this on. Don't bother with undergarments. We've got to hurry."

"No undergarments, but Mother……."

Mary pulled Colleen's nightgown over her head and began to tug on her dress while she was still seated on the side of the bed. "Why are you taking me with you? I've never gone before."

"If you are to marry Steven and be mistress of his house, it is something you will need to know how to do."

"Deliver babies?" Colleen asked incredulous.

"Yes," her mother said simply.

Colleen sighed, another duty for the mistress. She knew her mother had sometimes gone down to the cabins when one of the slave women's time had come, but she hadn't really thought her mother had done the actual delivery.

As they walked down the back pathway led by Dora and Matthew, who carried a lantern, Colleen became even more irritated that her mother had dragged her out in the middle of the night. She had been handed an armload of clean cloths and told to come along.

"Why can't the darkie midwife take care of this?"

"The midwife is there, but the girl is young, her first, and she's been laboring long. We just can't take chances with valuable property," her mother said shifting the medical bag she carried from one hand to the other. "Havin' a baby is one of the most dangerous things a woman can do. Half of the babies don't survive. If the midwife messes up and you lose the child or maybe the mother, that's money wasted, not to mention havin' to replace a worker. You have to make sure you protect your property."

Colleen watched Dora turn to them and saw that look in her eyes that she had seen in Bess's eyes not so long ago. What was she thinking? Did it matter to her that her mother had referred to them as property? What did Dora think of being a slave? Was she grateful she had a home and food, clothing and security, in exchange for her labor?

As they neared the slave quarters, Colleen could hear singing, low and soft, almost like a hymn. And then she saw a fire burning in front of one of the cabins. Several people were standing around it, some singing, others talking quietly. A few children were present, some sitting near the fire, others asleep in their mother's arms.

"It be this house, misses," Dora told them. "She be nearly ready."

Then Colleen heard the cries, wails really, and it made the gooseflesh stand out on her skin. The people around the fire didn't seem to react, they just continued their singing.

As they passed by the group, Colleen glanced over and saw an old woman seated in a rocking chair near the fire. She had her arms raised and her weathered face was tilted up towards the sky. She appeared to be chanting, her mouth moving almost automatically. Colleen suddenly realized she was praying.

The cabin room was starkly furnished, a table made of a plank of wood across two split logs, two chairs, a narrow bed upon which the woman lay, a few hooks fastened into the walls to hang their meager clothing and some cooking utensils and dishes. Beyond that, Colleen did not see many personal possessions.

Around the bed, besides her mother, stood two other people, an older gray haired black woman and a younger black man, anxiously wringing his hands. Colleen surmised the older woman to be the midwife and the man, the husband.

Finally, she looked over at the woman on the bed who was about to give birth. She was shocked to see how young she was, perhaps only sixteen or seventeen. Her young face was pinched with pain and her swollen body drawn up tightly. Her nappy hair was long and loose, spread out over the pillow, damp with sweat. Her arms were stretched up over her head, holding tightly to one of the bedposts.

Another pain hit the young woman and her grip on the post tightened, her mouth opened in a scream. It made the hairs on the back of Colleen's neck stand up.

Her mother pulled back the cover and Colleen saw the blood. The woman's gown was stained and so was the cover. "Oh, Lord," Mary said. "I certainly hope the sack is not in front of the baby."

"Gerald," she said to the young man, "go outside and bring in some hot water from the pot on the fire." Gerald hurried outside looking relieved to have something to do.

Mary motioned the midwife away and told Colleen to come closer. She inched forward hesitatingly. She was sure she didn't want to be here.

"The babes head is comin', Misses," the midwife told her.

Mary spread the woman's legs and peered down between them. "You're right, the head is crowning. She has torn some. I think that's where the blood is coming from."

At first Colleen didn't want to look, the sight of blood, the lack of modesty, the heat and sights and smells began to overwhelm her. She thought she might pass out, but then she saw the dark, round fuzz of the baby's head and she grew intrigued. She had had all the explanations about how babies came into this world, but she had never witnessed a birth before.

"Alright now, Lizabeth," Mary told the girl, "next time a pain comes, I want you to push. You understand?"

"The girl nodded. "It hurts, bad!" she cried.

"I know, but it's almost over," Mary said.

At that moment another pain rippled across her belly, the muscles tight, hard as a drum. "Push!" Mary commanded. "Come on, Lizabeth, push!"

Lizabeth pushed down, straining against the babe in her womb. She cried out in her effort. Colleen saw the head move further down, the eyes and nose showing. When Lizabeth stopped pushing, they slid back in. She was close to her mother, head against head, anxious to watch the birth.

The midwife wiped Lizabeth's forehead with a wet cloth from the basin next to the bed. "It'll be alright, child," she said reassuredly. "your babes nearly here."

Another pain came, causing Lizabeth to arch her back and pull harder on the bedpost. "Now give a hard push," Mary told her. "Come on! Push as hard as you can!"

Lizabeth bore down and strained to push. Colleen could see the baby's head coming down further and then she gasped as the entire head popped out.

"The head is out, Lizabeth," Mary told the girl and then to Colleen, "First thing to do is get the mucus out of the mouth and nose so the baby will be able to breathe."

Colleen watched as her mother ran her finger covered by a clean linen, into the baby's mouth and then its nose. "Now the baby must be turned so the shoulders will fit," she said as she rotated the baby's head. "Sometimes they turn all on their own, but others, like this one, you have to turn.

Alright Lizabeth, now push again, one more time," she instructed.

"I cans't!" the woman wailed.

"You hush now," the midwife told her. "You cans do its. You want's you little babes to die?"

Lizabeth shook her head. "Then you push gal, once mo'"

Another contraction tightened her belly and she pushed as hard as her tired body would allow.

Colleen's mouth opened in awe as she saw the baby's shoulders slide through and then in a flash, the baby had slide completely out of its mother's body.

Mary quickly wrapped the child in clean linens and began to rub it vigorously. Suddenly, a loud wail filled the room and Lizabeth began to cry.

"What is it, Misses?" she asked. "It be's alright?"

"It's a girl, Lizabeth," Mary told her. "And she looks just fine, a strong healthy baby."

Gerald had arrived back inside with the hot water to hear the announcement of his daughter's birth. "Glory! Glory!" he exclaimed. "I'se gots a baby gal!" He stood dumbfounded in the middle of the room, holding the pot.

"Well, get over here with that water," Mary commanded him. Gerald quickly brought the water and set it on the floor near her. She took out of her bag, a scissors and piece of strong string. She dipped these in the water and then tying the string around the cord, she cut it. Once the child was separated from her mother, Mary handed the swaddled baby to the midwife. "Wash her up and give her to her mother to suckle," she told the old woman.

"Oh, my Lordy," Lizabeth suddenly exclaimed. "Ise havin' mo' pains!"

"That'll be the after birth comin'" Mary told her. And no sooner had she said it then the glutinous mass was delivered into another linen. This was handed to Gerald and told to bury it deep where no animals would disturb it.

Colleen had walked over to the table where the midwife had unwrapped the child and begun to wash her. "Look how tiny she is," Colleen said quietly, almost to herself rather than to the midwife. She gazed at the round scrunched up face, the delicate fingers, complete with fingernails and the small round compact body. But it was the baby's eyes that fascinated Colleen the most. The child was looking directly at her and moving her tongue in and out of her mouth as if tasting her new environment.

"She seems to be looking right at me," Colleen said and reached out to touch the velvety skin.

"She cans't sees you yet," the midwife told her. "Babes is blin' at firs'."

"She looks as if she could see into my soul," Colleen observed. "She's so perfect, everything just where it should be." She marveled at how this small creature could have been curled up warm and snug in her mother's body just moments before.

Mary had finished with Lizabeth and was washing her hands in the basin. Then she began gathering her things together, preparing to go back to the house.

The midwife wrapped the child in a clean but tattered blanket and handed her to her mother. "Looks, Gerald," she said to the man hovering over her. "Looks how beautiful she iss."

He nodded his agreement and reached out nervously to touch the soft curl of hair.

"I suppose the child must have a name," Mary said getting out a ledger from her bag.

"I'se been thinkin', I'se gwine to name her Angel, "cause she be mine Angel gal," Lizabeth told Mary. Colleen could hear the baby making soft suckling sounds as she nursed at her mother's breast and it made her smile.

"Nonsense," Mary said opening the ledger, "that's not a proper name for this plantation. It must be something respectable."

"But Misses, I had's my hearts set on Angel if'n it be's a gal."

"I said no, that will not be the child's name," Mary said running her finger down the columns in her book. "Let's see, Gerald and Lizabeth, daughter born on November 5th 1860, named.......Sarah. Yes, her name shall be Sarah."

Colleen thought Lizabeth looked as though she were about to cry. "Yes'm," she replied quietly.

With that Mary put the ledger back into her bag and started for the door. "Dora, gather our things and lets be getting back to the house," she instructed the black woman who had been waiting just inside the door.

When they stepped outside, Colleen shivered from the cool air hitting her skin after the stifling heat inside. All the darkies around the fire suddenly grew quiet. Mary took a few steps towards them. "It's a healthy girl child," she announced "and the mother is fine as well."

"A cheer went up from the group and the old woman in the rocking chair raised her arms and declared, "Praise God!"

"Yes, well, then we'll be off," Mary said to Colleen motioning to Matthew to go ahead with the lantern.

As they walked back to the big house, Colleen thought about the small child who had just been brought into this world. She was a slave child, a new addition to their property. What would her life be like? Would she work in the fields, or the big house? Would she be a seamstress or weaver? At any rate, her life would not be her own. She belonged to them; even her name belonged to them.

Meanwhile the country remained in turmoil with Southerners fearing more and more that secession was inevitable. Many zealots would have been pleased if they had. And then on November 6th, Abraham Lincoln was elected president of the United States with an overwhelming electoral vote.

During a visit by the Covington's, Clifford and James retired immediately to the library to discuss the almost inevitable repercussions of the latest election. While they talked, Steven and Colleen walked to the gazebo. The fall air was cool and the fallen leaves crunched under their feet. Colleen wore a heavy shawl to keep warm on their walk. When they reached the gazebo, Steven leaned against one of the support posts and turned to face Colleen. Her cheeks were rosy from the crisp air, her long hair was down around her face in soft curls. He thought her to be the most beautiful woman he had ever seen.

"Do you know how desperately I want to kiss you right now?" he told her.

"Maybe as much as I want to kiss you?" she said looking furtively around. She leaned forward and pressed her lips to his.

He was astonished at her boldness, but he embraced her nonetheless, feeling the warmth of her lips, her soft breath on his cheek. She drew away and leaned against him, her head on his shoulder.

"What if someone sees us?" he asked her teasingly as he drew her even closer.

"I don't care," she answered almost defiantly. "Everything is in such a mess. Here I was so lookin' forward to the Christmas Ball and announcing our engagement, but now everything is spoiled. All everyone talks about is how Mr. Lincoln became president and how, now for sure, we will have to seceded and go to war."

Steven sighed at her naivete of the grave situation before them. How could he explain to her that this election would result in secession by the Southern states and they would become their own union? Did she really understand they could very possibly go to war for doing such a thing? Did he really understand it himself? How could anyone?

"Don't worry, darlin'" he said reassuredly. "Our engagement will be the talk of all Savannah."

Colleen looked up into his face. "Do you really think so?" she asked. "Do you think it will be the biggest event of the year?"

"I do," he said and then when spring comes, we will be married and I will be the happiest man alive."

She smiled at last and pulled away from his embrace. "It will be grand, won't it? And you promise our wedding will be the most important priority in your life, no more Lincoln, no more secession, no war?"

"My beautiful Colleen, how could anything else be more important to me than you are. I am counting the days when you and I shall be engaged." He drew closer to her and took her hands in his. "I love you Colleen, you are so precious to me, and I want to make you happy. I will do everything in my power to see that happens."

Colleen's heart was racing and in spite of the cool air, her face felt flushed. She looked into his blue eyes and knew if she didn't marry him soon, she would die. She wanted to kiss him and hold him, the way they had that day in the barn, only she wouldn't stop. She wanted to feel his naked body against hers, feel his warm kisses on her mouth, and feel him making love to her.

She knew her mother would be appalled at her thoughts, but she didn't care. She loved Steven with all her heart and she wanted to share every part of his life.

It wasn't long before the much planned for Christmas Ball was to take place. It was December 20th, just five days before Christmas. The house had been elaborately decorated with greens, garlands and several Christmas trees, the largest, an eighteen foot spruce, decorated with red ribbons, gold balls and dozens of miniature candles, and set up in the ball room at the rear of the house. The gowns and tuxedos were given the last final touches and the massive amounts of food were cooked and prepared.

Hundreds of people from all over the county were expected to attend so extra slaves were brought into the house to help with the crowd.

On the night of the ball, Colleen spent hours in her room preparing. After all, this would be the night of the announcement of her engagement to Steven. Her long hair had been piled onto her head with long ringlets hanging down onto her back. Her dress was of the finest velvet, a deep blue with a low bodice, showing off her soft amble bosom and a full wide hooped skirt, softly brushing the floor. The long sleeves tapered to small points over the back of her hands. Gold braid draped around her waist and hung down into the folds of her skirt. On her feet she wore gold slippers.

As she sat at her dressing table, putting the finishing touches on her hair and make-up, her mother came into the room. Her long green satin dress with the high ruffled collar, brushed softly against the floor. At her throat, she wore a delicate cameo brooch. Dora moved from Colleen's side to fuss with pretense of straightening up the room.

Mary went up behind her daughter and put her hands on Colleen's shoulders. "It's a big night, isn't it?" she said to her.

"I'm so excited, Mama," she said looking at her mother in the mirror. "Tonight Steven and I become officially engaged.

"Steven is a good man," her mother said. "He will make a wonderful husband." Mary put her cheek against Colleen's so that both of their faces were visible in the mirror. "I hope the two of you will always be happy and have lots of beautiful children."

Colleen smiled. "I can't wait to be Steven's wife, Mama. I love him so much."

Mary kissed her on the cheek. "I know you do, sweetheart," she said straightening up. She took a few steps back and reached into the pocket folded into her long skirt. She pulled out a small box and handed it to Colleen. "It's an engagement gift from your father and me."

Colleen took the box from her mother and looked up into her face. "What is it?"

"Open it," her mother instructed.

Colleen fingered the black velvet box, feeling it's softness. Slowly she opened the lid and stared at the exquisitely beautiful matched set of diamond earrings and necklace. The earrings were tiny teardrops on gold wires and the necklace had the same teardrops interspersed with small round diamonds. Their brilliance sparkled and twinkled in the light from her vanity lamp.

"Oh, Mama," Colleen sighed. "These are your best diamonds. The ones you only wear on special occasions."

Her mother nodded. "They belonged to your grandmother, then they were mine and now they belong to you. Someday you will pass them on to your daughter."

Colleen rose from her chair to embrace her mother. "Thank-you so much, Mama, I'll cherish them forever. Would you help me to put them on?"

Mary took the delicate necklace from the box and fastened it around Colleen's neck. "It looks wonderful on you darling."

Colleen removed the earrings and put them on her ears. "I will treasure them always, Mama and I will never let anything happen to them."

"Alright now," Mary said moving towards the door "it's time to come downstairs and greet your guests."

"I'll be right down," Colleen told her as Mary left to go down to the ballroom. She turned and looked at herself in the mirror, the beautiful dress, the sparkling necklace and earrings. Her hand touched one of the delicate teardrops at her throat. Her dreams were finally coming true.

"Dora, do you think Steven will think I'm beautiful?" she asked the servant girl.

"Yes'm missy. Massa Steven has no eyes 'cept you."

Colleen left her room, her many petticoats swishing along the polished floors. She walked down the long hallway to the wide grand staircase and paused at the top, holding on to the mahogany banister. Down at the bottom she could see several people being ushered into the house by Matthew, dressed in a fine tuxedo. The atmosphere was festive, everyone wearing their finest holiday apparel and greeting one another with embracing and kisses on the cheek.

And then she saw him, standing on the last stair, looking up at her, Steven. He smiled and she felt tears prick her eyes. He looked so handsome standing there in his black tuxedo and white shirt, his dark hair shinning, his face aglow with the love he felt for her. Oh, god, how she loved him!

She descended the stairs, never taking her eyes from Steven. When she reached the bottom, he held out his hand to her. "My beautiful, Colleen," he told her. "You are radiant."

She lowered her eyes, embarrassed at his compliment.

"Could I see you alone in the library for just a few moments before you see your guests?" he asked quietly.

She looked around quickly to see if anyone were watching. "Do you think we dare?" she whispered back.

He smiled and took her hand leading her towards the library. "I won't tell if you won't," he said shutting the door behind them. The only light in the room came from the fireplace at the far end, a large blaze burning within. Steven walked towards the large hearth with Colleen following close behind.

"What is, Steven?" she asked as they stood in front of the blazing logs.

He leaned over and kissed her gently on the lips. "I just thought you ought to have something before the official announcement of our engagement tonight."

"What do you mean?" she asked looking up into his beautiful eyes.

"I mean you should have something to show off when your father tells everyone we are to marry," he said reaching into his jacket pocket. He pulled his hand back out and took her left hand in his. Then onto her finger he slipped a ring.

Colleen's eyes opened in amazement. The large green stone sparkled and glowed in the firelight. It was the most beautiful ring Colleen had ever seen. She took her eyes from the ring to look at Steven. She saw tears shinning in his eyes and her love for him grew even more.

"I love you with all my heart, Colleen," he said huskily. "I've loved you since we were children. I could never imagine myself with anyone else. I want to spend the rest of my life with you. My darling, sweet Colleen McBride, will you do me the honor of becoming my wife?"

Colleen was so emotional she could barely speak. "Of course Steven, of course I will marry you, you know that." She threw her arms around his neck and he embraced her in return.

He pulled away and put her face in his hands. "I promise you my darling, Colleen, that I will be the best husband to you I can be. I will take care of you and give you everything your heart desires."

Colleen nodded and took his hands in her own. "And I will be the best wife to you Steven, I promise." She looked again at the ring on her finger.

"It's an emerald," he told her. "It fits you, your eyes, who you are……"

"I will cherish it always. I will never take it off," she told him.

He kissed her then, hard, forcefully, until it nearly took her breath away. "Now come," he said holding out the crook of his arm to her, "let's go to the ball."

Colleen smiled at him and put her arm in his as he led her out of the library. They walked together down the long hallway to the back of the house where a separate wing held the ballroom. As they entered, they stopped in the doorway to observe the splendor.

The long room held three large crystal chandeliers hanging down its length in the high ceilings. Many full-length windows lined the walls on each side. These were decorated with garlands of evergreens and small candles sat on the sills. The floors were made of gleaming marble and at the far end, double French doors led to a brick terrace. It was here the large tree stood, sparkling and glowing with tinsel and candlelights. An orchestra played in one corner of the room and on the other side, tables laden with holiday punches and a wide variety of foods.

Colleen and Steven appeared in the doorway and everyone turned to look at them. Both of their parents were there as well as Gerritt. A quiet applause filled the room as they entered. James motioned to the musicians and as they began to play, Steven led Colleen out onto the dance floor. Soon others followed until the room was filled with waltzers spinning and twirling on the polished floors. Colleen danced with Steven first and then with Gerritt.

"You look beautiful tonight, dear sister."

"Thank you, Gerritt," she told him.

"Do you think it may have something to do with that ring on your finger?"

She only smiled in response as he swung her about the room.

Others danced while still others grouped in corners, talking and eating. Young people giggled and gossiped about the adults while men and women stood discussing the subtitles of society and politics.

Finally about half way through the evening, James silenced the musicians and stood at the far end of the ballroom in front of the large Christmas tree. "Everyone, ladies and gentlemen, may I have your attention, please!" he called out as he gestured to Steven and Colleen to join him. He watched as the two of them moved toward the front of the room. He was about to announce the engagement of his daughter, his baby. When had she grown to be a woman? Wasn't it just yesterday she was small and he had bounced her on his knee? She was so beautiful, so grown up and now she would leave him and join with another man. It was a joyful time, a new step, but yet he felt sorrow, too.

After they were standing next to him as well as his wife and Anna Bell and Clifford Covington and the crowd had gathered around them, he raised his arms to silence everyone.

"Ladies and gentlemen, I want to make an announcement. Many of you have known our daughter Colleen her entire life. Now she is a beautiful young woman and has fallen in love with a wonderful young man. Most of you know him as well. So it is my great pleasure to announce the engagement of my daughter Colleen McBride, to Steven Covington!"

Anna Bell gave Colleen a hug and Mary did the same with Steven. The crowd suddenly surged forward as the young people pressed forward to surround their friends. Colleen held out her hand to show off her new ring, while the young men shook hands and slapped Steven on the back.

Colleen's friend Cynthia held her hand, as she looked at the dazzling emerald. "Well, darlin', it looks as though Steven has done right by you. That's a gorgeous ring," she told her.

"Thank-you, Cynthia."

"When's the weddin'?" one of the other girls asked.

"In the spring," she told them.

"Oh, you're so lucky!" another in pink organza said.

Colleen smiled. "Yes, I'm very lucky."

It was then Andrew broke away from the group of young men to come to her side. "Congratulations, Colleen," he said shyly.

"Thank-you, Andrew," she said remembering his attentions at the horse race last fall.

"I always knew you and Steven would end up together," he said, "although I was kinda hopin' I might have a chance, but I guess any hope of that is gone." He smiled and took her hand, kissing it.

"You're very gracious," she told him.

As they mingled with the crowd, the McBride's and Covington's friends congratulated them as well. While this was going on, servants went about passing out glasses of champagne. When everyone had received theirs, James again quieted the crowd and raising his own glass, made the toast.

"To Steven and Colleen, may they always be as happy as they are now and may their marriage be enduring and produce lots of children!"

Everyone else raised their glasses and in unison said, "To Steven and Colleen!"

As everyone was taking a sip from their glasses, there arose a commotion at the door. Colleen could hear shouting and there seemed to be a scuffle.

James began making his way towards the rear of the room, craning his neck to see what the fuss was all about.

"Mr. McBride!" a voice suddenly called out. "Mr. McBride! It's me Robert Banyon. I've some news from Savannah!

Colleen recognized Robert as another one of the young men at the picnic who had sought out her attentions. The ruggedly handsome young man was not dressed in party attire, his clothing disheveled and dusty, his hair mussed. At present two strong black slaves were holding him. He seemed excited and agitated.

James had finally reached Robert and directed his servants to release him. "Robert," James told him, "calm yourself and tell me what news you have."

"They've done it," he stated. "They've really gone and done it."

By this time the room had gone silent and all eyes were focused on Robert. "It's all over Savannah," he continued. "Everyone's talkin' about it."

James placed his hands on Robert's shoulders. "Calm yourself son and start at the beginnin'. I can't make head nor tail of what it is you're tryin' to say."

"Yes boy, what's the gibberish you're yammerin' about, disruptin' Mr. McBrides ball?" Clifford stated as he stood by James' elbow.

Robert took a deep breath. "As many of you may have heard," he began, "that afta' Mr. Lincoln got elected, the South Carolina legislature remained in session and called for a state convention."

"Yes yes, I believe we had heard somethin' to that effect," James said.

"Well today, December 20, that convention voted unanimously to secede from the Union." Robert paused and the room was deadly quiet.

"Did you hear me?" he said more loudly. "South Carolina has seceded from the Union!"

A loud cheer erupted from the partygoers, mostly the young men in the group. "Secession! It's begun!" someone shouted. "Yahoo!" People began breaking off into small groups talking about the news they had just heard.

Clifford slapped James on the back. "What do you think of that ole man?" he asked, a broad grin on his face.

"I'm not sure," James responded. "I think it may lead to trouble."

"It may lead to Georgia bein' next along with the rest of the South. It's about time we had our own Union," Clifford said vehemently. "Then perhaps we'll be able to live our lives the way we please, without interference from them damn Yankees."

"Perhaps Clifford, perhaps, but what if the rest of the South doesn't secede? South Carolina cannot maintain its independence alone," James said to his friend as they walked the length of the ballroom together.

"It won't happen. Now that South Carolina has declared its independence, the rest will follow."

"But, if they don't, because doing so could mean war, then South Carolina would be forced back into the union and no one else would dare secede."

"Why must you always play the devil's advocate, my friend?" Clifford said putting his arm around James' shoulder.

As they neared the large tree at the end of the room, Mary and Anna Bell broke away from a group of ladies. They wore worried expressions on their faces.

"What has happened?" Mary asked. "What does all of this mean?"

"Nothin' to worry beautiful ladies such as yourselves," James told them.

"But that boy said South Carolina had seceded from the Union. Does that mean they are no longer part of the United States?"

"I'm not really sure," James told her as he embraced her. "But, I do know this; so far Georgia has had no part in it."

"So everything's alright?" Anna Bell asked anxiously.

"Everythin' is just fine, for now," Clifford told her. He peered over the women's heads at James to warn him not to alarm the ladies.

James signaled the orchestra to begin playing and a few people moved back onto the dance floor.

Colleen stood alone near the Christmas tree. Her parents had gone back out to dance and Gerritt and

Steven were at the door with the other young men speaking to Robert. Cynthia and the rest of the girls hovered on the periphery of the cluster of boys, waiting for their attentions and the other adults were helping themselves to the food table.

Her throat constricted and she felt as if she were going to cry. What had happened to her engagement party? Everything had been so beautiful. All their friends had come; everyone was dressed in their finest. The house was decorated and the tables were laden with the best foods and wines. She was wearing the most beautiful dress she had ever owned and Steven had given her a gorgeous engagement ring.

It should have been the most wonderful day of her life, but now it was all ruined. Since Robert had crashed the ball and made his announcement, no one could talk of anything else. Even Steven was with a group of other young men talking politics. Not one person was paying her any attention.

Tears threatened to overflow her eyes and she did not want anyone to see her cry. She slipped behind the Christmas tree and though the French doors to the patio beyond. The night air was chilly and she shivered in her thin dress. There was a faint breeze, which blew the branches of the willow trees along the riverbank. Beyond, she could see the fires from the slave quarters and heard soft singing. Someone was down in the river collecting water and she could hear the soft splash of a bucket against the water.

The singing of the slaves seemed sad and melodious, which deepened her mood even more. Why did it have to be this way? Why were things in the country so in turmoil just at this point in her life? Why couldn't the northern states just leave them alone to live the kind of lives they had always lived? Why now was it so important an issue that they had slaves? They had always had slaves, even the generations before them. Even northerners had had slaves. Why tonight of all nights, did South Carolina have to secede from the Union?

She leaned on the white iron rail that encircled the patio and felt the despair wash over her and the tears flood her eyes. As her head was down and her back turned to the French doors, she did not hear Steven come out onto the patio. When he touched her shoulder she gasped and whirled around.

"Oh, Steven, you frightened me," she told him, trying to look away so he would not notice her tears.

But she had failed. He took her chin in his hand and turned her face to look at him. "What's this, tears? What's wrong my love?"

"It's.....it's just that everything's been spoiled. "It was such a lovely party and Daddy had just announced our engagement and then Robert had to burst in like that and….well, everyone's just talking politics and not paying the least bit of attention to us. And….it was supposed to be our night."

"It's still our night, Sweetheart," he told her. "No one can ever take that away from us. Tonight we declared our love for each other and announced it to the world. We shall remember it for the rest of our lives."

She looked into his face. "You're right, Steven. I shouldn't be so childish. It doesn't matter about the others. What is really important is you and me and our love for each other."

Steven smiled and held her tighter. His words did not show his true feeling for he wasn't sure at all what their future would be; if war came, then what?

"Let's go back inside," he told her, "you're shivering."

He led her back to the ballroom where, but for a few, everyone had resumed with the festivities, but for Colleen, somehow it just wasn't the same.

Finally, at 1:00 A.M. the guests began filing out. Each family's personal drivers, who had been eating and socializing with the McBride slaves, brought their individual carriages around to the front of the house to take their masters and mistresses home, some having to travel to Savannah and beyond in the dark. They had the carriage lanterns lit to help show the way. It would be several hours before they reached their destination.

The daunting task of cleaning up and taking care of the leftover food was left to the servants. Many of them would be up all night.

After Colleen had seen Steven and his parents off, she went upstairs to her room. Dora was waiting there for her as she slumped wearily into a chair near her dressing table.

"Is you tired, missy?" Dora asked. "I heerd it was a beautiful ball."

"The ball was wonderful until Robert Banyon came in and spoiled everything."

"Was he drunk?" Dora asked as she helped Colleen to her feet and started to undo the many buttons down the back of her dress.

"No he wasn't drunk. He had come all the way from Savannah to make this big announcement about South Carolina seceding from the Union."

"What dat means, secede?" Dora asked.

"It <u>means</u> South Carolina has left the United States…..to be a country of their own; all because of something as stupid as slavery." Suddenly she realized who she was speaking to and whirled around to face her, but when she looked into Dora's eyes, she didn't know what to say to her.

"Dora," she asked hesitatingly, "what's it like to be a slave?"

"What does you mean, Missy?" she said with down cast eyes.

"What does it feel like? What is your life really like?"

"It's jes' what's it is and dats all," Dora told her as she lifted Colleen's gown over her head and moved away towards the armoire.

"But it's not a bad life, is it? I mean, you're treated well. You have everything provided for you in exchange for some work you do. So, what else could you want?"

Dora slowly turned around to face Colleen, the dress still in her arms. She lifted her head and looked up at her mistress. "I'se could be free."

Christmas was only five days after the ball, but it too, was full of activities and visiting friends and relatives. Colleen and Steven were able to spend more time together. Colleen's thoughts were mostly of their upcoming wedding, the planning and working out all the details, while Steven seemed preoccupied, distant. She couldn't understand Steven's lack of interest in their nuptials. She felt he should be as excited as she and would want to participate more in the planning.

But Steven felt he had greater concerns, those of his family's plantation and the state of the nation, especially for the South. Talk was prevalent everywhere about South Carolina's secession and whether or not the other Southern states would follow.

He and his father Clifford, were trying to make sure supplies were in abundance and the overseer was diligent in his duties to watch the slaves. They were now even more concerned that slaves would try and run. It was no secret to either master or slave that an under ground railroad to the north existed and many from other plantations had already escaped through this method.

Even though James and Gerritt were occupied with similar concerns, Colleen and her mother could think of nothing else but the wedding. The date had been set for the first of May when all the flowers would be in full bloom. Colleen had asked her friends to be bridesmaids with Cynthia as her maid of honor. The dresses had been ordered from Europe, Paris to be exact and so had the groomsmen's tuxedos. Menus were planned and arrangements made for musicians and extra help.

Time passed quickly and it was soon February. After South Carolina's departure from the Union, other cotton states had followed; Mississippi, Alabama, Florida, Louisiana, Texas, and Georgia. Then, on February eighth, representatives from these states met in Montgomery, Alabama and set up a new nation, the

Confederate States of America. A temporary constitution was drawn up and Jefferson Davis from Mississippi was elected President, with Alexander Stephens of Georgia, as Vice President.

The new nation was the talk of all the plantation owners. Even though many were glad to see its existence come into being, they were still apprehensive. They knew their newfound independence could very well mean war.

Most were not worried about their prospects of winning such a war, believing the north was full of mudsills, poor immigrants and money mad Yankees. They believed no Northerner would want to fight to preserve the Union or to free a bunch of darkies. Any army thus encountered would run for home when confronted by a furious Confederate army.

From then on whenever the families got together or the men would travel to Savannah on business; the talk was always of war, whether or not the North would try to regain government holdings in the South.

Even the ladies at their embroideries and tea parties, could only discuss the aspects of war in regards to how it would affect their lives. Most had no concept of what war would mean to them. Those who were confident with the glory of the new Southern Union were sure if war did come, it would be short lived and the South would be victorious.

Then on March 4th 1861, Abraham Lincoln was sworn in as President of the United States. In his inaugural address, Mr. Lincoln reminded the Southern states of his desire to keep the nation unbroken and if war were to come, it would be because of their own initiative to be the aggressors. He reiterated his resolve to be President of the whole nation.

In spite of the turmoil within the nations, life went on at the plantation. The fields were tilled and planted as always. The gardening and sheep sheering took place, as did the laborious spring cleaning of the mansion from top to bottom. Windows were washed; linens were cleaned and hung out to dry. Quilts were aired and rugs beaten.

Colleen helped her mother to oversee the final preparations of her wedding. She had just gone to the seamstress for another fitting of her wedding gown and the last of the food and been ordered.

As Mary went over the guest list checking off the names of those who had already responded to the invitations. "We already have close to two hundred who have said they will be here," Mary told her as she moved about the music room with the list in her hand.

"How many more are on the list?" Colleen asked as she sat before the large mahogany piano, plunking quietly on the keys. She absently wondered if she could still play Beethoven's Fifth as she once had when she took lessons as a child.

"Nearly one hundred more have yet to respond," Mary told her, "and with only eight weeks until the wedding." She sighed and sank unto a settee. "How will this weddin' ever come together?

Colleen! Are you listenin' to me?" her mother said more sharply.

"What is it, Mama?" Colleen said finally looking up from the piano.

"I swear, gal, your mind is off somewhere else. I thought you wanted this weddin' to be perfect."

"I do, Mama, of course I do," she said getting up from the bench. She walked to the long windows against the south side of the houses. The afternoon sun was streaming through, creating a pool of light on the floor. Colleen fingered the white brocade curtains disturbing fractions of rays and causing dust to whirl in the air. "It's just that I hardly ever get to see Steven anymore, and when I do, he seems so preoccupied, as if he really doesn't care about this weddin' at all. Whenever I ask about what kind of champagne he wants or whether he'd rather have venison or pork, he just tells me to decide.

I mean, does he want to get married or not?" she said turning to face her mother. "Sometimes I wonder if he still loves me." Her head drooped and her lip stuck out in a pout. Steven's seeming lack of interest in the wedding preparations had made her feel depressed and despondent.

Mary rose from her seat and went to her daughter. "Now darlin', you know Steven loves you and wants to marry you. He's just preoccupied with the spring plantin' and lookin' out after his slaves. Besides, weddin's are women's work. The important part will be for him to show up."

"I know he's busy and now there's all this talk of war, but he promised he'd make our weddin' his top priority and besides, I love him so much, I just want us to be together."

"It won't be long now, darlin' and then you will be able to share your life with Steven." Mary put her hands on Colleen's shoulders.

"Have I told you how much I'm going to miss you?" she asked. "My baby is getting' married and going off with a husband of her own."

Then Colleen smiled. "I'll be close by and we'll see each other all the time. I promise.

Did I tell you the Covingtons are going to let us use the guesthouse on their plantation until we build a home of our own? They will also give us a couple of house slaves for our own."

"That's wonderful, darlin'," Mary told her, "and you know I've already told you, you could have Dora. Now can we get back to the weddin' plans?"

Meanwhile, Steven had by no means forgotten about his upcoming nuptials to Colleen. His love for her seemed to grow deeper every day and he looked forward to spending the rest of his life with her.

Whenever they were together, and it never seemed to be enough, he felt he never wanted to leave her side. The smell of her, touching her incredibly soft skin, drove him nearly to distraction. Whenever he kissed her lips, her mouth tasted so sweet his passions would rise, and he could barely control his hunger for her.

It wasn't as if he weren't interested in the plans for their wedding, he knew Colleen was frustrated with him. It was just that he was involved with so many other things. He had to help his father oversee the planting of the spring cotton crop and the running of the plantation was a major task in of itself.

The Covington holdings were just as vast as the McBride's, containing barns, stables, weaving houses, mill, bailer, and so forth. Along with field slaves, house slaves and their quarters, it was a massive business.

Now that Georgia had seceded along with the other Southern states and begun a new nation, there was even more cause for concern. The threat of war was ever prevalent. No one yet knew what that would mean to the plantations. Even now, several slaves had already tried to run. If it hadn't been for their diligent overseer Mr. Jenkins, they would have lost some of their valuable property.

Other plantations had already lost slaves to the Underground Railroad. Even with the hiring of more slave catchers, now with Northern sympathizers helping the runaways, they were becoming more difficult to recover.

He also thought of what it would mean to him personally if he were to go off to fight. He truly believed in his heart that their cause was justified and the glorious states of the Confederacy would prevail over the oppressive Northern Yankees.

However noble the cause, it was still cause for anxiety to think about donning a soldier's uniform and going off to kill men.

He also worried what all these ramifications would create for his marriage with Colleen. It was troubling times and Steven just didn't have time to ponder over wedding details.

Then on April 12th, the bottom dropped out of the Southern complacency. On an island off the harbor of Charleston, South Carolina stood Fort Sumter. It was still held by Union forces even though it lay within Southern territory and General Scott had advised Lincoln to abandon the fort.

And so, at 12:00 midnight on that fateful day, Confederate emissaries rowed out to the fort and delivered the ultimatum to the Union commander, Major Anderson Surrender by 4:00 A.M. or Southern batteries would fire upon them.

Receiving no word, General Pierre Gustave Toutant Beauregard of the Confederate forces, ordered the artillery fire on Fort Sumter.

After thirty-four hours of battery, Anderson surrendered to the whoops and cheers of Charleston civilians as they stood on their rooftops. The Union flag was lowered and the war had begun. In quick succession, Virginia, North Carolina, Tennessee and Arkansas joined the confederacy. Jefferson Davis promptly made arrangements to move the capitol from Alabama to Richmond,Virginia.

On April 15th, Savannah and the surrounding plantations received word of the battle and consequent declaration of war. The Covington plantation received word first and Steven quickly had his horse saddled and rode over to the McBride mansion to relay the news. When he reined his horse up in front of their porch, James and Gerritt hurried outside.

"Mr. McBride, Gerritt," he called out, "it's war!" He rushed up the stairs to stand before them. "Sir," he repeated, "it's war."

"Slow down son," James directed, "talk slower and give us all the details."

"They, the Confederates, fired on Fort Sumter two days ago. The Yankees surrendered! We won the battle!"

"Now that is a piece of news," James said thoughtfully rubbing his chin. "You say we're at war?"

"Yes sir, and four more states have joined the Confederacy."

"How large is our army?" Gerritt asked.

"Don't know," Steven told him, "but, they're signin' everyone up in Savannah. My father and I are goin' tomorrow."

"What's this? What's this all about?" They all turned to see Mary in the doorway and behind her stood Colleen. "What is it you're goin' to Savannah for, Steven?" Mary asked him.

"The war, Ma'am," Steven said smiling. "Fort Sumter was fired upon and the Yankees surrendered."

Mary and Colleen came out onto the veranda. "What does that mean?" Mary asked with growing apprehension. "James, tell me what this is all about."

"It appears my dear that we, the newly formed states of the Confederacy, are at war with the Union of the North. All able bodied men are required to report in Savannah to sign up for the army."

Colleen felt her heart leap to her throat and the blood drain from her face. She felt as if she were about to pass out. "No," she said in a whisper, "no, this can't be true. Steven, tell me this isn't happening," she said more loudly.

Steven went to her and put his arm around her shoulder. "It will be all right, Darlin'."

"But Steven, our weddin' is only a few weeks away," she said looking up at him.

"Don't you see? This is the chance we've been waiting for, the chance to show our stuff. Don't worry, we'll beat those Yankees in a couple of weeks. Why at most, we'll just have to postpone the weddin' for a little while."

"Will you have to go, too?" Mary asked Gerritt touching his arm.

"Yes Mama, Papa and I will go to Savannah with the Covingtons."

"James, not you too, not both of you?"

"Yes Mary, I'll be going as well. It's my duty. All along I was against war, but now that it's here, I will do my part like everyone else. Our homes, our way of life is now in jeopardy and I will do everything I can to protect it. I'm not so sure this war will be brief or easy."

Both Colleen and Mary felt overwhelmed by the news. They knew there was nothing they could do to keep their men from going to war and something deep inside themselves felt a dread they had never known before. It brought with it a fear that would remain with them for along time to come.

"Gerritt and I will come to your home tomorrow mornin'," James told Steven. "We can all go together to Savannah."

"Yes sir," Steven said moving towards his horse, "I'll tell my father." With a longing glance at Colleen, he mounted his horse and rode off.

That evening as Colleen lay in her bed, she thought about the news they had received that day. At supper everyone had been very quiet; each absorbed in their own thoughts. No one had eaten very much. The thing she had feared most had come to pass. War. It was almost too scary to think about; her papa and Gerritt going off to fight. And Steven, what would happen to Steven? And what about their wedding? All the plans had been made and now would they have to postpone it? What if something happened to Steven? She loved him so much she couldn't bear the thought of losing him. As she lay alone in her bed, her fears grew and she cried silently.

When she awoke the next morning, her father and Gerritt had already left for Savannah. She went to the dining room to find her mother having breakfast or not having breakfast as she was merely picking at the food on her plate.

Colleen went to the sideboard where Bess stood ready to serve her from the array of prepared foods. Colleen waved her away and asked just for coffee. When Bess had poured it for her, she took the delicate china cup and went to sit at the table with her mother.

"What will happen now, Mother?" Colleen asked her.

"I don't know, dear," she said laying her fork down. "I've never had any experience with war before. I do remember my grandfather talking about the Revolutionary war when I was small. He would only say it was a horror beyond words and many, many people died."

Tears willed up in Colleen's eyes. "Oh, Mama, do you think Papa, Gerritt, or Steven could be killed?"

"I don't think that's something we should dwell on right now," her mother said getting up. "I think we should be positive, support our men and do what we can to help."

Colleen wiped at her tears. "You're right; we need to be brave for our men."

"That's right, sweetie," Mary said going to her daughter and giving her a hug.

"This is going to be a difficult time for everyone and we're all going to have to be strong."

That evening the men returned, James feeling exhausted, Gerritt was ebullient.

"You should have seen all the men there signin' up, Mother," Gerritt said as he put forkful after forkful into his mouth. "It was something," he continued. "I didn't know there were so many men in this area, hundreds, there were hundreds. When you think about how this is goin' on all over the South, hundreds and hundreds of men signin' up to fight, why we'll win this war in no time!"

James looked up at his son. "Do you realize son," he said quietly, "that the North has three times as many people as the South; that most of the manufacturing companies are located in the North and the North also controls the major sea ports?"

"But Papa, the South has its cotton. We dominate the North in agricultural production. They rely on us and without Southern cotton, the Northern textile mills will stand idle, not to mention the foreign exchange the North enjoys by the oversea sales of Southern cotton. I wouldn't be surprised if the Northern financial structure will collapse. I believe the Unions entire wealth is imported to them through our labor."

"What has changed your mind on this matter, Gerritt?" James asked him. "I thought you were aware of the imbalance between Union strengths and our own."

"I just took a closer look at the situation and I believe our cotton could very well decree the destruction of the North's economy and because European markets rely on us so heavily, they could be forced to intervene on our behalf."

"It sounds as though you've been listening to all that rhetoric from Clifford and Steven Covington."

"It's more than that, Papa," Gerritt told his father. "When I saw all those men in Savannah today and I listened to their excitement about this war, how they would die to preserve our freedom to remain our own Union, why it's just like the Revolutionary war. They fought for freedom, to be an independent nation, to be free of England and her tyrannical rules, to be able to govern ourselves and live our lives the way we see fit. This is no different."

James sighed deeply. "I'm glad you have your ideology and convictions, Gerritt, along with all the other young southern bucks that are so anxious to fight for glory and honor. I only hope it's worth dying for."

"When will you have to go?" Mary asked her husband.

"We have one week," he said sadly, getting up from the table, "and then we must report to the Confederate camp outside Savannah for training."

"A week! How can that be possible?" she asked going to James's side. "What are we to do here? What about the plantation, the cotton crop, the slaves, the... the...everything!" she said in exasperation.

"Don't worry, my dear. You are such a wonderful manager, I'm sure you will be able to competently run the plantation in my absence. And Mr. Solomon, the overseer will be here to help and will manage the slaves."

"Oh, James, I just don't know……" Mary said putting her face in her hands.

James put his arm around her and began to lead her out of the dining room. "Come my dear, let's retire to our room." They left and went on up the stairs.

Gerritt and Colleen were left sitting at the table in silence. For a time they sat that way, thinking their own thoughts, watching their parents until they could no longer see them going down the hall.

Colleen thought about what it must be for her mother now. As awful as it was for her to think about Steven going off to war, she thought it must be worse for her mother. Her parents had been together for twenty-two years, built their plantation, had children together and shared many intimacies. How could her mother bear to let him go?

"We received our uniforms," Gerritt said breaking their silence.

Colleen suddenly realized he was talking to her. "Oh really? What does it look like?" she asked, mostly to be polite.

"Very sharp," he said. "We had to purchase them so of course, we bought the best. It's gray with fancy brass buttons and gold braid on the sleeves. The hat leaves something to be desired, however. It's a cap really, with a small brim and a squashed, flat top."

"I'm sure you'll look mighty dandy in your new uniform," she told him getting up from the table. Going behind him she rested her hands on his shoulders. "Just don't get any blood on it." She then left the room and went on up the stairs.

Dora was waiting for her in her room. She felt tired, depressed. How could all of this be happening? She began to undress. All she wanted to do was to crawl into bed and sleep, even though it was yet early.

"Is you sad, Missy?" Dora asked her.

"It's just awful, Dora. War, just think of it, war!"

"What's it all means, Missy?" Dora asked, helping her off with her dress.

"It <u>means</u>," she said irritatingly, "that all of our men are goin' off to fight and maybe be killed. All because the Union won't let us live our lives the way we want to."

"What happens if'n we lose?" Dora wanted to know.

Colleen looked at her Negro slave with contempt. "We will not lose, you hear me? I don't <u>ever</u> want to hear you say anythin' like that again, you understand me?"

"Yes'm, Miss Colleen," she told her, but secretly she wondered if the South lost, would it mean her freedom?

The next few days were spent in organizing the books of the plantation to make things easier for Mary. Directions were given to the overseer Mr. Solomon, in handling the slaves and making sure the running of the estate went smoothly. Mr. Solomon was allowed to hire several other men to help him, along with promises of additional salary for his extra responsibilities. None of these men were loyal to the Southern cause, concerned with only their own agenda, so had no qualms about not signing up to fight in the glorious cause unless forced to do so.

Two days before they were to leave, a special dinner was planned with the Covingtons coming to share with them. All the men's favorite foods had been prepared, roast duck, pork, sweet potatoes, chittlins, hot breads with sweet butter and several kinds of pies for dessert.

As Bess and Rose served the meal, tears shone in their eyes and they could be heard to sniffle now and then. But the men were in high spirits, looking forward to their great adventure and talked of how they would whip the Yankees in record time.

The women stayed silent, thinking only of the loneliness they would experience when they had gone. Colleen sitting next to Steven, kept looking at him, thinking how handsome he was, how much she loved him, could not imagine losing him.

Mary and Anna Bell too, could think only of their pain in having their men leave.

Anna Bell would be alone, having no other children to help her. She had her servants and overseer, but it would be a difficult time.

At one point in the meal when the other men were toasting the glorious Confederate army, Steven leaned over to Colleen and whispered to her that he would like to see her alone by the gazebo. He took her hand under the table and squeezed it, looking into her eyes. She nodded her head in response.

Once the meal was over, everyone retired to the library where the men got out the imported cigars and snifter of brandy, while the women sipped tea. Tonight was not the time for the sexes to be separated.

Steven rose from his seat and put his brandy on the large mahogany desk. "Colleen and I would like to take a walk down to the gazebo," he told everyone.

"Why, Steven, you know you can't……."Anna Bell began, but was cut off by her husband.

"Anna Bell," he said gently, "I don't think we need to worry about propriety at this time. It won't hurt for Steven and Colleen to take a walk without a chaperone."

The look on Anna Bell's face showed she disagreed, but she said nothing. Steven took Colleen's hand, helped her to stand and then lead her out of the room. Carlton was waiting to open the front door for them.

As they walked out onto the front veranda, the warm spring air caressed their skin. The stars shone brightly and a full moon trailed across the sky.

They went down the steps and started across the lawn towards the gazebo, still holding hands. They could see lights twinkling near the barns and workhouses from lanterns as slaves went about their evening chores and across the river the glow from the slave quarters fires lit the sky. Sounds of the slaves going about preparing their evening meal, talking and singing could be heard across the water.

They went inside the gazebo and stood silently for a few moments, each keenly aware of the others physical presence. Steven turned to her and took her in his arms. He held her tightly, feeling the warmth of her body, the pressure of her firm breasts on his chest. His hands trailed over her arms, feeling the softness of her skin. Suddenly he pressed his mouth on hers, kissing her passionately. He tasted her lips, his teeth biting tenderly. His mouth moved to her neck and then to the top of her breasts.

"Oh my Colleen," he whispered breathlessly, "my beautiful Colleen. I love you so much."

"And I love you, Steven," she whispered back. She could feel the warmth of his breath on her skin, causing the gooseflesh to rise on her arms.

Steven kissed her again and again, his passion rising. "Colleen, I need you. I can't wait any longer."

"No Steven, we can't. It's not right. We're not married yet."

He released her from his embrace, his hands on her shoulders. He looked into her eyes. "Colleen, I don't know anymore when we'll be able to get married. I leave in two days to fight in this war. I don't know how long it will last, when I will be able to get back, or if I ever will."

"Oh Steven, don't say that!" Colleen said alarmed.

"All I'm saying is, I want us to be close, Colleen. I want us to experience the most intimate act two people can experience. I've never had that with anyone before, Colleen." He took her hand and led her to a bench surrounding the gazebo. They sat down together and he turned towards her, holding both her hands in the fold of her skirt. She could feel him trembling.

"I know you've probably heard tales of how all the young bucks go into Savannah to sow their wild oats, to….to sleep with prostitutes or maybe with their slaves."

Colleen lowered her eyes. She had never heard him speak so frankly before.

"Well it's true some do that, but some don't. I never have because I've always been in love with you. I could never imagine myself with anyone but you.

I was so looking forward to our marriage, to being together for the rest of our lives. And I couldn't wait until we were joined as one…..in that special way that husbands and wives share. But now I don't know when that will happen or if it ever will. I don't think I can bear going away and not ever sharing with you in that way."

"Are you saying you want to get married before you leave?" Colleen asked looking into his eyes. She knew what he was really saying, but she needed to hear the words.

"There isn't time for us to be married, at least not with the minister or in a church, but we could make our vows to each other in front of God."

When she looked a little perplexed he went on. "Come to my home tomorrow, my parents are going to relatives to say good bye. We could be alone. We could say our vows to each other, make our promises. And then we could…..be together. Then when I leave we would know we always had that. It would be a special memory no one could take from us."

Colleen's mind was reeling. Everything was happening so fast. Steven would be going away to war in only two days. Their beautiful wedding they had planned for so long would have to be postponed. What if he never came home? The thought of it was almost more than she could bear.

She knew exactly what Steven was proposing. He wanted to marry her, even if it was only between them and God and he wanted to make love to her. Is it what she wanted also?

She looked into Steven's eyes, his beautiful eyes and saw tears shinning there. Her love for him was so over powering, she knew she couldn't turn him down. "I want it too, Steven," she told him. "I love you with all my heart. You know that. I've always planned on marrying you and I know you'll come back to me after this war is over and we'll have our big wedding in front of our families and friends. But before you go I want us to be joined together, in spirit and in body."

Steven closed his eyes and let out the breath he had been holding.

"I will come to you tomorrow," she told him.

They stood together and Steven held her in his arms. "Tomorrow darling, we will belong to one another."

They parted when they saw the Covington carriage being brought around to the front of the house. "It looks as though I must go for now," he told her, "but I will see you tomorrow. I can't wait for you to be my wife."

"And neither can I," she said touching his face.

They walked back to the house where Steven departed with his parents and Colleen went to her room to prepare for bed. She didn't speak much to Dora as she helped her undress. Colleen was lost in her own thoughts and Dora, sensing her mood, did not engage her in conversation.

As exhausted as she felt, sleep eluded her, her mind racing with all the recent events, the war, her father, Gerritt, and Steven all signing up to go and now she and Steven would say their vows to one another. Afterward they would make love. What would it be like? Would it be wonderful? She didn't yet know, but she did know it was something she wanted very much to share with Steven. There was a chance he might not come back. Just the thought of that possibility brought tears to her eyes. She wanted to have something to hold on to, to share something with Steven that no one ever had before, something so intimate as to be shared only by those who loved each other with all their hearts.

She knew of course, of the tales of prostitutes and masters with slaves, but she knew that did not apply to her and Steven. Finally, blessedly, she fell asleep and dreamed troubling dreams of war and chaos. She saw blood and death, the air filled with the sounds of battle. She could hear men scream, but in the dream she couldn't ascertain identity, only faceless skeletons of men. Everything jumbled together so that it made no sense. Upon awakening, there was only a feeling of deep loss.

The first thought that entered Colleen's mind that next morning was that it would be her father and Gerritt's last day at home and of course also for Steven. She felt nervous about their meeting that day, but excitement filled her heart as well.

Dora helped her bathe and then to dress in a simple camisole, bloomers and day dress, white with small pink roses. A small petticoat filled out the skirt. She brushed her long hair until it glistened, but left it down because Steven liked it that way. On her feet she wore soft kid skin slippers.

"What's you'se gwine to do today, Missy?" Dora asked as she made up the bed.

"Oh, nothing special," she said carefully. "I just wanted to look nice for my father and brother's last day home. And I might take a ride. I haven't ridden Princess in several weeks," she said in what she thought was nonchalance.

Dora had known Colleen her entire life and she knew something was afoot. But she also knew that whatever it was, Colleen didn't want anyone to know about it. So she chose to ignore it. "You'se gwine to be sad when your Pappy and Mister Gerritt leaves?" she asked.

"It'll be horrid," Colleen said with a deep sigh. "I don't know how mother and I are going to manage without them."

"Don't worry, Missy," Dora told her, "we uns will takes good care of you."

Colleen took her shawl from the chair. "It's not the same," Colleen said with tears in her eyes. "It's just not the same." She turned and walked out of the room.

Shortly after breakfast, James, Mary and Gerritt left to visit friends. Colleen begged to stay home, claiming she felt too despondent to visit anyone and perhaps she would take Princess for a ride.

After they had all left, Colleen walked casually down to the stables as if it were a walk she made every day. She went into the dimly lit cool interior, smelling the musky scent of manure and hay. Her footsteps echoed on the wooden plank flooring. She passed by her father's white stallion, Champion, then Gerritt's roan, then finally she arrived at Princess's stall. She called out to her and the black and white filly poked her head over the stall door.

"Hello beauty," she said to the horse as she stroked the soft muzzle. The mare nuzzled her hand and nickered, looking for the sugar cube. Colleen pulled it out of her dress pocket and gave it to the horse.

"You want's to go ridin', Missy?" a voice behind her said, causing Colleen to jump.

"Oh Henry, you frightened me," she told the groom. "Yes please, I would like to take Princess out. Would you saddle her for me?"

"Yes'm, Missy," Henry said, immediately going to the tack room to get her saddle.

Once Princess had been saddled and led outside, Henry helped her to mount, sitting sidesaddle. Colleen started down the wide sweeping, tree lined drive, walking Princess until she got out to the main road. Once there she put Princess into a canter, getting closer to being in Steven's arms.

It was nearly ten miles to the Covington plantation, but the closer she got the faster her heart seemed to beat. Today she would become Mrs. Steven Covington. Perhaps not in the eyes of the law, but she knew she would be in her heart. It was a day she had looked forward to as long as she could remember. Yes, she was disappointed there would be no expensive white dress, no vows before a pastor and her family, no friends to witness their love. But what mattered most at this time and place, was that she and Steven be together.

She finally arrived at the plantation called Briarwood. She followed the tree-lined drive to the two story sprawling mansion. Steven came down the wide stairs to greet her. He directed one of the slaves working in the garden to take her horse.

Steven was dressed in white pants, white coat and blue shirt. His hair shone and was combed back. To Colleen he looked to be the most handsome man in the world.

They walked up the steps together, Colleen taking Steven's arm. "You look beautiful, my darling bride," he told her. "Are you nervous?"

"I'd be lying if I said no," she told him holding tighter to his arm.

Once inside, Steven led her to the parlor located in the left wing of the house. They walked to the doorway and Colleen paused. She had been in this room many times, but never had she seen it looking so beautiful. Anna Bell had decorated it all in white damask and velvet with white drapes and rugs. Small tables were placed in strategic locations about the room which normally held lamps, but now brilliant bouquets of spring flowers graced the room in crystal vases. Their fragrance filled the room with a delightful aroma.

On the far side of the room were wide ceiling length windows which faced out onto the gardens. The morning sun flooded the room, making it dazzling in its brilliance.

"Oh Steven, it's beautiful," she told him.

"I wanted it to be special for when we say our vows to each other." He led her to the windows where they stood facing each other, bathed in warm sunshine.

Steven smiled and touched her cheek. "Are you ready to become my wife?" he asked her quietly.

"I've waited for this day my entire life," she told him.

He took both her hands in his own and then looking deeply into her eyes he began: "I Steven Covington, take you Colleen McBride, to be my wife. I promise I will love you and cherish you my entire life. I promise to share my life with you, in sickness and health, in riches and in poverty. I love you, Colleen and I always will. You are my heart and my life. Here to day, I promise to be true to you, to love you forever." He smiled and squeezed her hands.

Colleen took a deep breath and began her vows: "I Colleen McBride, take you Steven Covington to be my husband, my partner in life. I promise to love you and honor you. Where you go, I will go. Your lodging will be my lodging, whether a castle or home of logs, I will be by your side. I will share my life with you in sickness and health, in riches and poverty. I promise to be loyal to you and love you so long as I live." She stopped and her words came out a whisper as her emotions flooded over her and the tears filled her eyes. "I love you, Steven. You are my heart, my life."

He kissed her then, deeply and passionately. "We are now husband and wife," he told her. "We've made our promises to each other in front of God. Our hearts are joined as one and now there is only one last thing to do."

She nodded, knowing full well of what he was speaking. "We will join our bodies together, we will give ourselves completely to each other." She smiled at him, letting him know it was what she wanted also, that she wasn't afraid.

He kissed her again and then took her hand and led her from the room. As they walked down the hall towards the grand staircase to the upper floor, Colleen noted the lack of servants anywhere nearby. But she knew Steven would have thought of everything and made sure they were occupied elsewhere.

They ascended the polished mahogany staircase and went quietly down the hall towards Steven's room; each lost in their own thoughts. Upon arriving at the door, Steven stopped her. "It isn't a home of our own yet and I hope to make a repeat performance when that day occurs, but I guess this will have to do for now." He bent down and scooped her up in his arms and then carried her across the threshold. Once inside, he put her back on her feet and kissed her gently, softly. He parted from her and went to one corner of the room where a chair and table with lamp was located. Also on the table, Steven had placed a bottle of champagne and two tall glasses.

He took off his jacket and as he began to uncork the bottle, Colleen walked around the room. As many times as she had been to this house, she of course, had never been in Steven's room. It was decorated very masculine with a heavy, large four poster bed and matching massive armoire and clothes chest. A dressing table stood against one wall. Colleen fingered the gold handled brush and comb set, then the burl wood jewelry chest. She walked over to a pair of French doors, which went out onto a balcony surrounded by a white wrought iron railing. She opened the doors and walked out onto the balcony, the warm breeze blowing back the white lace curtains.

The room was on the opposite side of the house from the parlor and so looked out across the vast orchards, which were in full bloom, their delicate petals drifting slowly to the green grass below. Beyond the orchard was the river and the guest cottage that would become their home when Steven came back from the war.

He was suddenly there behind her, holding the glasses filled with the golden, bubbly champagne. He held one out to her and she took it from him. "This is to us, to our marriage," he said holding his glass to hers. "May God bless us and our union."

"And may He keep you safe so that when you come home we will be happy and blessed with many children," she said as well.

They clinked their glasses together and sipped at the champagne. Then he leaned over and placed his mouth on hers. She tasted sweet and warm. His tongue found hers and the kiss grew deeper.

He put his arm around her waist and drew her back into the room. As she sipped more of her champagne, he pulled the curtains across the doors, defusing the sunshine, making everything seem softer. The light in the room seemed to shimmer and move.

Steven went to the bed and drew back the comforter exposing the cool, crisp white sheets. He went to her and took the glass from her and set it down on the dressing table. He took her face in his hands and kissed her again.

"I love you so much," he told her and before she could respond, he kissed her again, deeply, passionately.

She kissed him as well, her lips moving on his. His mouth moved from her mouth to her jaw and down to her throat. She tilted her head back and let the sensations flood over her. She head felt light and her body was tingling.

Steven's lips had gone down to caress between her breasts. She held his head and moved her fingers in his hair. He moved up and kissed her mouth again. His breathing had become more rapid and he had begun to tremble. He reached behind her and began to unbutton her dress while she unbuttoned his shirt at the same time.

Her dress fell down around her ankles in a puddle on the floor, leaving her standing in just her chemise and bloomers. She pushed his shirt back off his shoulders and pulled it down off his arms.

Once his shirt was off, she ran her hands over his muscular arms and chest, feeling the softness of his skin. He held her close and she could feel his excitement, his hardness against her.

She untied the ribbons on her chemise until it fell open, leaving her full breasts exposed. She heard his sharp intake of breath and then tentatively reached out and touched her. She shivered at his caress, the gooseflesh standing out on her skin. She went to the bed and sat down, Steven following. He leaned over her, kissing her, touching and caressing her.

She fell back with Steven's body covering hers. Their passions grew; the kissing became more intense. "I can wait no longer," Steven told her. "I want you so much."

Somehow they both finished undressing and lay naked together beneath the sheets. Steven ran his hands over her body, her breasts, her flat stomach, her legs.

"You're so soft," he whispered between kisses.

She began to pull on him, urging him on. Her head was swimming. She felt she could never get enough. She loved to kiss him, to taste his mouth, to lick the salt from his body. She loved feeling the firmness of his muscles, the hardness of his manhood. And now she wanted more than anything to feel that inside her. He had awakened desires in her, she never knew existed. "Make love to me, Steven," she told him, her voice hoarse with passion.

She could feel him trembling as he placed his body over hers. He held himself up with his arms as he looked down into her face. "You're so beautiful," he said and kissed her again.

She felt him pressing into her, gently at first and then more forcefully. When the pain stabbed through her, she gasped and her eyes grew wide. He stopped, but she shook her head. "No please, don't stop, don't stop," she urged.

He continued until he had entered her completely. He lay still until the pain had gone. Then slowly at first, he made love to her. She never knew anything could feel so incredible.

Steven's excitement increased, his passion rising to a peak until he moaned and shuddered. Afterward, he held her in his arms, her head lying on his chest. "I hope I didn't hurt you too much," he said kissing the top of her head. "I never want to do anything to hurt you ever again."

"No, it wasn't bad. After the first part, it was wonderful."

"We truly are one now," he told her. "For you to share your body with me was the most precious gift you could give me."

She turned her head to look up into his face. "It was a precious gift for me, too. Now I know why married people share those little intimate secret looks with one another. It's that special knowledge of each other they share."

He kissed her and when the kissing became passionate, he made love to her again. This time she felt nothing but pure joy, the sensations in her body peaking to such intensity, wave after wave of such incredible sensations, she didn't know if she could stand it.

Afterward, he lay on his side, his head resting on his arm looking into her face. "This is how I want to remember you," he said as he ran his finger along her cheek and down her jaw onto her neck and down between her breasts. "While I'm gone I will always remember your beautiful face and your soft sensuous body. I want to remember how it felt to be inside you."

She reached up her arms to encircle his neck. Tears stung her eyes. "Steven, I can hardly bear to think of you going away."

"Don't worry, my sweet," he told her. "I promise to come home to you."

Before the rest of the Covington's had arrived home, Colleen had dressed and ridden home on Princess. That evening at dinner, she had conflicting emotions. There were her beloved father and brother, sitting calmly at the table with her when tomorrow they would be going off to war. It made her so incredibly sad to think of their going that she was always near to tears.

But another part of her would remember the afternoon spent with Steven, the vows they had spoken with each other and how it had felt when they had made love with each other. In spite of the chaos going on in her life, she felt incredible about what they had shared.

The next morning everyone rose early to say their farewells. Clifford and Steven, having already made their tearful departure, met the McBrides at their home. Anna Bell had been inconsolable, taking to her bed as soon as the men had left

Colleen had gone out on the veranda to see them off. There stood her father and Gerritt, Clifford and Steven; all dressed in their Confederate uniforms. They wore the flannel pants with a chambray shirt and over top, a gray jacket with brass buttons. On their heads, each sported a hat; Gerritt and her father wore the squashed cap with a brim. Steven and Clifford's' hats were wide brimmed with one side turned up. All four wore a good pair of boots on their feet, knowing they would be well used.

Behind them all stood Henry with their horses saddled, carrying bedrolls and knapsacks, and strapped to the side were their rifles. Gerritt and James carried the Sharps Breech loading, while Clifford and Steven owned the newer Spencer.

Colleen found Steven looking at her and her heart skipped a beat. He looked so handsome in his uniform and she remembered everything that had happened the day before; their beautiful vows to each other and how he had kissed her, the way he had touched her and how they had made passionate love. She knew he was thinking the same by the way he was looking at her.

A number of the house slaves and Mr. Solomon the overseer, were getting last minute instructions from James. Her mother clung to his arm and she looked as though she hadn't slept all night.

Colleen walked down the steps to stand in front of Steven. He took her hands in his and fought his impulse to take her in his arms. "Hello, my beautiful wife," he whispered.

"Hello, my handsome husband," she whispered back. Part of her felt so joyous at what they had shared together, but the other part felt devastated at his leaving.

James had gone to his horse and was preparing to mount. Mary held on to him, embracing him. He kissed her and she began to cry. Colleen went to her father and he gathered her in his arms. "Good-bye darlin'," he said giving her a kiss.

"Daddy, do you really have to go?"

"Yes baby, we must. Now that this whole thing's started, we have to see it though to the end. You be good and help your Mama, you hear?"

"Yes Papa," she told him, moving away as he got up on his horse. Next she went to Gerritt who hugged and kissed her also.

"I guess I don't say it enough," she told him, "but I love you, Gerritt. You're a good brother."

"And I love you too, Punkin'," he said stroking her hair.

"You come back Gerritt," she told him. "We need you around here. After all, you have to take over this plantation when Daddy retires."

Gerritt smiled at her. "Don't worry about me, little one. We'll whip those Yankees in no time and we'll be home quicker than scat. Why, you won't even have time to miss us."

She smiled back but her heart felt as if it were being torn in half. Finally, she went to Steven. Her knees felt weak. She really just wanted to break down in tears, but she knew she needed to be brave.

Steven took her hands again and she could feel him trembling. Then, not caring who looked on, he embraced her, holding her so tightly she could barely breathe.

"I love you so much, my beautiful, Colleen," he said his voice choked with emotion. "I can hardly bear to leave you." He looked into her face. "I know it wasn't suppose to be like this. We were going to be married here, at your home, with all our friends and we were to live happily ever after. I'm so sorry, my darlin'."

She took his face in her hands and looked into his handsome face. Her fingers trailed across his forehead, his eyebrows and then down his cheek, trying to memorize every detail so as not to forget. Then she touched his lips with her own, tasting their sweetness.

"I love you, too, my darling Steven. But please don't fret. What happened yesterday was the most beautiful day of my life and I will remember it always. You just come home to me and we'll still have that big weddin'. You keep that pretty uniform clean now. "

"I'll do my best," he said kissing her long and passionately, not caring who saw them. Then reluctantly, he let her go and mounted his horse, never taking his eyes from her. The others had already turned their horses and were headed down the drive to the road. Steven turned around as well and urged his horse to catch up.

Colleen, her mother, the servants, groom and overseer, Mr. Solomon, all watched them go. When they got to the end and headed out onto the road, dark clouds suddenly converged around the sun, blocking its rays. The sudden darkness made the gooseflesh stand out on Colleen's skin. It seemed an ominous sign.

She knew her mother must feel it too as she began to cry, her face in her hands. Colleen put her arm around her shoulder and led her back into the house. Betsy offered them breakfast, but they waved her aside and went on up to the second floor.

Colleen helped her mother to lie down and then she too, went to her own room. At first she just paced about looking at everything in the room, but not really seeing it. Her wedding dress was hanging on the outside of the armoire. It had arrived from the dressmakers last week. She had declared it the most beautiful she had ever seen, with a low cut bodice and yards and yards of imported Italian silk with hand embroidered white flowers on the skirt.

What was happening to their world? Nothing was as it was suppose to be. Would it ever be the same again? She felt exhausted and sat on the edge of the bed, holding on to one of the posts. She let her forehead fall forward onto the post and then she began to cry.

CHAPTER THREE
—Spring 1861

The four men rode most of the way to Savannah in silence; each lost in his own thoughts. Clifford and James dwelt on their plantations, how it all would manage while they were gone. They worried about this years cotton crop and whether or not it would yield a profit and also manage to be harvested and taken to market. They thought of their wives and hoped they would be strong and survive if anything happened to them. Their whole lives were there, on their plantations. They had been handed down from their father's father since Revolutionary War times and from them had built them up, greater and grander with more land, bigger house and many more slaves. But what would happen now? Would everything be lost?

Gerritt and Steven's thoughts tended more toward the future than what lay behind. They wondered what it would be like to be in the army, to go off and fight in a war. And in spite of proclamations to the contrary, they were afraid. Just the thought of war was a terrifying prospect. They feared the possibility of their own demise, but they also feared what they themselves might have to do on the battlefield, to the extent of taking another's life. What must that be like, to kill another human being?

As they neared the city limits, the roads grew more crowded with men. All were dressed in an array of uniforms. Some, like Steven and Gerritt's were gray with brass buttons and braid at the shoulders. Others wore blue with the now familiar squash hat. Still others, those obviously with less means, wore their everyday clothes, wool trousers, linen shirts and broad brimmed work hats. Nearly everyone carried a weapon in some fashion or another. A few had the newer Spence Sharps breech loader; still others had old muzzleloaders. Some only carried pistols; Sharps, Remingtons, and Wessons.

Hundreds of men swelled into the city limits, gravitating towards the wharf area where a temporary head quarters had been set up. People from the city lined the streets, women, children and old men, cheering wildly and waving the new Confederate flag.

Many men rode horses or rode in wagons, but still more walked, carrying their knapsacks filled with personal possessions. Those on the street patted them on the back and wished them well.

They arrived at the wharf where everything appeared to be in chaos. Hundreds of men milled about with no direction, while others in officer's uniforms were barking orders trying to create some semblance of decorum. Their horses were taken from them and told they would be used for the Calvary. They recognized the Hunters and Banyons in the crowd, others from nearby plantations.

Finally, without really knowing how it happened, everyone managed to be grouped together in companies. Gerritt and Steven were together in one, while James and Clifford were still in another.

A tall bearded man with Captain's bars on his uniform, stood on a large crate and placing his fingers between his teeth, blew a piercing whistle. The desired results were obtained. All eyes turned to him and everyone grew silent.

"Alright men, listen up!" he called out, raising his arms to be more visible. "My name is Captain Dean. You all have been divided into companies. If you have not yet signed up and have not been put into a company, go to warehouse A and see the man at the desk.

In a short time, a train will be pullin' into this here wharf area. You men will be loaded onto the train by company. From here we will be goin' to an area where trainin' will take place. You will also, at that time, be given your equipment, including weapons if you do not already have one."

The captain's voice lowered and everyone strained to hear his words. "This war has begun. However each of you might feel about it, just remember this, you will be fightin' to protect your homes, your wives, our sisters and children. You do your part, fight the good fight and we'll drive those Yankees into the ground!" His voice had risen as he spoke of their patriotic duty to the Confederacy. At the finish of his last statement, a loud cheer went up from the hundreds of men assembled on the wharf. Guns and arms were raised over their heads as cheer after cheer rose from the masses.

The clamor died when the shrill whistle of a locomotive and its great bulk came puffing onto the wharf area. The large beast with its huge smokestack bellowing black clouds into the air and its hissing, puffing engine, pulled a long string of boxcars behind it.

A man in his gray uniform began herding them towards the boxcars. "Company C," he called out, "company C, stay with me. I'm Sergeant Jennings, in charge of all you innocents." He was an imposing man in his early thirties, stockily built with heavy sideburns, a long handlebar mustache and piercing blue eyes. "Get movin' men!" he ordered. "Over here! Over here! Get on this here boxcar! Come on, double time!"

Steven and Gerritt moved along with the rest towards the train, climbing aboard one of the boxcars. Everyone was crammed together with barely enough room to sit down. Packs and rifles clashed against one another.

"I sure hope we aren't goin' far," Gerritt commented.

Even though the car was made of slotted boards, it quickly became sweltering hot inside. Steven could feel the perspiration running down his back and into the waistband of his pants. He glanced around at the many faces of the men who now made up the newly formed Confederate States. All ages were represented; young men barely out of their teens, their faces bright and expectant. There were middle-aged men of the aristocracy, well groomed with the finest of uniforms, bringing along their personal slaves to tend to them. There were others of modest means in their work clothes, looking resigned to the task of protecting the things they held dear. Still others were merchants, tailors, and well-muscled laborers. There were older men, some Steven guessed, well into their fifties, quiet, their eyes showing a calm and yet some kind of resignation of what was to come.

Fortunately for everyone crammed into the boxcars the trip from the wharf area to where the training camp would be was short, less than an hour.

"Hey, I know where we are," one man commented as he looked through the slates. "We're in a big field outside one of those big plantations. It's along the Savannah River." And indeed, as they all disembarked from the train, Steven and Gerritt recognized the area well.

"It's on the Mc Farland plantation," Steven remarked. "The main house and buildings are about a mile here to the north."

"This must be part of their land they didn't have in cotton," Gerritt said surveying the landscape.

"But look at it now," Steven said almost in awe. Before them stretched a huge camp with hundreds of small tents dotting the field. Large wagons and artillery pieces stood off to one side. A large pasture area had been set aside for the hundreds of horses which were to be used to haul wagons, caissons and for the Calvary. Near the river were larger sibley style tents where the officers were lodged and also where a large mess had been set up. They could see massive cooking pots steaming over large fires. The men suddenly realized how hungry they were, not having eaten anything since breakfast and now it was nearing dark.

They followed Sergeant Jennings to a section of the camp where the tents had been grouped together in large squares. They realized that the camp had been divided to act like a city block, with the squares of tents the block and the spaces between, the roads.

Sergeant Jennings directed them to pair up and store their gear in one of the tents. There were to be four men to a tent. Gerritt and Steven naturally chose each other and put their packs and guns in one of tents along with two others. There was barely room to stand or move about and even in April, the air was stifling hot and oppressive inside the tent. They stowed their gear quickly so as to get back outside as soon as possible. They found they had been supplied with a bedroll, a basic cooking pack, consisting of a tin plate, cup and eating utensils, a canteen and ammunition case and a slicker.

After putting their personal items away they were instructed to stand at attention in a straight line. Training began at once with directions in marching, turning and standing at attention. It was more difficult than one would think with men turning at the wrong time or in the wrong direction. Some would get their feet tangled together and slam into someone else, causing the whole line to misstep. Finally they were able to acquire some semblance of order and were able to maintain a straight line at attention.

Sergeant Jennings dismissed them to get their mess kits. Once this had been accomplished, they again lined up and marched to the area where the food was being served. It was now well past dark and everyone was very hungry, some stomachs could even be heard growling in protest.

They stood in line to receive their meal; this procedure they would repeat many times over. Once they had been served a plate full of an aromatic stew and a large piece of bread, they went back to sit in front of their tents to eat.

"Look at all this," Gerritt said as they munched on mouthfuls of the stew, "hundreds and hundreds of men here in this field. How many other camps do you imagine there are all across the South?"

Steven looked out over the massive camp; the hundreds of tents, the glow of fires and the drone of many voices. He wondered where his father and James might be in that mass of humanity. "I imagine there must be quite a few," Steven answered, "many in every one of the Confederate States."

"Isn't it amazin'," Gerritt said smiling, "so many. No doubt we'll beat those Yankees now."

"Don't count your chickens afore they're hatched," a voice nearby remarked.

Gerritt and Steven looked over to see an older man squatting on the ground as he ate his meal. He wore the gray uniform with the typical squash hat and long boots on his feet. He had long, shoulder length hair and his weathered face was covered in a heavy graying beard with bushy eyebrows above large dark eyes. His hands were dark and callused as though they had seen many years of toil.

"What makes you say that old man?" Gerritt asked him.

The man chewed his last bite of food before answering. "I'm jes sayin', don't be too quick to predict whose gonna' win this here war."

"Are you sayin', sir," Steven spoke, "that the South will not be victorious? That sounds very unpatriotic."

"Call it whatever you wants," he said as he pulled a piece of meat from his teeth, "but you gotta look at the facts."

"And what are those "facts"?" Gerritt asked the elderly man.

"I'd have to say and I am a sayin' 'cause you asked, that the South is overweighed right from the get go. Oh sure our enemy is the same race, equal smarts, but for one thing we the South ain't united. Our five richest states in men and money are divided 'bout which ways they gonna give their loyalties.

The North has one of the richest established governments in the world. They got no national debt and a solid currency. What we got? This here Confederate nation has jes got started, got us a new kind of currency. What's that gonna do? The North's cities are rich, got lots of people and are filled with shops, mills, factories, foundries, storehouses and arsenals. They've also got lots of farms with agrowing lots of food. They got a lot of railroads and waterways for transportin' all those goods.

You know what else they got, boys? They got a navy and a pretty good one at that. They can use that navy to reach the whole world, to get whatever supplies they need. And they can also blockade our ports so we can't get our ships out."

"We've got our cotton," Gerritt said a little desperately. "The South is rich in cotton."

"Ah, yes, our cotton; a good crop, but no good iffen you can't sell it. And except for Richmond, there isn't a mill or foundry with the machinery necessary to made firearms. There are no storehouses and no armory. We got only a few poor railroads, poor rolling stock with which to transport anythin' we're gonna need to fight this war."

"And how sire, do you know all this?" Steven asked him.

The old man took a drink of coffee from his tin cup, dribbling some on his beard as he did so. He swiped his sleeve across his mouth to dry it. "Oh I may not have the educatin' you boys did, I can see that plain. I didn't go to no fancy college, but I can read and write. I was born here in Georgia, loved a life on my daddy's farm, til I was twenty. Then I lit out on my own, went north, traveled all over there. I saw many things and I read everythin' I could get my hands on.

I won't bore you all with my life's history, but I saw the difference. I saw how powerful the North was and when I started hearin' tales of war, I knew what the odds were all about."

"Then why are you here?" Gerritt asked him. "Why didn't you stay in the North and fight with them?"

The gray haired man shifted his weight on the hard ground. "That's easy; I'm all of sixty years old. Could probably skip out on this one iffen I had a mind to, but this here's my home. This is where my kinfolk are. Winners, losers, my loyalty will be with the South to the bitter end."

"Tell me then old man," Steven said drawing closer, "have you nothing positive to say about the South?"

The older man packed his eating utensils away and then wrapped himself in his blanket, edging closer to the fire before answering. "Yes strengths, the strengths of the South. For one thing, we have immense territory with many rivers and vast mountains to hold refuge for our troops. We also have our slaves to work and toil for us, to grow grain and beef for the armies.

Another thing we got in our favor is our people, especially them on along the coastline; we're united, we're one. Our people fightin' in this here war are Anglos, descended from the same blood. We're fightin' for that heritage and for our homes and kin. Them northerners are all a bunch of immigrants and they, for the most part, jes don't give a damn.

'Nother thing we got goin' for us is superior leadership and lots of country folk who know their way 'round a gun; good shots, too."

"You seem like a good man sir," Steven told him, "but I'm not sure I agree with your assessment."

"That's your privilege boy."

Steven held out his hand. "I'm Steven Covington, and I'm pleased to make your acquaintance."

The old man took it and Steven was impressed by the firmness, the strength in his grasp. "Tom Hunter," he told them, "from Hunter Ridge, Georgia."

"And I'm Gerritt McBride," Gerritt said holding out his hand as well, "from Shannon Plantation, Georgia."

"Urmph, yep, I figured you boys fer aristocrats. Plantation boys, eh? Well, I guess we'se all equal now, ain't we?"

Taps was played and all the men retired to their tents, rolling up in their blankets to sleep for the night. But Steven lay awake for a long while thinking of what Tom had told them. Did he really know what he was talking about? Did the North really have the superior advantage? And if so, what would this war really be like? Could they win this thing in six months as everyone thought? Never before had so many doubts entered his mind.

The bugle awakened them and after a breakfast of eggs and fat back, the training began in earnest. Men, who previously had no uniforms or weapons, were given these accoutrements. Pickets were set up and guards posted, bringing home the fact they were now at war. They did not want to be surprised by the Army of the Potomac.

Then the real work of training began. Army officer Major Harlin McDowal took over the daunting task of whipping these untrained volunteers into fighting soldiers. The ten companies present made up this regiment of the 48th Georgia. Each company consisted of ninety-seven men and three officers, one captain, one first lieutenant, one second lieutenant, one first sergeant, four sergeants, eight corporals, two musicians, one wagoneer, and two hundred privates.

Major Harlin was a tall man in his early forties with broad shoulders and a barrel chest. When he spoke everyone listened as his deep, booming voice commanded respect. His uniform was sharp and clean with shinny buttons that flashed fire in the sunlight. There was braid on his shoulders and stripes on his sleeve. On his head he wore a broad brimmed hat with more braid around the brim.

His first order was to have the men salute the officers and say, "yes sir," whenever spoken to. Guards at the entrance to the camp were given orders that no one was to leave without a pass signed by himself. Drills were begun, marching up and down, back and forth across the parade ground. A break at lunch was given and then it was back to the drilling.

By nightfall the men were so exhausted, they literally fell into their bedrolls. The next morning at 5:00 A.M., they were awakened by the drum beating out reveille. Everyone scurried to put on their clothes while half-asleep. Then it was out of the tents for roll call with much yawning and blinking by many whom were still trying to wake up.

After breakfast Sergeant Jennings called out, "fall in for drill squad!" With a lot of grumbling the men lined up and began their marching back and forth across the parade ground, learning right face, left face and about face.

They began to learn the intricacy of battle formation. Major Harlin barked out the orders, directing the men into skirmish lines, which consisted of two companies forming two lines. Two more lines were formed approximately four hundred yards behind the first and then they marched forward, taking the place of those who might have fallen in the front line.

As Steven and Gerritt tramped and marched, creating skirmish lines and false charges, Gerritt couldn't help but comment. "God Steven, are your dogs as tired as mine?"

"I've never worked so hard in my life," Steven told him. "Everything in my body hurts and it's hot as Hades." The perspiration ran off their bodies in rivulets, depleting them even more.

"When do you suppose we'll stop with all this marchin' and get on with the fightin'?" Gerritt asked to no one in particular.

At noon they were allowed a break for dinner. They were given a meal and rested, some sitting around in groups talking, others reclining on the grass near the river. The water ran clear and sparkling, causing many to have an almost irresistible urge to jump into the cool waters. Along the banks small yellow flowers grew in profusion, their cheery faces bending in the breezes.

It was during this hiatus that Steven and Gerritt ran into their fathers. "Father!" Steven called out when he recognized the large man sitting near the mess eating his dinner.

"Steven!" Clifford called back. "Come see your old man."

Both boys sat talking with Clifford when Gerritt spotted James in a group of men. When he called to him, he too walked over and sat with them.

"How are you doing Father?" Steven asked Clifford.

His father shook his head. "Never been so tired in my life," he told his son. "And my feet are so sore; I've got blisters all over them. I can't wait until I can soak these puppies in some cold water. That river over there looks mighty invitin'."

"How about you Papa?" Gerritt asked James. "Are you holdin' up alright?"

"As well as everyone else I expect," he said. "The heat's what's botherin' me the most. Sure would be good to have one of your Mama's mint juleps about now."

They all laughed in agreement, but hidden beneath the laughter was sadness at the mention of those left behind.

The bugle sounded again and everyone roused themselves to go back to their own companies. As they rose from the grass, Steven looked into his father's face and saw the weariness there. He wanted to embrace him but knew it would be inappropriate, so he clasped him on the shoulder instead. "Take it easy Father," he said as cheerily as he could. "Don't get too worn out before we meet up with those Yankees."

Clifford gave him a smile, the creases around his eyes showing clearly and walked off to participate in battalion drill. As he did so, Steven felt a tightening in the pit of his stomach; an indescribable wave flooding over him that caused a weakness in his knees.

The battalion consisted of all ten companies practicing skirmish lines while others fired over their heads, with mock deaths and the second, third, fourth and so on lines moving up to fire at the non-existent enemy.

No sooner had they all limped back to their own companies, than they were ordered to re-form and practice company drill. But this was not to be the end of it. After more drilling, they were all ordered to appear for dress parade as if that were an important part of battle.

Finally at dusk the weary wretched feeling men hobbled back to their tents and were then given supper.

Before lights out Sergeant Jennings called for another roll call.

"Evidently they want to see if anyone died during drills today," Steven whispered to Gerritt out of the corner of his mouth. At least he got a small smile from Gerritt for that remark.

At nine o'clock, they were able to retire to their tents. Some stayed up playing cards, but others like those in Steven's tent, rolled up in their blankets and attempted to sleep.

"By golly, " Gerritt remarked once darkness had enveloped the tent, "I've never been so sore in my life. Not even when that white stallion threw me. What good do you suppose it does, all this drillin' and wearin' us down?"

"They ain't doin' it to wear ya down, They're doin' it to build ya up, make ya stronger," Tom told them.

"That's right, sure 'nough," the other member of their tent chimed in. He was a young boy of seventeen, hardly old enough to shave, from a small farming community north of Atlanta. He had joined up as soon as he had heard of Fort Sumter. His name was Charles Goss and none could be found more patriotic to the Confederacy.

"Oh, what would you know about it?" Gerritt said irritably. "You're just a pimply faced kid," he remarked, even though he was only two years older himself

"It's true," Tom broke in. "They're hardenin' ya up, getting ya ready for the fightin' ahead."

"As for me," Charles said, "they can work me hard as they kin. I want to be ready fer them Yanks."

"Well then, you can do my drills for me," Gerritt grumbled.

As they finally drifted off to sleep, they could hear the sounds of a fiddle being played somewhere in the camp. Many fellows had brought their instruments and many a night could be heard the sounds of a banjo or fife or as this evening, the Captain would solicit the melodious tunes of the fiddle.

The following day artillery practice commenced. Many of the fellows had never even shot a gun before. Major McDowal was becoming very agitated by the clumsiness of these recruits attempting to learn the intricacies of loading their rifle.

They were shown how to take the cartridge from its case, the powder end torn open with their teeth. They were then shown how to pour the powder down the barrel and the bullet pressed in with their thumb. The ramrod was taken out from under the rifle barrel. Using the cup end of the ramrod it was pressed down on top of the bullet and rammed in tightly until it was firmly on the powder. The ramrod was returned to its position, then the hammer pulled back to half cock while a percussion cup was taken from the capbox and pressed over the nipple.

When the shooter was ready to fire, the hammer was pulled back to full cock. Then aim was taken and the trigger pulled. All of this needed to be accomplished in rapid succession over and over. But many mistakes were made and either the guns would not fire at all or they would misfire.

Major McDowal ranted and raved at the men, walking up and down in front of their ranks declaring,

"Do you men realize how important it is for you to learn your weapon thoughly, inside and out? It can save your life! It is your weapon against the enemy! You will have to know how to load and fire your weapon in your sleep!" He stopped his pacing and stood before them, his hands clasped behind his back. "And if you don't learn how to shoot accurately, you will manage to kill more of your own men than enemy."

After many more days most of the men were able to learn the tedious task of loading, after much repetition, to fire accurately. If nothing else it served to instill a confidence and willingness to meet the foe on the battleground. Spirits were high and patriotism even higher.

What lurked in each man's breast was another matter. What doubts fester there, what fears caused sleepless nights, was known only to himself.

Around the campfires at night, bravery was the tale of the evening. Each declaring their fearlessness and course of action should they come face to face with the beast from the North. Bayonet charges were described in detail and if one's firearm ceased to discharge, the bowie knife would be used to carve up his foe. In this manner, this battalion of gray boasted and raved before engaging in deadly combat.

As time had passed muscles had hardened and fatigue was felt less often. It was nearing the end of May and everyone was becoming anxious to begin their own conflict, when the order came down to pack their belongings and strike camp. They were to travel by rail to Virginia where the fighting had begun.

Excitement filled the camp and as Steven filled his knapsack with personal belongings, his heart beat faster. The training was over and the time had come to show their mettle.

Steven's thoughts often turned to Colleen and he wondered if he would ever be returning to his beloved wife. But the thought was only fleeting as Sergeant Jennings called out, "Fall in men! Steady!"

They fell in line and marched to the waiting cars, all lined up behind the hissing, puffing locomotive. Everyone was loaded into the boxcars and soon the train was lumbering down the tracks towards Virginia and their destiny.

They traveled for many hours, cramped together in the hot cars. At first everyone was talkative, telling stories and complaining about the amount of drilling they had been required to do. The closer they got to the Virginia border, the quieter everyone became, lost in their own thoughts.

Steven opened his knapsack and pulled out a framed daguerreotype of Colleen. He traced the outline of her face with his finger; his beautiful Colleen, his wife. He remembered the fullness of her long hair, how it felt in his fingers when he kissed her. He remembered the incredible softness of her skin and how sweet her mouth tasted. He remembered the smell of her; like jasmine in the spring, and he thought, would he ever see her again? He felt a tug of hardness in his stomach when he thought of his own death.

"That there your girl friend?" a voice behind him spoke.

He turned to look behind his left shoulder. Charles was sitting on his knapsack, peering at the photo in his hand. “My wife,” Steven told him.

She sure is purty,” Charles remarked. “Bet she was sad seein’ you go off ta war.”

Steven only nodded, his eyes still on the image of Colleen.

“I ain’t got no woman,” Charles told him. “I was wishin’ I did, ‘cause, you know, it would’a been nice havin’ somebody waitin’ on me back home. I never had much time for girls, though. My Pa kep’ me purty busy on the farm. I ‘spose it be better not to have someone waitin’. You know, ‘case I gets kilt. “Course, I ‘spose my Ma’ll be sad iffin I die. Ever body needs somebody to miss ‘em iffen he dies, don’t ya reckon?”

“I reckon, Charles,” Steven told him. “I reckon.” And that tug of lead in his stomach soured the taste in his mouth.

They traveled all day and into the night making their way through South Carolina and then North Carolina and finally into Virginia, the steady rocking of the train cars lulling many to sleep. Others found a bare spot on the floor by sitting on their knapsacks and played cards. Still others merely crouched in the corners clutching their stomachs, motion sickness threatening to overpower their resolve.

They finally reached their destination on the Orange and Alexandria Railroad near Manassas, Virginia. As the train brakes squealed piercingly into the darkness of the night, they were finally able to disembark. As everyone pushed and shoved their way out onto the railway platform, they saw before them, stretched out as far as the eye could see, a massive camp of operations.

"Jeee hosaphat!" Charles commented as he hoisted his pack upon his back. "It's the gol durnest army I've ever seen!"

"Ain't it though," Tom said having come up next to them. "That there boys, is the great army of Virginia, consistin' of others too like, Kentuckians, Mississippians, South Carolinians and like us, Georgians, here to protect our new capitol of Richmond and the President, Mr. Jefferson Davis."

At the head of the camp flew the new Confederate flag, a bright red background, crossed with white, holding the stars. "Ain't that a mighty purty sight?" Charles whispered reverently. "Yup, mighty purty."

They passed through the immense camp, past the rows upon rows of tents, men drilling, men guarding post and those sitting or reclining on the ground. They were directed to bivouac under some trees with no means of shelter anywhere.

"Sergeant Jennings," one of the men called out, "is this where we are to sleep, no tents, no shelter?"

"This is it men and be glad for it," Sergeant Jennings spoke up amongst their members. "You'll be seein' a lot worse once you start seein' action. At least you've got the cover of these here trees. Shade in hot sun and cover from the rain if it comes."

"What about some grub?" Charles asked him. "My belly ain't seen a morsel since this mornin'."

"'Fraid you're outt'a luck on that score, soldier." Sergeant Jennings answered. "Found out from the higher ups that Governor Litcher somehow forgot to acquire extra provisions for all these extra troops. So until the wagons arrive with supplies, it's every man for himself."

"What does that mean?" Gerritt asked Steven. "Are we suppose to go to the nearby residents and shoot a cow?"

"I don't know," Steven answered. "I think it means we beg, borrow or steal or just go hungry."

They slept that night under the stars, rolled up in their blankets. The ground proved so hard, Steven had difficulty sleeping, not to mention the nearly incessant growling of his stomach.

The following morning the bugle call found the men with sore hipbones and even hungrier stomachs. But much to their disappointment, there was still no food for the new arrivals. To make matters worse, more troops were disembarking from the bellowing steam engine.

For the most part they spent their day roaming the large camp, meeting men from all over the South, listening to their opinions on the war, slavery and Mr. Lincoln and mostly about the lack of anything substantial in their stomachs. They also took this opportunity to write letters home. It was difficult to know what to say. Steven wanted to tell Colleen how much he missed her, how sometimes the ache he held inside for her was so overpowering, he wanted to lay down his gun and run home to her. But he did not want to make her sad. So he talked about the drilling and conditions of camp, of some of the men he had met and to tell her, her father was doing well.

Steven and Gerritt sat together under the trees, the shade offering some protection from the hot June sun, listening to two men debate the pros and cons of owning slaves, whether it was justified or condemned according to the Bible. They decided to stay out of the discussion. What was foremost on their minds was getting something to eat. The lack of any food had made them light headed and weak. Fortunately all drills had been suspended for the time being.

"Do you suppose they plan on starvin' us?" Gerritt asked Steven.

"Seems so doesn't it?" Steven replied, a blade of grass between his teeth. He was reclined, supporting himself on one elbow. "I do know I've never been hungrier. I'm about ready to eat the leather off my boots." He looked around at the thousands of men milling about in the massive camp. Voices floating on the breeze like the drone of millions of insects. Every now and then a word would become clear and then drift away again. Adding to the whole symphony was the din of the sounds of chopping, the clang of hammer against anvil, horse whinnys, the melodious music of a violin and someone singing a song.

The sky was a urethral blue, cloudless, piercing. The hot mid-day sun beat down mercilessly with the flies hovering in the shade to bother those who tried to find respite.

"Know what my favorite meal was back home?" Gerritt asked, his mind still on food, "suckling pig," he answered without waiting for a reply. "Our cook Ellen, would roast up the most delicious, juiciest pig you've ever tasted, slow cooked over a spit in the big kitchen fireplace, for hours and hours until the skin outside was brown and the juices were flowin' golden. Put that with yams and collards, baked apples, hot biscuits and sweet potato pie and I'd think I'd died and gone to heaven."

"Gerritt, you stop it now," Steven admonished. "You're just makin' matters worse. I can hardly stand thinkin' about food, I certainly don't need you describin' it to me in vivid detail."

"I'm sorry," Gerritt said laying on his back and looking up into the branches of the tree, saw the patterns the light made as it waffled through the leaves. "It's just that I'm so dog gone hungry.

Say, isn't this an oak tree? Do you suppose it's got any acorns? I heard you can eat acorns."

Steven laughed. "Not unless you're a squirrel."

Suddenly Charles burst into their midst, sprawling himself on his knees in front of them. His face was red, his hair sticking straight up on his head and he was breathing heavily.

"What in tarnation......." Gerritt exclaimed sitting up.

"I got....." he panted, "I got us......"

"Will you spit it out man," Steven said sitting up as well.

"Food! I got us some food!" He said it in a hoarse whisper so as not to alert those sitting close by.

"Food! Well, now what do you mean?" Gerritt asked, visibly getting excited.

Charles opened his jacket, exposing two large loafs of bread, all brown and golden, their fragrance wafting out to the hungry souls who gazed upon their beauty.

"Oh where did you get those?" Gerritt asked. "Did you steal them?"

Charles shook his head as he began to break off pieces and hand them to Steven and Gerritt. Unfortunately for Tom, he was off visiting friends in another company. "Me and my friend Jasper decided to walk along the roadside. We was thinkin' mebbe we could find us berries or sompin'. Anyways, we come up on this farm house and Jasper says, 'I bet ya, iffen I was ta go up ta that there house and tell 'em how hungry we is, they'd give us sompin' to eat." Charles broke more pieces off the bread, handing it to Gerritt and Steven who would immediately stuff it into their mouths so as not to be detected by others.

"Anyways," Charles continued, "ole Jasper kinda tousles up his clothes and messes his hair, wipes his grimy hands on his face and walks on up to the front door. He goes ta knockin''and soon as somebody opens the door, he grabs his stomach, see. It's an old woman a standin' there, wrinkles, all bent over. He's a kind'a moanin' and all. He says to her, 'Ma'am, I'se with this great army of the great Confederate States and we been marchin' and drillin' and getting ready to fight this way for our independence, but there just ain't enough food. I'se starvin', me an my buddy over there.' And then he points to me standin' by the fence. Then he says, 'We haven't et anythin' for three days. Please ma'am, iffen you could jes spare eny morsel of food, we'd be much obliged.' Well, dern, iffen she didn't go back inta the house and bring back a whole loaf of bread. Jasper thanked her and off we went. Wasn't long afore we came to another house. Well, this time it was my turn to try my hand at beggin'. Did a fine job iffen I do say so me self.

I got two loaves of bread." And with a last flourish, he broke into a broad grin, showing his broken teeth.

"You did real good, Charles," Steven told him as he stuffed another chunk of bread into his mouth.

"Yes sir," Charles said as he filled his own mouth. "I tol' my friend Jasper, I'se got to take these here loafs back to my tent buddies to share, knowin' they'se as hongry as me."

"We appreciate your kindness," Gerritt told him. "And when we get the chance, we will certainly repay the favor."

For a few hours they had some substance in their bellies and some of their weakness subsided.

Finally on the following day, supplies began to arrive from Richmond. More tents were erected with Charles and Tom electing to continue their bunking with Gerritt and Steven. The tents however, proved to be only a little less hot than a frying pan on the fire and no one spent any more time in them than necessary. They also bred flies in the warm moist interior so as to cause nearly a plague through out the camp.

The camp was divided into four messes with two cooks each. Unfortunately, none of them seemed able to cook anything palatable, but at least they had food in their stomachs.

The drilling and rifle practice also resumed with the arrival of General Beauregard who took command of the post. Eight hours a day were spent in drilling; running in double quick time until every man nearly expired from exhaustion. If any one failed to turn up for drills, he was ordered to police duty, involving the degrading work of cleaning the camp, carrying around shovel and spade to eliminate the soldier's waste and garbage.

Other duties after drilling practice involved digging entrenchments and erecting elaborate breastworks. This involved digging a large trench, deeper than a man was tall with the earth piled in front of it towards what would be the enemy. On top of this, large logs cut to spear points were crisscrossed along the trench, the points directed towards the pursuing enemy.

Beauregard allowed no rest for the weary, finding still more labor in digging the trenches in the hot June sun. The water around Manassas was stagnant and foul. Many who drank from it became sick and along with the hard labor in the hot sun, developed typhus and many began dieing, sometimes on a daily basis.

As Steven and Gerritt sat under the shade of the trees during a break in the drilling, the sound of the band playing the 'Dead March', could be heard and then the firing of a volley of shots.

"Another dead," Gerritt remarked. "When will it all end? It's that putrefied water everyone's drinkin'."

"I'm worried about my father...and yours," Steven said, his brow wrinkled in a frown. "How would we know if they became ill, or heaven forbid, passed on? Would they know to inform us, or even be able to find us if they did?"

"It is worrisome," Gerritt agreed. "We've not seen them since we left Georgia, even if the regiments have been divided up by state."

"I'll tell you this," Steven remarked almost angrily, "I'll not drink any water that's not been boiled first. I mean, what is Beauregard doing to halt the death toll in this camp? Are we all to perish before we ever get to fight?"

Steven's concerns were finally addressed when General Beauregard himself, alarmed at the daily mortality of the troops, finally had specially designed water tanks constructed on flat bed railcars. The tanks were then filled with pure water from the Blue Ridge Mountain streams and transported to the large camp at Manassas but not before many hundreds had died of typhus, fever, dysentery, scurvy and measles.

The days dragged on one after the other, the dull sameness repeating itself day after day until the entire month had passed them by. In the sweltering heat of July, Beauregard, at least for a time, halted the drilling and marching practices so that now the days were even more boring and the space of time seemed infinitely longer. Moral was low and the spirits of the men were being sapped.

Finally on that day of July 17th 1861, the boredom and tediousness was finally broken when the order of long roll went out. They were to pack up and begin to move out. They were on their way to battle.

Sergeant Jennings came around as they were packing their belongings. Many had too many personal items they were trying to stuff into their knapsacks; extra clothing, books, perfumed soaps, bowie knives, additional underwear and so on. Added to their burden, each man was given sixty rounds of ammunition. The packs were loaded on their backs, the bedrolls strapped on top. Their sacks with ammunition, powder and packing were slung over their shoulders. Sergeant Jennings reminded them they would be responsible for carrying their own supplies, but no one was willing to part with a sentimental item.

All those who had resigned themselves to tedious boredom were now full of excitement and vitality. The time had finally come, the thing they had been anticipating, the goal to all the drilling.

They lined up at attention and Sergeant Jennings called out, “Forward!” Everyone marched out of camp, a long line of men as far as the eye could see. Wagons lumbered behind carrying the cassions and supplies.

Steven’s spirits were high. He felt as if the reason for everything, the battle at Charleston, the frenzy of volunteers, rushing to defend their newly found nation, the bittersweet good-byes at home, had finally found fruition in this moment.

His father and Gerritt’s company was just ahead of theirs and the men could be seen marching along with the rest. Steven could see they looked in good health with no problems in carrying their heavy packs.

The road was good, hard packed and frequently traveled, so the march was not difficult. It was hot however, and soon the sweat was running down each man’s face in rivulets. Oh, for a drink of good, cool water. They had all been hasty in consuming the entire contents of their canteen early on and were suffering for it now. Their mouths became so dry their tongues would stick to the roofs of their mouths. Finally at the discovery of a stream, everyone broke ranks to fill their containers, this time being more careful in their rationing. Another lesson learned.

Steven looked about at the Virginia countryside. This place they were now in, was more lush than the county in Georgia where he and Gerritt lived. Many trees and brush grew alongside the road and one might even call it a forest. Further on were pasturelands with long grasses and berry bushes. Many of the men stopped to pick the delicious fruit, causing them to lose sight of their own companies. Sheep and cattle grazed peacefully in pastures lined with neat split rail or stone fences. Dirt paths led to quaint two-story farm houses. They saw farmers toiling in the fields while in other places, women and children lined the road and cheered them on.

Near dusk they finally arrived at a small stream called Bull Run which was located across from Blackburn's Ford. There they set up camp, posting pickets, stacking rifles and cooking for themselves around small fires, as the supply wagons had not yet arrived.

As Gerritt and Steven sat around their small cookfire, both of their fathers happened to come across them. They were all gratefully relieved to see each other and that all were healthy.

They sat with each other for a time, talking of the drilling and complaining about the food. But as they talked there were also those unspoken words, the words no one wanted to utter. They were on the eve of war and yet no one spoke of the battle to come. Nor did they speak of home, for that would cause the homesickness to settle in. The entire camp seemed to fall into a kind of quiet reverie, each man thinking his own thoughts of the day to come.

Steven looked into his father's face, a face he knew so well; the thinning graying hair over a broad forehead, his brows straight and arched, almost as delicate as a woman's. His dark eyes showed weariness, the lines around them more prominent than he remembered. His face was deeply tanned from all the days spent in the sun, but he could still see the humor lines around the corners of his mouth.

His father and Gerritt's could have escaped the war, there being a law exempting those who owned more than fifty slaves, but their loyalties ran deep and they felt it their obligation. This only caused Steven to feel even greater pride in his father.

But what would tomorrow bring? Would he ever see his dear father again? Tears burned his eyes at the thought, but he fought them back, knowing it was not appropriate.

Others seemed to have similar thoughts as the camp retired for the evening. There were only small sounds of men in hushed tones, a sound of a soft snore, the quiet gurgling of the stream and the croaking of a frog. On this eve there was no one singing, no violins, no card playing. Tonight was the night for each man's thoughts on what the new day would bring.

After Clifford and James had taken their leave to go back to their own companies, Steven and Gerritt rolled up in their blankets under the trees and gazed up at the stars and tried to sleep.

Steven wondered what the battle would be like. Would they all line up in formation and shoot at one another as they had done in drill practice? Would he be able to load his gun fast enough? And would his aim be accurate? What would it feel like to shoot a man; to witness that hot piece of lead piercing the body of another human, stopping his heart, killing him. He had never shot another person before, only deer, a squirrel, a rabbit, but this was different. This would be someone who had a family, perhaps a wife, a mother, brothers, sisters, people who cared for him. Would be able to do it when the time came? Would he be able to pull that trigger and snuff out the life of someone else?

Only time would tell the answer to that question. He gave a silent prayer, for himself, for his father and for everyone in the camp that night on their first ever battle on the banks of Bull Run.

CHAPTER FOUR
—July 1861

It had been nearly three months since Steven, her father and Gerritt had ridden off to Savannah and the war. They had had no word and since they as yet hadn't heard of any major battles, they hoped the men were still in good health.

Colleen and her mother at first had looked for the postal rider nearly everyday in the beginning, but as the days had lapsed into months and still there was no word, they stopped going to the end of the drive looking for the elderly man with his shay and horse. Instead, they went once a week, which was as often as he came by.

Life on the plantation was going well enough with Mr. Solomon the overseer, making sure the planting was done and many of the other many tasks of running their vast holdings. One grievance that Colleen and her mother held against Solomon, however, was that he beat the slaves more than they would have liked. When brought to task on this by Mary, he simply stated that on other plantations, many of the Negroes had begun to run away, some even to rise up against their masters and do them harm. He told her his reasoning for the beatings was only done when necessary to let the unruly ones know who was master and keep them in their place.

Mary had not argued, having so many more pressing needs on her mind. At first she had been nearly ill with the chore of keeping the books and making sure supplies were purchased when needed. But with the help of Colleen, they soon worked everything out and seldom did they lack for anything when it was needed.

Steven's mother Anna Bell would frequently come to their home as she was very lonely being on her own. Other ladies too, whose husbands and sons had gone off to war as well and some elderly already widowed, would gather at the McBride Plantation to work on projects for the cause. Sometimes they would tear long strips of cloth and then roll them into bandages. Other times they would knit socks and blankets for the men. They also sewed jackets and shirts for the men. They even had some of their darkies sewing up tents.

Sometimes this kind of work made Colleen feel sad, thinking of how Steven might have need of these bandages or how he may not have any socks to wear. She frequently wondered what he was doing, if he were well and if he was thinking of her.

At times Colleen felt frustrated being so far from Steven and her father and yet not be able to help in any substantial way. When voicing these feelings to her mother, she would protest the fact she was not contributing to the cause.

"My dear," she said to Colleen one hot July day, "you have helped immensely with your tireless dedication to your knittin' and makin' bandages for our poor boys who may be wounded in this war. Why, many of our soldiers will be proud to wear the clothing you have sewed for them."

"I know, Mama," she replied, "but I only wish I could be more of a help; perhaps as a nurse or some such."

"You aren't trained for that, my dear," Mary told her. "You are better served here, helping to keep this plantation runnin'. For if we are successful, we can raise money for our cause and perhaps even provide them with food. Just think of it! If every farm and plantation in the south contributed what they can in food, cattle, clothing and such, it will help to speed the end to this conflict and encourage our men in their efforts towards our victory over the Yankees."

"I know you're right, Mother," she told her, "but sometimes it just doesn't seem enough."

Mary took her hand and patted it. "I know dear, and sometimes I feel the same. But until the day they allow women to fight in wars, we will have to be content to do what we can here at home."

Often times, especially in the evening, when the crickets sang and the breezes blew their songs through the trees, Colleen would feel the achy loneliness for Steven. She would sit out on the terrace where they had gone the night of their engagement, where Steven had held her in his arms and declared his love for her.

Then she would feel overwhelmed with the pain of missing him. She could almost feel it flooding her like a tidal wave, filling her, engulfing her until she would sob and sob until the floodgates had been released. And then she would stare into the darkness and think about the day they had married, the sweet words of promise and the ecstasy in his arms.

That time seemed so long ago. Days dragged by as if the sun would forever stay overhead and at night the dark seemed to penetrate her soul and threaten to overtake her sanity.

She would wonder what all of it was for. Why did they need to fight a war? Why did brother want to fight brother? She didn't know much about politics and had no easy answers. She only knew she wanted the whole horrible mess to be over with so that once again Steven could be in her arms.

Her days were filled with the many tasks of helping her mother run the plantation. She remembered the talk her mother had given her regarding the mistress's duties. It had been there in the back of her mind, remembered, but by the wayside until now.

Not only did they still own the tasks of the household, but now they had to make sure the tasks of James and Gerritt were followed through as well. Soon it would be time to harvest the cotton and make sure it got to market. Everything regarding the cotton had become risky, not knowing whether the dirty Yanks would blockade the ports or whether they would get full price for it. Already news had reached them that a few of the ports in Charleston and down in Louisiana had been successfully taken by the Yankees.

They also, in time, had to harvest from the massive garden. In August it would be time to pick the apples and peaches just at their plump ripeness. All the produce, all the fruit needed to be cooked and canned, ready for the lean winter months.

Cattle and hogs needed to be slaughtered in the fall, the meat smoked and the hides tanned. The fat from the animals would be rendered into tallow for candle and soap making.

Winter clothing had to be made for the slaves as well as the arduous task of cutting firewood to supply not only the main house, but the slaves' quarters as well. And even though most of them grew some of their own food in gardens behind their cabins, meat and staples must be supplemented by the master. It was a daunting task to care for such immense holdings as Colleen was quickly finding out.

Their darkies were like children and needed to be watched over constantly. They required being told how to do something and when to do it. If one didn't encourage them in their chores, they tended to laziness and would slack off at any opportunity that came along. Their babies the pickaninies, were useless until at such an age they could be made to do small chores around the house or in the weaving barn. Once a slave became old enough to work in the fields or in the main house, they became more valuable and if they chose, could keep them on or sell them at auction in Savannah.

All these things Colleen was learning by reading her father's books. For instance, she discovered that her maid Dora, was worth less than her father's manservant, Matthew. This bit of information was a trifling distressing to her as she was rather attached to Dora and would personally have considered her worth more. But she had no intention of selling any of the slaves at this juncture anyway.

One evening as Dora was helping Colleen prepare for bed, Colleen asked her if she minded taking care of the family.

Dora paused a moment before answering. "I'se had a good life here, Missy," she told Colleen. "The McBrides been good to me, lettin' me stays in the big house and all when you alls were young 'uns."

Colleen nodded in agreement. "That's right. You've never had to do the hard labor of workin' in the fields like some of the others."

"But I cares 'bout them too, Missy," she said as she carefully folded Colleen's undergarments and put them in the dresser drawer. "They'se my brother and sisters and Mr. Solomon, he's been awful hard on 'em lately. Some's he's whipped."

"Oh I know," Colleen said as she brushed her long hair before retiring. "I don't like it either, but sometimes it's necessary what with many of them runnin' away now, or even risin' up against their masters. Can you imagine, tryin' to harm the folks who've provided for them, takin' care of them nearly their whole lives?" She spoke to her as if she were a close friend instead of one of <u>them.</u>

At first Dora did not respond, making as if she were tiding the room when it really didn't need tiding.

"Well, have you ever heard of such a thing?" Colleen asked again.

"Missy, you ever been to a slave auction in Savannah?" she asked her instead. She knew what she was about to say could get her in a lot of trouble, could even get her a beating, which was something she had never had. But she could remember being ten years old and standing on the wharf area of the Savannah Labor watching slaves being sold on the auction block; could remember as clear as if it were yesterday, how the hot sun had blazed down upon them, hot as a white hot poker in the sky, how hungry and thirsty she had felt, how loud and noisy the crowds had been. She remembered watching as men, women and children had gone before the crowds, shackled in chains, to stand on the platform. She could remember their faces, the look in their eyes, some with stark fear and others with defiance.

They had torn the linen shirt from one man's body. The sweat had run down his black body causing it to gleam in the sun. His wrists were bound and chaffed raw. She watched the man's face to see the way his jaw was set, how the muscles worked beneath as if he were clenching his teeth hard. She saw the sweat running into his dark eyes and him blinking hard to alleviate the stinging.

A tall man in a dark suit had begun a chanting, a kind of singsong and at the same time others in the crowd would shout out. Suddenly it had stopped and two large white men had dragged the man away.

She could still remember the look in the eyes of the man's woman, that look of horror and pain so deep it scorched the soul when she realized they were to be sold separately. And then the woman had screamed and fell to her knees; a scream so piercing it had caused the gooseflesh to stand out on her skin. And then the woman had sobbed, terrible wrenching sobs as she called out her man's name.

But the white men didn't care. They had jerked her to her feet and stripped the blouse from her small frame, exposing her breasts in front of all those people.

The man in the black suit began his chanting again, but she scarcely heard. All she could hear were the woman's sobs. All she could see was the anguish on her face. And then it had stopped, as if all sound had been sucked in from around them. It was then they had been led away. The auction block, she never forgot.

"I must say, I have never been to the auction in Savannah," Colleen admitted. "Why do you ask?"

"If you ever seed, what it be like for mens to sell other mens, to rip mamas from de babies, to sees mens whupped so bad they'se backs bleedin' and then goes someplace to work hard, always scrait they be sellin' you and to never be free. To hasta work most you life and never be free. Cans't go where you wants and iffen you runs, you hunted down likes a dog. Then mebbe you know why nigger mens runs away. Why they scarit to stay."

Colleen had never heard Dora talk so before and her instant reaction was one of defense. But then an image flashed in her mind of her mother and her traveling back on the road from Savannah when the runaway slave man had stopped them on the road and pleaded for their intervention from the slave catchers. She had not forgotten the look that was in his eyes that day, the fear, the panic, as if he knew the fate that awaited him.

"I guess I just hadn't thought of it before," she told her. "You can go now, Dora," she said dismissing her.

She went about snuffing out the lamps and then crawled in under the cool linens. Dora had started her to thinking about what it would be like at the slave auctions. Mostly she had heard about the sales from her father, how he had purchased this field hand or another. Or perhaps it was a woman who was known to be a good weaver and that she brought a child with her. It was like buying furniture; a chair, a table, a new stove. She had never really thought about it. It was in the Bible about folks owning slaves, how some group of people were just meant to be slaves. After all, slaves had been around since time immortal. But she hadn't thought what it must be like for those who were getting sold. She didn't think about families being torn apart, a father to one place, the mother to another. For the first time she put herself in their place. How she would feel if someone would sell off her Papa. What would it be like if she never saw him again?

"That must be so sad," she said aloud. "I'm so glad I wasn't born a slave." And she fell into a deep sleep. Near onto morning she dreamed.

In her dream she stood on the crest of a hill looking down into a great valley and in the valley a great battle ensued, with rifles firing and canon blasting all around. The clouded sky broiled and spun in great circles of turmoil. In the midst of it all was Steven, lying on the ground, wounded. His blood poured out onto the ground until it became like a great river. She began to run to him, but no matter how fast or hard she ran she could not seem to reach him. The distance between them continued to remain the same.

Suddenly strong hands grabbed her, hurting her arms, pulling at the joints. Large faceless men bound her wrists and dragged her to a waiting wagon. There were others in the wagon, bound as she was, silent, wide eyed, hallow cheeked. She recognized her father among them and called out to him, but he did not respond. He looked at her as if she were a stranger. She kept calling to him, "Father, father, help me!" But he did nothing, only sat silently as if he had no hearing, no senses.

The wagon arrived in a large city where she was roughly torn from the wagon bed. She was pushed and shoved among hundreds of people who jeered and laughed at her. Some struck her and pulled her hair, all the while pushing her forward. The times she fell, she was jerked roughly back to her feet and shoved forward.

Finally she was pushed up onto a platform where she stood trembling and crying. A man with no face began chanting, "What am I offered for this young woman? Eh, what's your bid? See how strong she is? She would be a good worker, many, many years of work. Come on now, what's the bid?"

She felt dizzy, her knees grew weak and suddenly everything went black. She awoke sitting bolt upright, her breath coming in gasps, the sweat running down her back and the tears wetting her face.

She felt the tears and lay back down on her pillow. "What's happening to me?" she said aloud. "What is this war doing to us all? It's making me crazy."

CHAPTER FIVE
—July 1861

The following day, Thursday the 18th of July, found the camp rousing before dawn. Their hurried breakfast consisted of a cracker, a slice of uncooked pork and coffee made from Bull Run water. When everyone was camp dressed and in formation, the bright sun rose over the horizon, filtering through the trees with dancing rays along the ground.

Steven and Gerritt, with most of the others, were silent during the early morning's toilet, which consisted of not much more than a quick wiping of the face and a rinse of the mouth with cold coffee.

Everyone was feeling trepidation in their hearts, this day of their first battle upon them. They checked and rechecked their muskets, loading them with a first round of shot. As the sun made its appearance, they lined up on the south bank of Bull Run, flat lowlands with long grasses. It was a long formidable line of men running from Blackburns Ford with the left flank curving claw like over the stone bridge at Sudley Ford. Thousands of men lining up for battle.

General Longstreet was there with the 17th Virginia, sitting on his horse, chatting with some of the men, as was General Beauregard with the Georgia brigade.

On the other side of the river was a heavy fringe of trees on top of a steep bluff which rose steeply from the banks of the river. In those trees somewhere, was the Union Army, the Yankees. As yet none had been seen.

Tom, Charles, Gerritt and Steven lay together on their bellies, looking up at the steep embankment, their guns pointed into the trees, their foe hiding somewhere within the forest.

"Jeehosaphat!" Charles exclaimed. "Lookee there. You can't see nary a one of them thar Yankees being up in them trees. Why they could jes shoot down here at us and we couldn't even sees 'em. And how we 'spose ta shoot up that big hill?"

"Yep, that's a dilemma alright," Tom answered him. "I guess we jes hope them there Yankees don't git a notion to attack first and iffen they do, we better hope they shows thereselves so's we kin hit 'em."

Steven glanced down the line at the older Tom. How could he act so relaxed? There he laid, his hat pulled down over his eyes, a blade of grass between his teeth, fingering the trigger on his musket. He looked cool as the river water. Steven however, felt nervous as a cat. His stomach lurched and his meager breakfast was making rumblings loud enough to be heard. The sweat was running down under his cap, even though the heat of the day had not commenced and his hands were trembling as they gripped the stock of his gun.

Down the line he could hear quiet comments by some of the men. One soldier was heard to repeat over and over, "Oh my Lord. Oh my Lord!" Another was saying the Lord's Prayer and someone else was calling for his mother.

Fear was a queer thing, Steven thought. It affected people in different ways. Why was it that it could paralyze some and cause others to action, whether it be to flee or attack? He knew he could die today. How did he really feel about that possibility? Previously he had imagined he would die if he must and hopefully with honor. Not that he wanted to die, but he thought he would be brave about it. Now he wasn't quite so sure. He had never felt so afraid in his life, a paralyzing, all consuming kind of fear. He had to do everything he could to muster enough courage just to keep from getting up and running away. But mingled in with the fear was also a feeling awe and curiosity about what was to happen.

"Ya know," Tom said breaking into his thoughts, "Henry the Fifth was known to have said, 'every soldier in the war should do as does every sick man in his bed, wash every mote out of his conscience.'"

"What's that suppose to mean?" Charles asked almost irritatingly, as if the quotation were an affront to his intelligence.

"It means if you believe in a hereafter, you better be confessing your sins," Gerritt explained.

"Oh Lordy, ain't that the truth," Charles whispered, the fear clearly showing in his voice.

Morning dragged slowly on, the hot sun nearly at its peak now. Since no action had as yet occurred, the men's tension had eased some. Relief clearly showed on some faces, the quickened heartbeats slowed. Having tired of the reclining position, many of the men were now sitting, talking amongst themselves, reading, writing letters to loved ones or smoking their pipes.

The four tent mates too relaxed, sitting in the long grass listening to the taunting that rippled down the line. "I'll bet there ain't no Yankees in them woods," one was heard to say.

"That's right! They're scairt, run on home," said another. "They seen this here mighty Confederate Army and turned tail."

"Boys," Tom said loudly enough for many to hear, "yer damn fools. You'll git your fill of fightin' and it won't be long now, either."

That silenced most of them, but some still thought the war had been won without firing a shot.

Soon it was noon and the sun had reached its zenith, beating down on the great army. Men removed jackets and caps. Many had retreated further back to the shade of the trees. The lookouts had relaxed to the point they were no longer looking out for anything but the bottle flies swarming around them.

Steven was lying on his back, his hands under his head, his weapon beside him, looking across the stream at the embankment above. The faint cawing of a crow could be heard above the droning of the flies and the calling of a kingfisher in a tree to the boys below.

"What do you suppose those fellas are doing over there?" Steven asked.

"Probably the same as us," Gerritt answered. "Wondering when this war's going to commence."

Their reverie was broken when not twenty feet away, a volley of shots rang out. Suddenly everyone scurried to take cover, flattening their bodies against the earth, readying their rifles, their hearts pounding in their chests.

"Fall in men! Fall in!" Sergeant Jennings called out "Right dress!" Everyone jumped to the line as more volleys burst around them.

Steven felt an icy shiver run through his blood, the sound of the minnie ball screaming over his head. As he lay flat on his belly, he could feel the ground hard and lumpy beneath him, a stick jabbed into his side. He smelled musket powder and the musky wetness of the river. The leaves on the trees stood out in sharp contrast to the black limbs they held. All his senses seemed more brilliant, keener, as if nothing else in the world existed but that which was going on around him. Looking to his left he saw with horror some of his comrades falling dead or wounded as the bullets thudded into their bodies.

Just as suddenly, a volley of shells began exploding overhead. "Oh my God, they're firing artillery at us!" Gerrit exclaimed, the terror sounding in his words.

The shells were landing high, tearing branches from the treetops and raining them down upon those below. Men became terrified beyond reason and were fleeing from the field, trying to put as much distance between themselves and the Yankees. Others stood their ground, firing across the river into the trees, not knowing if they were even hitting anything.

Steven felt paralyzed, didn't know what he should do. Everything seemed as if it were happening in slow motion, men running, others raising to their knees to fire, a man hit over there, another sprawled face down in the river. He knew he needed to do something. Finally when he saw Tom and Charles rise and fire their guns, he too rose up on his knee, his gun loaded and ready, aimed at the fire bursts he saw in the trees and fired. Immediately, he dropped down again and began to reload. Others, who had retreated, were emboldened by their actions and came back to the line.

The firing increased in intensity on both sides of the river as thousands of muskets were discharged. Fortunately, because the Yankees were firing down hill, many were landing too high. They were hitting the branches of the trees and thudding into the trunks. It was the artillery fire that was so devastating. The exploding shells and whizzing shrapnel was devastatingly effective. The violence of firing from the other bank doubled, causing a shower of minnie balls to rain down amongst them.

The officers kept screaming orders, calling for those nearest the river to move back closer to the trees.

"Steven!" Gerritt called above the din; "we're to move back! Let's get outt'a here before we're hit!"

Before they could inch their way backward, General Beauregard rode up and ordered a charge across the river. Before they could have time to think on it, to fear the continual volley of gunfire, they all rose up and made a rush for the ford. Crossing, they all realized what targets they made, had the Yankees wanted to pick them off one by one like a flock of ducks. But they were as green as they were and did not take the opportunity.

Steven felt the icy cold of the river streaming into his boots, soaking his pants legs. He held his rifle and ammo high to keep it from getting wet, his eyes scanning the far bank for signs of fire. But none came and they reached the other side safely.

The entire company, along with the 17th Virginia, climbed the bank and began patrolling the wood. Everyone spread out and scattered among the trees.

Steven was struck at how silent the woods were. No gun fire, no shouts, not even the birds called out to them as they moved furtively among the trees.

There ahead he saw movement; men running dressed in gray. Who were they; a part of Virginia Company gotten around in front of them? And then he saw the insignia, First Massachusetts Infantry! Why were they wearing gray? No one fired due to the confusion of who was friend or foe. The only difference Steven could see was their jackets; being ornamented with frogs and gilt buttons and on their caps in brass letters, 1st Mass.

They weren't what Steven had expected in his imaginings; not cruel looking beasts of men, but they were ordinary in every way, just like his friends or neighbors. He raised his weapon and sighted down the barrel at the back of a fleeing Yankee, but he couldn't pull the trigger. His hands were trembling and the sweat ran down his face from under his cap. His stomach felt queasy. What was wrong? Why couldn't he shoot? He had fired earlier when he hadn't been able to see them. He felt his worst fears were being realized; that he would not be able to kill the enemy when faced with the inevitable.

Gerritt came up behind him and Steven was glad he had not seen his cowardice. They roamed through the woods looking for more Yankees. Shots could be heard all around them and occasionally they encountered others from their own regiment. Some appeared highly excited, whooping and hollering, while others were silent, fearful.

A volley of shots suddenly began exploding into the woods around them. Men were running everywhere, aimless, without direction. Steven and Gerritt too, began running, not knowing where they were going; only trying to escape the deadly shells. It was then they heard Sergeant Jennings calling off in the distance to "fall back, Company C, fall back to the river!"

They ran towards the water and down the steep embankment. As they had come out of the woods, they saw hundreds of their fellow comrades already on the banks. Sergeant Jennings was there directing the cross. The men streamed to the other side and regrouped with Sergeant Jennings calling the roll. In Steven's regiment five men had been killed and fifteen wounded.

It was difficult to think of those men who had been with them just a few hours ago, men they had trained with, eaten with and now gone. Family and friends would grieve for them. It gave the men a queer feeling in their stomachs.

They moved back to the rear to the place they had set up camp, to rest and receive rations as well as more ammunition. Gerritt and Steven would not rest until they had roamed the camp and upon finding their fathers, embraced them and rejoiced to find them unhurt. They stayed and talked of the battle with them, all four speaking of the horrors. Soon they made their way back to their own company, stepping around and over soldiers who slept, reclined or were sitting on the ground.

"Do you think it's going to keep on being like this, Gerritt?" Steven asked his friend.

"What do you mean?" Gerrit said as they sat down near one of the fires where Charles and Tom were resting.

"Every time we go into battle, we're going to be afraid our fathers have been killed. Will we go onto the battlefields, turning over bodies to see if they are among the dead?"

Gerritt looked down at the ground, his arms resting on his bent knees. "I don't know, Steven," he replied quietly. "I know I'll always be afraid for my father, but going into battle today, I was afraid for myself. I've never known that kind of fear before. But I was also afraid for you and all the other fellows we've gotten to know. I didn't know how it would be if someone I cared about would be killed. It was a difficult thing to face."

Steven nodded. "It really wasn't what I expected it would be. In the abstract I knew men would die, but I guess I had pushed that to the back of my mind and it didn't have an impact on me until I saw those fellows who died and were wounded. All that blood and men with open wounds and legs shot to pieces….." he shook his head as if to clear away the spectacle he had witnessed.

"Now ya all have a better idea of what war's really all about," Tom told them. "But you ain't seen nothin' yet. We'se just got started."

"Jehosaphat!" Charles said quietly.

They listened to others around the fires as they regaled acts of heroism and boldness in the face of danger. Whether concocted or real, everyone seemed to have a tale to tell.

Suddenly, a signal gun was fired causing everyone to jump to their feet. They all ran to the edge of the clearing where the battalion of the Washington Artillery from Louisiana was firing at the Yankees across to the opposite bank, hidden by shrubbery.

The guns on the Yankee shore fired one after the other with the Confederate guns answering. They were repeated as quickly as the guns could be loaded. The air became filled with a huge roar, deafening to those watching the spectacle. Soon the surrounding area was so clouded with smoke that only the bright flashes of fire, like serpent's tongues, could be seen.

Finally the guns ceased one by one until it was once again silent. When the smoke had cleared, they could see great blackened holes in the earth where the shells had exploded. Several ammunition wagons were in splinters.

"Jehosaphat!" Charles declared and then voiced the thought no one wanted to say aloud, "what do you 'spose would happen iffen one of them hit a person?"

There was no answer to his question.

That evening no one rested well. They knew not what the morrow would bring but when the sun rose, everything was serene. "No guns!" one young man exclaimed. "I bettcha those Yankees have all run back North! They heard those mighty guns and they got scairt silly and run home."

"God bless your innocence," Tom told the young man.

Sergeant Jennings arrived and ordered their company to follow on a reconnaissance mission to find where the enemy was positioned. Everyone gathered up their ammunition and rifles and proceeded to follow the Sergeant across the ford. They quietly paced through the area on the other side where the fighting had taken place the day before.

Steven walked along with the others, glancing from side to side, looking out for any movement in the trees. His senses seemed heightened, his ears trained for any sound, his eyes darting back and forth. The hairs on his arms were standing up.

A cry of alarm was heard at the front of the line and Steven's heart raced, his hands perspired, ready for action. But no shots were heard, no volleys from artillery.

There were more cries and everyone ran forward double quick. The sight that greeted them made them recoil in horror; strewn around the ground lay the bodies of hundreds of Union dead. They had lain there in the hot sun for two days and the effects had wrought their devastation.

Steven had never seen such an appalling sight. These men who had only two days precious had been alive, talking, walking, laughing, were now disfigured. Their bodies and faces bloated and swollen to such a degree that even their own mothers would not have recognized them. The rank stench drew them back, many in the company retching and gagging.

Sergeant Jennings called for them to fall back to the river, but as they withdrew, Steven knew he would never forget those blackened features, those staring, sightless eyes. He looked over at his comrades, Gerritt, Charles, and Tom and he saw there the look that he knew must be reflected in his own face, the paleness, the absolute hideous horror of what they had seen.

Later, another detail of men was sent back over the river to bury the men they had discovered. A grim task it was and the mounds of earth left in the woods, a reminder of the great toll of war.

That evening in the trenches there was not much bold talk of bravery in battle, at least not for those in Company C. The men sat on the ground, huddled near each other in the dark, starless night. "Did you see those men?" Charles said quietly asking the obvious.

The men only nodded. Then after a cold supper, they rolled in their blankets to sleep quickly, to shut off the images they witnessed. But in sleep, the horror haunted them.

The enemy's firing of cannon awakened them. At first it was only sporadic, not really causing any panic among the troops. As they ate another cold meal of bread and fat back, the shelling became more intense and they were ordered forward to the river. Once there, they were given orders by General Beauregard himself to move down river to the main bridge to Washington, at a place called Sudley Church.

Major McDowal sitting astride his horse, called out for them to "fall in! Right flank! and forward march!"

They followed along the river for about a mile with General Beauregard riding with them. Joining him was Joe Johnston, a man who actually outranked Beauregard and was well known as a shrewd and canny commander. He had just arrived at Bull Run with nine thousand additional troops coming from the Shenandoah Valley.

They passed the two story brick church and continued onto Manassas Road. As they marched they could hear artillery fire increasing in intensity and frequency. Now, they also heard sporadic firing of rifles.

Steven kept his eyes glued to the front of the line, watching to see the fighting he knew was just ahead. His heart was pounding and his stomach lurched. How many of the Yankees were up ahead? Were they to be outnumbered? Would he be able to fight or freeze as he had before?

They continued on passing a large house on the left, someone called it Matthew's Hill. Some heavy fighting had already occurred here, the evidence lying about; a discarded musket, spent shot, blood stained grass. Steven was glad there were no bodies to be seen.

As they neared a wooded plateau, they could see the fighting down below on the stone bridge. The smoke from the artillery fire drifted up to where they stood. On either side were two white stone houses, now obviously abandoned, this place now having become a battlefield.

General Johnston ordered them into battle formation with two companies in front of them forming the skirmish line. They were to advance ahead of the main body approximately four hundred yards between. The regimental flag went with them carried by a young flag bearer not more than sixteen years old. Now was the chance to prove all the drilling practice had not been for naught.

General Beauregard sitting astride his horse along with Johnston, raised his saber into the air and called out….. "Forward!" and the first men ran towards the bridge, yelling as loudly as they could and firing their weapons.

Union artillery screamed over head, thudding into the ground and exploding into thousands of hot metal pieces. Steven could feel the pounding of the big guns in his chest. He looked to his left to where Gerritt stood. His eyes were glued to the first wave of men already on the front line. His hands were shaking and his face was paler that Steven had ever seen it. Beyond him stood Charles and Tom. They too, were shifting nervously, passing their muskets from one hand to the other.

Now it was their turn to move forward. They charged, yelling as had the first men. Steven could see the Union troops now, coming closer, firing as they ran. Minnie balls screamed past his head, smacked into the ground at his feet, sending up small sprays of dirt.

And then he saw him, a Yankee with his rifle pointed directly at him and everything seemed to happen in slow motion. The musket was raised, the Yank sighted down the barrel, his left eye closing, his finger on the trigger.

Without even knowing how it had happened, Steven had fired his rifle. Even the bullet leaving the barrel seemed to travel slowly, thudding into the body of the Yankee. His gun flew from his hands; his arms flailing out from his body, his head snapped back and his cap fell away. Then he just crumbled to the ground.

Realization struck him. He had just killed another human being. But before he had time to react, the man beside him splattered his blood on his face from a bullet in his brain. The horror of it, at first, paralyzed him. He stood there staring at the blood on his uniform. His hands were shaking and his legs trembled. Steven knew he needed to reload as quickly as possible. He dropped down in the grass next to the man's body, while others ran past him, firing as they went.

From then on he did everything automatically, blindly shooting, reloading, running towards the bridge, towards the enemy. It was as if everything had been shut out, as if his mind were numb.

He heard someone calling out orders, Major McDowal screaming for them to pull back. Steven looked over his shoulder, saw men retreating back towards the trees. He began to move back, firing, reloading as he went. Besides the first man he had killed, several more had fallen. He knew not whether they were dead or wounded. He couldn't think about that now.

He tripped over those lying on the ground, some dead, their eyes staring open, blank, some wounded, moaning, trying to crawl away. Some were gray and some wore blue, their red blood all mingled together, soaking the earth.

He saw Gerrit, then Charles and Tom. When they had regrouped, they stood together, breathing heavily, no one speaking, their eyes saying more than words ever could.

Off to the right they saw another brigade, standing steadfast against a barrage of firing, never wavering, never backing down and at their lead, Brigadier General

T. J. Jackson, a middle aged man with receding hair at the temples and a full broad mustache. Then one man among them called out, "Rally behind the Virginians men! See there is Jackson standing like a stone wall!"

They all cried out the battle cry, the adrenaline pumping through their veins and ran forward to join with Jackson and the Virginians. Fighting with the others, advancing closer towards the Union line they were suddenly aware of more of their troops joining them on their flank. They were wearing blue, confusing the Yankees, causing them to hesitate, to fire too late, until they were overtaken, the Union offensive collapsing, retreating. The Confederate troops followed crossing over the bridge in pursuit.

What greeted them on the other side astounded them. There among the fleeing Union troops, were civilians, Washatonians come out to watch the fighting as if they were socializing at a Sunday picnic. They sat in buggies and wagons on blankets spread out on the grass. They had picnic baskets filled with food and apparently had been watching the battle east of Bull Run.

Now however, with the Union troops running through their midst with wagons, ambulances, artillery, not to mention the wounded soldiers dieing at their feet, it became chaos.

Screaming, yelling civilians jumped into their wagons and started back to Washington as quickly as they could, choking the roads, and making it nearly impossible for any retreat.

Steven and the others watched the growing panic unfold before them, wheeled vehicles tangled together, horsemen riding up and back, screaming orders, troops on the ground milling about, trying to get down the road.

A Confederate shell whizzed overhead, exploding near the jumble of humanity, causing screams and general panic. Thousands of men dropped their weapons and began running away.

Steven could only stare at the spectacle. Women in their long, flowing dresses and parasols, men with their long coats and high top hats, mixed together with Union soldiers, all trying to escape back down the road to Washington.

Behind him more Confederate troops joined them, all cheering, throwing their caps into the air at the retreating foe. Everyone joined in until thousands of voices were cheering and calling out. They were all pressing together, trying to go forward to pursue the enemy while they had them on the run. The more frightened the Yanks appeared to be, the braver the Rebs became.

General Jackson, whom everyone was now calling Stonewall Jackson, rode up on his dark stallion calling to the men, "Fall in men! Right flank! Forward march!" His horse reared up into the air, his cloak flowing out behind him and upon coming down to the ground, Stonewall spurred him on, the troops following behind. The men marched on the run heading towards Centerville, a small village on the outskirts of Washington.

Steven felt exhilarated. His heart was racing and he joined in the yelling with the others. He never knew the victory could be so exciting, so inspiring. In the back of his mind he knew there were men lying dead back on the field, but he couldn't think of that right now.

For the time being, he could only feel exhilarated that the enemy had been beaten and he himself had gotten through the battle unscathed.

As they neared Centerville they came across the abandoned Union camp. It was obviously a rout, as the Yankees had left in such a panic that all their supplies had been left behind. The tents of the officers were still standing, filled with papers, official documents, some with the seals unbroken, clothing, beds, trunks filled with supplies.

Steven and Gerritt along with the rest of the troops, walked around the camp, helping themselves to guns, bayonets, boxes of ammunition. There were uniforms, knapsacks, camp equipage, swords, sashes, even food, still cooking over the fires, not to mention toiletries, and baskets of champagne among the personal supplies.

"Do you think we ought to be doing this?" Steven asked Gerritt as he picked up a box of ammunition and flung it over his shoulder.

"Certainly, why not?" Gerritt answered, "spoils of war and all that. After all, what else would they do with it, give it back? Let the officers get it all?"

"I suppose that makes sense," Steven said bending over to pick up a knapsack. He began looking through it, finding the usual items such as a razor, soap, cologne, and letters from loved ones. But there were also pictures; a young woman and one of a small child. As he held them in his hand, the sun glinting off the metal of the derrgerotype, his hand began to shake. What if these pictures belonged to someone who now lay dead out there on the field? What if he had been the one to kill that man? Was this woman his wife, the child his son?

A lump rose up in his throat and he stuffed the pictures and letters quickly back into the bag. He laid it carefully on the ground where he had found it. Perhaps they would all come back for their things, at least the personal ones. Perhaps the man wasn't dead after all. He needed to believe, to have hope or he would go crazy.

They passed on through the camp with everyone exclaiming, "Forward, don't stop and we'll be in Washington by day break!"

They pressed on believing they could march on and conquer Washington that very day. But it was not to be. As General Longstreet rode forward, leading them on, a courier galloped up to the General and handed him a message halting the troops.

As he read it his exclamation could be heard to the back of the column. "Retreat! What the Hell! The Federal Army is broken! They're retreating!"

The order was given to about face and go back the way they had come. Mumblings and curses could be heard throughout the ranks.

"Why are we retreating?" Gerritt asked, as were many others. "We've got them beat!"

"It would appear that way. But perhaps they know something we don't." Steven said, trying to be rational. He too, felt disappointed. If they had pursued, would they have gone on to conquer Washington and thus ended this war?

He looked back at Tom and Charles who were in rank behind them. Tom carried his rifle across his shoulders, his mouth beneath the bushy mustache set in a hard line.

Charles walked with his head down, his face scrunched up as if he were trying hard not to cry.

It had been so exciting, so exhilarating, to have been in battle, their lives on the line, the enemy fleeing in terror, the pursuit and then to have it all ripped away, was devastating.

They retreated all the way back to their old camp on the banks of Bull Run where they settled in and built fires, cooked their evening meal. Once again Steven and Gerritt sought out their fathers and found them alive and well. They exchanged greetings, but did not stay long to talk. Their uniforms were dirty, their faces showed the anxiety of battle, but no wounds were seen which relieved both of them.

That evening, the entire camp was quiet, everyone talking in low tones. Some men sat around their fires reading the letters they had picked up from the Yankee camp. Others regaled stories of the battle. But most sat silently, feeling despondent over their bright dreams of an early peace with Southern independence, dashed.

Steven went to the stream to try and wash some of the blood off his uniform. The battle relived itself in his mind, the rebel cry, the sounds of the guns, the clash of blue and gray, the dead and dieing, men with their legs blown off, their arms missing, dieing agonizingly slow, men dead at the first shot. He knew that horror would live in his mind forever. He had seen the detail going out to collect the dead, the wagons filled with the wounded. A sense of dread filled him and in spite of the days victory, he feared what the future would bring.

CHAPTER SIX
—September 1861

Colleen had finally received her first letter from Steven. She had gotten it in August, but it had been written nearly a month previous. She remembered when it had arrived. It had been so long with no word, that she had stopped going to the road to watch for the postal carrier. When his shay arrived at the front door, she suddenly felt fear.

She had watched the short, thin man step out of the carriage and walk up the long steps to the front door. In his hand he held a letter, something she had waited for so long. Then why did she feel such fear? And then she knew it was the anxiety over receiving bad news.

She met the man at the door herself, recognizing him from past deliveries. He smiled at her and tipped his hat as he handed her the envelope. She thanked him and took the letter in her hand. She looked down at it and recognized Steven's handwriting. The paper was a little tattered and soiled and she wondered what trail it had taken to get to her. Her hand was trembling and her other hand went to her mouth, the tears springing to her eyes. When she turned back to the carrier, she realized he had already gone, climbing back into his shay and was clucking to his horse.

She had closed the door and walked into the parlor where it was quiet. Her mother was seeing to the meal in the kitchen house and the servants were occupied elsewhere.

She sat near the window, the fading light of the day streaking across her shoulder. She felt the warmth of it as she held the envelope in both hands. She touched the writing with the tips of her fingers as if somehow she could feel Steven through the ink on the page.

She drew in a deep breath and it caught in her throat. Why did she feel so apprehensive? If it were bad news, he would not notify her first. He would write his mother, because after all, no one knew she was his wife.

She turned the white paper over noticing the smudges acquired from all its travels. She broke the seal and slowly drew out the fine parchment paper she knew Steven had taken with him.

My dear Colleen, my sweet wife," he had written. *"Do I dare say the words? I think of you all the time. You are my heart, my life. I look forward to the day when I will be in your arms again.*

We have as yet not seen any action. Our days are spent in drilling and marching, drilling and marching. I have not felt so exhausted in my life. It would almost be a relief to finally face our foe and be done with this war. Why the Yankees in Washington cannot just leave us in peace, to live our lives the way we choose, is beyond me. After all, wasn't this the same reason as to why we fought the British, in order to gain our freedom and not have others tell us how we should be living?

But, I digress and apologize for boring you with political rhetoric. Your brother Gerritt and I are in the same company and have become tent mates along with a feisty old timer named Tom who fought in the Mexican Wars and has given us a good deal of insight on what to expect. The other is a youngster, Charles, who although coming from a poor family, is nothing but a delight. His spontaneity is very refreshing and is always willing to give us a laugh.

Your father and mine are together in another company. We see them occasionally and they too, are well.

On a sad note; we had an epidemic of typhus sweep through the camp and many died. It was a terrible tragedy and just another horrible aspect of this war.

There are rumors we may be moving soon, on the march towards the action. So be it. The sooner we drive the Yankees back to Washington, the sooner we end this war and I can come home to you.

I look forward to that day, when I can hold you in my arms and kiss your sweet lips. When I can tell the world you are my wife and we will spend the rest of our lives together.

Until that day my love, we will all do what we must do. Be brave and try not to worry. I will write again when I get the chance. I love you with all my heart.

Your loving husband, Steven

Finishing the letter, Colleen clasped it to her bosom, tears filling her eyes. "I miss you, too, Steven," she whispered, "if you only knew how much."

For the next several weeks Colleen read and re-read the letter, touching it, kissing it, keeping it with her at all times, putting it in the pocket of her dress during the day while she went about her chores. At night she placed it under her pillow. It was her last link with Steven.

She had written several letters to him, but she had no idea if he had received them. He had not mentioned them in his letter. She had tried to sound casual, writing of gossip and everyday plantation happenings. But he was at war and she did not want to worry him. She didn't tell him how desperately she missed him, how many nights she cried herself to sleep. She didn't tell him how much she wanted to be held in his strong arms and have him make love to her.

She had not written how difficult things had been on the plantation since the men's departure; how the Yankees had blockaded the ports and none of their cotton was being shipped to England, or how several of their darkies had run away.

She did tell him how much she loved him and was praying daily for his safe return. In her letters, she had written of their future and how much she was looking forward to the day when they would have their own home and raise their children.

Her mother too, had received a letter from her father. The news was pretty much the same as Steven's had been, writing of the terrible epidemic that had struck the camp. He too, had reassured Mary that Gerritt and Steven had survived safely.

Colleen and her mother had taken to overseeing most of the running of the Plantation, not trusting everything to Mr. Solomon. It was exhausting being out in the fields, making sure the cotton was being picked according to schedule, going to the barns to oversee the running of the cotton mill, the weaving house, candle making and now with fall coming on, the harvesting and preserving of the garden stuffs. There was also the large supply of wood that had to be cut, split and stacked near the big house as well as the slave cabins, to keep them warm in the colder months to come. There was also the usual running of the house to contend with on a daily basis.

Everyone in the surrounding area was in the same situation with the men now gone. Many darkies had taken advantage of this and run away, there being rumors of an under ground railroad helping them to get to the North. Even several of their own slaves, mostly field hands, had slipped away in the middle of the night.

As soon as Mary had made the discovery she called on the slave catchers to retrieve their property, but because so many had run away from all over and there being so few slave catchers, the likelihood of recovering those men was slim.

Even though the tasks of running the plantation were daunting, Mary insisted on weekly gatherings of the closest neighbors to sew and knit for their men in gray. Much of their own cotton was spun and woven into cloth for shirts, jackets and trousers to be sent to the men in Beauregards brigade.

The talk during these sessions was always about the war. Everyone attending had a loved one in battle, a husband, a son, a father. They had heard about the battle at Bull Run, but as yet no one had received any word of casualties or wounded. It was on everyone's mind whether their loved ones were killed, buried somewhere in the Virginia soil or maimed and lying in a hospital. Most tried to be positive, not dwelling on the morbid.

Anna Bell however, was nearly certain that either Clifford or Steven or both had met a horrible end and spent a great deal of her time at the McBride's dabbing tears from her eyes. If things had been difficult for Mary and Colleen, they were doubly hard for Anna Bell, especially since she had no support, was alone on her plantation. The financial and agricultural aspects had confused her to the point where creditors had begun to pressure her for their due. Many more of her slaves had escaped and her overseer seemed incapable of preventing it from happening. She was afraid if things continued the way they were, the plantation would fail before her husband could return.

Mary and Colleen did what they could to guide her, but their own burdens were great enough and the distance between homes, far enough to render them helpless at most times.

After each sewing session, the ladies would hold a prayer meeting, gathering together in a circle to offer supplication for their men in gray, the cause and a speedy peaceful end to the war. Then each would get into their respective carriages and go home to deal with running their homes, worry and wait until the following week when they would gather again.

One evening, late, Colleen was having trouble sleeping, not an uncommon occurrence of late and decided to go downstairs to find a glass of buttermilk. She left her room and began to go down the back stairway to the kitchen, something else she seldom did, when she heard voices coming up the stairwell from the pantry below. She recognized Dora and Carlton's voices and they were discussing the war. Curious, Colleen sat on one of the steps to listen.

"How's come you'se can't see what's happenin'?" She heard Dora say. "Iffen the Yankees win this here war, we's gonna be free!" Colleen was shocked to hear her loyal servant apparently siding with the North.

"I'se skeert of this war," Carlton told her. "I'se don't wanna be free."

"How's you say somp'en likes dat? How's you not wanna be free?" Colleen heard anger in Dora's voice when she asked Carlton this question. "You likes havin' white folks ownin' you, telling you'se where's you can goes or not goes? You likes 'em takin' away our men folk, womens, chilins, being sol' iffen you don' do what's they be tellin' you to?"

"I was born on this plantation," Carlton told her. "The McBrides, they'se good white folks. Dey always done treat me real good. I don' knows what's I'd do, where I'd go iffen I'se free. I could mebbe starve or freeze!" Carlton's voice sounded whiny, almost as if he were about to cry.

"Is you tellin' me, you wants to stay a slave, that you'se too lazy to work for your self, to has your own house, your own land?

How 'bout that woman from the Covington place you wanted for you wife? When you axed Massa iffen he'd buy her for you, he says no. How's come you don't gets mad? Them white folks won't lets you be with the woman you loves?"

Colleen heard no response from Carlton and scooted down a step to hear more clearly. She was beginning to feel chilled being away from the warmth of her hearth with just her nightgown on. She wished she had thought to grab her shawl. She hugged her arms about herself to feel warmer.

"You ever been down to them cabins wheres the fiel' hands lives?" Dora asked Carlton.

"Course I'se has," he answered. "You knows dat. We'se been dere together. We goes lots when somebody jumbs de broom and there's a party, or iffen we'se has a dance."

"Then hows come you can't see's hows it is? How hards they works, hows they'se whupped and sold iffen they don' do as they'se tol'"

"Mebbe, mebbe, freedom be good for somes, but jes not fer me," Carlton said and the sound of a chair could be heard scraping across the floor.

Colleen heard Dora audibly sigh as another chair scraped on the wood planking. "I'se tellin' you this, I'se hope 'en and prayin' the Yankees win this here war and iffen they don', then mebbe I'se jes gonna has to runs away."

"You does dat an' they be sendin' the slave catchers afta you and iffen they catches you, they be beatin' you and mebbe kills you!"

"Enything's worth bein' free, even iffen I'se gots to die!"

Colleen heard the two of them walk out of the room. She stood up slowly and quietly walked back to her room, her buttermilk forgotten.

Dora and Carlton's conversation kept running through her mind. She felt hurt by some of the things Dora had been saying. Her Dora, the woman who had taken care of her her whole life, bathed her, dressed her, someone who was like a second mother to her.

She had always thought Dora was happy with them. She had never complained, had never tried running away like some of those field hands. They had clothed her, fed her. She always had a warm bed to sleep in and they had treated her well.

Why would she be so disloyal? Why would she run away? Was it so horrible here that she would rather be dead? How could she want the Yankees to win, their enemy? Didn't she realize their men were out there fighting, dieing for their independence, for their way of life, for her?

She blew out the small candle on her bed stand and crawled back under the comforter. The tears began to fall, wetting her hair and pillow. It was just one more disappointment, one more heartbreak.

The following morning when Dora woke her, she sounded pleasant and cherry as usual without belying the conversation of the previous evening. Colleen kept watching her to see if there was any hint of the feelings she had expressed the night before. She wanted to confront her, to let her know that she had heard the conversation between her and Carlton. But she wasn't sure how Dora would respond. Surely she wouldn't admit to hating it here or having the desire to run away.

She sat down at her dressing table and looked at her reflection in the mirror. She touched her face, the soft smooth skin of youth. "Sometimes I wish I were a man," she said aloud.

"Lordy missy," Dora said, "Why would you wish such things?"

"Because then I could go into the army with Steven. We could fight side by side like he and Gerritt for the things we believe in and perhaps get this war over with sooner."

"Oh missy, Colleen," Dora said taking the hairbrush and beginning to brush her hair. "You don't wanna go fights no war. Ain't it bad 'nough Mr. Steven, Mr. Gerritt and yo Pappy don gone without you wan'ta go fights you self? Your Mama needs you here, to helps with the cotton and such."

Colleen sighed. "I know, but it's so difficult stayin' here carryin' on as if nothing unusual were goin' on, while our men are somewhere in Virginia, fightin' for their lives."

During breakfast, her mother talked of the Cookes, her good friend Cynthia's family, having a fall cotillion. Mr. Cooke had not signed up with the army, using the newly enacted Southern law which allowed anyone with more than seventy-five slaves to stay home. Her own father and Steven's could have gotten out using the same excuse, but their loyalties would not allow it. Colleen felt angry that he would not go while her father had. His son Ben however, was also with Beauregard in Virginia.

But to plan a cotillion, a gay time of dancing and ballgowns, seemed inappropriate at such a time. So when her mother began talking of what they would wear and who would be there, she had to excuse herself.

She went for a walk past the gardens, past the stables and down to the river to the little gazebo where only a few months before, she had been in Steven's arms. She held on to one of the support posts and looked out at the rippling river and across to the slave quarters. Men, women, and children were moving about, carrying on with their daily chores, going off to the fields, or work barns, washing clothes, cooking or caring for children.

Colleen remembered the slave girl Lisbeth, who she had assisted in delivering her baby and she wondered how the child was doing. She would be several months old now and probably accompanied her mother to the weaving house each day.

How queer life could be, she thought. While children are born every day, at the same time men were dieing on the battlefield in some far away state.

How many had already died in this insane war? How many wounded? And when would it all end? When would their men be able to come home? She wondered if she would ever again look upon Steven's handsome face, be held in his arms, or taste the sweetness of his lips.

She closed her eyes and the ache in her heart spilled over as tears. "We must be brave, Colleen," she suddenly heard her mother say.

She spun around to see her standing at the edge of the path. She had not even heard her approaching. She wiped quickly at the tears and left the gazebo to join her mother. They turned back towards the house and Mary put her arm around her daughter's waist.

"I try Mother, but sometimes I just get to thinking about Papa and Gerritt and Steven and I can't help but feel sad. I miss them so much."

"I know sweetheart, and I miss them too, very much. But think how much more they're suffering, so far away from home; death and dying all around them, fighting for us, for our Confederate States and our families."

"Yes mother. I'll try harder to be brave, but it does bother me that the Cookes are having a cotillion when our men are off to war and Mr. Cooke stays home putting on parties. How can you be involved in that?"

"It's for the cause, dear," Mary said turning to her. "Mr. Cooke will have several of our fine officers of the Confederacy there, along with cabinet members in President Davis's office. All the gentry of Georgia are invited and also invited to make a generous donation to our glorious cause. I have already allocated three thousand dollars to give for our men in battle."

"Oh I see," Colleen said as they reached the house. "Then it's alright I suppose."

"And you might even enjoy yourself," her mother told her smiling. "All work and no play, you know."

Later in the day as Colleen and her mother were taking a break from overseeing the chores, by having tea in the parlor, Colleen waited for Betsy to leave before questioning her mother.

"There is something I've been wanting to ask you," Colleen began.

"What is it my dear?" her mother said lifting the cup to her lips.

"Do you think it's wrong to own slaves?"

Mary choked on her tea, coughing until she regained control. "Why would you ask such a question?" Mary said scrutinizing her daughter's expression carefully.

"Many are saying so. After all, isn't that one of the reasons for fighting this war?"

"Yes, it is one of the reasons for fighting this war," Mary said choosing her words carefully. "But it's so much more than that. You see, Northerners, they live in cities, labor in factories. They have many European emigrants to do their work, but we in the south are mostly agricultural. We grow the food, cotton, tobacco and sugar cane for our country and the world. We need our slaves to produce.

As for the slaves themselves, well, it's beneficial for them also. They are a primitive people, backward, rather like children. They have a good life with us. We care for them, give them housing, clothing, food, in exchange for their labor.

Think about it, my dear, what would these poor ignorant Negroes do without us? They wouldn't know how to take care of themselves. Why, they would literally starve to death."

"I suppose you're right," Colleen said aloud, but she kept remembering Dora's words of the night before.

"Of course I'm right," her mother said standing up and sitting her cup on the Queen Anne table. "Can you just imagine what would happen if all the darkies were free? They'd be runnin' loose all over the place, theivein' rappin', killin'……. Why, it would be chaos. You just better pray our brave men win this war."

CHAPTER SEVEN
—Spring 1862

Steven and Gerritt were now near Yorktown, having spent the fall and winter in Centerville, the same area where they had fought their first fight. After Bull Run, General Johnston had had them build extensive lines of entrenchments. Also built were many wooden guns carved out of massive logs, which looked like real cannon and hopefully would fool the enemy.

Patrols were moved forward to the hills surrounding Washington on the Potomac and batteries were erected downstream to prevent access by the river. And although they continued to drill and patrol, the troops had settled in for the winter.

They had been given double wall tents trenched around on the outside and staked to the ground. They accommodated four persons, so the old tent mates had elected to stay together.

Inside arrangements consisted of a stove, which the four had pooled their money together to purchase, having finally received their pay of forty-four dollars each for four months service. They were crisp, new bills of the Treasury of the Confederacy.

Also in each tent were two bunks for sleeping. They had also acquired cooking utensils, which had generally been stored under the bed.

Late fall had brought abominable weather with much rain and cold temperatures. Everyone had generally stayed in their tents, except when ordered out on picket duty and occasional drills.

On one occasion a report came down that the Yankees were advancing. Everyone gathered their arms and ammunition and headed out on the double. After marching for an entire day, they had finally camped in a stand of trees.

Huge fires had been built with the men huddling around them to warm themselves and dry out their clothing. Steven had never remembered being so wet and cold. Everything he wore was soaked, including his underwear and the socks inside his boots. Before they had had a chance to get dry, they heard the sound of the long roll and were ordered to form in line and move out.

Never had there been more cursing and grumbling as when they were required to pull on wet boots and clothing. Back they had gone down the same road to Centerville, but by that time the road had become a quagmire and with every step, mud clung to the soles of their boots.

Steven remembered the shivering, the clammy cold, the rivulets of water that had run off his hat and down his back. He remembered how much he had ached and having felt so tired, he could have slept on the march. They had returned to their camp without having seen one Yankee.

The rest of the winter had stretched interminably on, with no action regarding the war whatsoever. On occasion, they would hear of a skirmish being fought, mostly in the west, but nothing more came their way.

They had spent their time playing cards, betting and reading when they could get their hands on books, washing clothes and sleeping. During the coldest months, drills were suspended entirely, bringing on more boredom to their already monotonous lives.

One positive element of their confinement had been to spend more time with their fathers. They would periodically visit one another's tents to spend time sipping hot coffee and sharing tales of life back home. Sometimes when one or the other would receive a letter, they would share parts of it with the others.

Steven cherished the letters he had gotten from Colleen, reading and re-reading them. She always seemed cheerful, but underneath, he could tell things were difficult for them back home. He only wished he could be there to help, to take his place as her husband and fulfill their dreams of being together for the rest of their lives. He had also used this time of quiet to write back to her and his mother, but after awhile he had run out of things to write about, considering the lack of activity.

In March the winds had begun to blow cold and blustery, bringing down nearly all of the tents in camp. Several times with much profanity, the tents were again erected, only to have them blow down again.

It was during this time of unpleasant weather that they had been notified the enemy was on the march and that they were to pack up and move out. Many of the supplies they had accumulated over the past months had to be left behind.

They had started marching southward, thousands on the long winding road. Steven and the others had never known such walking as they had done then, especially after so many months of inactivity. Their backs and feet ached and if they had been allowed, many would have fallen by the wayside.

The weather had remained inclement and tortuous to those on the march. On one particular day they would have snow, another rain, soaking and chilling them to the bone. The next day it might be sunny and warm, with the next sending shards of sleet into their faces.

Added to their discomfort had been trying to traverse the woeful conditions of the roads. Wagons, caissons and horses had turned the highways into rut filled quagmires, barely passable by the troops and cause for extreme hardship.

Whenever darkness had come on, they camped in the woods, cutting down trees, using any available fence rail for firewood, building immense fires to dry their clothing and warm their frozen extremities.

They had marched for a week until they reached Orange Court House where they had camped until the first week in April. After that, they had continued their march towards Richmond.

Having received word that Yorktown had been attacked and that the assault on Dam #1 had been repulsed with the loss of the enemy, there was renewed energy in the troops and they reached their destination in a very short time.

They had marched through Richmond with much pomp and circumstance, brass bands had played the fife and drum for each regiment, the entire town coming out to watch, and then had gone on to Williamsburg.

Steven remembered the history of Williamsburg, the old colonial town from his history books in school. He had been looking forward to seeing the town for himself, but it was not to be. They had passed it by a few miles distant and now lay in the trenches at Yorktown, helping General Magruder and his troops. General Beauregard had been sent west to Tennessee, their troops now in command by Joe Johnston.

The weather had turned dreary once again, raining ceaselessly, soaking everything in its range. Large breastworks, six and eight feet high had been put up by Magruder's troops. These were logs laid crisscross at the top of the trenches, creating a large wall. Along with these, there were deep trenches they had taken shelter in. Across the way, only three hundred yards distant, was the enemy, in full force with heavy batteries of columbiads, a ten inch cannon mounted on a casemate carriage, mortars, and mounted siege guns, the roar being heard for miles. They had not seen any action for such a long time; the expectation of battle was unsettling. The battles they had already participated in were fading in memory, the horrific scenes, blurring.

The four tent mates were together, trying to stay as dry as possible in the pouring rain with their feet in three inches of water. They were not allowed to fall out of ranks because of the threat of an imminent attack.

Gerritt and Steven sat huddled together; their slickers on and their caps pulled down, trying to keep the rain out of their faces. As a Union shell exploded nearby, they flinched.

"I don't think I've ever been so miserable," Gerritt commented and then sneezed. "On top of it all, I think I'm catching cold."

"I think I might be able to warm up a bit if I could just get my feet dry," Steven said shifting around as if trying to find higher ground.

"My teeth are chatterin' so bad, they ache," Charles said trying to pull his arms up under his slicker and keep his musket dry at the same time. Another shell burst nearby and he jumped, causing him to fall in the water. Tom helped him to stand, but his pants were now soaked.

"Damn!" he said holding his gun up out of the water. "There ain't no way this here thin's gonna fire now. I think my powder's wet, too."

"It's gonna be alright," Tom told him as a rivulet of water ran from his beard like a small stream. "Them Yankees can't fight in this here mess either."

"That's right. Their guns are just as soggy." Steven told him, trying to pick up his spirits. He could see the terror in his eyes, the way his hands were shaking and it wasn't from the cold.

"I don' know; them shells is getting' purty close. I wonder what happens to a body iffen it gets hits by one of 'em."

"Well, let's not think about that. We'll just wait out this rain and then we'll whup those Yankees," Gerritt told him.

Darkness came on and still the rain continued until nothing, not even the clothing beneath their slickers, was dry. No fires could be built to warm their chilled bodies and the night was black as a deep cave.

Some tried to light pipes, hoping to glean some comfort from the glowing tobacco, but no flint was dry and no pipe would light.

The men could not sleep, could not lay down anywhere, and only prayed for the morning to come with hopes for the rain to cease at its dawning.

But, it was not to be. Morning light brought more rain, never seeming to cease even for five minutes. They ate crackers washed down with dirty water and no coffee, as they still could build no fires. The day was spent patrolling the perimeter and socializing with each other. Some even indulged in singing, trying to lighten the mood.

Still the rain continued and soon the trenches were knee deep in water with no hope of dry feet. It wasn't long before dejection set in with all the troops and silence prevailed among them all.

Another night was spent standing in the water filled trenches, darkness enveloping everything around them.

Steven stood leaning against the breastworks, his arms wrapped around himself, trying not to shake hard enough to drop his rifle. He closed his eyes and listened to the sounds around him, the quiet talking, indistinguishable murmuring, the splashing of someone walking along the trenches, the aroma of a pipe finally lit, the explosion of a shell nearby.

His thoughts turned to home and Colleen and wished he were with her now. How good it would feel to hold her in his arms, to kiss her lips. He longed for the times he strolled with her along the river under the swaying magnolias, the scent of apple blossoms in the air and the warmth of the sun on their shoulders.

Suddenly he felt himself falling, could not catch himself in time until he had splashed into the water, his entire body submerged. Before he could gain his feet, strong hands lifted him from the swirling pool.

"Are you alright?" Gerritt asked him.

"You must'a fallen asleep," Tom told him. "It's happenin' all over; men so tired, they'se fallin' asleep as they stand. You kin hear 'em splashing inta the water."

Steven could only nod as he emptied the water out of his cap. Now his head was wet as well, chilling him even further. He felt so miserable and homesick, if he had been a lesser man, he would have wept.

By morning the rain had finally stopped, but not before many had fallen ill with colds, chills and fever. "At least they got moved to the rear to a hospital tent where they could be up off the ground and dry," Steven lamented as they climbed up out of the trenches.

"Yeah, I'm sure it would be much better to be sick and lyin' in the hospital," Gerritt said sarcastically.

"Alright, alright, but at least they're dry! I haven't been that in days!" Steven said yelling in Gerritt's direction.

"Boys, boys," Tom said putting his arms around their shoulders. "We're all a little testy here. Why, who wouldn't be with bein' soaked to the bone and no sleep? Let's git over to them there trees. I sees the fellows got a fire goin' and some grub. Iffen we can sleep awhile and have some nice warm grub, we'll all be feelin' better."

The days of torrential rains finally abated and the warm sun of Spring warmed the earth. The blossoms and flowers were in abundance filling the air with their aromatic fragrance.

The regiment was now camped outside of Richmond where supplies were numerous and food abundant. The troops were only required to perform occasional drills and the mandatory guard duty. The men relaxed and enjoyed time for letter writing and socializing with friends.

It was during this respite that Gerritt and Steven spent time with their fathers again. Steven's father Clifford, had suffered from a fever and cough during the many days of rain, but had recovered sufficiently, except for a lingering occasional bout of coughing.

It was from them they learned of the bloody battle of Shiloh in Tennessee on April 6th and 7th. The Union forces had been led by a General Ulysses S. Grant and the Confederates under Generals Johnston and Beauregard.

It was not good news. The rebel troops had been defeated. It was reported the Federals had lost 13,000 men, while the Confederates lost 10,000, including General Johnston. It was a sobering statistic, jolting everyone in camp back to the realities of war.

As the men sat around their campfires that evening eating stew and smoking their pipes, they talked of the battle at the little country meeting house, now known as Shiloh Church.

"Jehosaphat!" Charles exclaimed. "Kin you jes imagine, 10,000 men. I cans't even count that fer."

"And 13,000 Yanks," Steven commented. "It's hard to imagine that many lying around dead."

"Tis a purty powerful imaginin'," Tom said as he took a long draw on his pipe, temporarily lighting his face. Each of them only nodded, their pictures of the horrific battle in their minds.

May—1862

Near the end of May, the bulk of the Confederate troops were camped at a little town five miles from Richmond, called Mechanicsville. They were across the bridge on the Chickahominy River with the Yankees occupying the high ground below Seven Pines. Everyone knew the conflict was about to escalate and a battle was imminent.

The men sat around their small cooking fires late at night, sipping coffee in their tin cups and talking quietly, listening to the rumble of distant thunder.

"I sure hopes we ain't gonna be getting no rain likes we a had afore," Charles commented. "I done 'bout drownded."

"I hear what you're sayin'," Tom said as he took a drink from his cup.

"Somethin' else I been hearin'," he said peering over the rim of his cup.

"What is it you've been hearin'?" Steven asked him.

"I heerd the Confederate Congress passed a law sayin' we can't go home after our year's up like we signed up for. They say now we half ta stay for three or the duration of the war."

Gerritt nodded. "Yes, I heard that too. I'm not quite sure how I feel about it."

"What's it mean," Charles asked poking the embers of fire with a stick, "that duration thing?"

"It means as long as the war lasts," Steven told him. "at least three years, but if it ends before or if it goes longer, we have to stay in."

"It shouldn't take a whole heap longer to whup them Yankees, I spect," Charles said encouragingly and then with a longing in his eyes even the others could see in the firelight, "And then well, I guess I could go on home."

"I heerd somethin' else," Tom continued. When no one spoke, he went on. "I heered another thin' them Congressmen did, was to say that them who owns more'n twenty slaves can go on home."

Steven and Gerritt exchanged glances. "I figger you rich fellows probably got way more'n twenty slaves, ain't that right, Mr. McBride and Mr. Covington?"

When Gerritt and Steven were silent, Tom continued with sarcasm in his voice. "So I 'spect you boys will be leavin' soon, eh? I guess this war's become a poor mans war, us fightin' for you 'uns, so's you kin keep them fancy lives on them plantations with all yer slaves."

Steven took another sip of his coffee before answering. "Well, Tom, you're right about us owning a lot of land and having more than twenty slaves. It's more like three hundred, each."

Tom gave a big sigh and rolled his eyes. Charles stared at Gerritt and Steven, his mouth open, not really understanding what was being said.

"I'm not ashamed of that or of what I am. But, I want you to look closely at the men you've been sharing a tent with, eating with, fighting side by side with, and tell me what you see. Are we some snobbish, aristocratic prudes who look down our noses at everyone else? Are we like some of those fellows who brought their slaves with them to wait on them, or those who hired someone else to take their place in the fighting?"

"Well………"

"Just because the Congress has made some legislation saying we don't have to fight, doesn't change anything. We came to fight and fight is what we'll do until this thing is finished."

"We're fighting for our freedom to have our own government, to live our lives the way we wish without the Yankees tellin' us how we must," Gerritt said. "A lot of us plantation owners believe in that, including our fathers who are here as well. Yes, we have a lot of slaves, a lot of land, but the cotton, tobacco, and sugarcane we grow helped support the south and its economy. If we cotton growers stop sending our product overseas to England, then they'll have to join the war to break the blockade. Their loyalties are with the south. Once England joins us, we'll beat those Yanks in no time."

"Sounds alright to me," Charles said, a grin on his face.

"I'm sorry for doubtin' you fellows," Tom said, "You've been damn good soldiers so far."

That evening the sky burst forth with a violence that rivaled a major battle. Lightening flashed almost incessantly, with the following thunder so loud, conversation was impossible. The men sat huddled in their small tent, the rain pounding so hard on the canvas, it soaked through and thus, thoroughly soaked those inside. Sleep was impossible.

By morning the storm had abated and as the divisions formed rank, they could see the Chickahominy was swollen to over flowing. Bridges were gone and no one could fathom how the right wing would have been able to come to the aid of the left, should that maneuver become necessary.

Sergeant Jennings came around and distributed sixty rounds of cartridges to each man, forty for his cartridge box with the remaining twenty in his haversack.

"We're movin' out, men," he told them as he moved down the line. "We'll be facin' those Yanks again. Be ready." The commissary sergeant followed behind him handing out three days rations.

Everyone knew a big battle was about to occur. Each one knew the other was thinking of Shiloh and the thousands who had died there. What would tomorrow bring? Would each of them be counted among the dead or wounded?

They were ordered to move out and were soon on the Williamsburg Road. The march was made difficult by the rains, turning each step into a tremendous effort. Streams that previously had meandered gently alongside the road, were now overflowing and required fording.

It wasn't long before they began to hear the booming thunder of artillery fire which grew louder as they got nearer.

Steven's heart began to beat faster, his senses sharpened for any appearance of the enemy. He heard small arms fire off to his left and the company returned fire even though the Yanks could not yet be seen. Here and there a man would fall, struck down by some phantom sharpshooter off in the tree.

Above them could be seen the puffs of white, left by the bursting cannon shells. Smoke from the rifle fire rose like the mist, surrounding them in a surreal blanket.

Suddenly Steven spotted them, a long line of blue, moving forward, firing as they came. The blood pounded in his ears so furiously, he could hear it and in spite of the chill, he broke out in beads of sweat. He began to return fire, reloading as quickly as the bullet was sent on its deadly mission.

The officers called out the orders to march double quick and they began to move forward towards the opposing enemy before them.

Men began to fall as minnie ball or shell would penetrate their fragile bodies. The mutilation was horrendous, arms, legs, shot off, an entire body blown to unrecognizable small pieces and the blood, everywhere there was blood, staining the ground, the men upon it.

Steven felt sick to his stomach with the sight of it. There was no time to stop and vomit because of his churning stomach. He continued firing, moving forward, dropping to reload. A bullet whizzed by so closely to his head, he felt its breath on his ear. It struck the man behind him in the throat. He knelt quickly beside him, but the man was dead, the blood pouring from the gaping hole in his neck.

Steven moved on, Gerritt beside him, Colonel McDowal urging them on, waving his sword as they went on the run. Ahead of them was a large woodpile and barn with several batteries of foe behind them. Shell, shrapnel, and grape shot burst around them. More men dropped dead or wounded.

They broke over the woodpile, screaming the Rebel cry as they went; the Union soldiers scattering before them. On the other side was a camp, tents and supplies still intact. Steven saw a four gun battery deserted, every one of the horses killed, dead men all around. But huddled behind one of the dead horses was a boy, the powder monkey, cowering and shaking, his skin pale and his eyes wide with terrified fright. It startled him nearly as much as the mutilations around him. Small boys should not have to be a witness to this horror.

Things suddenly became chaotic as more and more men moved up, surrounding the camp. Steven had no more time to think about the boy, with more artillery fire raining down upon them and now being surrounded by their own men. No one dared fire their guns for fear of hitting one of their own.

Meanwhile the enemy continued their barrage upon them, bullets flying everywhere, ripping through the canvas of the tents, through men's bodies, their screams filling the air.

The flag went down, another picked it up and he too was shot. A third raised it up and bore it on throughout the day.

The Captain called out for them to take cover and they dove behind the woodpile. There they found rifle pits dug by the Union soldiers and there they took refuge. They could at least for the moment, have time to catch their breaths.

As the bullets hissed around them like snakes in a pit, Steven was able to glance around at those others in the trench with him. Gerritt was there beside him, eyes wide, hands shaking. Charles and Tom were no where in sight and Steven wondered if they had met their fate out on the field like so many others. Several more men cowered there as well, afraid to move for fear of being shot.

One soldier, a Yank, lay at their feet, severely wounded in the chest. Blood poured forth, staining his uniform and running unto the ground. He groaned horribly and looked desperately up into their faces.

"Please help me," he pleaded. "I'm dying. Please sir, help me!"

Steven removed his handkerchief from his pocket and went to bend over the man, pressing the cloth to his wound. It was quickly saturated and the warm, sticky blood oozed unto his hand. He literally could feel, with every beat of his heart, the man's life slipping away. He watched his face pale, his body went lax.

"Tell her," the soldier whispered.

Steven put his face closer to the man's mouth to hear him more clearly. "What is it, soldier?" Steven asked him.

"Tell Cora, I….love her."

"Who's Cora, your wife, mother? Soldier?" Steven looked over at Gerritt, both knowing the man had died. Steven removed his bloody hand from the man's chest and wiped it on his pant leg. He looked down into the sightless eyes.

"Someone named Cora will miss him very much," Steven said quietly.

More men began climbing over the breastworks trying to find shelter, but the shelling was so intense, twenty men fell dead. Bullets ricochet off the woodpile and thudded into the ground sending sprays of dirt over them

Several men tried to rise up, to fire back at the constant barrage from the Yankees and were rewarded with a bullet in the head. No one dared move from the breastworks.

Because of the heavy deluge of rain the previous night, the rifle pits were filled with mud and ooze. To the men's horror, they discovered that buried beneath the mire, were corpses that had sunk beneath the surface and now they were standing upon them.

Just before dark, the firing suddenly abated and in the ensuing silence, Sergeant Jennings jumped out into the open and called for the troops to form. Steven and Gerritt came out from the rifle pit, along with others from behind the breastworks, barn and other concealment's. They all formed into a line and advanced through the open to the abattis the enemy had set up; the long line of fallen trees, sharpened to a point on one end and placed with the sharpened part, facing the Rebels. They reached the relative safety of this construction without a shot being fired by Union troops.

Once several hundred of them had gathered, Sergeant Jennings moved them through the woods to the very edge of the Union camp where they had previously seen the large array of tents. On the edge of the woods they could see where the Yanks had held them at bay. Cartridges, shell casings, and broken weapons were strewn about the ground. Now being closer to the Union camp, they could also view the spoils that had been left behind. Supplies littered the ground. Food still cooked in pots, tents spilling over with blankets, haversacks and personal items.

But they were halted on the low ground just on the edge of the camp and were prevented from going in. They could only stare at the riches before them, out of reach.

The low ground they cowered on was full of wet, black mire, covering their feet, their legs, oozing into their boots.

"I guess it wasn't enough we were barraged with bullets, had our friends dying all round us, pinned down in a water filled, corpse covered rifle pit; now we have to stand in this mud suckin' quagmire, while all that booty waits just a hundred yards away," Gerritt commented.

Unbelievably, while the wet and miserable men watched, new troops, who had not even fired a shot, were brought in to hold the camp and were allowed to partake of the spoils, bringing out meat, flour, fruit, sugar, rice, bottles of wine and brandy. They found swords and rifles, clothing and other luxuries.

Wounding their pride even further, they were ordered to retreat back through the woods to the breastworks were many of their comrades still lay where they had fallen. The medical company had come forward to tend to the wounded and had only just begun to remove the dead.

They were finally reunited with Charles and Tom who had survived the onslaught, but Steven and Gerritt wondered about their fathers, as they had not been able to locate them. Darkness was coming on and they were exhausted from the grueling horror of the day. The men lay down on the wet ground and fell into a deep sleep.

When they awoke in the morning, stiff and wet from sleeping on the cold ground, they were better able to assess their losses. Under the direction of General Longstreet, roll call was given and it was made apparent the causalities that had befallen their regiment. Two field officers had fallen; three companies had lost all of their officers, with their own brigade losing half their men. All told it was fifty-nine killed and one hundred fifty-six wounded. They knew not the numbers of the other brigades nor what might have befallen their fathers who were under General Johnston. The official report stated that since the Union forces retreated with heavy losses and had abandoned their main camp, the Rebels forces had obtained the victory.

Steven, Gerritt, Tom and Charles, along with the others, built fires and proceeded to warm themselves as well as make breakfast. Steven reached into his mud-encrusted haversack and pulled out a strip of rag, inside of which was a large strip of fat. From this he cut off a slice and skewered it on the ramrod from his musket. Then he drew from the bottom of his haversack, his hardtack or crackers. These, he propped in front of the fire to toast while he cooked the fat, holding the ramrod over the flames. Once the fat had begun to cook and drip juices, he held it over the crackers for flavor. After the meat had been cooked, Steven filled his metal cup with water and gingerly placed it on the coals so as not to spill any. Once the water started to boil, he threw in a handful of roasted rye for his coffee.

Everyone else had prepared their breakfast in the same manner and so they all settled down to eat. "Ah, who would have thought I would be eating this stuff and actually thinking it's wonderful," Steven said as he chewed a piece of the fat.

"Especially when you haven't eaten in twenty-four hours," Gerritt remarked.

"You should'a seen what we had'a eat durin' the Mexican War," Tom said as he chewed a piece of hardtack. "You think this stuff's bad, why what we all had then wasn't fit for man nor beast."

"Alright Tom," Steven said holding up his hand, "you've already told us many times before. You had to eat lizards and scorpions and chewed cactus for dessert. Hands down, you had it much worse."

Tom nodded, pulling at his beard. "You got that right."

"Let me ask you something Tom," Gerritt said quietly. "You've been in a war before. How do you handle all the death?"

Everyone grew silent, thinking of the battle they had just fought, of the hundreds who had lain dead. Many were men they had known for over a year, shared meals, tobacco, and stories of home. Now they were gone and it left a hollow achy feeling inside.

"Ain't no easy answer to that," Tom said. "Some gets cold inside, so's it don't touch 'em. Others, it breaks, they gets crazy in the head, teched. For most, I guess it's someplace in the middle. When you first sees it, the death, the mutilations, it makes you sick, you feel the horror of it in the very pit of your soul. Then you kin's of gets use to it, not that you even think it's a good thing, but it's not quite so horrifying, you know?"

"I don't know," Steven said, leaning back against a tree as he sipped his coffee. "I don't think I'll ever get use to it. Every time I close my eyes, I see those men on the field, in the ditches, eyes wide open, arms, legs, missin', blood everywhere."

Charles nodded, the pain obvious on his face belying his own thoughts.

"So young, Steven thought, to be engaged in this horror of war. But then, most of them were young, so young to die. He thought of the man in the rifle pit who died with the name of Cora on his lips. He knew most of the dead were hauled away to some designated place where they were buried, never to go home again. He was beginning to wonder if it was all worth it.

Having finished his breakfast, Steven reached for the small bag hanging on the buttonhole of his jacket. From it, he removed a small portion of tobacco and taking his pipe from his pocket, packed it into the bowl. Once this was done, he struck his flint, causing a spark and lighting the tobacco. He drew deeply on the stem, inhaling the sweet smoke.

He thought about how the simple pleasures in life had become so much more important. Back on the plantation he had taken so many things for granted, had enjoyed every luxury without wanting for anything. Now a warm bed, dry clothing, a full belly and a good smoke were all one could ask for to be completely satisfied.

The brigade was called to fall in line and they marched back to the abandoned Union camp and the scene of the previous days' battle. The dead Yankees still lay thick around the ground. They were informed that they were to be ready, as the enemy would most likely try to re-capture the camp.

They were placed in position behind the breastworks with sharpshooters all around. This time they felt more confident as they would be the defenders and the Yanks would have to cross the Chickohominy and charge them.

As they waited, more brigades joined them, including stragglers who had either run away or gotten lost during the battle. It was then they saw General Johnston and their fathers' brigade. They could see from a distance they were well, but were not able to speak to them.

A tremendous feeling of relief swept over Steven and he had not realized until then, how concerned he had been. For now they were all safe, which was amazing considering the landscape around them. The ground itself had been trampled swamp like, with bodies lying in the mud. The nearby barn was shattered and riddled by bullets and shell to the degree that not a space larger than a man's hand was left untouched. There was no more time to think on how anyone could have survived such an assault, as the thunder of guns could be heard in the distance.

"Here we go again," Steven thought as he readied his musket for the battle. He was startled when Charles suddenly stood, not always a wise decision with a battle imminent.

"Jehosaphat!" Charles exclaimed looking over towards where General Longstreet had been conferring with his officers.

Steven and Gerritt stood also and looked to where Charles was pointing. Sitting on a splendid black horse was a handsome looking man of about thirty-five years of age. His face was tanned; his eyes were a striking deep blue, sparkling as he laughed at some remark. He wore a large, full, flowing beard like a Norseman of old. He sat straight in the saddle wearing a splendid uniform, gold braid on the sleeves extending nearly to his elbows. His fitted blue pants were decorated with silver cord and were met at the knee by shiny black cavalry boots which had large silver spurs attached to the heels. His head sported a wide brimmed slouch hat with a golden cord around the crown. One side carried a gilt star with a large plume, which nearly touched his shoulder. His voice was deep and musical, a pleasant sound to the ear.

He rode off and then reined in short at the edge of the clearing. Beyond him were hundreds of mounted men, battle smoke behind them, their bayonets glittering in the morning sun.

"Who is that man?" Steven asked in wonderment.

"I knows who he is," Charles told them. "That there's General Jeb Stuart, Commander-in-chief of the Cavalry!" Charles was smiling and nodding his head as he made his announcement.

Steven could see why he admired the man. He looked positively splendid and from the tales he had heard, was a brilliant and courageous general. "Hey boys," he said, "maybe we joined up with the wrong outfit." They all began to laugh, but suddenly a shell burst over their heads causing everyone to drop flat on the ground.

General Stuart called out his troops and the regiment rode off down the Williamsburg road in a cloud of dust to confront the enemy from the south.

"Go gets 'em!" Charles called out to the retreating cavalry from his position on the ground. "I sure wishes I could rides a horse like they does. I'd a jinned up with Jeb Stuart."

A few more shells had burst over their heads, but they soon realized they were out of range. The regiment was formed together and they began their march back down the road towards the camp they had been in the day before. The roads were difficult to traverse with deep ruts and mud caused by the heavy artillery which had gone before them.

They finally reached the camp, exhausted and foot sore, but they saw General Johnston's brigade flag and sent to search out their fathers before resting. After several inquiries they finally found them, sitting by a warm fire, sipping coffee. They were dirty, unshaven, with torn clothing, but they were in relatively good condition.

Gerritt was at first anxious when he realized his father James's arm was bandaged. "It's alright, son," he reassured him. "It's just a scratch. A bullet whizzed by just a little too closely and nicked my arm."

"Have you had a doctor look at it?" Gerritt asked him moving closer to inspect the arm. "It might be more serious than you think."

"Yes, yes," James said waving him away. "The medic was the one who bandaged it."

"How are you boys?" Clifford asked them. "We heard about Longstreet's men being in the thick of it up there."

"It was pretty bad for awhile there. A lot of good men went down, but praise to God, we made it through."

"We worry so about the two of you," James told them. "Being in different regiments is difficult, not always being in contact."

"We know, it's the same for us, worrying about you. But please know, we don't take risks and we stay as safe as we can," Gerritt said touching his father's arm.

"I know you're both good boys, have level heads, but when you see so much death…..it's just frightening."

"We'll be careful, we promise," James told them smiling, trying to be reassuring.

After a bit more conversation, they went back to their own regiment where they obtained some food and drink. Sitting by the fire, Steven put his forehead in his hands, resting them on his drawn up knees.

Gerritt came to sit next to him and handed him a cup of rye coffee. Steven raised his head to take the steaming cup. "What is it?" Gerritt asked seeing the sadness in his friend's eyes.

"I keep thinking of my father, our fathers," he said sipping the coffee. "They looked so weary, so worn out. I'm very concerned."

Gerritt nodded sitting next to him.

"How much of this war can they take; how long will they last?"

"I know it's difficult to see them this way, beaten down, filthy…"

"They are not young men, Gerritt. This war is too much for them, the hardships too great."

"I'm as concerned as you are," Gerritt told him. "I was scared out of my wits when I saw my father had been wounded. It makes you think what might have been. But they believe in this cause as much as we do. They too, know that we cannot just let the Yanks overrun our country, our cause. And our fathers are much tougher than they let on."

"I'll try to remember that," Steven said. "But I still can't help but worry."

Weariness overtook them all and they dragged themselves into their tents to fall into an exhausted sleep.

So ended the battle of Seven Pines.

CHAPTER EIGHT —Spring 1862

Colleen sat in the morning sun of a warm spring day reading a letter from Steven. It was only the sixth letter she had received from him; six letters in a year. It seemed so little, so small a piece of the man she loved. She knew it was difficult for him to write while he was out in the trenches, fighting the battles. In fact, four of the letters had been written while he was in winter camp. There was also the difficulty of getting the mail delivered from the fields where the men were, to all the homes of the loved ones, desperate for some word.

It was now early June and this was the first letter she had received since February. In previous letters while whiling away the cold winter months of winter, he had spoken casually, lightly of their daily lives. He told of the men, especially of Tom and Charles who he and Gerritt had shared a cabin with. He told tales of card games and snowball fights. He explained about the feast they had all shared on Christmas, singing carols and exchanging small gifts of tobacco, toiletries and such. But there had been little written of the war, of the hardships they were facing. She knew he was only trying to spare her, to shield her from the brutalities, but she wanted to know; wanted to know what it was really like to be out there in the trenches, what Steven felt as he faced the enemy.

This letter she held in her hand was different. He had been in another battle and she could tell it had affected him deeply. He had written:

War is a horror. I'm not sure what I expected, perhaps two opposing teams meeting on the battlefield to spar with one another; clashing of swords, the fire of cannon, like knights of old. In the back of my mind I knew there would be bullets, killing, but I pushed it to the background, like some distant scene in a painting.

The reality is so much worse than I could have imagined; artillery fire blowing off arms, legs, bodies into unrecognizable pieces, blood saturating the ground like spring rains. The dead and dying are all around. It crushes the spirit, causes a deep kind of sadness that never seems to dissipate. There is no glory in killing, only the satisfaction of knowing you saved yourself for the moment. There are times when one asks himself what it's all for, especially the times when I get homesick and lonely for my beautiful wife.

But I apologize my dear. I did not mean to write of such depressing news. On a positive note, I am well and so is your brother Gerritt. The Lord has spared us to fight another day. We are still in Virginia but will again be on the march soon. Then it will be more digging of trenches and building up breastworks. Again we will face the enemy and hopefully, with every victory we come closer to gaining our freedom, which is the ultimate goal of this tragic conflict. And then, my sweet, I will be able to come home to you, to feel your arms about me, to taste the sweetness of your lips.

I wonder how things are with you. I hope you are well. We hear so little of what is happening in Georgia, only pieces and parts. We hear of many of our Southern patriots, starving, losing their homes. I know from your last letter that up until then you and your mother were still faring well. I hope your condition remains the same.

I worry about you, my dear, with Yankees now infiltrating more and more into our beloved South. I feel so torn, wanting to be here with my fellow comrades, fighting for our freedom and our beliefs and then wanting to be there with you, to protect you from harm.

I miss you so much my sweet, Colleen. Our time together was so short, but it stays in my mind always. It is what keeps me going through the rough patches, that day we spent together. It fills my dreams and keeps my hopes alive for the future..........

Colleen stopped reading and clasped the papers to her breast, closing her eyes. How she missed him! She never knew a heart could ache so. If only she could feel him through these thin pages of parchment.

She brought the letter back down to her lap and looked at the words. He had written those words, had touched the pages with his hands. She drew the tips of her fingers over the creamy surface, as if somehow she could feel his touch. The letters began to blur together as tears filled her eyes.

"Steven," she whispered, "I love you so much. When will you be coming home to me?"

She was startled when Betsy came into the room to announce lunch. She wiped at the tears and carefully folded the letter and put it into the envelope. She rose and left to go to the dining room where her mother was waiting for her. She sat down across from her at the long table while Carlton served them.

"Have you read the letter from Steven?" her mother asked.

"Yes, three times," Colleen answered.

"So, does he mention Gerritt?"

Colleen could see the look of concern in her mother's eyes. Even when she would not vocalize her worry, Colleen knew she thought of the welfare of her father and brother on a daily basis. "He has not been injured and neither has father," she told her. "I'm not so sure about how they are doing emotionally. The war sounds so horrible."

Mary nodded looking down at her plate. "I hear the same from your father. It's been difficult for everyone, even those who are left at home."

Colleen knew her mother was referring to the fact that many Southern civilians were suffering. The Yankees had successfully blockaded the harbors, thus keeping any supplies from coming in or from going out. Their hopes of a cotton strike with England in order for them to join the conflict on the side of the Confederacy, was fading. There had been no indication that they would ever be an ally. Many of the poorer people were literally starving. Their homes had been burned or confiscated. There were bands of people roaming the countryside living in woods or caves like nomads, gathering food anyway they could, including robbing homes if need be. Amongst them and on their own, were also deserters from the army who either had no home to go to, or were afraid to do so.

Many more slaves had run away from all over the south. They too were hiding out, sometimes committing acts of violence against whites. Even more of their own slaves had run in spite of Mr. Solomon the overseer, hiring some unsavory characters to help keep them in line. Consequently, there had been more beatings and whippings for infringements of the rules. Mary did not like the practice, but tried to leave the matter of security of the slaves to Mr. Solomon and hesitated to interfere lest she should lose him. She also knew that he and some of his cohorts were pilfering from their stores, but she felt helpless to stop them. It was a frightening time.

"Did you hear the news from the Hunters," Mary asked Colleen as she sipped water from a goblet.

"What news?"

"Andrew was killed at some place called Shiloh," she said quietly.

"Oh my god! I've known him my whole life. Why, he was such a sweet boy," Colleen said as tears stung her eyes.

Mary nodded. "I know, I've always liked Andrew. His parents are devastated. He was their only son, you know; three girls and only one boy. And now he's……" Mary let her words drift away.

Colleen felt sick. She could no longer eat. It was hard to believe Andrew was gone, would never be coming home. She remembered his sweet face, the times he had gone riding with her, the picnics with their families together. She remembered the times he had danced with her at the balls and how he had always been so kind to her. She put her elbows on the table and rested her head in her hands.

"I know sweetheart," her mother said gently, "it's very difficult, this war, the sacrifices we have to make. We always need to think about what it's all for."

"What is it all for?" Colleen asked lifting her head to look at her mother.

"It's about our freedom, of course."

"I've heard that all before, but what does it really mean, fighting for our freedom?"

"So that we in the south can be our own nation, to live the way we choose."

"But, that's why we fought the Revolutionary War, to be free from England," Colleen said getting up from the table. "Why has that changed?"

"You know why; our culture is different. We have much agriculture and need our slaves to produce. The Union wants to take that away from us. They want us to be just like them, to take our culture from us, our way of life."

"What happens if they win, mother?" Colleen asked. "What would it be like if all the slaves were freed?"

"Then we would be ruined," Mary answered simply. "We would lose everything. Is that what you want?"

Colleen just shook her head. "I just wonder if it's worth the sacrifice."

Before her mother could respond, Betsy came into the room clearly agitated.

"What is it, Betsy?" Mary asked her. "What's wrong?"

"Oh, Misses, it's one of the de fiel' hands. He gots hurt real bad. He needs you, Misses."

Mary got up from the table and headed towards the kitchen. "Did Luna see him yet?" Mary asked Betsy referring to the slaves' healer woman who treated her people for minor ailments.

"Yes Misses, Luna done seen 'em, but dis bad, dis real bad."

"Well, get my medicine bag then and we'll see to it."

Betsy ran to get the bag while Mary grabbed some cloths from the pantry cupboard. "Please come along with me," Mary said to Colleen who had trailed along behind her mother. "I don't like going down to the slave quarters by myself anymore. Things have changed. It's as if they all look at me differently."

"Of course Mother, I'll come," Colleen told her.

They went out the back through the kitchen; past the house slave quarters, the gardens and stables, and across the river bridge to the cabins of the field hands. They walked down several rows and back further from the river. Finally, they saw a group of darkies clustered around someone lying on the ground.

Before going to the man, Mary turned to Betsy. "What happened to him?" she asked.

Betsy looked down at the ground and spoke so quietly, she could barely be heard. "He done been whipped."

Mary drew in her breath and broke through the crowd, Colleen following after her.

A pallet had been laid out on the hard packed earth and the injured man placed face first upon it. Colleen gasped and covered her mouth with her hand, nearly vomiting when she saw him. He was a large man, probably a good six feet five inches with wide broad shoulders and muscular arms. His shirt had been removed, his body exposed from the waist up.

But it was his back that had taken Colleen's breath away. There was no doubt he had been whipped. However, there were not just a few whiplashes crisscrossing his back. The flesh had literally been torn away, the bone showing through in some places. It was a bloody, pulpy mess, blood flowing onto the ground and soaking the brown trousers he wore.

Mary knelt on one side of the man and on the other was Luna, the slave's healer. Mary looked at the torn flesh and muscle that had once been this man's back and did not know where to begin. Her knowledge of medicine was limited to stitching wounds, applying salve to burns and helping with the birthing of babies. She looked up hopelessly into Luna's eyes and saw the same helplessness reflected in hers.

"I knows not whats I can do, Misses," she told Mary. "It's too bad, too much. I has no medicine, no herbs, no voodoo can fix this!" she gestured over the man's back. Her eyes filled with tears and spilled down her cheeks.

The man's strong face was turned towards Mary, his full lips trembled and his broad nose flared with pain, even though he was unconscious. Betsy was there at his head, stroking his hair.

"White mens has better medicine," Luna told her. "You'se can heal him?"

Mary shook her head. "I don't know, Luna. This is very, very bad. I'll do what I can, but I'm afraid he may die."

As soon as she had expressed these thoughts, Betsy began to wail great tears.

Colleen still stood by her mother, looking from the man to Betsy. What had happened? How could someone beat a man so horribly? The wounds were appalling. It made her gag to look at it. And what was wrong with Betsy, the woman who worked in their house everyday? Why was she so distressed over this man's injury? Did she know him?

"Get me clean water," her mother ordered. "It must be clean, fresh from the river, not anything standing around." Someone in the crowd rushed to do her bidding.

"What is this man's name?" Mary asked, looking at Betsy. It was nearly impossible to know all the darkies names, there were so many. They knew the house servants well and some of those who worked in the gardens and stables. The ones they knew the least were the field hands because they had less contact with them.

"His name be Jonah," Luna answered for her. "He be on dis here land fo seven years."

"Who did this to him?" she asked her.

At first she hesitated, not sure if she should speak up. "It be dat overseer man, Massa Solomon," she finally answered.

Mary felt incredible anger towards Mr. Solomon. How could there be any legitimate excuse for this kind of brutality? She touched the man's face. "Jonah, I'm so sorry. We'll do the best we can for you."

The man finally returned with a bucket of water which Mary began pouring slowly over Jonah's back.

Blood washed away, but also with it went bits of flesh and tissue. Even Mary, who had seen her share of illness and wounds from accidents in her time, had never seen anything as horrific as this. She felt helpless as to what she should do.

Once she felt most of the blood and pieces of skin had been washed away, she took the cloths she had brought and began to apply them to Jonah's back. She directed Colleen to rip others into strips and then with the help of several others, got him into a sitting position and began to wrap the cloths around him to hold the bandages in place.

As they attempted this maneuver, Jonah began to regain consciousness. Colleen watched his face as the pain filled his awareness. He cried out and began to struggle.

"Jonah!" Betsy said to him. "Let's the Misses helps ya."

Jonah looked into Betsy's eyes with the most incredible pain Colleen had ever seen and then he passed out once more.

"It's more of a blessing he be unconscious right now," Mary said as she finished wrapping him. "Now let's get him inside. He shouldn't be out where he might get a chill. Several men came forward to carry him into the nearest cabin. In the process, the blood oozed through the bandages Mary had just applied.

"Try to keep him as comfortable as possible," Mary told Luna. "I'm afraid I don't have any morphine to give him. And…..he may not make it through the night. But if he does, I will be back in the morning to change the bandages. And I will see if I can find some laudlum."

Tears again filled Luna's eyes as she silently went in to tend to Jonah.

As Mary and Colleen turned to go, they realized the crowd of people was still standing around, silent, waiting. Mary turned to them knowing they were expecting her to tell them something. The faces she saw were young and old, male and female. They were dressed simply and wore the look of people who had worked hard every day of their lives. She realized she knew very few of their names, these men, women and children who worked their fields, labored in their gardens and barns.

"I am truly sorry for what happened to Jonah," she told them. "I want you all to know I had nothing to do with this. I am completely against beatings. You know Master McBride never beat anyone." Some of the men and women only looked at her coldly, as if they didn't believe her. The others appeared sad or afraid.

"I will make a promise to you. I will speak to Mr. Solomon and get this whole thing straightened out," Mary said holding out her hands as if she were pleading with them. "I know things have not been the same since Master McBride has been gone. It's been difficult, but if we all work together, we can make it through this war. One of the reasons our men are out there fighting is for you all, so that you will be able to keep your homes, your security." Mary paused and then said quietly, "so please, people, let's co-operate, work hard, don't get into trouble and everything will turn out alright."

Why did it suddenly sound as if this incident had been their fault? Colleen wondered. She joined her mother as she turned to walk towards the overseer's cabin.

"What is wrong with that man?" she muttered as she raised her skirts to step over a log. "I can't believe I'm having to deal with this."

Colleen could tell her mother was angry, but she wasn't quite sure at whom, Mr. Solomon, or Jonah the slave. The closer they came to Mr. Solomon's cabin, the angrier she became.

When they finally arrived at the two-room cabin, they saw Mr. Solomon sitting outside in a straight-backed chair. It was tilted on two legs to rest against the cabin wall. Across his lap rested a long shot gun. Sitting around him on the ground were four of his sleazy companions, ragged, dirty and chewing on pork ribs, the grease dripping off their fingers and onto their pants. Lying amongst them were two large hound dogs, biting into discarded bones, which littered the ground around them.

Mr. Solomon grinned at them as they approached, but did not get up. He was stroking the stock of the rifle as if it were a cat.

"Mr. Solomon!" Mary began. "I demand to know your justification for the severe beating you gave Jonah, the field hand." Her face was red from anger and the exertion of the walk over.

Well, Ma'am, it's like this, ya see," he began slowly. "That there nigger done tried to run. Yep, he was way over near 'bout to the next county. But me and my boys...we catched 'im. Yep, and then we brung 'im back here and beats 'im in front of everbody. You know, to teach 'im, alls of em. So's nobody else gits the idea of runnin'."

"Mr. Solomon, do you realize you beat that man so severely he may not live?" Colleen could tell her mother was doing her best to contain her anger.

"The way I sees it, iffen you don't do it good 'nough, they'se jes gonna run agin."

"Of course he won't run again if he dies!" Mary said stepping closer. "And if he dies you will have cost us valuable property! Do you understand what I'm saying?"

"I was only tryin' to keep……."

"I know what you were tryin' to do, Mr. Solomon," Mary broke in, "and I think you have abused your new found power. That slave cost a lot of money and dear sir, if he dies, you will pay back the cost from your wages including the loss of his labor and what it has cost us to keep him all these years."

Mr. Solomon's chair thudded down on all four legs. ."Now ma'am, I don't think that seems quite fair."

"Perhaps you don't understand. My husband was never this harsh with the darkies and he never had any trouble. I do not approve of this kind of punishment. For more severe infractions there is the block house, you should have put him in there for a period of time."

Colleen knew her mother was referring to the six by six foot brick building equipped with a heavy wooden door, no windows, and only a small slat in the roof that let in air and sunlight. Mortared into the floor were steel shackles onto which a person could be chained. It was this solitary blockhouse about which her mother spoke. Her father had only used it one time that she knew of.

"Or perhaps you should have equipped him with the metal, spiked collar with the bells and kept him chained to someone else for a period of time," Mary continued.

Now Mr. Solomon had risen to his feet, still clutching the gun. "mebbe you don't understand. This here war goin' on has caused these niggers to act all upitty. More'n more of 'em's been runnin' off. Way I figger's it, is even if this here nigger dies, it jes might keeps the three or four who was a thinkin' on runnin', in their place. So's I guess that would a saved ya all money."

"I just don't believe it's the proper way……." Mary began to falter.

Mr. Solomon took a step towards them. "That's jes it, ma'am, things ain't proper no more. Your husband left me in charge of these niggers and I'm only doin' my best.

Now why don't you ladies go on back to your big house and leave the workin' to us." As he took another step, the other men on the ground stood up.

If their intention was to intimidate, it was working, Colleen thought. She wondered if these men would ever do anything to harm them. Her mother must have been feeling the same as she had taken a few steps back.

"We done everthin' we'se suppose to ma'am," Mr. Solomon had continued. "The cotton's all been planted and even them acres of food crops you wanted. Them niggers is out there every day earnin' their keep, hoein', shovelin', haulin', and such. Now iffen you wants things to keep runnin' smooth like, you best leave the nigger tendin' to us uns."

Mary's rage had gone and in its place was a fear, a fear of these men and what they might do and Mr. Solomon knew it, could see it in her eyes and the way her nostrils flared like a trapped animal.

"I…I don't want the slaves beaten like that ever again," she said trying to sound authoritative, but failing. "Understand me? No more beatings like that!"

Mr. Solomon only nodded, smiling, but there were no assurances in that smile.

The two women moved off, hurrying to cross the river and back to the safety of their home.

Colleen went to her room, sitting in a chair and putting her head in her hands. She realized she was out of breath and shaking. It had been such a horrible ordeal, the way that man had been beaten, the way his back had looked and the attitude of Mr. Solomon had been, well, frightening.

Dora came in and found her still sitting that way. "Is you all right, Missy?" she asked her.

Colleen removed her hands from her face and looked up at her maidservant. Ever since she had overheard the conversation between her and Carlton, she had not been able to look at Dora in the same way. What if someday she decided to get it in her head to run? What would she do without her? She was forced to realize that Dora was more than a servant; she was a friend and second mother.

"It's that horrid overseer, Mr. Solomon. He frightens me."

"Yes'm," Dora responded simply. "How be Jonah, Missy?" she then asked.

"Not good, I'm afraid," Colleen told her getting to her feet and walking to the window. She pulled back the long curtain and looked out onto the gardens. Spring flowers bloomed in profusion, their beautiful heads bobbing in the breeze. Beyond were the apple and peach orchards, with their delicate flowers perfuming the air.

So much beauty here, Colleen thought, and so much ugliness elsewhere; that overseer and what he did to Jonah, and the war.

"Dora," she said turning to her maid, "would you ever try to run away?" knowing as she asked, she would not hear the truth.

"Oh no, missy. Where I goes? I gots no other place. This here's my home and whose gwine ta takes care of you and your Mama?"

Colleen nodded. "I'm glad you feel that way Dora, because you're right, I do need you."

The lunch bell rang and Colleen was spared saying anything further. She joined her mother in the dining room, realizing she was ravenous, not having eaten any breakfast.

"That man is impossible," her mother said as she put a forkful of brown rice into her mouth.

Colleen knew her mother was referring to Mr. Solomon. "I don't know what I'm to do with him. I can't have him fired without someone to replace him first. What on God's earth would we do without someone to oversee the slaves and make sure the work is done? But where will I find a replacement? All the good men have gone off to war. All that are left are the dregs and soldier deserters.

I know for a fact that that man and his white trash cronies are stealin' from us. That pig they were eating and there have been other things, clothing, food stuffs from the root cellar, tools, utensils……"

"Perhaps you could advertise in the Savannah newspaper for a new overseer," Colleen offered.

Mary shook her head. "I just don't think I could find anyone suitable. Anyone who's had any experience at any rate. Any candidate would have to know how to run a large plantation with hundreds of slaves. No, I'm just afraid it's nearly an impossible task. In the meantime, Mr. Solomon is robbing us blind and may do who knows what. I suspect he and those other men may also be raping the women. He…he frightens me." She put her head in her hands. "I just wish your father were here. He'd know what to do."

Colleen got up and went around the table to where her mother sat. She put her arms around her to offer comfort. "I know Mother, it's very difficult right now, but the war will be over soon and then Daddy will be home."

She raised her head and patted Colleen's hand. "I hope you're right, my dear. I really don't know how long I can continue."

"You'll do what you have to," Colleen told her, "because you're a strong woman. Daddy knows that. It's why he could leave things in your hands with confidence and it's also partly why he loves you so much. He and Gerritt are out there doing their part for the cause and we're here doing our part here at home."

"Thank-you darling, for your confidence. I'm just not sure I'm as strong as you think I am. Now go finish your lunch."

Later in the evening as Colleen and Mary were sitting in the parlor with their reading and sewing, Betsy came to the doorway. She said nothing but when they looked up they could see she was clearly agitated. She was trembling and there were tears on her face.

"What's wrong? Betsy, what happened?"

"Misses, Carlton says I should tells you," she faltered and seemed to have trouble beginning again.

"Well, what is it?"

"It be Jonah, ma'am. He's passed on."

"Oh no," Mary said closing her eyes. "I'm sorry, Betsy. Thank-you, I'll deal with this." With her dismissal, Betsy left the room hurriedly.

"I was afraid of this," Mary told Colleen. "Damn that Mr. Solomon! I have to do something about him. I can't continue to lose slaves!" She threw her sewing onto the floor and got up and left the room.

Colleen suddenly felt an overwhelming sadness. The man she had seen in the slave quarters, beaten, bloody, had died. Even though she hadn't known him, even if he had been just a slave, he was still a man and perhaps a man who had had a family, those who loved him.

Colleen rose to go to her room, but before she had gone up the stairs, she heard a commotion coming from the rear of the house. She decided to investigate. She passed the library and further on, the wing containing the ballroom. How long ago had it been since she and Steven had danced there, since they had announced their engagement? She remembered it had also been when they had first heard of the outbreak of the war. It seemed like forever ago.

On the other side of the hall, Colleen passed by the dining room which led to the pantry. Beyond the pantry was the portal leading to the kitchen house. It was in the pantry from where the sounds were coming. Yelling and screaming could be heard, her mother's voice, Carlton's, Dora, who else was there?

She entered the room and saw Betsy collapsed on the floor, wailing and tearing at her hair. Bess was there, too, kneeling by her side, her arms about her. Both Carlton and Dora stood over them, talking, but Colleen could not make out their words.

Her mother too, was yelling at all of them, creating havoc in the room. Finally, she heard her mother saying, "Take her out! Take her to her cabin, now!"

Carlton and Bess stood, lifting Betsy with them, holding her under the arms. She appeared not able to walk, her face wet with tears and her wailing unceasing.

"Please ma'am," Bess said looking up at Mary, "may I stays wif Betsy tonight?"

"Yes yes, you have my permission. Just take her out." The two took Betsy outside, past the kitchen, beyond the gardens to the house servants' quarters.

Once the noise had subsided for a brief moment, when the pantry door had been open, Colleen heard an even louder wail, the sound of many voices rising together. She felt a chill flow over her, the gooseflesh standing out on her skin.

"What was that all about?" she asked, turning to her mother.

"Jonah," Mary told her wearily, "apparently he and Betsy were to be married. Your father had promised them before he left."

"But if they were to marry, why would he try to run away?"

Mary glanced over at Dora who was still in the room, not sure if she should speak in front of her. She decided Dora probably already knew everything she was to say. "Mr. Solomon told Jonah it would be a cold day in hell before he would allow a field nigger to marry a house nigger. Then he told him he was going to sell him to the slave trader," she said referring to the unscrupulous men who went about plantations, buying slaves and selling them for profit further south, severing people from their families forever.

"He told him that?" Colleen asked incredulous.

Mary nodded. "He has absolutely no authority to do either one, but apparently Jonah didn't know that. When he thought he wouldn't be able to marry Betsy and he would be sold, he ran."

"Oh, my god,"

"I'm exhausted," Mary said giving her a kiss on the cheek. "I'm going to bed." Her mother left, going up the back stairs off the pantry leaving Colleen alone with Dora.

Dora kept her head down, looking at the floor. "Did you know him, too, Dora?" Colleen asked.

"Yes'm, some. We see's de field han's on Sundays at church and somes at gatherin's."

"I'm sorry. I didn't even know Betsy and he were to marry."

"Yes'm," Dora said, her eyes still cast down. "She be powerful grievein'."

Carlton came back in just then, returning from helping Betsy to her cabin. The wailing could be plainly heard again.

"'Cuse me, Missy. I'se not knows you still be here," Carlton said backing towards the door.

Colleen held up her hand. "No, don't worry about it. I was just going up.

Dora, what's that horrid wailing sound?"

"Dat be de slaves 'cross de river. Deys cryin' for Jonah."

Colleen nodded. She had heard that sound before when one of the slaves had passed on. It was the way they grieved for one of their own. It always sent chills down her spine. She headed up the stairs, the way her mother had gone, to her room.

As Dora was helping her undress for the evening, Colleen asked, "What will happen to Jonah?"

"Your Mama say we all kin buries him tomorrow night, afta de workers comes in from de fields."

The following day Colleen could not help but think of the death of Jonah and how Betsy had collapsed. She must have loved him very much, she thought. She had been clearly distraught when she had learned of Jonah's death. She had never really thought of the slaves loving each other before. Oh, she knew they married, had children, but to have passion for one another, the kind of feelings she and Steven had.

She remembered that morning when they had gone to the slave quarters to nurse Jonah and Betsy had been there, stroking him, talking to him. She had seen the look in her eyes and she knew it was true. They did love, just as deeply as she.

It made her wonder what she would do if something happened to Steven. How would she behave, what would she feel? She would not want to live without Steven. Just thinking of the possibility caused tears to come to her eyes.

That next evening as Mary worked on the books in the library and Colleen sat with her reading, they were startled to see all the house slaves standing in the doorway. Even Ellen the cook and Matthew, James's personal manservant, were there. They waited for acknowledgement before speaking.

"Carlton, what is this all about?" Mary asked him.

"Um, Misses, we uns, we wuz jes wonderin'," Carlton stammered, looking down at the floor. "we wants to goes to Jonah's funeral, ober in de fiel' han's quarters."

Mary gave a deep, audible sigh. "Oh my; well, Ellen and the other kitchen help may go and Betsy, of course. But I need you here, Carlton, to secure the house and Miss Colleen and I need Rose and Dora to prepare our rooms and help us ready for bed."

"Yes,m," Carlton said without another word.

As they began to move away from the doorway, Colleen spoke up. "Dora, it's alright if you wish to go. I can prepare myself tonight."

"Thank-you, Missy," Dora replied hurrying away.

After the servants had left, Mary turned to her daughter. Colleen was surprised to see anger on her mother's face. "Don't you ever change one of my orders to the servants again," she said quietly.

"I only thought it would be permissible for Dora to go. I can take care of myself."

"It doesn't matter if you think you can. I told her not to go and you went against my orders. That undermines my authority and gives the servants the idea they can get out of working for any little thing."

"I didn't think….."

"That's just it, Colleen," Mary said rising to her feet, "you didn't think."

"But, it's for Jonah's funeral," Colleen protested again.

Mary pointed her finger at her daughter. "I don't want anymore sass from you, young lady. Hear me, don't ever do that again!" And she left the room.

Colleen felt despondent. As far as she was concerned, her mother had been too harsh with the servants and definitely with her. She rose from her chair and extinguished the lamps before going out.

She went out into the foyer and saw Carlton going about snuffing lamps and closing the house for the night. "Is you'se gwine up now, Missy?" he asked her.

"Not right now," she told him. "I'll go soon. I want to go outside for a few minutes."

"Yes'm, Missy."

She walked out the front door and stood on the wide porch with its large pillars. A soft, warm breeze was blowing, brushing past her face. She looked out at the vast yard with its neatly trimmed hedges and spreading trees. Beyond, at the rivers edge was the gazebo where she and Steven had liked to go.

It had all seemed so long ago, she thought; a lifetime. And then she heard the drums and saw the fire across the river. She went down the stairs and started across the lawn. The nearer she came to the gazebo, the louder the drums became. It was a rhythmic, primitive sound that thudded in her chest and sped up her heart.

She slipped into the shelter of the small structure on her side of the river. On the other side, in the center of the slave quarters, a large bonfire spread its flames skyward. Hundreds of men, women and children stood around swaying and singing to the beat of the drums. At the center of the crowd, she could see a large wooden box and she realized it was Jonah's casket.

Bits and pieces of the songs reached her ears, sad and melodic…..*Swing low, sweet chariot, comin' fo de carry me home. …Swing low, sweet chariot, comin' fo de carry me home. I looks ober Jordan an' what'd I see, Comin' fo to carry me home. A band of angels comin' afta me. Comin' fo ta carry me home.*

Then someone else started another; *"No mo' rain fall fo wet yo, Hallelujah!*

No mo' sun shine fo burn yo,
Dere's no hard trails
Dere's no whips a-crackin'
No evil doers in de kingdom
All is gladness in de kingdom.

The drums increased their rhythm; the people's dancing grew in intensity. Colleen could see them raising their arms towards the sky, praising Jesus. The crowd parted and she could see clearly, in the light of the fire, the crude wooden box that held the broken body of the slave known as Jonah.

Six large men surrounded the coffin and raised it up onto their shoulders and began carrying it through the quarters. Several others carried torches to light the way. They headed towards the fields where the slave cemetery was located, A small section with a few spreading oaks had been set aside behind the cabins and in front of the vast fields.

All the rest of the people began following behind, humming a low cadent song. Then the wailing began, a high mournful sound that caused gooseflesh to stand out on her skin. She saw Betsy walking there, touching the coffin, being held up by two others on each side. Her wails and crying could be heard all the way across the river.

She wished she could join them, be a part of their mourning, be able to feel their grief as they did. But she knew she would not be accepted, wouldn't be welcome to participate in this, their private grief. After all, she was a part of the system that had caused his death in the first place. Two different people, two different worlds and where one could go, the other could not. But, were they really so different inside? Colleen wondered.

CHAPTER NINE
—August 1862

It was now the middle of summer with its stifling heat and swarms of flies. All the men in camp were suffering from their insipid infestation. They settled on their food, on their faces when they attempted to sleep, on the inside of the tent, until the men were crazy with their pestilence. They felt as if the Lord's wrath had sent another plague as he had on the Egyptians. They didn't know what was worse, the fear of battle or the torture of the flies. But, of course, each man knew who had already experienced the horrors of war, that anything else could be tolerated.

After Seven Pines they had moved the brigade to Richmond. As they, along with other regiments, passed through the streets, the people cheered and waved their hats. Behind them rolled the heavy artillery, the drivers urging the horses to a trot through the streets.

But then came the ambulances and wagons filled with the wounded and the dead. The crowd became hushed as the moans and screams of the injured filled the quiet. Those who were not as severe were made to walk, leaning on the shoulder of another. A trail of blood followed them down the street, the men's lifeblood pouring from their veins.

Every hospital room had been filled and yet more wounded kept flowing into the city. Every room available was used to capacity and then the citizens themselves began taking the men into their homes. Each and every one had been given the most tender of care as if he were their own son. Indeed, many women would have wished that her own dear, sweet boy might receive the same, if the need should arise.

All told, over five thousand maimed and dieing had passed into the arms of Richmond. And the shell and bullet knew no rank; private to General had felt their blow. Steven had never seen such horrors of maiming, arms, legs, faces blown off, entrails exposed, blood flowing everywhere.

When he and Gerritt had walked the streets, screams could be heard as wounds were tended to. And there had been wailing in sorrow as a husband, son or brother was recognized. It made them all realize what a horrific sacrifice was being made for the cause.

Late in June they had marched to Machanicsville, approximately three miles from Richmond. There they had participated in another battle with more casualties and wounded all around. Citizens from Richmond had again come out to treat the men; this time Union soldiers mixed in amongst them all. They were given no less care, uniforms knowing no boundaries to suffering. Blue and gray alike had lain together, shared the same canteen, and smoked together. Steven had felt the irony of that, fighting each other to death on the battlefield, and once wounded, they were again brothers.

It was here they first heard of a new general, who was taking over command of the Army of Virginia.

Steven and Gerritt, Tom and Charles had been sitting under a tree, smoking their pipes, when a horseman, followed by an aide, rode by slowly, touching his hat to the men. They saluted him back, the older man with the iron gray beard, riding the white horse.

When Steven had asked who the general was, Tom had replied, "That, Mr. Covington, is General Robert E. Lee."

The battle had continued later in the day with Stonewall Jackson's forces taking the brunt of the assault. Voracious gunfire could be heard, while the shelling of artillery had set the woods on fire. An orange glow had cast its errie fingers towards the waning light of day. When their brigade had finally reached the scene, they found the ground literally covered with the dead and the stream red with blood. But, it had grown dark and they had been ordered to bivouac for the night while many had gone out on the field to collect the wounded, others, not so honorable, had plundered the dead.

The next morning Steven and Gerritt's brigade was marched back to Richmond, the wounded following behind, swelling the already burgeoning hospitals beyond their limits.

While there, they received reinforcements. Some were green troops, never having seen a battle. Reports of Lee's total forces had been bantered about in the ranks. He was in command of Smith's division, Longstreet's, Magruder's, D.H. Hill's, one cavalry brigade, Ripley's brigade, Holme's, their own Georgia brigade now under Lawton and two divisions belonging to Jackson. Estimates were Lee was in command of eighty thousand, seven hundred and sixty men.

However, reports from spies and operatives in the field, gave the Union count under General McClellan, one hundred fifty thousand men.

On this morning of June 29th, they had left Richmond and crossed the Chickamoniny River towards White Oak Swamp. There, they had found the Union line, over eight miles long, extending all the way to Malvern Hill. They had heard distant fire, but had not engaged the enemy until they met them at a place called Frazier's Farm, a point where the road leading from the James crosses that from Richmond.

There they had been ordered to charge, but the opposing forces were too great and after many losses, were forced to withdraw. They had charged again and were with drawn. It was then decided to move the brigade back over the Chickahominy to an area where they had been greeted by a large chain of breastworks, redoubts and rifle pits. It was there they had taken refuge, it being occupied by the Rebels. No sooner had they done so, than the shells began bursting all around them, followed by musket fire.

Almost immediately they had been ordered to line up in battle formation. They had charged the enemy, bayonets pointed forward like lances of knights of old. But the firing from the front had been too intense and they had again, been called to retreat. Regimental officers and men alike had broken and scattered. The fire had become so intense the men were falling by fives and tens. They had finally reached the safety of the breastworks, but not before many had fallen wounded or dead.

It was now August sixteenth and they were camped at Orange County Court House. The brigade sat at their campfires, eating, reading, and talking. As Steven looked about the camp at the fellows he had been fighting with, he thought them a general rag tag lot. Some came from wealthier families and wore light gray uniforms with gilt buttons. Others from the poorer lot wore nearly black jackets with wooden buttons. Caps ranged from the squash hats to slouch wide brimmed Stetsons. Shirts were of all different colors and material depending on the availability. Pants were nearly all the same, gray wool and obviously dirty. On their feet some like Steven and Gerritt, wore boots, but many like Charles were barefoot. All were in rags and tatters as no new clothing had been issued since they had begun this campaign a year and one half ago.

But in that time, they had fought battles together, seen men die, had slept together, eaten together and shared their life's miseries. And in the end, it mattered not what they wore, or where they were from. It was why they were here, in this place together, fighting for what they believed in.

They no longer brooded over the length of the war or its hardships. They followed their superior officers without question and had learned to adapt.

This was a time of rest, to renew and reflect. Steven tried to get caught up on his writing to his mother and Colleen. Three of her letters to him had finally found him and he had gotten much pleasure from reading them. He could discern that Colleen was trying to keep any hardships she might be enduring, to her self. She had written of how she and her mother were running the plantation on their own and how the Union blockade of the ports was hurting cotton sales. But, it was when she spoke of how she missed him and how much she loved him that brought back the loneliness. Sometimes he felt if he didn't get to touch her soft skin or kiss her sweet lips soon, he would die from heartache. The war had been so much more tragic than he ever had imagined and being away from Colleen made it even more so.

Gerritt had watched him reading the letters and knew how much he must miss his sister. He knew too, that they had been planning their wedding and now Steven probably wondered if he would ever be returning.

He himself had left no serious love at home. He had always enjoyed seeing many different beautiful belles, and had not as yet met anyone that would cause him to think of matrimony. His mother, Mary, was always trying to set him up with this influential person's daughter or that ones, stating he should settle down so as to run the plantation when his father would pass it down to him. But he tried not to let his mother influence him in any way. He was waiting for a love, deep and abiding. The kind Colleen and Steven shared.

He went to sit near Steven, bringing his tin coffee cup with him. Steven sat holding a letter in one hand, his forehead in the other. "Letter from Colleen?" he asked.

Steven looked up at his friend and nodded. "Things seem to be going well for now," he told him, "except for the blockade of the ports."

"I know, mother wrote me." He paused for a moment. "You must miss her very much," he said quietly.

Just having Gerritt say the words made tears come to his eyes. "Sometimes I miss her so much I feel like deserting and running home to her."

"Don't worry," Gerritt said placing his hand on Steven's arm. "You'll see, this war will be over before you know it and then you and Colleen will have the grandest weddin' ever." He smiled at him, trying to reassure him.

Steven looked into Gerritt's eyes and saw the kindness and concern there. He knew he could trust this man, his brother. "We're already married, Gerritt," he told him simply.

At first there was only a stunned look of surprise on his face. "When, how?" he finally asked.

"Before we left. It wasn't an official marriage. One day when my parents and yours were gone, we had a little ceremony of our own. We married ourselves, said our vows before God. She's my wife in every way, Gerritt."

He looked at Steven closely and then realizing exactly what it was he was telling him, he broke into a broad grin and embraced him. "Congratulations, that's wonderful! I couldn't be happier for you. Does my father know?"

Steven shook his head. "No one does. We haven't told a living soul, until now. I just felt I wanted to tell you, for you to know; in case….in case anything happens to me."

"You're my brother now, as well as my friend," Gerritt told him. "We're going to make it through this together; you'll see."

Steven smiled back at him knowing there were no guarantees. “You’re not upset,” he asked, “that we married secretly, that it wasn’t in a church?”

Gerritt shook his head. “Far be it for me to condemn. I love my sister and I love you. I know the two of you wouldn’t have done it unless it meant everything.”

For the next week they marched along toward Kelly’s Ford, listening to the screaming of the Yankee shells. They did not engage the enemy there, but kept on until they reached Rappahannock Run and there they saw the long line of Union infantry, moving their artillery in place, daring them to advance.

That evening as they rested beneath the trees, a violent storm suddenly burst forth upon them. Normally, they detested getting their clothing wet, but it had been many weeks since any of them had been able to bathe. Nearly all of them now sported beards as it was easier than trying to shave, many times without the benefit of water. Now they all stood out in the downpour, allowing the refreshing deluge to wash away some of the dirt and grime from their bodies and uniforms. The only disadvantage to the rain was the mud it created. They knew the next days’ advance would be a difficult one.

The sun shone hot and sultry the following morning as they marched on to Salem. The heat wearied many of the men and drained them of their strength. Provisions had been slow in coming, causing hunger all around. After routing the Yankees from Salem, they marched on to Throughfare Gap at the base of a mountain where they were allowed to rest for the night. Off in the distance, the booming of the cannon could be heard.

As they sat around the fires that night, the camp was generally quiet. They all knew there would be a battle the following morning and each man was lost in his own thoughts, reading letters from home or a Bible, making his peace with God.

"Thar's blood on the moon tonight," Charles said breaking the silence.

The others glanced up at the orb in the sky, watching a cloud pass in front of it.

"What's that mean, Charles?" Gerritt asked.

"It means lots o' men gonna die tomorrow," he said solemnly. "I feels it in my bones."

The others only nodded, not knowing how to respond. Men always died in battle. That was nothing new. Just the fact that the four of them had all remained alive this far, had been remarkable. Even Gerritt and Steven's fathers, having survived relatively unscathed, seemed impossible, given the horrendous number of deaths. Each time, before a battle, every man questioned whether or not this would be the battle that ended his life. Each time they stood on that precipice, waiting for that unseen bullet or shell.

Here, at the base of the mountain, the air felt so fresh and pure, so sweet; never had dieing felt so loathsome.

In the morning more troops arrived filling the gap, spreading out over the meadow and the railroad track. Officers rode about barking orders, gathering the men. And leading them all was Stonewall Jackson.

Sargent Jennings had them lined up and marching toward the north to a place they had been before; at the junction of the Orange and Alexandria Railroad. A place called Manassas. They were halted on the outskirts of a cornfield just a half-mile from the famous Chinn House, a large plantation home, long ago abandoned.

The men suddenly broke ranks and began running though the cornfield, grabbing the fat, sweet ears from the stalks. The officers yelled themselves hoarse until they too, joined in the gleaning. Thousands of men tearing through the stalks made it appear as if a tornado were passing overhead.

Men reappeared with their arms full of succulent corn. Not being able to build fires, they began eating it raw. They had had no rations for four days.

Gerritt, Steven and Tom laughed as they watched Charles devour the juicy kernels. They were all struck how young he looked, his face so boyishly excited about the unexpected treat.

Soon after, Union cannon could be heard and the troops once again became solemn; hearts beat faster and nervousness set in. Sergeant Jennings called for them to "fall in!" and ammunition was passed around.

"Forward march!" Sergeant Jennings called out. "To the colors!" They all moved out following the flag bearer.

All that could be heard was the rattling of equipment and the pounding of thousands of feet on the road. It wasn't long before shells were shrieking overhead and bursting at close range.

Their Captain drew his sword, placed himself at the head of their ranks and called the charge. They all yelled the blood curdling Rebel cry, and followed their Captain towards the Union line.

The men in blue appeared from behind an old stone wall and fired a deadly barrage into their midst. Many fell with this first assault, but others filled in the gaps and kept moving forward, loading and firing as they went.

Steven kept his eyes on the brave Captain, following his lead, listening for his orders, but soon the air was so filled with smoke, he could no longer be seen nor could he be heard. Now it was time to muster his own bravery and move forward in spite of the danger.

Every time the smoke cleared sufficiently enough to see the line of blue, Steven would carefully aim his shot and fire. The Yankees were so close now, only fifty yards away, that he could see the determined look on their faces. It was at this interval, when the fighting was the hottest, the bullets flying past their heads, that Steven saw several men running to hide behind the Chinn House or in a wide gully nearby. Fear could make cowards of any man.

Steven kneeled down on one knee to reload, getting ready to fire again, when Charles suddenly jumped in front of him and fired his own weapon. In that instant, before he could lower his rifle, a Yankee bullet thudded into his body, throwing him back into Steven's arms.

Tom and Gerritt, having seen Charles fall, ran forward and the three of them dragged him to the rear where they would be in less danger. Tom held the boy in his arms; the others huddled over him.

"Charles, Charles my boy!" Tom called to him, hoping upon hope, the boy still lived.

Charles made a rattling, gasping sound in his throat the others had come to recognize as the death rattle. They had heard it many times before.

Tom too, knew what it meant and grabbed the boy's jacket, shaking him and calling his name. "No! Charles! Stay with me, boy!" But it was too late. Charles's eyes had gone glassy and they all knew he was dead.

Tom tore open his shirt and they all could see the fatal hole in his chest where the bullet had pierced his heart. Tom leaned over him and began to cry. Charles had become like a son to him. He had taken him under his wing and had always looked out for him, giving him advice and pointers on how to keep safe. He had stayed by his side in battle and saw to it he was taken care of.

"He…he just jumped in front of me," Steven whispered, his face stricken. "Why would he do that? That bullet was meant for me. Why?" Steven's eyes filled with tears as he looked into the sweet innocent face of the boy he had come to care so much about.

Gerritt placed his hand on Steven's shoulder. "Only God knows," he said. "But it was only the tragedy of war and there was nothing you could have done to stop it."

Steven shook his head and looked up into Gerritt's eyes. "It should have been me." Steven could not shake the feeling he was somehow to blame.

The battle was continuing, the brigade scattering everywhere over the grounds. Sergeant Jennings came to where they had clustered around Charles, one arm hanging limply at his side. "Come on men!" he called to them. "You are needed in the front! No time for the dead; we need to save the living!"

All three knew he was right. They were needed to help their comrades. They rose up from the grass and ran toward the front line where the sounds of musketry and cannon could be heard. The battle still raged hot and furiously. They had gained ground, now being even closer to the Union lines. They volley of firing was horrendous, the men falling dead all around.

Steven kept loading, firing, loading, firing as if on automatic. Some men forgot to fire their guns and would load six, eight bullets into the barrel, rendering them useless.

He still felt in shock over Charles's death, causing him to take risks. He, along with others, reached the wall and stormed over it, yelling their Rebel yell as they went. Fighting hand to hand with bayonets drawn, stabbing, smashing with the butts of their guns, the Union troops began to scatter, but the Rebs continued to pursue them.

Steven ran up next to a large cannon, preparing to fire at those hiding behind it, when it suddenly went off, knocking him to the ground unconscious.

When he awoke it was dusk and the air was filled with the fog of musket smoke. He sat up slowly, his ears ringing, not yet hearing the sounds of battle. All around wherever he looked were thousands of Rebel reserves brought in under General Longstreet, who had come forward to rout the Yankees. Littering the ground were hundreds of dead, most of them wearing the blue. Over to one side, he saw a large group of Union soldiers being held prisoner.

His head was throbbing and when he tried to stand, the world began to spin, so he sank back to the ground noticing as he did so, that the grass around him had been burned and blackened. He knew he was fortunate to be alive.

Tom and Gerritt were suddenly by his side, leaning over him in concern. “Steven, is that you? Are you hurt?” Gerritt asked him pulling aside his jacket looking for wounds. His face was so blackened by the powder, he had been difficult for them to recognize. “Please tell me you aren’t dieing.”

Steven could hear the fear in his voice. They could not have borne to lose two friends in one day. “No, no I’m alright,” he told them. “Just got knocked out when the cannon fired.

What happened?”

“The reserves came forward and it was one fearful struggle,” Tom told him. “Cannon’s blazin’, muskets firin’….

Can ya stand?” he asked offering his hand.

“I think so,” Steven said accepting the help. He stood shakily and took another look around. The sun was sinking below a wooded hill, casting its blood red glow across the body-strewn meadow. The carnage was appalling; over four thousand lay dead, disfigured, maimed and torn. The living moved among them, looking for survivors, the burial detail beginning to drag away the lifeless forms.

“I reckon I’d like ta go back to Charles and collect ‘im afore the burial detail gets to ‘im,” Tom said quietly. “I’d kind’a likes ta bury ‘im myself.”

Steven and Gerritt both nodded, the same thought having crossed their minds. They began their trek back across the open, treading around the broken bodies, listening to the moans of the wounded.

Everywhere they looked lay abandoned Minnie Muskets, the pieces having proved worthless. After several shots the barrel would foul and the bullet would be driven home. The ramrod was so slender and weightless; it would become greasy and slip through the hands. Steven and Gerritt were never more grateful to possess their Enfield rifles.

It had now become so dark they had become lost on the field and kept tripping over dead bodies, or worse, someone wounded would cry out making their blood run cold. They could see torches in the distance and headed towards them, hoping they belonged to their own brigade.

Steven wondered if they would ever get out of these killing fields; if life could possibly ever be normal again.

Having reached the lights, they discovered with relief, they belonged to their own detail, out looking for wounded. Tom grabbed the lighted stick from one and headed towards the spot they had left Charles' body, Gerritt and Steven following behind. After much searching, looking over many of the dead, some with heads missing or limbs frozen in grotesque positions, they finally found Charles.

With Gerritt holding the torch, Tom and Steven carried him back to one of the many campfires that had sprung up around the perimeter. There, he was laid gently on the grass, his face looking peaceful and serene. The front of his shirt was stained with his life's blood and Steven couldn't help but recall how he had jumped in front of him at the last moment.

"You can't bury him now," Gerritt told Tom. "It's too dark."

"I'll stay with 'im," he said calmly. "I don't want none of them burial niggers takin' him away in the night. He jes wouldn't likes being thrown in pit with hundreds of others."

"I'll stay, too." Steven said sitting next to him. "It's the least I can do."

Gerritt went off to find them some rations while Tom and Steven huddled closer to the fire. Off somewhere around another fire, someone was singing, sweet clear and sad, Danny Boy.

Steven looked into the flames, staring, not really seeing. His mind and body felt numb. He had seen and experienced so much this day. So many had died on both sides; including their friend Charles. One minute he had been with them, alive, well and full of patriotism and the next, he was gone, cold and lifeless.

He looked over at Tom who kept touching Charles; straightening his hair, brushing dirt from his coat. His eyes would fill with tears and spill down his face. He had cared so much for the boy.

He rested his head on his arms, the exhaustion overwhelming him. He had tried not to think of the negative before, but now he let them flood over him. What if he never made it back home? What if he never again could hold his precious Colleen in his arms? Was this to be the end of it all?

"I nev'a noticed afore how his ears kinda stuck out," Tom said breaking into his thoughts.

"Wha…what was that?" Steven asked raising his head to look at Tom. He still sat staring at the body of Charles.

"His ears, see how they kinda stick out?"

"Oh, sure, funny, I never noticed that before either.

He was right, wasn't he?" Steven said.

"Right 'bout what?" Tom said without looking away from the boy.

"That moon thing. About there being blood on the moon and that a lot of people would die today."

"He said he had a feelin'. I wonder iffen he knew it would'a been him. I seen lots of death in the Mexican War," Tom said quietly. "You'd a thought I'd be use to it. I guess you never does, and this here boy was kind a special." Steven could only nod.

Gerritt arrived back without rations, but no one felt much like eating. They sat by the fire, staring into the flames, remembering everything they had seen that day.

"Someone ought to tell his mother," Gerritt said breaking the silence.

"I'll do it," Tom spoke up. "I knows where she lives. He use to tell me 'bout her all the time, how much he loved her. I kin mebbe write her a letter." He choked up on the last words and had to stop talking.

Steven couldn't recall falling asleep, but soon the soft light of a new day began to break over the horizon. He sat up slowly, his head still hurting from the blow the day before. It took a moment for him to realize that someone was calling his name. He saw a medical aide walking amongst the men calling for Private Covington.

He stood and met the man half way, calling to him; "I'm here. I'm private Covington."

The man handed him a handwritten note and then hurried back through the troops. He was gone before Steven had opened the folded piece of paper. Reading it, a large knot filled his throat and he felt as if he had been punched in the stomach. The note read:

> Steven: I am sorry to inform you that your father was seriously wounded. Please come to the hospital. He is asking for you.   James McBride

"What is it?" Gerritt asked, becoming concerned for his friend.

Steven looked up into Gerritt's face. "It's from your father." A look of puzzlement crossed Gerritt's face until he said, "He says my father's been wounded and I should go to the hospital."

Gerritt nodded, "I'll go with you."

"Where is the hospital?" Steven asked, panic starting to creep into his voice.

"I saw it last night while I was searching for rations," Gerritt told him. "I'll take you there.

Wait," he said, stopping him. "Let's wipe your face first or your own father won't recognize you," he said wiping at Steven's face with a handkerchief. But his effort at levity was not appreciated.

They started off without a word to Tom or anyone else. For Steven, his only thoughts were for his father. "My god, Gerritt," he said, "how bad do you think it is? You don't think he'll die do you?" he asked without waiting for answers.

They finally arrived at the house along the road that had been set up as a hospital. A yellow flag flew from its porch indicating a medical facility.

In spite of their single-mindedness to find Steven's father, both he and Gerritt were taken aback upon reaching the two story wood structure. Around the house and about the grounds, spread out for over an acre, lay the wounded, both blue and gray. Their moans filled the air. Screams could be heard coming from the open windows of the house and under one was a pile six feet high, of amputated limbs; arms, legs, hands, Yankee and Rebel alike. It was an appalling sight. They stopped at the foot of the stairs looking out at the suffering mass of humanity.

"My god!" Steven whispered. "What if he's out there somewhere? How will we ever find him?"

"Let's go inside and ask. My father wrote the note, he must be with him," he said reassuredly. He could hear the frustration and panic rising in Steven's voice.

Steven nodded, accepting his friend's help. All he could think of was finding his father.

They walked up the steps and entered the building. Covering the floor were pallets with wounded men lying on them. On one of them, they saw their own Sergeant Jennings. His arm had been removed. They spoke to him and he reassured them he would survive. They continued searching the room, but did not find Clifford. Doctors and aides were moving about them, washing wounds and applying bandages.

They went on to the next and what they saw horrified them. Down the center of the room was a long table where a man laid, his right leg mangled to shreds. Several men stood over him, holding him down, while the surgeon cut with his saw. Blood covered the table, the floor, running down in rivulets between the cracks, covering the arms and clothing of the doctor. Steven gagged and hurried from the room.

They walked down the hall where there were more rooms filled with the wounded. Finally, in a room at the back of the house, they saw James sitting near someone lying on a cot by the window.

Steven's heart beat faster as he came closer. He could see the form on the cot was very still. He saw no movement. James stood as they approached. He looked haggard and worn, his face dirty and now covered by a beard. The front of his uniform was smeared with dried blood.

Steven stood next to his father looking down at his shattered body. His eyes were closed, but he saw he still lived, his chest rising and falling. Below the waist he saw his father's legs had been amputated below the knees, the stumps wrapped in bloody bandages. His throat constricted and the tears sprang to his eyes.

"Father," he whispered.

"It was a shell," James told him. "It shattered both his legs. They....they couldn't save them."

Steven tore his eyes from the still form on the bed to James, who had moved to embrace his own son. "Will he live?" he asked him.

James released Gerritt and looked back at Steven. "It doesn't look good. He's lost an incredible amount of blood.

He was asking for you. I thought it wouldn't hurt to try and find you."

"Thank-you," Steven said kneeling next to his father's bed. He touched his forehead and it felt warm. "Father, father, can you hear me? It's Steven."

Clifford began to stir and then he opened his eyes. They were glazed with pain, but Steven saw recognition in them.

"I'm here, Father. I'm right here. Everything's going to be all right. You'll be going home soon, back to mother and she'll take care of you."

"Steven?" Clifford said in a hoarse whisper. "Steven, I'm…so glad…you're here." Every word was an effort, as if it took every once of strength he possessed to speak them.

"Don't try to talk," Steven told him. "Save your strength."

"I…just wanted…to see you…my only son….one last time."

"No, father, there'll be many more times. You'll see, it will be just like before, the dances, the horse back riding….." The tears flowed down his face unheeded, for he knew it wasn't true.

Clifford feebly raised his hand and Steven took it in his own. "I…love..you, son." His hand grew lax and his eyes stared unseeing.

"He's gone, Steven," James said with tears in his own eyes.

Steven's head dropped onto his father's chest and he wept. Gerritt stood behind him, his hand on his back.

"I'll take care of him," James said, sitting again beside the bed. "I still have connections. I'll make sure he's brought home, back to Briarwood, where he can be with his family. I'll pay whatever it takes."

Steven looked up, wiping the tears from his face with his sleeve. "You could do that?" he asked.

James nodded. “Yes, I’ll have him put on a train and taken back home to Georgia.”

“Thank-you,” Steven told him, “my mother would be grateful and so would I.”

“We should get back to our unit,” Gerritt said quietly. “They’ll be doing roll call and if we aren’t there, they’ll assume we’re dead.”

“I don’t care,” Steven said sadly. “Let them think I’m dead.”

“Are we going to desert?” Gerritt asked him. “Because where you go, I go.”

Steven was silent for a moment, his head hung down. “No,” he said at last. “I can’t do that. Father wouldn’t want me to be a coward. He wasn’t.”

Steven rose to his feet. “Did you mean what you said about getting him home?”

“I promise,” James said, “And Steven, I’m so sorry about your father. I loved him too.”

“I know you did. The two of you have been friends for as long as I can remember.” His head hurt and the pain in his heart was unbelievable. How could his father be gone? He leaned over and closed his father’s eyes, touching his face. “Good-bye, Papa,” he whispered.

Gerritt took his arm and helped to lead him out of the house. Steven felt in a daze, no longer seeing the suffering all around him. As they walked back to where they had left Tom, Steven kept turning around to look at the house where he had left his father.

“I always knew it could happen,” Steven finally said. “I just didn’t think it would hurt this much.”

Gerritt was silent, not knowing what to say to his friend, but he had wondered the same thing himself. How would he feel if anything happened to his father?

"I guess you're never really prepared for the loss of a parent, do you think?" Steven said looking at Gerritt.

"No, you're right. I don't think you ever are."

"First Charles, and now my father," Steven said as they came within sight of their brigade. "I hope I never see that blood on the moon again."

That night as Steven lay in his bedroll, trying to sleep, the events of the day kept swirling through his mind, making it impossible to sleep. He thought of the battle, of Charles jumping in front of him and falling into his arms. He thought about the hospital with its suffering masses and of how his father had looked. And he thought about his own dieing. There was a pain in his chest that threatened to overwhelm him with grief.

He also thought that if his father had lived, he would have hated going home an invalid, having to be waited on, dressed, bathed, not being able to do all the things he loved. He remembered how as a child his father had taught him to ride a horse, to swim in the lake, would take him all over the plantation, teaching him everything he knew.

He lay on his back looking up at the stars, the night quiet for a time, and wondered what would happen to his mother when she found out. She had never been a very strong woman and he knew this would devastate her. He realized when the war was over he would be the one to run Briarwood, if he survived. But Colleen would be by his side and with her help he knew he could do anything.

He missed her now, more than he ever had. If only she could hold him in her arms, he knew she would be able to help ease the pain. She would know just what to say, what to do. God, he needed her so desperately! The tears ran freely down the corners of his eyes onto his blanket.

On towards morning the clouds had moved in and it began to rain, rousing them from their sleep. A hurried breakfast was eaten from meager rations, which had finally been distributed, and the troops were assembled. They were all congratulated on their overwhelming victory of the day before. The Yankees had been routed from the area with five captured colors. Four battery pieces had also found their way into Confederate hands because all the horses had been killed and they could not be hauled away.

Many soldiers were in good spirits because of their victory, but others were despondent, having lost friends or relatives in the last battle.

Tom had shown Gerritt and Steven where he had buried Charles. It was near a maple tree and he had affixed a crude cross with Charles' name burned into it.

"I think he would'a liked it here," he had told them. "Always did likes to sit under a tree."

"It's a fine spot," Gerritt told Tom. But all Steven could think about was his own father and where he might be right then. Had James been able to obtain passage for his body to be sent home, or was he even now in some unmarked grave near the battlefield?

They moved out and marched towards Fairfax Court House, the rain continuing to pour down upon them.

They walked all day with no food to sustain them and towards evening they camped at a place called Chantilly Plantation, a stately old homestead that had seen the ravages of war. One wing had been completely burned to the ground, with the rest of the house having been scavenged for firewood. All the fences were down, the out building torn apart, the furniture inside had been smashed to pieces, the plaster knocked from the walls with rifle butts. Even the forest around it had been cut down along with all the fruit trees. It made Steven pause to think of his home, Briarwood. What would happen to it if the Yankees ever got to Savannah? As he looked at the devastation of the once splendorous mansion, he could only pray it would never happen.

The rains had finally abated and they built fires to dry out their clothing and take the chill from their bodies. The lack of food had caused them to be weak and lethargic. Several of their numbers had fallen out along the way, no longer having the strength to go on. Many wondered if they would starve to death before they would face another battle.

Still others nursed painful feet because of being barefoot. Not only had there been no rations, but they also had not been issued any clothing in months. They wore the same tattered pants and shirts which had seen many battles, waded streams, endured downpours, sloshed through quagmires, and slept in.

Instead of this army being reinforced, it's losses recovered, instead of being properly fed, they were allowed to march day after day with no rations, no boots for their feet, and allowed to fall out of ranks. Instead of having a thoroughly equipped army to face down the Yankee army, they had long lines of limping, starving soldiers, carrying wearily on, disheartened and miserable. It was as if Richmond and President Davis had ceased to care about them. Many became embittered towards those in command.

By six the next morning they were on the march again. There still had been no rations and along the way, even more men fell alongside the road from weakness and injured feet.

In the evening they would camp near a cornfield or orchard and glean what they could from the fields. Such was their diet for many a day, causing digestive upset and even more of their numbers to fall out.

Lee had sent orders to General Toombs Georgian brigade to advance to Antietam Creek and hold it against the advance of the Federal troops, led by General Burnside.

It was now September and Lee's army of Virginia was divided. Generals Longstreet and Hill were in defense of South Mountain Pass against McClellan's attacks, while McLaws division went against the whole of Franklin's corps. This separation would prove to be disastrous. When they would again meet on the battlefield, their divisions would consist of skeleton regiments, which in many cases were not even as large as a full company.

They had marched toward the Potomac River and were required to cross to the other side. This proved to be a task more formidable than first anticipated. Many of the men did not know how to swim and in some areas the river was deep owing to the deluge of rains they had suffered with. Another problem was how to keep supplies and ammunition dry.

Fortunately, Steven and Gerritt were among those who did know how to swim and prepared for the crossing. They packed their meager belongings into their haversacks and tied it to their muskets. On top of this bundle, they perched their ammunition boxes. Some in their number took all their clothing off, while others, perhaps more modest, stripped only to their undergarments.

Steven and Gerritt were among the first to cross, wading out as far as they could, holding their bundle laden rifles over their heads. They were pleasantly surprised to discover they could cross without the water rising any further than their shoulders. Once on the opposite shore, they encouraged those who were terrified of the swirling waters.

The river bottom, however, was strewn with rocks, allowing for unsteady footing at best. What a scene it caused when naked and half -clad men began slipping and falling, drenching their bundles. Every profanity known to man was uttered as the soaking wet troops finally emerged from the river. Those watching the spectacle were driven to laughter as more men ventured to cross.

Ten of the more cautious decided there might be safety in numbers and hung on to each other in a long line. The first fellow was purported to be a swimmer and thus the illusion that he would get them all across safely.

Once they had gotten in the middle of the river, however, the lead man suddenly stepped into a hole.

Down he went pulling the man holding him down, and then the next and the next and so on like dominos in a row. Steven, Tom and Gerritt were laughing so hard; the tears were rolling down their faces.

Finally, once everyone had crossed safely, including the camp darkies who had been in charge of burial detail and totting their cooking supplies, they all stretched out in the warm sun to dry. Many shot off their muskets to make sure they would fire, making it sound as if a battle had just ensued, causing more laughter from the men.

Steven lay on his back, his arms under his head, his eyes closed to the bright sun. "It's good to laugh again," he said.

"Yes it is," Gerritt agreed. "I guess it's a testament to the human spirit, that no matter what the adversity, we will go on."

"That we will, my friend," Steven told him. "And we have somethin' those Yanks don't have, a will and tenacity to protect our homeland. In spite of fightin' in rags and no shoes, without rations and in spite of the losses," he paused for a moment, "we will continue to pursue until we win this war, until we drive the Yanks back north and then, only then, will we return to our homes. My father's death, all their deaths, will not be in vain."

Having crossed the Potomac, the brigade moved on through Maryland towards the town of Frederick and then to Sharpsburg.

CHAPTER TEN
—September 1862

The cotton was ready to be picked, the bolls bursting from the confines of their shells. Mr. Solomon would waken the slaves every day at dawn and march them to the fields for the harvesting, but no one knew whether or not it was wasted effort or prudent necessity.

No one had been able to sell their cotton while the ports remained blockaded by the Federals. As yet, in spite of the most earnest pleadings by the Confederate Congress, neither the British nor French would join the fight on the side of the South.

Harvest time of the remaining crops was also upon them, the corn, wheat, fruit and vegetables. A call had gone out for donations of foodstuffs to help feed the troops. When she had first heard the plea, Mary could not refuse. After all, how could she, when she might be helping to feed her own husband and son? The disadvantage; their own barns were full of bales of unsold cotton and their pantries were meager.

Conditions concerning Mr. Solomon and the slaves had continued to deteriorate. More beatings had occurred for various infractions, but there had been no more deaths. However, the pilfering and rapes of the slave women had continued. Mary had been at a loss to know what to do about it. Even though she had warned and threatened, her words had fallen on deaf ears.

Then a horrible tragedy had entered their lives. Steven's father had been killed on a battlefield in Virginia. Anna Bell had received word by way of a telegram from James. He had also called a friend, a member of Congress, to do him the favor of sending Clifford's body home. The Congressman was happy to oblige and not long thereafter, the simple wooden crate arrived at the rail station in Savannah.

Anna Bell had been so devastated by grief, she had not been able to get up from her bed. She barely ate and cried nearly incessantly. After her overseer and a few of the slaves had buried Clifford in the family cemetery, the minister had arrived and Anna Bell's maid had dressed her in mourning clothes. It had taken two people on either side of her to hold her up during the service.

Colleen had watched the proceedings almost passively, the minister speaking eloquently about Clifford's life, his accomplishments, and his service to his country. Her mother too, stood with tears flowing down her cheeks. She saw the other mourners in their black, silent, somber, while Anna Bell moaned her grief. She couldn't help but remember the funeral she had witnessed for Jonah, the singing, the praising and yes, the loud wailing.

She knew if it were Steven down in that cold ground, broken, still, she would not be able to stop wailing either. She would feel as if her heart were torn from her body.

She shook off the morbid thoughts and tried to concentrate on the ceremony, a man had died, a friend, in a horrible war that tore men apart. He had been her father-in-law, Steven's father. She wondered how he was handling all of this. Her father had written and told of the circumstances of his death and how Steven had been there at the end.

She cried then for Steven, but not for Clifford. It was Steven who would carry the pain in his heart. It was always Steven she thought of. In the past months she had been thinking of him more than ever. She thought perhaps the longer time had gone on, the less she would miss him, but just the opposite was true. The longer he was gone, the more she felt the desire to be with him.

After the funeral, Mary invited Anna Bell to come and live with them for a time. She accepted readily, bringing a few of her personal slaves with her and leaving the running of the plantation to her overseer, a much trusted and loyal employee, unlike Mr. Solomon.

Mary settled her into a room near her own where she could be available to her if needed. Anna Bell stayed in her room a great deal at first, but having others in the house, encouragement from them, helped to bring her to socialize. But she was a changed woman, distracted, seldom smiled and easily brought to tears.

Unfortunately, the fate that had befallen Clifford was not a rare incident in these times of war. Many families around them had felt the sting of death. Every week the lists of those dead and wounded were posted at the hospital in Savannah. Most did not have the luxury of hearing the news of a loved one by telegram and had to rely on the official lists. They knew James's telegram and intervention for Clifford was probably something that could not occur again.

Colleen worried about Steven and what might happen to him should some disaster befall him. Would they discover his name on the list someday or would he forever lie beneath Virginia's soil?

Ever since Jonah's death, Colleen had been more interested in the lives of those around her; those who lived their lives to serve them. Before, she had never questioned how they themselves felt about their lot in life, but now she did. Before, she had always just assumed they were mentally slow and needed white people to take care of them. Now she wondered about her assumptions. Why was it, for instance, that the darkies were not allowed to have schooling? Was it possible they were actually capable of learning more than just simple tasks? She felt very curious to learn more and decided to talk with Dora.

She wasn't quite sure how to broach the subject with her, or how she would respond.

She was given the opportunity very soon after, when it was discovered that Betsy had run away. She lived in a cabin with Bess and had slipped out unobserved in the night, or so it was said. Mr. Solomon had immediately hired a slave catcher, but after a week, there had still been no clue of her whereabouts.

One evening while Dora was helping Colleen to prepare for bed, she asked her why she thought Betsy had run away.

"I'se don' know, Missy," she answered.

"You must have some idea. You both work together in the house and I know you talk," Colleen said slipping her nightgown over her head.

"Mebbe she jes powerful sad 'bout Jonah," Dora said turning her back to Colleen to hang up her dress in the wardrobe.

Colleen walked over to stand behind her. "Please Dora, I really want to know. You don't need to be afraid. You can talk to me."

Dora turned to look her mistress in the eye, to see if there was any mockery or threat there. She had been taught not to trust white folk. Some of them had done unspeakable things to her people. On the other hand, she had known Colleen her whole life and knew her to be kind and compassionate to everyone. She saw openness, sincerity about her and thought perhaps she could trust this woman with the truth.

"I guess she jes feels ain't nothin' keepin' her heres, since Jonah dies," Dora explained without looking at Colleen.

"But this is her home, isn't it?" Colleen asked not wanting to appear defensive.

"This be your home, Missy," Dora said walking away.

"But where would she go?" Colleen asked following behind her.

"Can't say, mebbe north. We hears some white folks helps black folks to be free."

Colleen sat on the edge of the bed. "Do you want to be free, Dora?" She asked quietly.

Dora paused and when she answered, she did not look Colleen in the eyes. "Yes'm, I sho' does wish I was free."

"But why, Dora? Aren't you well taken care of here?" Colleen asked carefully, afraid to show anger; that she might frighten her off.

"Yes'm," Dora answered. "I'se gots clothes to wear, foods in my belly, a warm place to sleeps, but I ain't free." Colleen was quiet, waiting for Dora to continue. "Your family owns me. I cans't go where's I wants to go. I cans't do nothin' when I wants, only when other people says. I has to gets up when Mam says, helps you when you say, eats when I'se tol to. I can'st get married iffen I wants, has to gets Massa's permission. Iffen I doesn't do what I'se tol', I could mebbe be sol' or beat. I'se jes not free." Dora was afraid she had said too much. She had never spoken to any white person about her feelings of slavery before.

"I guess I….never thought about it that way before," Colleen said. She didn't voice to Dora how she had grown up believing that darkies were a lower class, less intelligent, a whole race of people who were like children and suited to slavery, actually preferring it. Maybe, just maybe, what she had been taught was wrong. She saw that Dora's body was firm and youthful, her face soft and beautiful. Her dark eyes were large and sad. Those things she had grown up with, those beliefs had changed. When the change had begun to occur, she couldn't recall. Perhaps it had been the look in the run away slave's eyes on the road, or the look in Dora's eyes when her mother had referred to them as property. Maybe it had been the new baby born in the quarters without the name Lizabeth had wanted. It might have been the time she had seen the look on the faces of the field hands when Jonah had been beaten, or perhaps it had been Betsy's grief when he died and the way they had sung for him at his funeral. It was if she were looking at them with new eyes.

"You know I've never asked you before," Colleen ventured, "do you have a family, Dora?"

"Iffen you mean does I has a Mammy and Pappy, no nots no mo. I had a man once, when you was little, but he be on Massa Covington's plantation and gots sol' afore we could jumbs de broom."

"I'm sorry," Colleen told her. "I didn't know about that, but I'd like to hear about him sometime."

Dora looked at her quizzically. No white folks had ever expressed an interest in her personal life before. She wasn't quite sure how to react. "I thinks it 'bout times fo' you to be getting' in bed," Dora told her pulling back the sheer drape around her bed.

The next morning as she sat at the breakfast table with her mother and Anna Bell, Colleen again asked what would happen if they lost the war and the slaves were set free.

"You've asked that question before and I don't understand what's behind it," her mother said as she buttered her biscuit. "Are you afraid of what will happen?"

"Perhaps, I know you have told me that we could not run our plantation and house without the slaves, but…."

"After you've seen what it takes to bring in the crops, to raise our food, the candle making, weaving, and everything else," her mother interrupted, "are you trying to tell me you think we could do it all ourselves?"

"Of course not, I only wondered how……."

"We would be ruined, that's what," her mother said with anger growing in her voice. "What do you think our husbands are out there fighting and dieing for?" With Mary's words, Anna Bell began to tear up.

"To keep people enslaved?" Colleen ventured.

"I'll have none of your sarcasm, young lady," Mary said, her eyes flashing angrily at her daughter. "There are just certain things we believe in, a style of life that those damn northerners can't understand. They want to tell us how to live our lives, to take away our rights. That's what this war is all about, our freedom, the freedom to govern ourselves, to live our lives as we choose."

"Couldn't we just hire darkies, pay them to do our work?" Colleen asked, finally getting to the question she had intended all along.

Her mother sighed and sat back in her chair. "We could never afford it. We would surely go broke in no time and can you imagine trying to get those lazy darkies to work if they were free and being paid? Why, the least bit of hardship and they'd walk off the job. Then where would we be?"

"I'm not sure that's entirely……" she began, but this time was interrupted when Anna Bell suddenly stood at her place. Tears still shone in her eyes.

"You insult the men on the battlefield who are dieing to maintain our way of life. My husband did not die for us to lose everything we have. I would think you would be a little more patriotic. After all, you have a father, a brother, and a fiancée out there trying to keep the Confederacy intact, to be able to maintain our way of life and that includes keepin' our slaves!" Her voice had risen to the point where she was shouting, then she sat down. "I'm so sorry," she said to Mary. "I didn't intend to get so emotional."

"It's quite alright, dear," Mary told her patting her hand.

Colleen then stood at her place, putting her napkin on the table. "I'm sorry if I upset you Anna Bell. My intention was not to be disloyal to the Confederacy. Perhaps I've begun to question whether or not slavery is right. Nevertheless, if we lose or if slavery is abandoned, I think we need to be prepared for what we might do.

Now if you would excuse me," she said walking from the dining room.

She went to her room and sank into the chair near the window. She looked out at the orchards and fields. Everything on the surface seemed normal; most things in their life going on as before, except everything wasn't normal. Life was not the same. For the last two years men had been dieing on the battlefield and for what purpose, she was no longer sure.

Dora entered the room just then, her arms laden with clean linens. She was startled to see Colleen there. "Sorry Missy, I'se thoughts you was still ats breakfast."

"I wasn't very hungry," she told her.

Dora," she said turning away from the window, "would you tell me how you got to be here? I mean, I know you were young, but where were you before this?"

"I'se been on a plantation up in Virginy," Dora told her as she stripped the linens from the bed. "Can'st rightly members the name of its now. It bes somepen likes Para, para…"

"Paradise? I know that place," Colleen said with interest. "I've been there with my family."

Dora nodded.

"How old were you?"

"I believes I was ten."

"How did you happen to come to Shannon?" Colleen asked pressing her further.

"I was sol' by my ole Massa. You daddy buys me and here I is."

"Would you tell me about it, your life before?"

"Not much to tells, Missy. Befo' I lives in Virginy and then I lives here." Dora was beginning to feel uncomfortable with her mistress's questions. She was afraid if she said the wrong thing, it would be used against her.

Colleen got up from the chair and went around to the other side of the bed where Dora had begun to put on the clean linens. "Stop a moment and come over here," Colleen said taking her by the hand. She stood her in front of the chair and told her to sit down.

"No'm, Missy. Misses don' allow us to sits on the furniture."

Colleen saw a look close to fear on Dora's face. "It's alright. I say you can sit. I want you to."

Still, Dora had not done as she was asked. "My mother and Anna Bell will be taking their morning walk in the garden. If you like, no one will know, I promise."

Hesitatingly, Dora finally sat gingerly in the chair, just on the edge without touching the arms.

"Good, now please Dora, tell me about your life before you came here." Colleen saw she was fidgeting, nervous, so she tried to make her feel more at ease. "It's alright, Dora. I just want to learn more about you. You've been with me, taken care of me, my whole life.

Could you tell me about your parents, do you remember them?"

"My Mammy and Pappy? I sho' does. They was fiel' hands. They growed tobaccy there in Virginy and they worked powerful lots of times in the fiel's, but they always finds time fo me. When they come in home aft'a dark, my Mammy cooks stew and biscuits and we'se sing songs and plays games. She learns 'um from her pappy who was from Afriker."

"Your grandfather was from Africa?" Colleen asked sitting cross-legged on the unmade bed. "Did you know him?"

"My grandpappy lived on the sames plantation. He be a big, ole back mans, tall, wif big arms and chest and he learns the blacksmithin' from the ol' blacksmith. He still be there when I sol'."

"So you had to leave your mother, father and grandfather. Did you have brothers and sisters?"

"Yes'm, I has a younger sister and a baby brother, lest they was when I lef'."

Colleen saw tears pooling in Dora's eyes. She had never before thought about their slaves' lives before they came to them, whether they had had families. It gave her a queer feeling in her stomach. "It must have been very difficult when you had to leave," Colleen said quietly. Dora only nodded and hurriedly wiped at her tears.

"Tell me about your grandfather," Colleen said, thinking if she talked about him, it would make her feel better.

"Well, it be likes I says, he been from Afriker and when first was here, he only speaks Afriker. Times be, even afta' he speaks English, when he gits mad at us chillin's he talks Afriker."

"Did he teach some of that language to you?" Colleen asked.

"Yes'm, he would tell me names of things, but I done forgets what they is. Sometime I done feels sad 'bout that 'cause I thinks iffen I could 'members some, I could hold on to parts of my grandpappy."

Colleen nodded thinking of the things she held dear of Steven. "What else do you remember about your grandfather?" she asked.

"I does 'member stories he done tol us 'bout Briar Rabbit and some 'bout Afriker," Dora said, a smile on her face. She was obviously recalling some pleasant memories.

"Your grandfather could still remember when he lived in Africa? What did he tell you about it?" Colleen asked as she wiggled on the bed to get more comfortable.

"Yes, Missy, he 'members a powerful lots. He be twenty-five years when he got cotched. He belong to a tribes be named Akan. They lived in a village with grass huts with his Mammy and Pappy and sisters and brothers. He done tol' me he love bein' in Afriker. He be free there and that they has wild animals that they hunts for food. He say little chilluns jes play all de live lon' day wid no troubles. Older chillun's learn to hunt and helps the grownups.

He says it beautiful there in Afriker, not like Virginy, different. He say there be flat lan's and scrubs and then there be bushes and lots o' trees and long grasses what blows in the win', and it be warm there." Dora stopped speaking, wondering if she had said too much, if she was telling this white woman more about herself than she wanted her to know. But it had felt good to talk about her grandfather. It wasn't as if she had forgotten him or her parents. It was just that she had not spoken of them in a very long time. All the other slaves on the plantation had their own stories to tell.

"Go on, Dora. I'd like to hear more," Colleen told her feeling as if she were listening to a story from some novel.

"He tol' me 'bout when he comes a mans, how they takes the boys inta the jungle and makes 'im lives on their own fo awhile. They puts 'em through tests, to sees if they be a man, you see. Then, iffen they passes, they tattoos they faces with dots on they nose and cheeks. Then they haf' a bigs celebration with dancin' and singin', lots o' food, all nights long. They wore cloths wif lots a colors. They paint their faces and wore feathers in their hair. My grandpappy still has them dots on hiss face to this day."

The door opened and Mary entered the room. Dora sprang to her feet and stood looking terrified. "What's going on here?" she asked hurrying over to Dora. "Why aren't the beds made?" she asked looking at the rumbled linens on the bed.

"I'se sorry, Misses, I….."

"It's my fault," Colleen broke in, "I distracted her. We were talking."

"First you upset Anna Bell by your disloyal talk and then you keep the servants from their chores. Haven't I enough to deal with without you bein' disruptive," Mary said angrily. "And as for you," she directed at Dora, "what makes you think you're good enough to sit on my chairs?"

"I'se sorry, Misses. It won'st happens again," Dora said with her head down, almost as if she expected to be struck.

"Get back to work," Mary ordered. Dora hurried out of the room, gathering up the dirty linens as she went.

"It wasn't her fault," Colleen told her mother. "I told her to sit down. I asked her to tell me about her grandfather."

Mary turned to face her daughter. "I don't understand what's going on with all of this. Dora is a servant, not your friend. We don't socialize with darkies. Before you know it, they'll be thinkin' they're on our level and want special privileges, and we can't have that now, can we?" Mary touched her daughter's face and then she left the room.

"We can't have that now, can we?" Colleen said mockingly. She picked up a glass dish from her dresser and threw it against the wall, shattering it. "I hate this!" she screamed. "I hate all of it; daddy, Gerritt and Steven fightin' in war, having to deal with everything here by ourselves…. Why are we doing this, why!" Her screams turned to tears and she stood in the middle of the room crying.

The next time Colleen saw Dora, she said nothing to her about the incident that morning, but she had not forgotten it. Even though she had grown up with slavery, had them taking care of her, her whole life, it was only now that she was beginning to see them in a new light. Perhaps it was the war and the idea that the Yankees would actually fight to free them or that she was older now and questioned things she had grown up with, but she saw herself as having her eyes opened to them for the first time.

Later, after Dora had settled her in for the night and gone back to her own cabin, Colleen quietly got up from her bed and put a warm shawl on over her nightgown. She then crept stealthily down the hall, past her mother and Anna Bell's rooms, to the back stairs and down to the pantry.

It was dark, the blackness enveloping her like a shroud. She felt the gooseflesh prickling her skin. She made her way to the door and went outside. She held her breath as the heavy oak squeaked on its hinges. She did not want anyone to hear her. She walked under the portico to the kitchen where a small fire still glowed in the hearth, giving her some comfort.

Colleen went to a shelf and found several candles. Taking one and lighting it in the fire, she continued back outside to the gardens. It was a moonless night and very dark. Her candle gave her but a small light to guide her path.

There were sounds in the night, frogs croaking, crickets chirping; nothing she hadn't heard before, but somehow being out here alone, in the dark was cause to make her heart beat faster.

She followed the path through the gardens, stepping gingerly so as not to trip. She finally saw the glow of lights coming from the row of cabins where the house servants lived. The small structures were set close together containing a door and one window. The brick chimneys on each one had smoke rising lazily from them and Colleen could smell the burning wood.

In front of each, the dirt had been raked smooth and a few bright flowers grew alongside. She paused, realizing she didn't even know which cabin belonged to Dora. She had never been to visit her in her home before.

She knocked at the door of the first cabin and shortly Ellen, their cook answered.

"Missy, Colleen," she exclaimed, obviously surprised to see her mistress at the servant's cabins. "What you doin' down heres?'

"I'm sorry to disturb you," Colleen told Ellen. "I'm looking for Dora."

"You'se in trouble, Missy? You'se needs help?" she asked moving her large frame outside. From inside, Colleen could hear the voices of her husband and two children.

"No, no, I'm fine," Colleen reassured her. "I only need to know which cabin is Dora's."

"She be three mo down the path dat aways," Ellen said pointing into the darkness.

"Thank-you and again, I'm sorry I disturbed you. And Ellen, I would prefer you not saying anything to my mother about me being down here."

"My mouf is shuts. Now ya'll be careful. I doesn't wants you Mammy getting' afta Ellen iffen sompen happens to you."

Colleen cupped her hand around the small flame on her candle to keep it from going out as she continued on down the path. As she walked up to the door of the third cabin, she suddenly wondered why she had come all the way down here in the middle of the night. She knew she had wanted to talk with Dora again, but perhaps she was sleeping or wouldn't want to talk again. She nearly turned back until the door suddenly opened and there stood Dora, framed in the light from behind her.

"Missy Colleen, that be you?" She asked peering out into the darkness. She was wearing a simple cotton dress with a shawl wrapped around her shoulders. "What you be doin' here?"

"Oh, I just thought I'd come visit you. I've never been to your home before."

Dora frowned, always suspicious of white men's or women's strange ways. "Well, you comes all de way down here, you better comes in," she said standing to one side.

Colleen went on in to the small interior. Her first impression was of how clean everything was. A small wooden table sat in front of the fireplace, scrubbed and worn to a shine. Two chairs were pushed underneath as if waiting for company. A cabinet against one wall was filled with plates, cups, kettles and pans. Along the opposite wall was a single cot, made up with clean linens. The wall contained several nails where Dora's clothes were hanging. Colleen recognized the flowered cotton dresses and starched white aprons she wore while working in the house. The plank wooden floor was scrubbed and swept clean.

Dora followed behind her, shutting the door. "Missy, you wants some tea?" she asked her. She was feeling very uncomfortable having her mistress in her cabin. She already felt as if her life were not her own, being scrutinized, watched over as if she would do something wrong at any moment. Her home had been her only sanctuary, a place she could go without prying eyes, to be herself, to get away from the white people who owned her. Now, here was her mistress invading even this small space.

Colleen sat in one of the chairs at the table while Dora took the steaming kettle off its hook over the fire. She carefully set out two china cups and while holding the strainer of tea, poured the hot water into the cups.

Colleen recognized the cups as part of an old set from the house. They had a few chips and fine cracks, and Colleen supposed her mother had given them to her.

Dora stood near the hearth sipping her tea and looking very uncomfortable. "Dora, sit down please," Colleen told her.

"No,m, I cans't sit with my mistress."

"This is your home," Colleen told her. "Please sit down."

Dora pulled out the other simple wooden chair and sat gingerly down. "Please tell me more about your grandfather," Colleen said eagerly.

"I'se don' know 'bout that. Your mammy don' likes me to be tellin' you those things," Dora said. "And what she say you be down here wif me? She jes might whup me. She be powerful angry afore."

"My mother was upset by something else when she was sharp with you. It's alright for you to speak with me. And if you like, she never has to know I was here.

Now, please tell me about your grandfather. How did he come to be a slave?"

Dora hesitated before answering. She still wasn't sure she should be telling this white woman who owned her about her family, but perhaps it would cause her to understand the truth of what had been done. "He be in his village," she started out, the same one he grows up in. At that time he be's married wif two little chilins'. He says his woman be young and beautiful wif soft brown skin. He say she has most pretty brown eyes he has ever done sees. Her name bes Shamyra.

There be another tribe, closer to the big water what's be terrible furious and they be paid by the slave traders to comes and cotch the peoples.

I still does 'members how he be tellin' us chillins 'bout that time, sittin' front of his cabin, us chillins on the grass listenin's.

He tol' us 'uns he neber forgets dat night. There had beens a big celebration; two young people had jumbs de broom togethers, only it weren't called that there. They had been dancin' and singin', lots o' foods ta eats. He says afta everbodys has gones to sleep, it be quiet, onlys the sounds of the crickets. His woman Shamyra and chilins lay together in the hut when yellin' and screamin' a goin' on. Grandpappy run outs the house and sees peoples runnin' everywheres and screamin'.

Then he sees strangers, mens from a different tribes, hittin' peoples and chainin' 'em all up."

Colleen was becoming more intrigued by Dora's story. A story of a different people in a far off land, living a completely different life from anything she had heard of before, simple and yet somehow savage as well.

"Grandpappy goes backs insides and tell his wife to gets their chilins and run to the bush," Dora continued. "The baby girlchil', she be a babes in arms and the boy chil', only three years ol'. Shamyra grabs the chilins and escapes out the back through the reeds on the hut. Meantimes, Grandpappy goes to distracts the strange mens in the village. He finds a stick and goes to smackin' somes, but then they be four of dem and de hits 'im on the head and he fall down likes he be dead.

When he wakes up, he be chained wif hafs the village, men's, womens, chilin's. And then he sees Shamyra and his babes; they be caughts, too. This makes him very sad for he doesn't know what's gwine to happens to them. He thinks mebbe they mights be all kilt.

Them slave cotchers, they makes 'em all starts walkin', walkin' and walkin' for days through the jungles. Grandpappy helps Shamyra to carrys the babe but they gets so tired. Them bad men whups 'em iffen they don's walks fas' 'nough and they don' gets 'nothin' to eats. All the chilin's they be cryin' fo food. Grandpappy say it be hot and the chains hurts they ankles and necks powerful much. Somes of the people dies, people he knows his whole life. Shamyra, she be cryin', but Grandpappy makes her goes on, so she don't dies, too.

After a spell, they got to a river and puts ever body into boats and takes 'em down river to the big water where they is big rocks and sand. On the sand there is a big building made of rocks. That's where they sees the white mens fo' the first time. They never done sees white mens afore. Grandpappy say they be afraid of them. They whups 'em and talks strange like." Dora stopped, fearing she may have said something insulting to Colleen. She had gotten caught up in her own story, remembering how her grandfather had related it so many times to them. It seemed so much a part of her; the words had simply flowed out. But now she was afraid she had said too much. You always had to be careful what you said to white folks.

"Please Dora, go on," Colleen said encouragingly.

"Missy, it be late. I'se gots to gets up early to helps in de house."

"Oh, of course," Colleen said getting to her feet. "I was just so interested in your story. I'll be getting back, but Dora, you've got to promise me, you'll finish telling me about your grandfather real soon."

"Yes'm, Missy," Dora responded lighting Colleen's candle and handing it to her.

Colleen took the candle and began to walk carefully back down the dark pathway.

Dora watched her until she had turned a bend toward the house. She felt so ambivalent about talking to her mistress about her family. On the one hand she was always suspicious of white folks and their motivations, but on the other, this was Colleen, her sweet little

Colleen. She had raised her, cared for her as if she were her own daughter and she had to admit it to herself; she loved her. She had no children of her own and she was as dear to her as if she were. She didn't believe Colleen asked the questions to hurt her. She believed she really was just curious.

It had forced her to think again of her life before Shannon, when she was young and felt relatively secure with her Mam and Pa and Grandpappy. They had all lived together in the same cabin. During the day when her Mam and Pa were off working in the tobacco fields, and Grandpappy was in the smithy shop, the old women would care for her and her sister Cassie and little brother Samuel, along with the other small children. Then in the evenings when they would come home, Mammy would cook and sometimes after the meal, they would get together with others in the quarters and sing and dance. It had seemed to her to be like the village in Africa that her Grandpappy would tell them about.

When she was eight, she had begun working in the big house, helping the other servants with making beds, sweeping floors, and fetching for the Massa and Mistress who had a young daughter and teenage son.

Then at ten years, her whole world was turned upside down when Massa McBride had bought her and took her away from her family, never to see them again. As she lay on her small bed in the dark, thinking of her Mammy and Pappy and Grandpappy, the tears slipped out and fell silently down her face.

Colleen had finally found her way back to her room, tiptoeing up the back staircase and stealing quietly down the long hall to her room. She slipped off her slippers and crawled in under the quilt. Her feet were cold from her walk.

She lay in the dark trying to sleep. It was very late, but the thoughts kept whirling in her mind. She couldn't help but think of the story Dora had told her of her Grandfather.

She had imagined in her mind the village of people in a far away place called Akan, living their lives as they always had. People being born, people dieing and everything in between; loving singing, dancing, and having children. What must have it been like for those people when they were captured? She imagined they must have been terrified, confused. They had been ripped from their homes, their lives, their loved ones and made to walk many, many miles to the ocean. She thought how it must have been an arduous journey, some even dieing on the way. She imagined women crying, children screaming.

She closed her eyes, not wanting to think of it any further. She tried instead, to think of Steven and the day they married each other. But that only served to make her sadder yet. It seemed so long ago; a year and a half. She sometimes wondered if they would ever be together again. When she had these thoughts, it always depressed her. Was there any joy left in the world?

The following day Dora seemed to avoid her whenever she could, and Colleen wondered if she were sorry she had spoken so honestly with her about her grandfather. Everytime she tried to corner Dora alone, she would find some excuse to rush off on some errand or another. Colleen however, was determined to hear the rest of the story. It was as if Dora's past had become a fairy tale in a book and she needed to see how it came out.

That evening in the waning hours of the day, the three women, Colleen, Mary and Anna Bell, sat on the terrace watching the glow from the setting sun. "Here it is September and we've done nothing about plannin' a Christmas dance," Mary was saying.

"Do you really think that's appropriate considering the war and all?" Colleen asked. "After all, a lot of the men are gone fightin', in case you've forgotten. Many of our friends are hurting, they've lost so much with the blockade and of course, there's the fact that so many have lost loved ones," she said more quietly looking over at Anna Bell.

"All the more reason to hold a dance, to lift everyone's spirits," Mary said as she lifted her teacup to her lips. "And besides, most of the plantation men are home."

"Only because they own slaves and got out on some technicality, favorin' the rich while the poor are the ones left to fight," Colleen said angrily.

"I don't understand your attitude," Anna Bell said to her. "Your own father and brother chose to stay, not to mention your fiancée. They believe in what they're doin' and my Clifford died for it."

"Really, Colleen," her mother said, "those men who came home needed to see to their families. Further north, people are goin' hungry; they have lost their homes."

"I'm sorry, but to me it just doesn't seem fair."

"Well, war isn't fair, my dear," Mary said dismissing her with a sentence. "We didn't hold a ball last year and

I think it about time we did. Oh, perhaps not a big ball, but a dance none-the-less. For those of us who still have some abundance to give to those who have less."

"Then why don't you just give them some of our livestock and food stuffs, if we have so much?" Colleen asked her.

"You miss the point entirely," Mary said. "It's to give the people a chance to forget the war for awhile, to have some fun, to dance."

"You're right. I guess I do miss the point," Colleen said getting to her feet, "because it's difficult for me to be frivolous when my father, brother and fiancée could be killed in this damn war!"

"Colleen! You will not speak to me that way." Mary stood, knocking her teacup to the brick terrace, shattering it.

Colleen did not wait for any further lectures from her mother and walked back into the house. As she went down the hallway towards the stairs, she heard her mother apologizing to Anna Bell.

"I'm so sorry for her behavior.

Well, what do you think? Don't you agree a dance might be a good idea?"

"Perhaps," she heard Anna Bell reply quietly.

Colleen went up to her room where she found Dora preparing her bed for her to retire. She was still angry with her mother and threw a shoe she had removed across the room.

"My mother is unbelievable! Imagine havin' a ball while there's a war goin' on!"

"Yes'm. Misses do likes the parties," Dora said coming closer to help Colleen with the buttons on the back of her dress.

She held up her hair that Dora might reach those on the high collar around her neck. "Dora, did it bother you to have me come to your cabin?"

"No'm," she replied quietly.

"I really didn't mean to intrude. I was so interested in your grandfather's story. I merely forgot the lateness of the evening."

"Be no harms done, Missy," Dora said finishing with the buttons.

Colleen turned around to face her. "Would you be willing to tell me the rest about your grandfather?"

Dora cast her eyes down, stepping slightly backward. "I'se jes don't know iffen I shoulds."

Colleen closed the space between them and took hold of Dora's hands. "I will not force you to tell me if it makes you feel uncomfortable," she told her, "but I truly would like to hear."

Dora looked up into her mistress's face and saw her smiling. Then she nodded.

"Oh, thank-you," Colleen said clasping her hands together in delight. "Come, let's sit and you tell me about your grandfather and Africa." She brought Dora over to the bed, but she refused to sit in the chair by the window.

"I be fine jes sittin' on the floor," she told Colleen.

Colleen climbed up on the bed, sitting cross- legged in just her chemise and bloomers. She looked down at Dora sitting on the rug beside her bed. It made her feel like she did when she was young and her cousins from Atlanta would come to spend a few days. It also reminded her of the better times when everyone was happy and they had fun traveling, visiting and having wonderful parties. She had no cares then, no war; she was happy.

"What happened to your grandfather after he was taken to the ocean?" Colleen asked Dora.

Dora thought back to when she was young and listening to the stories of her grandpappy. "The white mens kep 'em in that there rock buildin' for weeks. He say it be col' and dark. They don't gets much food to eats and them babies cries all the time. While they be there, more peoples come, black peoples; the slave cotchers bring 'em.

Then one day, the white mens come and chains 'em all up again by their feets and takes 'em outside. It be so bright, it hurts their eyes. When Grandpappy looks out in the water, he sees a big boat, the biggest boat he ever done sees. It has tall poles with white fabric ties to it. They starts takin' the black peoples on the boat. They makes 'em go downs in the bottom where it be dark and smells bad. He says downs there in the belly of the boat there be long rows of wooden planks and then 'nother row, jes rows and rows. All them peoples had to lays on the boards, the nex row jes above 'em. They can'st even sits up or turns over. They was all chained there."

"How awful," Colleen said. "I can't imagine what that must have been like."

"Grandpappy, he say it be terrible. Womens and chilins be scarit and screamin'; somes were sick. When they clos' the hatch it be so dark, they can'st see nothin', nots even the person next to 'em.

Then the boats starts movin' and it be swayin' and rockin' in the waves and then even mo' peoples gots sick. Grandpappy say it made him sick, too. And the smell be even worse.

Grandpappy , he be separated from Shamyra and his chilins, sos he calls out, but ever' body else is callin' and he can'st hear 'em."

Colleen listened, appalled at the conditions Dora was describing to her. She had never heard anyone's story of what it had been like for the slaves coming over across the ocean. "How…how long were they on the ship?" she asked.

"Grandpappy say it be weeks and weeks."

"Did they have to stay down there the whole time, chained to the planks?"

"Grandpappy tol' me, ever few days, they brings 'em up on top to gets fresh air and sun. It be so not so many dies. When they does die, they jes throws the body in to the water fo the sharks to eats. They also gets mush and water fo' food. When they up on top Grandpappy sees Shamyra and it breaks his heart to sees how poorly she look and the chilins be so scarit and sick. He say it makes 'im cry.

Likes I say, it be weeks and weeks on the boat, many sick, some they die. Finally the boat stops in Ameriker, but he doesn't knows that den. All he sees is lots an' lots of whites people who be speakin' languages they can'st understand. An' there's buildin's an' houses an' such likes they never sees afore. Some mens they puts 'em in a big cage wif Shamyra and his chilins."

Dora stopped for a moment and looked down at the floor. Colleen was silent; realizing how emotional this must be for her.

"They be powerful scarit, not knowin' where they be or what's gonna happens to 'em," Dora said quietly without looking up. "Grandpappy say he couldn't makes Shamyra stops cryin'." Dora looked back up at Colleen as she continued. "Afta a few days they takes all the peoples outside on the docks. Grandpappy saw hundreds o' white folk all crowded 'round a big ole platform. One by one and sometimes chilins wid they mammy, they sol' the peoples to the white folks. "Course Grandpappy doesn't know that then 'cause he don't understands nothin'. All he knows then is the white mens take Shamyra and his chilins on the platform. Some mans took Shamyra's blouse offen her. Then theys all this loud talkin' wif one man talkin' fas'. Then suddenly some mens was takin' 'em away. He tries goin' to them but the chains hol' 'em fas. Then he hears Shamyra screamin' and screamin'. That be the las' time he ever see her or his chilins again."

Colleen felt stunned. She really didn't know what to say to her. I'm sorry, seemed so inadequate. And she felt ashamed. It was her people who had done these things to hers. "So then your grandfather was sold to someone else?" she asked. She knew it was growing late, that Dora had exposed her vulnerability in telling her family's story, but she wanted to hear all of it. She didn't know why, she just knew she needed to hear it.

Dora had nodded in response to her question. "This man from the tobaccy plantation buys him and two other, one man and one woman. They makes 'im work in the fiel' and it be hard work. All the time he be thinkin' 'bout Shamyra and the chilins and he be powerful sad. Two times he tries runnin', but they always cotched 'im and beats 'im for it. Afta' two years he be so lonely and sad and one woman, she be so kind to 'im. So they jumps the broom together. It be my grandmammy Grace. She be helpin' granpappy's heart to mend. They has two chilins, a boy chil', who died when he be three month ole and then my mother, Leah was born. My grandmammy Grace died of the cholera afore I was born. Grandpappy say he never marry agins.

Mammy met my pappy when she be sixteen. Our massa done buys 'im from a slave trader. I 'members Mammy sayin' he be the bes' lookin' mans she ever did sees." Dora stopped and smiled at the memory.

"And then you were born?" Colleen asked encouragingly.

"Yes'm and then came Cassie and Samuel. Grandpappy, Mammy and Pappy works in the day, but in the night we be a family and that's when Grandpappy tell me the stories. He tells 'em over and over, so's I knows 'em by heart. He tells me never forgets and to tells my chilin some day.

When I'se eight, I works in the big house wif Misses. She be sick and I tries to works hard like my Mammy, but ole Misses, she done yells an' hits me all the time.

Then one day Massa McBride comes a visitin' on the plantation and Massa sol' me. They jes comes in the house where I be wif my Mammy, Pappy, Grandpappy and they drug me out and puts chains on me so's I don run. I done never had no chains afore, and they puts me in the wagon. Mammy be screamin' and cryin', sayin' nots to takes her girl away. Then we all be cryin', Pappy, Samuel, Cassie and Grandpappy. Pappy had to hol' Mammy back afore she be comin' afta me.

That be the saddest day of my life. I cries and cries til I can'st cries no mo'. I never done see's them ever again." Dora had stopped talking and Colleen could see she was crying, the tears running unheeded down her cheeks. She kept silent, waiting for her to compose herself. Finally she was able to continue.

"That's when I comes to Shannon. I be a house slave 'til you babies comes along. Then I be your nanny and takes ker of you ever since. When I be nineteen or so, I falls in love wif a young man who worked in the stables. You probably don' 'members. You was a babe then. We was gwine t jumps the broom, but afore we coulds, your Pappy sol' 'im. That be the second saddest day of my life."

"I'm so sorry," Colleen whispered. "I didn't know. I mean I've always known how slavery works, but I just didn't think……."

Dora was silent and Colleen didn't know what else to say to her. Finally, when the tears were gone, Colleen told Dora she could go.

As she was leaving the room, Colleen stopped her. "Dora, thank-you for telling me your story. I know it must have been difficult for you and that means a lot to me."

Dora only nodded and quietly went down the back stairs, wondering if she should have told her so much. But once she had started, it had been difficult to stop. The words had just flowed like water out of her mouth.

After Dora left, Colleen finished preparing for bed. It was now late, but she could not sleep. Dora's story kept going around and around in her mind. What her family had gone through, what all slaves went through, was horrible. She had always known that the slaves came from Africa, but she had never known the details. She didn't know what she had thought about, how she imagined they would have become slaves. They surely would have never volunteered willingly. Perhaps she had intentionally shut it off from her mind, not wanting to think of the responsibility they all bore.

She saw in her mind what it must be like on those slave ships, the horror of it. Then to be sold, ripped away from family and friends in a strange land and forced to do labor for someone else, must be traumatic.

They were people, human beings with feelings, emotions, loving their children and spouses and grieving when they lost them. What had made her think they were less; just because they came from a place more primitive, or because their skin was a different color? That was what she had been told her whole life, by her parents, her friends, and other slave owners. If they seemed less intelligent it was because they came from a place where they spoke another language, where the culture was completely different. When they arrived here, were they given English lessons? They were not even allowed to learn to read and write, let alone be given a mastery of English. She understood now, the way they spoke was a combination of their African dialect and what English they had picked up on their own.

She remembered what Dora had told her about being sold away from her family when she was just a child. What must have that been like, her mother screaming, tears running down her face, trying to get to her child. And Dora must have been so frightened, put in chains, fastened in a wagon and driven away, away from the only home she had ever known, away from her entire family. She couldn't even imagine what that must have been like. And then once again, to have the man she loved torn from her, gone forever. Why was it she didn't hate them all? No wonder so many ran away. Tears formed in her eyes and ran down the sides of her face. "What are we doing?" she whispered aloud. "This is why, isn't it? This is why the north is fighting so hard to free the slaves. They know it's wrong and we don't. What happens if we win? More and more people forced to be slaves? And what happens if we lose? How many people will have to die? Why couldn't I see it before?

CHAPTER ELEVEN —September 1862

After crossing the Potomac, Steven's brigade continued their march through Maryland. As they walked along the lush, fruitful fields, they couldn't help but compare them to the battle scarred land of Virginia. The citizens they encountered gawked, open-mouthed as they marched, long lines of infantry filing past for miles. They had not ever seen Rebels before. Some looked panicked, as if they thought the soldiers might bring them harm. But when they saw that not a single man broke ranks, or even attempted to cross into their yards, they became sympathetic of their poor conditions. They brought food, bread, smoked meats, fruit, until they had enough to last them the day.

They marched on to Hagerstown where cornfields and orchards abounded. They bivouacked there for the night and helped themselves to the plenty of the fields.

As Tom, Steven, and Gerritt sat near their fire eating corn and apples, Gerritt began a persistent itching, not unlike a pastime shared by them all.

"Damn, these lice," Gerritt said scratching even harder. "Will they give us no peace?"

"It's no use," Steven told him. "You'll only make yourself raw. We've tried everything to rid ourselves of the vermin, you know as well as I."

"Yeah boy. We'se tried boilin' our clothes, holdin' our underdrawers in the water, scrubin', rubbin', and even buryin' them suckers and nothin' gits shed of 'em," Tom said detailing their efforts.

"This infestation is just intolerable," Gerritt continued as he plucked the creatures from his skin and tossed them in the fire. "I think I'd rather endure almost any kind of affliction rather than this."

"Careful what you'se wishin' fer, son," Tom told him.

The following day, September 15th, they marched on to Sharpsburg. As they neared the town, they could hear the booming sounds of cannon fire. When they entered the village, they found it empty, the citizens having already abandoned it.

Just a mile outside of town was Antietam Creek, spanned by a bridge that the Yankees would have to traverse in order to acquire the town. Orders were sent from General Lee himself, for Toombs Georgia brigade to proceed there at once to guard the bridge and keep the Yankees from crossing at all costs.

Steven and Gerritt looked at each other as they heard the orders, for all that was left of them was barely a skeleton command. Death, wounding and those who had fallen out from illness, starvation and injured feet had all but decimated them.

"Is Lee insane?" Gerritt asked. "How does he expect us, with these paltry numbers to hold a bridge against the Yanks?"

"Mebbe he's got some plan we jes don't knows about yet," Tom said. "Mebbe he'll bring us reinforcements."

"I guess we just go where we're told," Steven said resigned. "That's what we've been doing all along anyway."

Their new sergeant Porter Davis, a slight nervous man, ordered them to fall in as they began their march towards the bridge. The seventeenth Virginia surrounded the town of Sharpsburg on three sides. It sat in a valley with undulating hills all around, enclosing pasture and miles of wooden split rail fences. It was behind these, the Virginians took cover. But no one else went along with the Georgians to the Antietam Bridge.

As the bridge came into view, the shelling could now be felt and seen, as the earth was split apart and spewed out in all directions. Steven could hear their wild war song, the song of death. Nothing else sounded like the Hotchkiss's shriek, putting fear into the bravest of hearts. It wasn't any deadlier than other shells, but the jagged edge on the shell as it left the gun, caused it to scream like a devil. Steven hated that sound.

As they neared the bridge, rifle fire broke out and they quickly got into their formation. The minnie balls were zipping past furiously; causing them to realize they were vastly outnumbered. They crouched down behind whatever barriers they could find, but they were few. Most lay prone on their faces.

Steven could see the vast solid mass of blue and he wondered how they would ever survive this encounter. Shells kept bursting around them, shattering trees, boulders and human flesh.

Steven and Gerritt lay close to one another, waiting out the shelling, expecting at any moment to be blown to pieces. They had to keep their eyes shut because of all the flying debris. After fifteen long minutes, it ceased. At first there was a deadly silence where each click of the hammer on each gun could be heard.

Then the infantry attack began, the Union soldiers firing as they began pouring across the bridge. They could hear their officers calling commands, the clanking of their equipage, the broad flag with its Stars and Stripes flying unfurled in the front of their ranks.

Steven and Gerritt stood with the remaining men in their company and charged into the advancing Yankee line. Everyone fired at once, sending a shower of bullets into the opposing foe. Many of them fell, but many more came up to fill their places.

The next volley of bullets came from the blue line in front of them. Many more of their number lay dead and dieing. The air was filled with smoke, and the noise was deafening.

Steven could see the black muzzles of their guns not twenty feet away, the sun glinting off the barrels. A bullet thudded into his hat, knocking it from his head. He could not stop to think how closely he had come to dieing. Grabbing it back on his head he could only load, fire, and reload.

But the onslaught was too fierce and their numbers too small. Sergeant Davis called the retreat as they began withdrawing back to the trees. The Union soldiers kept advancing, continuing to fire as they did so.

Tom was in the lead with Steven following and Gerritt behind him. They loaded their guns on the run, stopped, turned and fired, then continue their retreat. There seemed to be no stopping the wave of blue.

They had nearly reached the cover of the trees; only a few feet more. They could hear the bullets thudding into the branches, stripping small twigs from overhead. Tom and Steven ran into the trees, ducking behind a large fallen log to catch their breath.

"My god, what a rout. There were just too many of them," Steven said then he paused, realizing Gerritt was not with them.

"Where's Gerritt?" he asked and the two men stood, looking back over the log.

There just outside the tree line, in the clearing laid Gerritt; face down on the ground. Steven felt all the breath being sucked out of him as if he had been hit hard in the gut. The blood drained from his face and his heart pounded madly in his chest.

"Gerritt, no," he whispered. He kept expecting his friend to get up and run, but he lay still. "I've got to go get him," he said starting to climb over the log.

"You can't go out there," Tom told him grabbing his arm. "Them Yanks is too close."

"I don't care. I've got to get him. He could still be alive," he said shaking off Tom's hand.

"Then I'm goin' with ya."

They both ran towards the edge of the wood and stopped. Just beyond lay Gerritt and only a few yards past was the Union army. Steven hesitated no longer. Still holding his rifle, he ran towards the motionless form of his best friend. Tom too, ran towards Gerritt, reaching him at the same moment as Steven.

They picked him up under the arms and began dragging him towards the safety of the trees. The bullets were flying past, thudding into the trees and the ground around them.

They finally reached the trees, dragging Gerritt to the spot where they had rested behind the fallen log. Steven knew that their gallant effort to retrieve Gerritt had all been for naught. There in the back of his head was a small round bullet hole, the blood flowing profusely over his back, the ground and Steven's hands.

"No, oh no," Steven moaned. He turned his friend over and held him in his arms, the blood staining his uniform. The tears came and would not stop.

Tom sat near them, the tears flooding his eyes as well. He could hear the Yankees breaking through the tree line and he knew if they didn't move soon, they would be taken prisoner. He watched Steven holding on to Gerritt, sobs wracking his body, not wanting to release him to death and he knew right at this moment, it didn't matter.

The air was suddenly filled with shouts and yells. A fierce volley of bullets sailed over their heads, right into the Union line. Men in gray poured over the ground around them, pushing back the Yanks. They were Texans under John Bell Hood. They were their reinforcements and were now re-taking the bridge, pushing the Yanks back into a cornfield.

Tom touched Steven's shoulder. "Let's take 'im back to camp," he told him. "We kin takes ker of 'im there."

Steven looked up at Tom, the tears still pooling in his eyes. "He was my best friend," he said, his voice ragged with emotion. "We grew up together."

"I know boy, I know. But we needs to move back."

"What am I going to tell Colleen?" Steven said looking into the face of his friend, his gentle, kind friend who never had a bad word to say about anyone. "What will I tell his sister, his mother? They loved him so much. Oh, god!" he put his head back looking up into the trees as if the Almighty would give him the answers.

Tom could see that Steven was overcome with grief, not thinking clearly. He knew the boy had been through so much already. He was so young to be in war with all the killing, the hardships. First Charles was killed, then his father and now his best friend.

"Steven, I'll helps you git Gerritt back to camp," Tom said trying to lift Gerritt's body from him.

"No!" Steven yelled holding him tighter. "You're not taking him away!"

Tom knelt beside him and looked into his eyes. Steven was shaking, his breathing was coming in short gasps and his lips were trembling. He had pulled Gerritt's lifeless body close to his chest and had begun to rock back and forth.

Tom touched his arm. "Steven, Gerritt is powerful needin' to go back to camp. You wants to help him don't ya, Steven?"

At first there was no response, so Tom called his name again. "Steven!" This time he shook him.

Finally Steven looked up into Tom's eyes. "That's right boy, let's git Gerritt to the camp where's he'll be safe."

Steven finally nodded and allowed Tom to take Gerritt from him. He hoisted the body up in his arms and began carrying him through the woods, back to where they had camped near Sharpsburg. The battle still raged on nearby on a sunken county road. The road had become a rifle pit and the fighting could be heard as fierce, nearly continuous firing.

Steven had gotten up and followed Tom as he carried Gerritt. By the time they reached the camp, he had regained control of his emotions. Tom laid Gerritt down on the ground near to where a rudimentary hospital had been set up with a series of crude tents. Others, who had been wounded, lay on pallets, moaning and crying out.

A weary, blood spattered doctor walked over and kneeled next to Gerritt. "This boy's dead," he said looking up at them. He stood to his feet and pointed to a grassy area where several darkies were hard at work digging a large hole. Nearby; a long line of bodies.

"You need to take him over there for burial," the doctor told them. "There's nothin' I can do here." With that he turned his back and went to a man whose leg had been blown off.

Without a word, Tom picked up Gerritt's body and carried him over to the burial detail and laid him in line with the others. Steven began pulling on Tom's arm trying to get to Gerritt, but Tom held him back.

“You can’t put him here,” he told Tom frantically. “He can’t be buried here with these others. He has to go home to Shannon, to his mother and sister!”

Tom turned to him and grabbed his upper arms with both his hands and looked him directly in the eyes. “Son, I know you all’s rich and Gerritt’s daddy pulled strings and got your papa’s body sent home, but you don’t even knows where he’s at. He’s somewheres with General Cobb’s Georgia’s troops. I heerd they’se on their way to Fredricksburg. Even if you did find ‘im, he can’t do nothin’.

Look here,” he said pointing down the long line of bodies,” they all be common men, but all eats together, slept together, marched together, fought together and we dies together.” Tom stood out of the way so that Steven might see down the entire line of bodies. “We’se all equal in death; Gerritt’ll be with his comrades.”

Tears again filled Steven’s eyes and he nodded. “I know you’re right. It’s just so hard to let him go.”

“I know, son.”

“Do you think it would be alright if I stayed with him until…….”

“I’ll tell Sergeant Davis. I’se sure it’ll be fine.” Tom walked away leaving Steven alone with Gerritt.

Steven sat with Gerritt’s body as the sun began to fade behind the horizon. Long shadows crept over the fallen forms, the battle’s slaughtered children. He thought perhaps if he stared into the dear face long enough, he might perhaps stir and open his eyes.

But, he knew it wasn’t so. His friend had already gone cold to the touch. He could see the burial detail moving down the line of silent forms, gently laying them into the ground. By the time they reached Gerritt, it had grown dark, the stars the only other witness to Gerritt's burial.

The men lifted him up and a sob escaped Steven's lips, choking him. He had an overpowering urge to stop them, but he said nothing. He too, was laid next to the rest in the long grave. They began filling in the hole, the dirt thumping against the bodies.

Steven watched as if mesmerized until they had nearly gotten to Gerritt's body. Then finally, he turned away; not able to watch them cover him, to watch him disappear under the earth. He wanted to remember him in life, happy, carefree.

The battle sounds had stilled as darkness had surrounded them. Now he could hear the chirping of tree frogs and crickets, the low murmuring of the men. He wondered how everything could just go on the same. How could the sun come up in the morning, the rain fall from the sky, the stars twinkle in the heavens, when so much death went on? His father was gone, his dear friend; who would be next? Surely this must be hell.

He found his way back to his decimated company where Tom was sitting by a small campfire. He looked up as Steven sat down beside him. "Is it done?" he asked simply.

Steven only nodded, not being able to say the words aloud. Tom held out some rations, knowing he hadn't eaten since the day before. But Steven rejected the proffered food.

"Y'all needs to eat, son. We may finds ourselves doin' battle agin tomorrow, or iffen not, we'll be marchin'."

"It doesn't matter any longer," Steven told him. "If a bullet finds me or I fall along the way, I will at least end this pain I carry inside."

Tom signed loudly and wiped his hand across his eyes. "I know you'se hurtin' right now, but you gotta go on. There's people countin' on you; this here Confederacy for one. Y'all must'a jined up to fight fer somethin' beside that you thought it might be a lark. Those reasons still exist. All these men; yer pappy, Charles and Gerritt, should not die for nothin'. And if that don't convince you, then think about your Momma and fiancée back at home. Who's gonna take care of them now?"

"Colleen," Steven whispered.

"That's right," Tom told him, "your fiancée, Colleen. Think how heart broke she'd be iffen anythin' was to happen to you."

"My wife."

"What's that you say?"

"I said Colleen is my wife. We secretly married before I left."

"Well then son, all the more reason to keep on agoin' and git on home."

Steven put his head in his hands. "I may never see my darlin' Colleen again."

"Don't you think you otta try?" Tom asked. "Ain't she worth it?"

Steven looked at Tom with tears shinning in his eyes. "Yes, yes she is. Of course, you're right. I need to go on."

On that day, the losses were fearsome. It was the single bloodiest day of the war. Federal killed and wounded was twelve thousand five hundred men. Rebel losses exceeded eight thousand, but it was nearly a quarter of Lee's men.

Following a night of encampment, they marched south, crossed the Potomac once more and re-entered Virginia. Once onto home ground, they rested, their forces once again increased by new recruits and provisions handed out all around. Once again their bellies were full.

While there, news came down that Lincoln had issued an Emancipation Proclamation, declaring that beginning on the first of January 1863, anyone who was being held as a slave would be free, whether they be in slave or free state. For them this proclamation meant nothing. "Nice of 'im to jes be givin' away our property with no call," one of their number remarked. And no one was heard to argue.

After this respite, they headed out on the march towards Fredericksburg to rejoin General Lee. Steven knew that if he found James, he would have to tell him about Gerritt. He did not relish the task.

It was now December and the wind carried frost upon its wings and the colorful leaves lay scattered on the ground. They finally arrived at Fredericksburg, a sleepy little town on a branch of the river. This river made a bend a mile above Fredericksburg and for a great distance ran between heights on either side, each falling steeply to the riverbank. It was on the crest of these heights that half of Lee's army lay under the direction of General Longstreet.

On December thirteenth, the Union General Burnside, replacing McClellan, began the attack on the

Confederate line by repeated and continuous charges on the height of Marye's Hill.

Steven's brigade was not actively participating in the battle, being held in reserve at the crest of the hill. From this vantage point, they were able to watch the entire battle as it unfolded.

Across the river could be seen the stars and stripes unfurling in the breeze; the Union earthworks with their huge guns and down below them in the town of Fredericksburg, swarms of blue coats.

The guns began firing at ten o' clock, straight into the town, igniting it on fire. The charge on Maryre's Hill had also begun. It proved to be a fatal mistake, for at the crown of Maryre's Hill were two batteries of artillery with fifty more guns placed half a mile back to repulse all approaches.

Steven and the rest of his brigade, watched as wave after wave of Union troops attempted the attack on the hill, only to be slaughtered by the big guns. All day long, the carnage continued until it made them all sick at heart.

Just before sunset, Meagher's brigade of Irishmen from New York attempted a final assault. Never before had any of them seen such gallantry and bravery. Even though they had watched brigade after brigade rush forward only to be struck down by the hailstorm of lead, they pressed forward undaunted. Even from their hilltop vantage point, could be heard the cry, "Erin go Bragh", and they could be seen waving their green banner.

Batteries fired upon them and then the muskets began their deadly birage. Men fell, but others took their place time after time until the ground became littered with their bodies. They finally advanced within twenty yards of a stone wall, behind which lay the Confederate infantry.

"That's Cobb's Georgians," Tom said quietly. His voice sounded loud to Steven in spite of the battle raging below. He realized not a man had spoken since the assault began, as if everyone were holding his breath.

They heard the infantry fire as one simultaneous burst, hurled against the enemy. The force of their iron hail drove them back and no waiting men came forward as they had all been swept away by the fire from the surrounding gullies and ravines. Suddenly, there was silence and when the musket smoke had cleared, they could see thousands lying dead, scattered over an area not more than eight hundred yards wide.

Steven's regiment looked over the scene with horror. In spite of the fact that these men were the enemy they were men nonetheless; brave and valiant men.

"Damn, them were brave men," one of their group commented.

"Aye," said another, "hats off to the Yankee Irishmen from New York."

So ended the battle of Fredricksburg with all military operations ceasing for the winter. A long rain followed the battle and then a hard freeze. The streams and the ground were frozen and the men could only huddle around fires, wrapped in blankets.

Steven's regiment, as did all others, finally went into winter camp, constructing every manner of shelter, be it hut, hovel, shack, or cabin. Tom and Steven put together a crude hut with a firepit. It was something to give them temporary shelter for a few months.

Winter camp was a chance to relax, to socialize with friends and to rest from their many months of battle, but it was also a time of reflection. The long days of inactivity caused Steven to think back to better times in his youth, when parties, horse racing and gambling were his prime concerns in life. Now he worried about where his next meal was coming from and whether or not he would live through the next battle.

His thoughts turned more and more to Colleen and whether he would ever see her again, whether he would ever truly claim her as his wife. He still remembered that day they married, how the sun had shone through the window making gold shimmers in her hair. He remembered how her face had glowed with absolute radiant love and joy. And he remembered too, how she had felt naked in his arms, the way her body had felt next to his and how glorious making love to her had been. Thoughts such as these only caused him to feel depressed and he would sometimes sit for hours at a time staring into the fire.

He thought about that day at Fredricksburg when he had finally found James and told him what had happened to Gerritt. It had been awful to watch the spirit drain from him, to see him crushed and devastated. He had cried and Steven had tried to comfort him the best he could, but what comfort can there be for a father who has lost a son?

He had had to write to Mary and Colleen about Gerritt. It had been the most difficult letter he had ever composed, to put into words something that he knew would be devastating, was a painful task.

Christmas brought with it a severe snowstorm, driving everyone inside to escape. Those soldiers from Virginia who had family in the area, were provided with many a treat for the holidays. The others, which included Steven and Tom, were not as fortunate. Their Christmas dinner consisted of a pound of fat pork, crackers and a quarter pound of dried apples. Considering some of the meager rations in the past, they considered themselves fortunate.

At times they would break the monotony of the long winter by engaging in snowball fights. Toombs Georgians, sporting a red undershirt flag, while the Virginians heralded a gray pair of breeches, charged each other with haversacks full of snowballs. It was fierce fighting with all participants covered in glory with snow.

Finally, the cold winds of winter declined and the breath of spring blew across the land. With it came the wetness and mud, which adhered to everything unfortunate to come in contact with it. Men, horses, artillery, pontoons and wagons became marooned in it. Mules actually drowned in it. Along with it also came illness, colds, and afflictions of the throat and lungs, sending many of the men to the hospital. Many died there of scurvy, dysentery, typhoid, diphtheria and pneumonia. They were just more victims of this interminable conflict.

Spring finally broke forth with all its glory, flowers blooming, fragrant petals drifting like snow upon the green grass. It was May and Virginia was in all its beauty.

The troops had been moved to Richmond for respite after the first battle since winter quarters, at Chancellorsville. Steven and Tom's regiment had not participated in this battle either, but reports had told of a glorious victory. The only fly in the ointment was that Stonewall Jackson had been wounded.

Spirits were high, with the talk of ultimate victory on the lips of everyone. The Confederacy's many victories had put confidence in the hearts of the whole city. Then came the devastating news; Stonewall Jackson had succumbed to his wounds. The great, beloved general was dead. The word traveled quickly, in the streets, in the shops. Women were weeping openly as if he had been a near and dear relative.

He had been an idol, a hero to the soldiers; the General who had stood steadfast at Manassas, who had bested the hail of lead at Gaines Mill and had faced death at Sharpsburg and Bull Run. It was almost unthinkable that he could be gone, to lead them no more. The whole Confederacy felt the grief.

The next day at 3:00 P.M., every bell in the city began to toll as the train bearing his body drew into the station. A mass of humanity filled the streets as they took the coffin unto the platform. Soldiers and citizens alike were crying openly as they lifted their fallen hero into the hearse.

The following day, all the troops lined up by company and marched behind the casket cassion, Jackson's horse was led riderless, behind the hearse. In spite of the heat thousands lined the streets as their beloved general passed by. Even men who had been wounded, made their way outside to salute the man who had led them to many victories.

After Sonewall Jackson's death, the army was given a reprieve. It was a time to mend, a time to heal, a time to replenish. New troops were brought in, vigorous, ebullient in their confidence to whip the Yankees in short order. They were anxious to participate in their first battle.

Steven and the other seasoned soldiers looked on their exuberance with understanding and sadness. They remembered a time when they too, looked forward to facing the enemy, to prove their mettle, when glory seemed so honorable. But they also knew that all too soon, too many of them would die in their determined effort to be a part of the struggle for their independence.

Near the end of May, Lee divided his troops into three corps. Steven and Tom were with another Georgian, James Longstreet, who asked his men to call him Old Pete. Lee, referred to him as his old warhorse.

They began to advance north, right into Union territory, into the fields of Pennsylvania. On July 1st they found themselves in a sleepy little town called Gettysburg. On the outskirts of town was a seminary and nearby, a cemetery surrounded by a white picket fence. Everywhere they looked were fields and orchards with split rail fences surrounded by rolling, wooded hills with mountains in the background.

The sky was azure blue with pale, low hanging clouds, but it was July and the heat was oppressive.

"Neva knew the north could be so hot," one man from Alabama remarked as he wiped his brow.

"Did ya think it all snow and cold?" Tom asked him.

"I dunno," the man answered, "I reckon I hadn't thought much on it."

Tom grinned, "When them Yankee artillery opens up, it'll get lots hotter, I 'spect."

They didn't have long to wait. Union forces had gathered in the town and at the Seminary on the outskirts. Confederate troops were spread out along the hills, surrounding the town.

Attacking Confederate troops pushed the Union line through the town, causing a retreat to twin hills; one Little Round Top, the other Big Round Top. These were rock and boulder strewn hills, rising up from the trees and fields below.

Steven's company was prepared to advance on the hills under General Longstreet, wanting to strike while the iron was hot, but General Lee over ruled him and requested the men stop and rest for the evening.

They sat around their fires after dark, new recruits and old, contemplating the coming day. Union fires could be seen flickering in the distance, the men knowing that they too, were apprehensive about what the morrow would bring.

Steven sat silent, staring into the flames. He was becoming weary of this war. It was difficult to imagine he had been fighting for nearly two years. His principles about why they were fighting were still strong, but he had lost his desire for the fight. Too many men had died; too many would carry for the rest of their lives, the mutilations and scars. Mothers, daughters, wives, on both sides, grieved for those who would never return.

So many good souls who had suffered so much; they had endured sleep deprivation, starvation, lack of even meager supplies, days of forced marches, living in intolerable weather conditions with no shoes, or adequate clothing.

How long would they have to continue? When would the breaking point come? Which would be the decisive battle? So far, the Confederate states had done well, claiming victory in the majority of battles. But how many more lives would it claim? When would the supply of fresh bodies run out? He looked into the faces of the new recruits and saw the fear shinning in their eyes, remembering when it was so for him also. Now, for those who had seen many battles, there was a kind of resignation, a fatalistic attitude. Not that their hearts didn't beat faster or feel panic when confronted with a barrage of rifle fire, but the constant terror did not live inside them any longer. Part of his resignation was also due to the grief he still felt for his father and Gerritt. At times when it was quiet and he had time to reflect, the hurt would come crashing down and everything seemed hopeless.

The following day broke clear and hot. There was no breeze and the sun felt oppressive. No movement was taking place and the men laid about in camp, trying to rest and keep out of the sun. Some gambled and played cards, others made sure their rifles were clean. Steven spent his time shaving off his full beard, using a straight razor and a borrowed mirror.

"What made you think on takin' off your whiskers?" Tom asked as he fingered his own long beard.

"Just got sick of it, is all," Steven told him. "First I was just sick of shavin', but now I'm sick of havin' it full of dirt and lice, so it's comin' off."

"Seems, you jes picked a mighty peculiar time for it, is all," Tom said squatting next to him.

"I figure it's as good a time as any, even if I have to go into battle with whiskers on half my face and the other half not. If nothin' else it'd give those Yanks a start."

Tom laughed at the picture of Steven charging the ranks, screaming the Rebel cry with his face half shaved. Steven joined in the laughter, enjoying the release it provided.

It wasn't until 4:00 in the afternoon that the artillery fire began. Longstreet put John B. Hood in charge of the troops while Dan Sickles went to occupy Cemetery Ridge. Steven's regiment lined up and they marched towards Little Round Top where Union troops held the uppermost position. If they could gain the stronghold, they would be able to overtake the main body behind it. Simultaneously, Lee planned to attack the other Union flank.

Steven marched with his company through a peach orchard and across a wheat field to the base of the steep incline called Little Round Top. He gazed up the slope and observed the rocky, boulder-strewn approach. Shielding his eyes from the sun, he looked up at the summit. He could see flashes of light as the sun glinted off the bayonets of the men in blue.

Sergeant Davis assembled them in their ranks and as Longstreet's guns opened up, they began the charge. Steven tried maneuvering his way across the rocks. Some were as large as a fist, others the size of his head and still others, as large as a horse. It was difficult to traverse, his feet turning over between them. He had to put out his hands to keep from falling. He found the rocks hot to the touch from the scorching sun. Bullets flew all around from the men on top. Some hit the rocks, ricocheting off and hitting men.

He and Tom crouched down behind one of the larger boulders. "How's we suppose to shoot up hill and hit somethin'?" Tom asked above the din.

"Good question," Steven answered. "They can just sit up there and pick us off."

"This here be the devil's den," Tom commented.

Sergeant Davis ran ahead of them, calling orders, encouraging them to move forward. They scrambled out from behind the rock and began their assault again, stopping occasionally to fire their muskets.

They finally reached the base of the hill where a tree line began and rose to the top. There, they stopped to re-group. General Hood shouted orders, explaining how they were to charge the hill and take the top from the Yankees. If they could seize Little Round Top, the Union line on the other side would be exposed to their deadly fire.

They lined up in formation again and with the call, they all surged forward, firing as they went. Steven began running up the hill, dodging rocks and trees, firing up into the blue line at the top. All he could see were hundreds of muskets firing down upon them, smoke filled the air, minnie balls whizzed past so close, he could hear the air passing. They slammed into the trees, the rocks, the ground. Many of those around him were falling, wounded or dead. His heart was racing, the blood pounded in his ears, and still he kept firing. The closer he came to the top, the easier it was to see the determined look on the faces of the Yanks firing back at him.

He hid behind trees whenever he could. He stepped over his fallen comrades and then he saw General Hood wounded, lying on the ground in front of him. He kneeled next to him and began lifting him under the arms to drag him to safety. "Call the retreat," he told Steven. "We are being over run, call the retreat!"

"Retreat men!" Steven yelled to his comrades. "By order of General Hood, retreat!" Steven continued backing down the slope, pulling the General with him. Once they got to the bottom, they regrouped around their fallen General.

"Take them around to the left and try again," he told the Captain. "Storm that blue line and claim the hill top."

Again, they formed their lines and began their assault, following the colors. They gained more ground and more men fell dead.

Steven could see the faces of the Yankee soldiers, scared, determined, their rifle muzzles glaring down at him. The order came to fall back once again and re-group. They picked up unused ammunition from their fallen comrades. They were running dangerously low.

Steven saw Tom across the line from where he stood. His face was scratched and bruised, but he appeared otherwise unhurt.

They were directed not to fire until they were close enough to see the enemy's face. Once more they stormed the hill, closer and closer to the Union held top. Fire, stop, re-load, fire again. It became automatic.

Everywhere Steven looked, there were bodies strewn about, piled on top of one another, blood pooling in the rocks, saturating the ground. Others, wounded, moaned or cried out. But he had no opportunity to stop.

Up ahead, those who had reached the Union line before him were fighting hand to hand with the Yanks. Now he was close to the top, his bayonet fixed, ready for the battle. A soldier in blue pointed his gun at him and for a brief moment he thought he was about to die. Quickly he ducked down and then rapidly rose up underneath the man's arm, thrusting his bayonet into his side. The soldier's eyes widened, his mouth opened in a silent cry and then he fell over dead. He didn't have time to think about it, as another man charged him bayonet first. Before he could be impaled, he fired his gun, killing him.

There were too many of them, swarming over the ground with a fierce determination, stabbing, shooting at close range; men falling everywhere.

Someone came up behind him, stabbed, but he moved quickly and the blade caught him in the arm. A hot, white fire spread through the upper part of his arm. He felt blood flowing out onto his shirt.

Then he heard Sergeant Davis calling the retreat. His remaining comrades were fleeing back down the hill and

Steven quickly followed. The scattered remains of their regiment met together at the base of the hill, dragging their wounded with them. The assault on Little Round Top was a failure and they moved back to where they had camped the night before. The wounded, General Hood among them, were moved to an abandoned house, now a temporary hospital. They were not able to gather their dead as the Union troops still swarmed over the hills.

Steven found Tom near the Plum Run stream, washing the blood from his face. "How are you?" he asked.

"Feelin' like a fool," he said looking up at Steven, water running from his beard. "I jes fell plum on my face, broke my nose. Other than that, I made it through that hell alive.

Hold on, son, you've been wounded!" he said noticing the blood on Steven's arm. "You should be at the hospital." He led Steven to the bank and sat him down in the grass.

"It's not that bad. Yankee bayonet just caught my arm. The doctors have enough to do with the serious wounds."

"Iffen you don't takes care of it, it'll fester and kills you," Tom told him helping him remove his shirt.

Steven looked at the wound for the first time. "See, I was right. It went clear through the skin, didn't hit the bone or anything."

"That sucker still's deep," he told Steven wiping his arm with the wet cloth he had been using on his face. "Lookee, it's still bleedin'."

Tom washed the wound and then bound it with strips from the cloth. It was beginning to be quite painful. He remembered when James had received a similar wound back at Williamsburg. He wondered where his father-in-law was now. He did know Cobb's Georgians were somewhere right here at Gettysburg.

The following day the Virginians renewed their attack on Culp's Hill, but the Yankees were too strong and they withdrew. The day was dry and hot, no clouds could be seen. It was scorching and the men felt debilitated in the heat.

By one o'clock in the afternoon cannon after cannon was brought up to Cemetery Ridge, and pointed directly at Union General Meade's vast regiments of troops.

Lee had put General Pickett in charge of the Confederate troops. Rebel forces were gathered in the woods and over a mile away, across broad, open fields were the Union army, taking cover behind a long stone wall. Regiments from all over the south were gathered in these woods, Virginians, Alabamans, North and South Carolinians, and Georgians.

Steven saw James once again. He thought he looked fairly well, considering; considering the toll of war, months and months without adequate sustenance, witnessing friends and comrades dying, the death of his own son. Physically he appeared to be healthy, but there was a haunted look in his eyes that hadn't been there before.

He had hugged him and called him son, something he had not done before. Steven was tempted to tell him about his and Colleen's marriage, but he knew this was not the time.

They were lined up in the woods, a mile long and nearly as deep, waiting to storm over the fields to attack the Yanks on the other side of the wall. Men talked quietly amongst themselves, others prayed. Everyone looking across that wide expanse of ground felt they would surely die crossing so vast an open area. It was too far, too open. What could Lee be thinking?

As soon as every cannon in their arsenal had been assembled, they loosed their torrent of shot and shell. Union batteries returned fire, the shells hitting in the trees over their heads. The noise was deafening, constant and relentless. The air was filled with smoke until the wall at the other side of the field could no longer be seen.

General's Longstreet and Pickett called the orders to resume their formation. Line upon line moved into position behind the trees. Steven and Tom were about half way back in the line, completely surrounded by their comrades. Some of the men fidgeted in line, nervous, others stood silent, staring straight ahead.

The battery fire had ceased, the Confederates having depleted their supply of ammunition. The silence was nearly as deafening as the shelling had been. No one spoke, waiting for the orders to begin the assault.

Steven looked over at Tom. There were no words spoken, but each knew they were experiencing the same emotions. They had a feeling of dread, that this could be their last day. How could anyone possibly cross that wide field, out in the open, with the full assault of the Union army firing down upon them, and survive?

The order was given for the ready. Each man checked his weapon and ammunition; bayonets were fixed. Then they heard the call, "Forward, march!" and every man surged towards the field, yelling the Rebel cry. Each man carried with him, not only his gun and ammunition, but also his haversack, blanket and heavy cartridge case. Steven's arm was still sore. He could feel stabs of pain running down his arm like small needles.

The troops swarmed across the open space, line after line, thousands of men; the sun glinting off the muzzles of their guns. They marched and marched, covering the distance between them and the Union lines. As soon as they were within range, they began firing. Men in front of them were dropping, others taking their place, closing in on their flag; as they did so the line behind kept shortening up. So many muskets were all going off at once, it was deafening. Smoke obscured their vision, but still they moved forward.

Steven could feel the heat baking on his shoulders, the sweat running down his face and back. The bullets were close, thudding into the ground near his feet, whizzing past his head, smacking into the body of the man ahead of him.

Sights and sounds assaulted him. The blinding sun and dense smoke obscured his vision. He couldn't even see the blue line he was firing into. He saw the men lying on the ground, stepping over their bodies as he went. He could hear the shouts of the officers as they yelled encouragement. General Armistead could be seen riding straight for the Union line, his hat on his sword, cheering his men.

Steven heard men screaming and moaning, the ripping of flesh, the thud as a body hit the ground. He could hear the Union soldiers yelling: “Fredricksburg! Fredricksburg!”

He was getting closer now, running towards the wall, firing his rifle. Men in front of him had flattened themselves to the ground to avoid being annihilated. He could see the Yankee faces, the determination, the hate.

Then a massive pain ripped through his leg, fiery, horrendous and he fell, his gun flying through the air. He was looking up into the blue sky while others stepped over him. He tried to rise, to go on, but the pain ripped through his leg so horribly, he cried out. He suddenly realized he was wounded. He tentatively looked down at his left leg and all he could see was pieces of flesh and massive amounts of blood. He felt as if he were going to pass out and lay back down on the ground. As he lay there he was surprised to feel a kind of calm. He could hear his heart beating, could feel the blood flowing from his leg.

“I’m dieing,” he whispered to himself. And then his thoughts turned to Colleen. “I’m so sorry my sweet, Colleen.” And then as the shells burst around him and men screamed, the world went black.

CHAPTER TWELVE —July 1863

Colleen couldn't believe it was now over two years since this horrible war began; so much suffering, so much loss of life. The war had touched everyone. She didn't know of a single family who had not lost a loved one in this terrible conflict. Her friend Cynthia had lost her cousin, that sweet boy Andrew Hunter had died somewhere in Virginia, and of course Clifford Covington. But now their own family had been touched. Just this past spring, they had received word of Gerritt's death at some far away place called Sharpesburg.

When they had gotten the news, her mother had collapsed. They had put her to bed and she had not been able to get up for over a week. Her sobs could be heard all over the house. For a time, she was so hysterical; she was out of her mind with grief.

Colleen, herself had wept almost continually, not being able to accept the fact that her brother would not be coming home. They couldn't even bring the body back as they had Clifford's, to bury in the family cemetery.

She had thought so many times of their growing up together. The way Gerritt had played games with her, sometimes taking her down to the slave quarters where she would play marbles, jump rope, tag and other games with the little darkie children.

Gerritt had held her hand as they took walks together and always, always protected her. She had remembered one time when she was perhaps three and had wandered down to the river following a pair of ducks. Standing on the bank, she had nearly fallen in, but Gerritt had caught her by the edge of her skirt and saved her. He had been the one to teach her to ride and had been the one to comfort her when she had fallen off. The thought of Gerritt lying cold in the ground caused her to cry and cry until she thought she could cry no longer and then she would cry some more.

Once her mother had finally come downstairs from her room, she was a changed woman. She spoke little and stared into nothingness, even when spoken to. Both Colleen and Anna Bell had tried to comfort her, but for many months nothing would console her.

Even the servants had gone about their chores with tears in their eyes, for they had truly loved Gerritt. He had always been kind and compassionate towards them, frequently asking after their welfare. Dora especially, had grieved a great deal, for she had been like a mother to him, caring for him since a baby. Colleen saw her despair, but she could say nothing to ease her pain. Her own was so great she had no energy to be able to help anyone else. She had felt tired of life, weary of just going on, of hearing dread news of the war.

The Christmas Ball her mother had wanted to put on last December had never happened. So many of their friends were grieving and had already lost so much to the war that they had refused to participate. So her mother had reluctantly cancelled and they had spent a quiet Christmas with just the three of them. It had been so sad celebrating without their men, wondering, but never voicing whether it would always be this way.

Everyone was suffering, whether from loss of a loved one or physical with loss of property and means of living. They too, lived in a kind of managed chaos. Confederate officials had come and told them what they must plant and when and when the crop came in, they were to turn it over to the Confederacy. Their own supplies were dangerously low and while more and more of the slaves were idle, they still needed to be fed. Flour was all but impossible to get and sugar was just as scarce. Slaves had their own small gardens to supplement what they received from the big house. The cattle and chickens were slowly being killed off as the need arose. They had received no imported items since the blockade such as coffee, bananas and clothing from Europe. The food in their own home was rationed, not knowing how long their supplies would have to last. Even oil for the lamps was only burned when absolutely necessary. The cotton they had left was stored in the barns. Some was used to spin for cloth and made into simple clothing for the servants. Shoes could not be had at any price. They had even read in the papers that many of their own troops were barefoot. No one complained.

At the news of Gerritt's death, Colleen had also worried about Steven and her father, but shortly after she had received a letter from him telling her they were well and how grieved he was over Gerritt's death. He had told her he had been with him when he died and had seen to his burial. She had wept again over the letter.

Now it was July and they had gone on, just as everyone else had who had lost loved ones, but it was not easy. Her mother, like Anna Bell, seldom smiled anymore and would cry at any reminder of Gerritt. Colleen too, grieved for her brother, but she was young and it was difficult being in a house of sadness all the time. She took to riding her horse nearly every day to get away and enjoy the countryside.

One warm sunny day, she had taken Princess out for her daily ride. She had stopped by the river to avail herself of the shade under the weeping willows. She even took off her riding boots and waded part way into the water, letting the coolness flow over her hot, sticky feet, while Princess drank at the edge. She dipped her handkerchief into the water and then wiped her face and neck. The cold felt refreshing. She put her head back and looked up into the sky.

What was Steven doing right now? She wondered. Was he looking up into this same sky? Was he fighting a battle or marching down some dusty road?

She sighed, knowing she had no answers to her questions. She gathered up Princess's reins and began leading her back to the stable. Once she had been safely unsaddled and put into her stall with fresh hay, Colleen started back to the house. She hadn't gotten very far when she heard the screaming. She began to run and as she came around the side of the house, she saw the telegraph boy's horse disappearing down the lane. She knew that could only mean one thing and she felt her heart skip a beat. Her hand went to her throat and her legs felt weak.

When she neared the front of her house, she saw her mother and Anna Bell sitting, collapsed on the veranda. But, it was Anna Bell who was screaming and holding the scrap of paper in her hand. Her mother was next to her, holding her.

Colleen stopped. "No!" she whispered, and then louder, "No! Not Steven!" She began to run again until she was standing in front of the two women. Her heart was pounding so hard, it felt as if it would rip from her chest. She wanted to ask, needed to ask, but the words would not come out.

Anna Bell was crying and screaming hysterically. She knew it had to be Steven, but how could she ask if her beloved husband were dead? She kept looking from her mother to Anna Bell, but neither was saying anything.

Finally she could bear it no longer and tore the paper from Anna Bell's hands. The telegram read: *Dear Mrs. Covington stop I regret to inform you that your son Private Steven Covington was wounded at the battle of Gettysburg stop He was taken prisoner by the Union forces stop He is believed to be in a military hospital somewhere in Pennsylvania stop Sincerest regrets stop Sergeant Davis C.S.A.*

The paper fell from her hand and fluttered to the ground unheeded. "He's not dead," she finally said. The two women looked up at her. "He's not dead," she repeated. "My god, be grateful he's still alive!"

"But he's wounded and in a Yankee hospital," her mother said. "We don't know how serious he is or if he will survive. And if he does, what will those Yankees do to him?"

"I don't know," Colleen told her. "I can't think about that right now. I only care that he's alive. We've got to get him home."

Mary stood up to face her. "And how do you purpose to do that?" she asked.

"I don't know," Colleen said the tears beginning to form in her eyes. "Isn't there some important person we can wire that will be able to get him released?"

"He's a prisoner, Colleen and the only people we know are Southerners. They are enemies. They can't do anything."

The tears overflowed and spilled down her face. She rushed past the two women and into the house. She went up the stairs and down the hall into her room. Once there, she collapsed on her bed in sobs.

Dora heard her cries and came into the room. She stood by the side of the bed, silent, allowing Colleen to cry. Finally she spoke. "Missy, there be anythin' I kins do?"

Colleen ignored her at first, the ache inside so powerful. "Does it be Massa Steven?" Dora asked with trembling in her voice.

Colleen rolled over on her back, her eyes wet and puffy, her moans still audible. "He's not dead," she told Dora.

"Missy?"

"Steven, he's not dead, but he was wounded and taken prisoner." She covered her face with her hands.

"What that means?" Dora asked.

"I don't know," Colleen said sitting up on the edge of the bed. "I just don't know. The telegram said he had been wounded, but we don't know how seriously. He…. he might not…..have survived." She began to cry again just saying the horrible words.

"But, you say mebbe he be alive?" Dora asked hopefully.

Colleen nodded. "They say he was taken prisoner, probably in Pennsylvania."

"Pennysl……" Dora struggled over the unfamiliar word.

"It's a place up north, very far away."

"Dem Yankees, they takes ker of 'im?"

"Oh, god, I hope so, Dora. I certainly hope so."

That night she could not sleep for the constant thoughts of Steven. She could still hear Anna Bell sobbing in her room down the hall. They were only able to calm her somewhat by reminding her that Steven was still alive. They tried to reassure her by telling her that he was in a hospital and surely was being cared for by a kind hearted Yankee woman. Only a mother could know the grief of the loss of a son and therefore, they would take splendid care of him. But Colleen was not sure she believed it herself.

Where was he, her handsome beloved husband? Was he truly still alive and if so, in what condition? Was he in a lot of pain? Did he think of her? Would he ever come home to her again?

It was so difficult thinking of him as a prisoner of the Yankees. What would they do to him? Would they torture him? She finally fell into a fitful sleep, dreaming of battered and torn bodies, screaming men as battle raged around them. She awoke with tears running down her face. She reached for the portrait of Steven she kept on her bedside table. She ran her fingers over the profile of his features. "Where are you, my darling?" she whispered.

The following morning was raining and dreary, fitting all their moods. Colleen and Mary came down for breakfast, but Anna Bell stayed in bed. Mary went to her daughter and gave her a hug.

"How are you doing, sweetheart? I know this news of Steven must be devestatin' for you."

"I'm alright," she said going to the buffet. She put some fruit on her plate. She really didn't feel like eating at all. "I refuse to believe he's dead," she told her mother as she sat at the table. "The telegram said he was a prisoner and I'm going to believe he'll be alright. We just have to get him home."

"Well, I explained to you yesterday that it's impossible for us to do that," Mary said folding her napkin on her lap. "We'll just have to pray for him and wait for this war to be over. Then they'll have to release him."

"What if that's too late?" Colleen asked leaning forward towards her mother. "What if this war continues for years? He could die in prison before that happens."

"I don't know what you want me to tell you. It's all we women can do. We wait. I have to wait for your father to come home and you'll just have to wait for Steven."

"I hate waiting. I want to do something."

"You're just going to have to accept it and live with it. There is nothing you can do."

"I refuse to sit back and allow my husband to die in some Yankee prison!" Colleen yelled, standing and slamming her hand on the table. Too late, she realized what she had said.

"What was that?" Mary asked. "I believe you misspoke. You meant to say, your fiancée."

Colleen sat down slowly, turning everything over in her mind. Should she tell her mother the truth? "No, I did not misspeak. Steven is my husband," she told her quietly.

"How can that be? No, you were never married. He left before that could happen," Mary said beginning to get agitated.

"One day when you and father and Gerritt had gone visiting, I went to Steven's and there, on that day, we were married."

"But how, who married you?" her mother asked.

"We married ourselves. We said our vows to each other before God," Colleen told her mother.

"Well, there you have it then. The marriage wasn't real, not legal."

"It was very real, Mother. We are married. We took our vows very seriously. Just because there was no clergy there, doesn't mean we aren't truly married in the eyes of God, just not for the state."

"Of course, you're not married. Don't be ridiculous, Colleen. It isn't real if you don't have a minister." Her mother had gotten up from the table and had started pacing the floor.

"Listen to me, mother," Colleen said patiently. "Steven and I are husband and wife in every way."

"No!" Mary said putting her hand to her heart. "You don't mean to tell me, you… and Steven have……."

"Yes, Mother, that's what I'm telling you."

"How could you!" her mother shouted. "You're tarnished, no longer a virgin."

"Is that all you care about, whether I'm still a virgin? Doesn't it matter that Steven and I love each other; that we wanted to marry and be close before he left?"

"All I know is, that Steven took advantage of you because he was going off to war and you….why you're no better than a common whore! What would have happened if you got pregnant?"

"If you weren't my mother, I'd slap you for saying that. All you care about is your little improprieties and what the neighbors might say. People are dieing, mother," she shouted throwing her hands in the air. "Who cares about the neighbors and who is wearing the right style or was seen with the mayor, or who threw the largest ball? We're in the middle of a war. People are suffering. I would think you'd have a little more compassion, be a little more understanding." Her anger had turned to tears and she turned to leave the room.

"Colleen, it's not that I don't understand being young and in love, but what you did was wrong!"

"No, it wasn't mother," Colleen said turning back to face her. "We love each other very much and we <u>are</u> married." She left and went up the stairs to her room.

At first she paced about wringing her hands, so angry with her mother that she was brought to tears. "I know I shouldn't have told her," she said to herself. "She just doesn't understand. The only thing that should matter is getting Steven out of that prison and home, but how, how can I do that?"

She sat in the chair near the window and put her face in her hands. Slowly, an idea began forming in her mind. She stood and went to her dressing table, looking herself over, turning first one way and then the other. Dora walked into the room just as Colleen was pulling her hair back from her face.

"What you be doin', Missy?" Dora asked.

"I think I've thought of a way to find Steven," she said excitedly.

"How's you gwine to be doin' that?"

Colleen turned to her, her eyes wide. "I'm going to join the army and make my way to Pennsylvania. Most of the fighting has been in Virginia and that's close to Pennsylvania. Somehow I'll find my way there."

Dora laughed. "That be a joke?"

"It's no joke, Dora. I'm seriously thinking of doing it."

"They don' lets no womens in the war, does they?" Dora asked.

"No, but if they don't know I'm a woman……"

"What's that you talkin' chil'?"

"I could cut my hair, dress like a man and join the army."

"I thinks griefs gots you teched in the head," Dora said walking over to feel her forehead.

Colleen's mind raced. The more she thought about it, the better she liked it. "I'll get myself some men's clothing, boots, whatever else men use, and I'll….why, I'll just become a man."

Dora covered her mouth with her hand and broke out into giggles. "'Cuse me, Missy, but you jes ain't no man. What you thinks you gwine to do wif them breasts you gots?"

Colleen looked down at her bosom, cupping them in her hands. "Oh well, I'm not really that big and I'm sure we'll think of somethin'."

"We, what's dis we business?"

"I'll need your help and you've got to promise to keep it a secret."

Dora looked closely at the excitement shinning in her eyes, the flush on her cheeks and she realized she was serious. "Missy, I scairt. You can'st be doin' this," she told her mistress.

"Dora, I am going to do this, with or without your help. Now, I just have to figure out the details and when would be the best time to go. I want to get started as soon as possible. I've got to find Steven before anything worse befalls him and bring him home.

Now find me a haversack. I think you might find one in the stables. Then I need some men's clothes, perhaps someone in the servants quarters would have something that would fit. I'll try to gather some things here."

"I jes thinks this be a bad idea," Dora said again. "How you thinks you gonna fights?"

"I can shoot a gun as well as any man. Gerritt taught me and I can reload, too."

"But what 'bout the killin'?"

"I.....well, I'll just cross that bridge when I come to it."

"I can'st 'llow you to do this," Dora told her. "I takes ker 'o you since you was a bare butt baby chil' and I say it be too dangerous."

Colleen stared directly at Dora and took hold of her arm very firmly. "Who do you think you are talkin' to? You will not allow me? Let me tell you, Dora, if you do not co-operate with me, or if you tell anyone, even your friends in the quarters, I swear I will sell you. And don't think I wouldn't. You know I never threatened you before. That should tell you how serious I am."

Dora only nodded, realizing she had stepped over her bounds. "I does what you say, Missy," she said quietly.

"I'm sorry, Dora," Colleen told her more gently, "but this means everything to me. After all, what's the worst that could happen; they find out I'm a woman and send me home?"

"You could dies, Missy," Dora whispered as tears shown in her eyes.

"If I don't do something to get Steven out and he dies, then I don't want to live either."

Dora said no more, but began following Colleen's instructions. By the end of the week, she had collected all the items she had requested and.Colleen herself had found some things on her own. She had gone into Gerritt's room. She hadn't been there since the notification of his death. Everything was the same as it had been the day he left. It was eerie being there, as if his spirit somehow dwelt there. She had touched some of the things on his dressing table as though she could feel him through his belongings. Then she had gone into his armoire, his clothes still hanging neatly, shirts crisply pressed. She had held her nose to them, smelling his scent, bringing the tears to her eyes again.

Finally, she had found a couple of shirts he had only worn for working in, plain, muslin. And at the bottom, among his dress shoes and riding boots, were an old worn pair of boots, obviously too small for him. She had no idea why they were there, but she was grateful.

The last item she needed was a gun. Late at night, after her mother and Anna Bell had gone to bed, she snuck down to her father's study in the library. She had been so afraid, she could hear her heart pounding in her ears and every creak of the floorboards caused her to gasp. But then she found herself in front of the glass-encased cabinet, which held James's gun collection. She removed a Springfield and its ammunition. It was the one she had been taught to shoot with. Then carefully, she had locked the cabinet and replaced the key in the desk drawer.

Later, she packed the haversack containing some change of clothing, a few toiletries and a bedroll. These, along with the gun, she hid under the bed. Dora was there to help her.

"I still don' sees hows you thinks you can be a man," she told Colleen.

"It'll work, it just has to. It's the only way I can think of to get Steven back.

Now I want you to go to where my mother keeps her sewing and bring me her large scissors and several rolls of those bandages she's been rolling. And make sure no one sees you."

"Yes'm," Dora answered as she hurried away to do as bided. When she returned with the requested items, she found Colleen sitting at her dressing table staring into the mirror.

She stroked her face with one hand while holding her hair back with the other. "Do you think I'll make a good boy?" she asked Dora as she came into the room. "I'll have to tell them I'm sixteen," she said without waiting for an answer, "young enough that I haven't started shaving yet. I'll have to always remember to speak in lower tones," she said speaking gruffly.

"What you wants wif this scissors?" Dora asked.

"I want you to cut my hair off, of course," she told her. "I can't very well pose as a man with this long hair now, can I?"

Dora's mouth fell open and there was an audible gasp. "Oh, no missy; I can'st do that. You gots the mos' beautiful hair. I can't jes cuts it all off."

"Oh yes you can," Colleen said turning to look at her. "If I tell you to cut it, that's exactly what you'll do."

"Yes'm Missy," Dora complied, coming up behind her with the large scissors. Her face betrayed her disappointment and Colleen could see tears in her eyes, but she didn't care. She was doing this for Steven.

She gathered all her hair into a ribbon at the back of her head. The long auburn tresses reached all the way to her waist. "All right now, cut it above the ribbon," she instructed. "After all, I can always grow it back," she said encouragingly.

Her hands trembling, Dora grasped the thick bundle of hair and began sawing across with the scissors. It wasn't long before the full length was separated. For a moment, the two of them stared in silence at Colleen's reflection in the mirror. She touched the sides, which still hung below her ears.

"It needs to be shorter," she told Dora quietly. It was trimmed and trimmed until it was as short as some men's. Then Colleen took a comb and combed it back away from her face.

"You still looks like a woman wif really short hair," Dora commented.

"We'll just have to wait until I have all the clothes on."

"Iffen your Mammy sees you, you in big trouble," Dora said still holding the length of hair.

"My mother is not going to see me. Now listen carefully. I want all this hair cleaned up. I want no strand left, you understand?"

"Yes'm, but cans I keeps this?" Dora asked holding up the beribboned tresses. "Please missus?"

"Alright, but you take it to your own cabin and hide it. You mustn't allow my mother to see it.

I also need you to go to the stables before first light and have a horse saddled for me. I do not want Princess and it must be a man's saddle. Then bring it around to the kitchen entrance. Make sure no one sees you, not Ellen or Rose, not anyone. Can you remember all that?"

"Yes'm, Missy. I does what you wants."

Colleen went to bed, trying to rest for a few hours before she planned to leave, but she could not sleep. She was so apprehensive about what she was about to do. Actually, she was terrified. What made her think she could actually pose as a man, join the army and find Steven? Even to her, it seemed ludicrous. What if she was found out? Would they send her home or put her in prison? And if they found her out then how was she to find Steven?

She finally fell into a fitful sleep, waking a few hours later. It was still dark, but she rose and lit the lamp next to her bed. She woke Dora who had been sleeping on a quilt on the floor, to be ready to assist Colleen.

Dora left sleepily, to go to the stables to acquire a horse for her mistress while she dressed. Taking the strips of cloth Dora had gotten from Mary's sewing room, she wrapped them around her chest, flattening her breasts as much as possible. Once this was accomplished, she put on the men's underwear, an undershirt and long drawers, she had taken from Gerrit's room. Next, a linen shirt and the worn pants Dora had confiscated from a young field hand. Then, men's stockings and the boots she had found in Gerritt's closet. Lastly, she put on a wide brimmed, felt hat Dora had discovered in with some discarded clothes.

After dressing, she observed herself in the mirror. The change was startling. To her, she did not see the voluptuous young debutante any longer, but a young man. She only hoped the army and the men she would be serving with would see the same. She was pleased when Dora came back into the room and gasped at her appearance.

"Well?" she asked.

"You shore does look different," she told Colleen. "Effin I seed you on the street, I mights not knows you."

As she stood in front of her dressing table, Colleen held up her left hand. There, on her fourth finger shone the beautiful emerald engagement ring Steven had given her. She pulled it off and stood looking at it for just a moment. Then, carefully she put it into her velvet lined jewelry box.

"I told Steven once he put it on my finger I would never take it off. I think he'll understand and I'll put it on again when I get home," she said sadly, the tears threatening to come.

Dora could only nod, her tears already streaming down her face. She had only just realized the dangerous mission her mistress was about to undertake. She might never come home again. She loved her, this beautiful girl she had cared for her whole life. She almost felt that this white child, of the plantation aristocracy who had bought her away from her family, was her own child.

Dora no longer argued with her, but followed her quietly down the back stairs. They went through the pantry, out under the portico to the kitchen. There was the horse, saddled and ready, hitched to the post by the door. It snorted when they drew closer and Colleen spoke softly to him so he would not become alarmed. She stroked his neck, feeling his flesh quiver under her touch. She tied the haversack and bedroll on the saddle, strapping on the rifle as well. Then she reached down and grabbed a hand full of dirt, rubbing it through her hands and then some on her face, just enough to look a little worn and scruffy.

Untying the reins, she proceeded to mount the horse, turning first to Dora who stood there in the dark wringing her hands. "You don't tell anyone where I've gone or what I plan on doing, you understand, Dora? Because I'm very serious, if you do, when I get back,

I will sell you." She spoke harshly, but quietly. "You act as if you know nothing, that I left while you were sleeping in your own cabin." And then more gently she added; "I know I'm asking a lot of you, but you've been with me my entire life and I trust you. I trust you with my life." Then impulsively, she hugged the black servant woman.

Just as quickly, she released her and climbed up onto the horse's back and without another word, she turned the horse and rode off. She circled around behind the barns and then followed the river out to the road instead of taking the main drive from the house.

As she took the main road leading into Savannah, the orange glow of the sun began spreading its shards over the horizon, waking the world with its light.

She practiced her speech to the army recruiters and her voice and mannerisms she would need to use as a man. She had even thought of a name she would use, Colin Malone, something close enough to her own, so that hopefully she would respond to it when called.

She finally arrived in Savannah just as the sun came fully into view. As she rode down the street she remembered to tip her hat to the ladies she encountered along the way. She was met with disgust and a cold stare. Even when she smiled, they would not respond. It was the first time she had ever been rebuffed because of the way she looked. She tried not to allow it to become personal, but she couldn't help but feel angry.

She finally arrived at the army headquarters, near the docks and tied her horse outside. It was a large imposing brick building, three stories tall with the red and blue cross of the Confederacy flag flying above it.

She began to feel extremely nervous, her stomach churning and she wondered if she were going to be sick. She nearly turned around again, but then she thought of Steven hurt, lying somewhere in a Yankee hospital and she drew up her courage to go inside.

She entered into a large open room surrounded by long open windows to allow for any passing breeze to enter. In front of these was a row of chairs where a few men sat around silently, looking nervous. In front of her stood a massive desk with a man dressed in a Confederate uniform sitting behind it. He had long hair and a handlebar mustache.

He was slight in stature with a long thin neck. The man barely looked up from his paperwork, but Colleen would not be deterred.

She stepped up to the desk and loudly cleared her throat to get the man's attention. Finally, he looked up in annoyance. " 'Cuse me," she said in her deepest voice. "I want to sign up to fight."

At first he just folded his hands in front of him and looked her over carefully. One eyebrow went up and she felt very uncomfortable. Could he tell she was a woman in spite of binding herself and the loose shirt? "You look mighty young, boy," the man told her. "How old you be?"

"I'm sixteen, sir," she told him "old enough to fight for the Confederacy."

"Where you from?" he asked unfolding his hands and rifling through some papers.

"From a little farm 'bout twenty miles outside Savannah," she lied. "My older brother already is fightin' for the cause and now that I'm old enough, it's my turn."

"Well, then you need to fill out this form. You know how to read and write?"

"Yes, sir."

"Very good. Just fill this out, name, where your home's at, next of kin, that sort of thing. That way, anything happens to ya'll, we can notify your family."

Colleen was taken aback for a moment. She hadn't thought about filling out forms. If she lied and something really did happen to her, no one at home would know. She hesitated no longer and took the paper from the man and began filling it out using the pen and ink on his desk.

"You gotta gun, son? The sergeant asked her.

"Yes, sir, it's outside on my horse."

"First off, boy," he said pointing a finger at her, "don't ever leave your gun out'a your sight. From now on, it's your lifeline, part of your body. You got that?"

"Yes, sir," she responded.

"Second of all, you'll have to get rid of that horse. You're goin' to the infantry. You can probably sell it at the livery down the street, or you can donate it to the cavalry. They can always use a good horse."

"That's what I'll do then. I'll donate it."

The sergeant nodded and took her paperwork from her, looking it over. "Let's see here, Colin Malone, eh? Well, Mr. Malone, raise your right hand."

When she had complied, he continued. "Do you promise to be loyal to the Confederate States of America, to follow all orders given by your superiors and to fight to the best of your ability?"

"I do," she declared.

"Fine then, you are now Private Malone. Go get your gun and personals. I'll have someone see to your horse. Once you've done that, have a seat over there with the others."

"Yes, sir," she said turning to go out and get her haversack. The sergeant had turned back to his paperwork without a second glance. She felt elated, feeling she had passed the first test.

Having retrieved her gun and haversack, she joined the men sitting in the large room. She smiled at them when they looked up at her, but they did not return her greeting. She sat quietly with them, staring at a portrait of Jefferson Davis.

Surreptitiously she began looking at the other men in the room. One was a man about her father's age, probably in his forties, well groomed with a haunted look in his eyes. Two others, sitting together were young men in their twenties, fidgeting, wiggling their feet, nervous. The last was a boy about her age, dirty, worn, holey clothing that appeared not to have been washed in years. His skin was actually stained from the grime smeared all over it and she could smell him from where she sat. He had a sharpened piece of wood, which he was using to pick at his blackened teeth. She remembered hearing stories of their own Confederate troops pillaging and ransacking homes right in the south and she knew that not all men in the army were gentlemen. She knew too, that many more Southerners lived in poverty than the wealth she had enjoyed. Many of her own countrymen, whether from desperation or greed had become thieves and turncoats.

She was just beginning to wonder how long they would be required to sit there, when a tall, bearded man in a neatly pressed uniform entered the room and asked them to stand. He introduced himself as Captain Ambrose. He directed them as to how to stand at attention and how to address an officer. He then explained to them that they would be spending the night there at the headquarters where upon, they would be taken by wagon to field camp. Once they had learned the rudiments of fighting, they would then be shipped to the front.

Colleen wondered where that would be. If they sent her to Mississippi or Arkansas, or any place other than where Steven had been, it would make it more difficult to find her way to Pennsylvania. On the other hand, if she were to go to Virginia, she just might be able to slip over the state border and follow the trail to Steven.

They were all taken up to the second floor, which was a large open barracks room with cots along the sides in rows.

"This is where you will sleep for the night," Captain Ambrose instructed. "You are free to move about the city during the day, but you must return here by dusk. If you do not, you will be considered a deserter and deserters will be shot." He looked them squarely in the eyes, never smiling. "First light you will be moved to the training grounds outside Savannah where you will be taught to be soldiers, how to fight in formation and how to properly fire your weapon." He paused, "Any questions?"

"Yeah, when we gits grub?" the dirty young man asked.

"You will address me as sir and you're on your own for meals today," the Captain answered. "Once you're in the field, you'll be given supplies."

"Damn! I'se hongry now," the boy exclaimed.

"Silence!" Captain Ambrose boomed. "You will not speak unless directed to do so," he yelled at the offender.

The young man saluted, almost mockingly, but Captain Ambrose ignored him.

When Colleen looked over at the boy, he winked at her. The Captain told them to stow their gear and then they were free to go for the day, warning them to be back at dusk.

The other two young men had finally relaxed enough to become more talkative, laughing at the antics of the shabbily dressed boy. The older man still had not spoken and after storing his haversack, lay down on one of the cots and turned his back to them.

The four left him and went down onto the street. Once there, they introduced themselves. The two men in their twenties were brothers, Stuart and Reid Bates, who had resisted the war to this point, staying on their farm to plant and harvest the crops. Once, most of these had been confiscated by the Confederate army, and there was no more seed to plant, they had come to fight.

The young man with the dirty, torn clothing said his name was Joe, no last name offered. He simply told them he was seventeen, had no home, was starving and decided to join the army to get a bed and some food.

Colleen told them her alias and the story she had given the sergeant, that her brother was fighting in

Virginia and she wanted to fight as well. Then she asked about the older man still upstairs.

"I think he said his name's Miles," Stuart told her. "His son died at Manasas and then his wife died of a broken heart. He said he had nothin' left to live for so he might as well sign up to fight."

"That's very sad," Colleen said.

"Hey, it's a war," Joe said shuffling his feet. "People dies. Who ain't knowed somebody who'se died?"

They all simply nodded and then Stuart and Reid went off on their own leaving Colleen and Joe standing in the street. "So, you'se got any dough?" Joe asked her. "I sure could use some grub. I ain't et in three days."

Looking at his appearance, Colleen was repulsed. He was filthy and unkempt. His clothing was so torn; they were practically falling off his body. His teeth were blackened and rotten. His speech was uneducated and coarse, but she tried looking underneath and what she saw was a boy, a boy younger than she, with no home, never knowing where his next meal was coming from and a frightened look in his eyes that belied his cockiness.

"I've got a few Confederate bills," she told him, "Come on, I know a place we can get a cheap meal."

As they walked down the street, Colleen noticed Joe was shuffling and realized the soles of his shoes were coming off. She wondered how he could have gotten to this place. Surely, at one time he must have had a family. What had happened to them? Why didn't they take care of him? Why was he on his own, so young? She also wondered where he had been, how had he managed to survive?

They arrived at a small diner along the waterfront where Colleen bought soup and bread for herself and Joe. She had never been to this particular part of Savannah before. It was mostly men, rough, hard working men, who sat eating, drinking and talked of the war. Some had already been in the fighting and were now home because of wounds or mental incapacity. It was very sobering for Colleen to see the men with empty sleeves or pant legs, or sit with vacant stares, trembling. She felt she had been very sheltered living on the plantation. She wondered what it would really be like to fight.

After wandering about the city for most of the day, savoring her last bit of freedom, Colleen finally returned to the army headquarters. She was the first to return and found Miles sitting on the edge of his cot. His head was down, his arms across his legs. She unrolled her blanket and laid it on one of the cots. Still, the older man had said nothing.

"I heard about your son," she finally said to him, "and I'm terribly sorry."

Miles nodded and then looked up at her. "He was a lot like you," he said quietly. "Just about your age, nice looking, always had lots of girl friends. It broke his mother's heart, you know, when he died. She just kind of faded away."

Colleen nodded, not really knowing what to say to this sad man. She too, had felt the pain of loss, knew that heartache inside, but it was not something she could share. She had told everyone her brother was alive and in Virginia. "I'm sorry. Too many people have lost loved ones in this war," she said finally.

The other men came back to the headquarters and it was apparent Joe was drunk. Colleen wondered where he might have gotten the money for liquor. She knew he probably begged, borrowed or stole it. At any rate, he fell on his cot and was sound asleep, snoring loudly in seconds.

Colleen lay on her cot and covered herself with her blanket, but try as she might she couldn't fall asleep. Fear of the unknown, what was to come, her family back home; all these thoughts kept flooding her mind. The loud snoring in the cot just two down from hers helped contribute to her sleeplessness.

She felt she had only just gotten to sleep, when Captain Ambrose was calling for them to get up. She felt groggy, disoriented. Her head was throbbing and her breasts hurt from being bound. But worse, her bladder felt as if it were ready to burst. How could she relieve herself without the rest discovering she was a woman?

She could wait no longer and asked the Captain where she could find the latrine. There was no chamber pot here. He directed her behind the building where she gratefully hurried; hoping none of the others would follow. By the time she had unbuttoned her pants, pulled them down and squatted over the hole, her teeth were grinding together. She gagged at the smell and tried not to touch anything.

She had nearly finished when someone began banging on the door. "Hey! this here a two holer? Can'st I come in?"

Colleen recognized Joe's voice and started to panic. What if he came in and found her like this? She would be found out before she had really begun. "No, no only one," she called out in her deepest voice, "almost finished." She hurriedly fastened her pants and stepped out of the latrine.

Joe was hopping around impatiently. "'Bout time," he said his voice husky, his eyes bloodshot. He rushed inside and began to urinate without bothering to close the door.

Colleen hurried back inside the building. Escaped that time, she thought to herself.

The rest of the men had gotten their gear together and were waiting for further instructions. Captain Ambrose came into the room carrying a stack of clothing. He laid them on the nearest cot and motioned for the five of them to stand at attention.

"Men, I have here your uniforms," he told them. "We only have jackets in Confederate gray, and the caps with insignia. Our men already in the field are in need of clothing and shoes. So this is the best we can do. You stay in uniform unless otherwise directed. You don't want to be mistaken for a spy or a Yankee."

The five of them began rifling among the jackets and caps, trying them on to find the best fit. Colleen settled on the smallest one in the pile. The caps, however, were all too large, the brim nearly covering her eyes, but she thought it might be beneficial for hiding her identity.

Joe was issued a rifle, a muzzleloader, as the rest had their own weapons, but no ammunition would be given out until they reached the firing range. When they went out onto the street to get into the wagon, the stifling heat hit them in the face like a furnace.

Stuart and Reid scrambled up into the back with Miles following behind. Joe pulled himself up slowly as if it hurt him. When Colleen tried to get in, she found the bed of the wagon too high, with no step to help her up. She struggled for several minutes while the others watched.

Joe looked at her with disgust. “Come on prissy,” he taunted her. “What’s the matter? You too weak to even gets in this here wagon?”

“Give the kid a break,” Miles said as he offered her his hand. She took it gratefully as he helped pull her up into the wagon.

“What kind’a soldier you gonna make?” Joe said angrily. “Can’t even get inta the wagon. I shore don’t want you to be fightin’ with me.”

“Stop it, now,” Miles told Joe. “Just because you’ve got a bad hangover from all that drinkin’ you did last night, doesn’t mean you have to take it out on poor Colin here.”

Joe was silent, but he had brought up something she hadn’t thought of before. She was so concerned with her disguise as a man and finding Steven, that she hadn’t considered whether or not she would actually be able to withstand the harshness and rigors of army life and would she ever put anyone else’s life in danger because of her lack of ability? It was a sobering thought.

The darkie driver called out to the horses and they started out towards the outskirts of town. It took them several hours to reach the camp whereupon they were directed to an area near the headquarters and mess.

Colleen glanced around the camp, wondering if Steven and Gerritt had been here. It lay next to a river, a wide-open area which obviously had been a field, growing crops. Now, large Sibley tents, four man pups, fire pits, cooking messes and supply buildings graced the land. There appeared to be several hundred men about the grounds. Some were drilling off in the distance, others patrolling the perimeter, while some sat near the river relaxing.

They were told to store their gear in one of the four man tents and then report to the mess for some grub. They would begin their training afterward. Colleen hefted her haversack on her back, carried her rifle and walked down the paths with the rows of tents. Men were gathered around small fires or in small groups talking. They would glance her way and then back.

She finally found an empty tent and went inside to set up. She unrolled her blanket and put her haversack and rifle on top of it. She sat on the hard bed and looked around at her surroundings. It was stifling hot inside, with mold and bugs trailing along the roof. It wasn't tall enough to stand and the ground was hard and full of stones. It certainly wasn't the spacious mansion or the soft feather bed she was used to. She felt a sudden desire to flee back to her safe home, but she endeavored to push those thoughts from her mind. She was determined to see this through.

She felt suffocated in the oppressive enclosure and stepped out into the fresh air. She went to the mess as directed to get something to eat. She received a bowl of stew and a hunk of bread. She sat on the riverbank to eat it. It turned out to be bland and watery. Certainly not like the delicious banquets that Ellen prepared back home.

When she got back to her tent she found another man had moved in as well. He was a rather skittish looking young man with long hair and eye glasses, which he kept nervously pushing back up on his nose. He had trouble making eye contact with her, which Colleen found unsettling.

She stuck out her hand to him. “Hello, my name is Colin Malone,” she told him.

“Ah, yes, well, I’m Henry Osbourne,” he said taking her hand. He quickly dropped it and looked over at the river.

“So, where are you from?” she asked finally, since Henry hadn’t offered any more information.

“Um, outside Atlanta,” he said pushing up his eyeglasses and looking into the sky. He hadn’t asked any questions of her, so she stopped trying to make conversation.

Soon, the bugle was blowing for them to assemble. The next several days were spent marching, learning to fight in formation, and shooting their weapons. Colleen had never been so sore and so weary in her entire life. Up to this point she had never had to do physical labor, had been waited on hand and foot. Her body had never been through such rigors; but so far, she had been holding her own and in a strange way, she was enjoying it; the pure physicality of it. Even though it was challenging, she was keeping up with the other men and in some instances even surpassed some of them in shooting.

At night she fell exhausted unto her bedroll. And even though Henry had the tendency to talk in his sleep, he never bothered her and she seldom heard his ramblings as she fell into exhausted slumber.

By the time she had finished with training it was now September and the Confederate forces had suffered several more losses in small skirmishes. Men were desperately needed at the front to replace those killed and wounded at Gettysburg. Both armies had been devastated there. The more Colleen heard about the horrific losses, the more she feared for Steven.

The new troops were divided into companies, with each being sent all over the south wherever the greatest need. Colleen felt immense relief when her company was assigned to join the great army of Virginia; the same army Steven had been part of. The thought crossed her mind that it was possible she could run across her father. She didn't think any disguise she could create, would fool him. She felt he would know her anywhere. She knew if that were to happen, her quest would be over. He would betray her identity to keep her safe and send her home.

Each company was put on a train traveling to each separate destination; some leaving on different days. Colleen watched as Stuart, Reid and Henry boarded a train for Chattanooga, Tennessee to be under General Bragg. She wasn't too pleased, however, to discover Joe in her same company and traveling on the same train as she. She had taken quite a dislike for the young man, in spite of the fact he had cleaned up a bit and was now wearing the Confederate jacket and cap. She never found out the fate of the sad Miles. She hoped he was able to work out his grief. Nor did she ever see Henry Osbourne again.

It was finally time for the train to take them north to Virginia where Lee's army had retreated following Gettysburg. Besides men, the train was filled with much needed supplies for those already at the front. Men were packed into the one available car, where they settled in for the long ride, as best they could. Colleen found a spot against one side where she could lean her back. She noticed Joe had already curled up on the floor and was falling asleep.

For the first part of the journey, the group talked with one another, some slept and others even sang songs. Spirits were good now that they had gotten the training out of the way and they had a destination. But the closer they came to where the fighting had taken place, the quieter the men became, each lost in his own thoughts, each wondering about his own fate.

They stopped several times for meals and for the men to relieve themselves. Colleen was fortunate to find abundant brush and trees where she could be secluded from the others. She did feel it was more convenient to relieve herself wearing pants, instead of the cumbersome ordeal it had been with all the slips, corsets, skirts, hoops and pantaloons. She thought men certainly had the advantage in that regard, especially when they didn't even have to have their pants puddled around their ankles. With just the manipulations of a few buttons, they were finished.

As they continued on into the evening and darkness enveloped the car, many of the men settled into sleep. Colleen shifted her haversack into a position that she might rest her head on it. With the clacking rhythm of the train, she was soon asleep. Her dreams were disturbing; of battles and death, Gerritt bleeding alone, Steven screaming in agony.

When she awoke, the train was coming to a stop, with screeching brakes and hissing of steam. The door slide open and they all poured out into the darkness. Off in the east, the sun was just beginning to throw its golden rays over the horizon. Some told them they were at Brandy Station, Culpepper County on the Virginia Midland Railroad, a desolate area which showed the scarred ravages of war. Alongside ran the Rapidan River. Just on the opposite bank was the Union Army.

Colleen blinked sleepily, still feeling groggy. Before her spread out a vast camp, the likes of which she had never seen before. Hundreds of tents dotted the land with triangles of white in neat rows. Other shelter consisted of crude lean-tos with tree branches for a roof. Beyond was a vast corral filled with every color and description of horseflesh. Surrounding the camp were the accoutrements of war; large artillery pieces, cannon, formidable in appearance and deadly when alive with shells.

They were directed to set up camp according to company. They found a few empty spots in tents near the end of the vast camp. As they walked through, Colleen gave sidelong glances at the men sitting about their morning fires. There was a look about them that differed from those at training camp; a worn, fatigued look that she knew must come from looking death in the face. Many wore tattered clothing, their uniforms barely recognizable. Some even wore parts of Federal uniforms, while others had no shoes and were unusually thin. A dread filled her belly as she realized this was an army lacking; lacking proper supplies to even clothe or feed its soldiers. The thought crossed her mind that perhaps the entire Confederate army would starve to death before they would win their independence.

Once ensconced in camp, they were given a few rations of hard tack and pork, which Colleen chewed on distastefully, but owing to the fact she hadn't eaten since breakfast, she ate without complaint.

Some of the veterans welcomed them into the company, while others only greeted them with silence. Colleen found herself sitting with four other men, drinking strong bitter coffee. Three of them had been in nearly since the beginning; having seen many battles while the fourth was a new recruit like herself. She found herself being drawn more to the young man named Patrick O'Leary. He was perhaps just a little older than she, with a quick smile and a lively sense of humor. He was also the handsomest man she had ever seen. She never imagined anyone could have been more handsome than Steven, but now she had met someone who was. Patrick had sandy brown hair with striking dark eyes and a dimple in his left cheek when he smiled. He was tall and his body hardened from his years at war. He had sensuality about him that Colleen had only felt from one other person. Her attraction to him was baffling to her and she felt almost a disloyalty to Steven. But then she rationalized, Patrick thought she was a man.

"I hope you barines got someone to show you the ropes," Patrick was telling the new recruits. "If you dinna know what your doin', you'll end up six feet under."

Colleen was enamored by his Irish accent. She wanted to listen to him talk some more. "Who do you think would be willing to teach us these things?" she asked him in her deepest voice. "Would they be somethin' besides shooting and marching in formation?"

"Aye, they'd be more like keepin' yer arse down so's you don' get your head blown off." The others all laughed, but Patrick looked directly into her eyes without smiling. She quickly looked away, afraid he would see something that would betray her true identity.

"Nay, truly boys, you need a protector. We lose too many a young 'un by just plain ignorance."

"Do any of you know how to set up a breastworks?" one of the older men with a full thick beard asked.

"N-n-n-no sir," the other young recruit said stuttering. "Wh-what's a breastwork?" Colleen learned his name was Sam.

"It's them delicious round orbs on a lassie's chest that's so comfortin' to snuggle with on a cold evenin'," Patrick said smiling.

Colleen found herself blushing as the others laughed and had to remember she was suppose to be a man now. She had never been exposed to the exclusive company of men before. Always, whenever the men she knew had been in the presence of women, they had used proper language, never anything bawdy to offend a lady's senses.

Patrick noticed her discomfort and proceeded to tease her. "What's troublin' you lad? Have you never afore seen a lady's breasts? 'Cause I would'a thought, if you'd seen a'nough of 'em, t'wouldn't bother you now to talk on it."

Before she could respond, William, the bearded man in the group, spoke up in her behalf as he wiped the grease from his beard with his sleeve, which had collected there from the piece of fatback he was eating. "Aw, leave off the kid," he told Patrick. "Can't you see how young he is? Prob'ly still a virgin."

"S-s-s-so, really, w-what is it?" Sam asked, trying to discover if this might be important information he would need to know and saving Colleen from further embarrassment.

"Biggest damn wall of rocks, dirt and pointed logs, you ever did see," the fourth man who had a handlebar mustache said, having been silent up to this point. He told them his name was Gordon. "You work your ass off to build it and then you hide behind it, so you don't get shot. "Course it doesn't help if the Yank artillery hit it. Then they'll just be pieces of you lying around."

Sam simply looked at the man in disbelief, his mouth hanging open, not knowing what to say next. "Better to be blown to bits than just get wounded," Gordon continued. "If you get wounded you're likely to go to some damn field hospital where they seem to have a tenacious passion for cutting off parts of a man's body. Then if you don't die from that, you're likely to die from typhus or dysentery or the like. There's been more of our good men die in the hospitals than on the battlefield."

His comment was met with silence, the new recruits having had no previous knowledge of the conditions of the field hospitals. Not only did the men have to contend with the horrors of war, but also of the place where healing should occur.

"Were any of you at Gettysburg?" Colleen asked them.

"Aye, all of us were in that great battle, we were," Patrick answered, "lost many a good man."

"We all lost good friends," William told her with sadness in his voice.

"The men who were wounded and taken prisoner," Colleen said, "where would they be taken?"

"Don't know," William told her, "but if they survived, they'd be taken to Point Lookout Prison. That's the closest."

"Point Lookout, where would that be?"

"Maryland," he told her, "enemy territory."

Silence prevailed until the young recruit Sam, spoke up. "Y-y-y-you'll see," he said exuberantly. "We'll w-w-win this war yet. G-g-g-general Lee w-will c-c-come back and push those Y-y-yanks from Virginia and then w-w-we'll go back to our cotton, r-r-rice and sugar a t-t-tobacco fields and become the r-r-r-richest country in the world."

"That's right lad," Patrick said. "You just keep them thoughts, tis always good to have a cause."

"And you, sir, what is your cause?" Colleen asked him.

"Ah, now there's the question. Here I t'was mindin' my own business, helping my father to run our farm, when them politicians tells us the dirty Yanks will be takin' away our land and our slaves if we don't fight for what's our'n. So I go off to fight like any good Irish Confederate. But, let me tell you laddie, after seeing men die, maimed and broken, I've begun to see it in a whole different light. Me thinks now, my cause is to stay alive and kill as many Yanks as I can."

Colleen was sobered by Patrick's words. Where was the great cause they had all gone off to fight for? Where was that fire she had seen in all the men's eyes? "Don't you want to be an independent nation any longer?" she asked him. "Has it only become about the killing and dieing?"

"I'm not sure any longer. If the South losses this war and I have to free my slaves, than what's that to me? Perhaps they's men after all and should be free. Is my life on my farm going to change 'cause of it? Perhaps it shall, but I'm thinkin' maybe all this killin's not worth the cause."

"T-t-that's n-not very patriotic," Sam said almost angrily.

"Aye, perhaps laddie, but we'll just see how you'll be feelin' after your first battle."

They spent the remainder of the day performing various chores about the camp, cleaning the garbage from the perimeter and spending time on guard duty. Pickets were posted twenty-four hours a day owing to the fact the Yankees were just on the other side of the river. Times were, they even exchanged pleasantries and would trade goods, such as tobacco and perhaps a tin of meat; wading into the river to accomplish this tryst with the enemy. It was definitely an advantage that they spoke each other's language.

At night Colleen tried settling into sleep, but she had discovered Patrick was in the same tent as she, and she found it difficult to fall into slumber, listening to his steady breathing. All about the camp she could hear the sounds of an army; low talking, the words indistinguishable, someone waking past, horses softly nickering, a splash as someone gathered water from the river. And then she heard the screams, men crying out in their sleep as they relived the horrors of war.

For the next few weeks, they stayed in the big camp with Patrick taking Colleen under his wing, thinking she was a young teen boy who needed guidance and instruction. He was always patient and kind with her, explaining things she would need to know should they ever go into battle. It only caused her to admire him the more and she found herself searching camp for a sight of him whenever he would go off on some errand.

There were times when they had sat around a fire and talked late into the night. He, telling her of his roots in Ireland, how poor he had been and wanting a better life for his family, his father had packed them all up, his wife, Patrick, and Patrick's sister Molly, and come to America. After working hard on the loading docks of Georgia, his father had saved enough money to buy a good share of land, build a house and later, purchase some slaves to help with the labor. They grew tobacco and had become comfortable in their lifestyle, although not wealthy.

Colleen felt somehow pleased that he had not yet married and had no serious love interest. She asked herself why she would care when she herself was already married and in fact, on a quest to find her beloved husband.

What she had shared with Patrick was half-truth and half falsehood. She told him that she too, had a heritage from Ireland and the story of her grandparent's settlement in America. But she had also told him she was of modest means, that her brother had been in the army since the onset of the war and now that she was old enough, she too, wanted to fight the Yankees. But then he had asked what company and regiment her brother was in and she had not been able to think of an accurate answer. She simply told him she knew he was in the Army of Virginia and had been at Gettysburg.

"Well, then laddie, what be his name?" he had asked her. "Perhaps I know him. Perhaps even he was in this great camp."

She had faltered, not having the forethought to have put a name to her brother. She could not give him Gerritt or Steven's name, as it would be different from her own. She had paused, thinking. "He was at Gettysburg," she told him again, stalling, still trying to think of a name.

"Ah, perhaps I do know the lad, then. Do you know his commander's name?" he had asked her. "Would it be Longstreet, Hill, Pickett, Hood, Early?"

"I never knew whom he served under," she had replied, but my brother's name is Joseph."

"Ah, Joseph Malone, tis a good Irish name. Can't say I know him, though. Myself, I fought with Jubal Early at Cemetery Hill," he had said with the pain of remembrance in his eyes.

Near the middle of the month, Lonstreet called for several companies of men to join him in reinforcing General Bragg's army of Tennessee who had been involved in fighting near Chattanooga. General Rosecrans of the Union Army of the Cumberland, had virtually snuck up on Bragg from the southwest, forcing him to evacuate the city and flee to northwestern Georgia where he awaited the reinforcements.

Both Colleen and Patrick, along with Patrick's comrades, William and Gordon and the young Sam, all in the same company, were assigned to go along with Longstreet. General Hood, still nursing his wounded arm from Gettysburg, also brought several companies to join Longstreet.

The troops, who were leaving, packed up their supplies in their haversacks and lined up to begin their march. Everyone had grown silent, knowing they were headed towards another battle. For Colleen and Sam, it would be their first. She had heard of men deserting during battle because of stark fear and she prayed she wouldn't be in their number.

"Y-y-you mean to t-t-t-tell me, we gots to w-w-walk all the way to Tennessee?" Sam asked as he stood in position in line, his red hair sticking up all over.

"Yup," William answered. "Besides fightin', that's 'bout all we does is walk."

"That's the truth," Patrick agreed. "Why, we've already walked enough miles to go to the moon and back. That's why so many of our boys haven't shoes. Why myself, I took these here fine boots off'a dead blue coat," he said holding up one foot to show them the nice pair of boots he sported.

They hadn't much time to admire Patrick's boots as the long line of men, spread out nearly three miles long, began its trek towards Tennessee. Leading the regiment was General Longstreet. Sitting astride his horse, Colleen could see the tall, proud man, his sword held high. His long hair reached to his shoulders and he wore a full beard and mustache, but his eyes were kind. Colleen saw the great burden he bore, the responsibility of directing thousands of men into battle. Behind them came the covered wagons, ambulances and light artillery pieces.

They walked all day and into the night, finally stopping just at dusk at a small stream. They only took enough time to eat a quick meal of fat back and hard biscuits, before laying out their bedrolls on the hard ground to sleep.

Colleen had never walked so far in one day in her life. She felt exhausted and her feet were sore, but couldn't seem to fall asleep. All around her were the sounds of snoring as men drifted off. But try as she might, sleep eluded her. There was a rock under her bedroll that kept poking her. Her breasts were hurting her from being bound all the time. Occasionally, while on private excursions into the brush to relieve herself, she had loosened them a bit. She only wished she could remove all her clothing and bathe. The only times she had gotten wet were when they had crossed a few streams, but the dirt underneath remained. She didn't know how these men could stand being so dirty all of the time. She had also seen many of them scratching, belying the fact that vermin lived on their bodies.

Her mind would not stop racing as well. She knew men died and were wounded in battle, but what would it really be like? And by going into Tennessee, how could this be getting her any closer to Steven when she believed him to be in Pennsylvania or Maryland. And Chattanooga was extremely close to Georgia. The fact that Bragg had retreated there showed the war was coming to her backyard.

She felt as though she had just fallen asleep when the bugle call sounded for them to awaken. They barely had enough time to gulp down a bitter tasting cup of coffee before they were again assembled to be on the march.

By the end of the second day of marching, Colleen's feet hurt so badly, she didn't know how she would be able to go another step. She moaned and pulled her boots off. She began rubbing them with her hands to ease the pain. She was developing calluses on her heels and the inside of her toes. She had watery blisters on the bottoms of her feet and they certainly didn't look like the feet of a lady. She wondered what her mother would think if she could see her now.

Thoughts of her mother caused her to think back to over a month before when she had left to sign up for the army. She wondered what her mother had felt when she had discovered her missing. What must she had thought happened to her? Did she think she had just run off like some disobedient child, or had she imagined her being kidnapped and killed in the middle of the night? Of course she would have discovered the missing horse. She hoped she had not put Dora in too much jeopardy. Henry, the groom would have known Dora had requested the horse. In either case she felt her mother would grieve and she was sorely contrite for having to put her mother through that agony. It had been difficult enough for her when Gerritt had been killed and now, she was gone too.

Finally, on the evening of September 19th, they arrived near the banks of the Cickamauga River near Chattanooga. They joined Bragg's Army of the Cumberland who had already seen action that day. Colleen saw men lying about, smoking, talking quietly, while others near the hospital tent lay bleeding, waiting for attention. Colleen looked away; tried not to be appalled by their injuries. By looking in the other direction, she witnessed the colored burial detail, dumping the casualties into a long mass grave. Her stomach lurched as she thought about Gerritt being thrown into such a crude burial.

They gathered with the others near General Bragg's tent as General Longstreet and his officers conferred with him. Bragg still wore his arm in a sling from his injury at the battle of Gettysburg. Colleen thought he looked pale and sickly. He was quite a handsome man otherwise, she thought; deep-set eyes, with a neatly trimmed beard peppered with gray.

Owing to the fact it was already nightfall, they grabbed some hastily provided hardtack and rolled up in their blankets for the night. Once again Colleen found it difficult to sleep. For one thing, Federal troops were only about a mile away and in spite of vigilant pickets, it was an eerie feeling knowing the enemy was so close. She also kept thinking about the following day and what it would bring. There was no doubt they would be engaged in battle. She wondered how she would fare. Like all others before her, she worried whether or not she would be able to pull the trigger when face to face with the enemy. Or what should happen if she were required to fight hand to hand; stabbing with their bayonets? What if she weren't strong enough? She realized there was a real possibility she could die here tomorrow and then what if no one knew? If she were thrown into an unmarked pit to rot in the ground, who would know? Her family would never know what had happened to her. Steven, if he survived, would never know of her gallant attempt to find him. "I'm so scared," she whispered to herself. "God, I'm so scared."

"Are you scared, laddie?" a voice near her asked, startling her. It was Patrick bringing his bedroll near to hers.

"Yes," she said honestly, rising up on one elbow to look at him.

"Aye, everyone's scared their first time out; only natural. Fact is, it be a good thin' to be scared; keeps you cautious. Anybody who ain't scared is a fool and more careless and he's more likely to be killed. Why laddie, I still gets scared right before a fight; tis only natural.

But you try to sleep, now. I'll be a watchin' out for you."

"Thank-you, Patrick," she told him, but in spite of his reassurances, she still found it difficult to sleep.

The following morning dawned bright and clear. They sky was an azure blue with just a few wispy clouds floating lazily along as if they had not a care in the world. Colleen wished she could be that carefree.

She had just come back from the line of trees where she had relieved herself, when a thunderous booming commenced. She hurried back to where the others were still casually sitting on the ground. All but Sam, who stood at the ready, his gun clutched in his hands, a look of terror on his face.

"Calm yourselves, laddies. It be only the Yanks, tryin' to warn us they be comin'. As if we dinna already know. That's just their light artillery a talkin'," Patrick told them.

It was difficult to believe the shells couldn't reach them, the sound was so loud. Colleen could feel the vibrations from it in her chest.

"I-I-it c-c-c-can't r-r-reach us th-th-then?" Sam asked, his stutter worsened by fear.

"Naw, they jes kind'a likes shoot 'em off ta let us knows they's a comin'," William told them.

Just as he spoke these words, a loud roar arose across the air, the shouts of thousands of men; the Yankees. It made her skin crawl to hear it. They were lined up in formation, rank after rank, with Bragg's men to the right while Longstreet's regiment was directed to the left. Bragg sent Polk to advance against the heavily fortified breastworks.

They began to move in double quick time, closing in on the men in blue. They marched across fields, past homes, through orchards, when suddenly in front of her, Colleen saw them, Yankees, a mass of blue, pointing their rifles directly at them. Her heart raced, her breath came in rapid gasps and she heard herself whimper, but she couldn't stop.

"Steady as she goes, laddie," Patrick said next to her, "calm and easy. Just watch for the fire. When you see it from directly in front, get down." He kept up the talk as they moved forward. "Aim a little high and squeeze the trigger nice and easy like. Make your shots count. Then drop and reload quicks you can."

The entire formation suddenly rushed forward, yelling the rebel cry, shooting as they went. Colleen found herself swept along, yelling too, her adrenaline coursing through her body. Men in front of her were dropping while others kept going, stepping over them.

A soldier in blue was suddenly in front of her. She saw the muzzle of his gun spit fire and she dropped to the ground. The bullet went whizzing over her head. Immediately she got back to her feet in time to see Patrick shoot another man directly in the chest. He waved her on and she went forward, firing her rifle when she saw the line of blue in front of her. She didn't know whether or not she had hit anyone. She dropped to one knee to reload while others swarmed around her.

They passed around a two-story farmhouse and out onto a road, still pushing back the Yankee line. Colleen fired again and this time she saw a man fall, but she had no time to reflect, only to reload and fire again.

Men were falling all around her, some mortally wounded; others with severe injuries to bodies and limbs. The ground was soon saturated with their blood, their screams filled her ears. She began to falter as the line began moving left. She was shaking and dropped to her knees. She had an incredibly strong desire to flee, to run back into the trees behind the line as fast as she could go. She nearly did it; nearly got up to run, but suddenly Patrick was there by her side.

"Are you hurt, lad?" he asked. She shook her head. "Then up with you. It's harder for them Yanks to hit a movin' target." He put his hand under her arm and helped her up.

By the time they had reached the Confederate line, it had once again swung back north, spilling through a hole in the Yankee line. Chaos ensued with the men in blue turning to run.

They were able to pause in their fighting; resting behind a large red brick home surrounded by a neat garden and small orchard. Colleen wondered what had become of the family who had lived there. She wondered if they would ever be able to return, ever live normally again. Would any of them return to what had been?

She found herself shaking so badly her teeth were chattering and it took all the strength she could muster to keep from crying. What was she doing here, she wondered? She didn't belong and she wanted to go home.

Their sergeant came around handing out more ammunition, telling them they were doing a good job, they had the Yanks on the run.

Patrick, William and Gordon huddled with her in the grass. "Are you alright, boy?" Gordon asked her, his mustache twitching as he spoke.

"I think so," she replied. "It's pretty awful though; all those men dead, wounded."

"Aye, laddie, the tragedy of war," Patrick agreed.

"Thank-you for helping me back there," she told him.

He held up a hand. "No need. We're all in this together. We look out for one another."

Once into the afternoon, the Union Army again regrouped and began their charge. The rebels formed their line and charged back over a hill, heading toward a stand of trees. Colleen kept firing and reloading as fast as she could, afraid if she stopped long enough, she would run, or a bullet would find her.

It was so horribly terrifying, the bullets whizzing past, thudding into the ground, the trees, the man beside her. Any moment she expected a bullet to fly into her chest or her head. It was a horrible feeling. But, she kept on.

Incredibly, the Union army kept up a steady retreat, past a split rail fence, over plowed fields. On the left, a large log home had been occupied by Union General Thomas, had also abandoned his headquarters.

General Bragg gave the order not to pursue and while they watched, the men in blue swarmed down the road to Chattanooga, bringing with them their wagons, ambulances filled with wounded, horses pulling artillery and the hordes of men.

"Why ain't we goin' after them bastards?" William asked, spitting on the ground. "Now's the time for defeat; we've got 'em on the run!"

"Came from the top, General Bragg says not to pursue," Gordon told him. "Story is he's wounded; caught one in the leg."

They began making their way back to where they had been camped, stepping over the dead and wounded; both blue and gray. She was struck how, in death, everyone looked the same, only different uniforms.

Colleen was appalled at the devastation dealt to the human body. Men lay with shattered legs or arms, some with no heads. Others appeared only to be sleeping while a pool of blood trailed from under their bodies. She felt sick to her stomach as she stepped over a dismembered leg. Besides the human carnage, there were dead horses and shattered caissons. By the time she reached the camp, her stomach was heaving and she had to lean over to retch. The tears began pouring from her eyes unabated. She had had no comprehension of the horrors of battle.

"It's alright, laddie," she heard Patrick say as his hand lay on her back. "No cause for shame. It happens to us all the first time."

She looked up at him, his dark eyes sympathetic. She wanted nothing more than to collapse into his arms and sob as she had never sobbed before. She wiped at her face with the sleeve of her jacket. "How do you do this, time after time, battle after battle? How do you do it and not go crazy?"

Patrick shrugged. "You gets kinda numb to it, unless it be someone your close to. I guess if you didn't, you'd go crazy. I've seen it happen."

"I don't know if I could do this again, Patrick. I don't think I can ever be in battle again. My god, I think I killed someone!" She had gotten a little hysterical, her voice rising.

He was looking at her strangely when she remembered she was in disguise. As quickly as she could, she tried to regain her composure. "You did fine, lad," Patrick told her quietly, "for your first time. I saw you out there and you was doin' your part. When the next time comes, you'll do what you have to, just like the rest of us."

The other young recruit, Sam had been missing and they feared he may have been wounded, or worse had been killed. But soon after the shelling had stopped and everyone had returned to camp, here came Sam from the cover of the trees, shame-faced and apologetic.

"Don't let it worry you, boy," Gordon told him. "Many a brave man ran scared his first time out. You'll stand up and fight next time." And she thought; if it hadn't been for Patrick by her side, she would have run too.

That evening as she lay in her bedroll, the battle replayed itself in her mind; all the horrific sights and sounds. The unofficial count from that day was 17,800 casualties. It was then she remembered Stuart and Reid had been sent to fight with Bragg's army of the Cumberland and she wondered if they had been out there today. She hoped if they had, they had survived. It had all been so much more horrible than she could ever have imagined; so much death, so much destruction. What had Steven been enduring all these years? The burning tears fell unabated from her eyes.

The following morning, what remained of Longstreet's regiment, began their long trek back to Virginia and Lee's army. It had been a harrowing experience for Colleen, one that would haunt her dreams for some time to come. She was ready to leave this place of death and move further north on her journey to find Steven.

CHAPTER THIRTEEN

When Mary awoke that hot morning of August 1863, she could hear shouting and running footsteps. Hastily, she put on a dressing gown and went out into the hall to see what all the commotion was about. Her own maid Rose was just on her way down the back stairs, when she stopped her.

"What's the meaning of all this noise?" she asked her.

"It be missy Colleen," Rose told her. "She be gone."

"What do you mean gone? Where did she go?" she asked as a strange sinking feeling began in the pit of her stomach.

"We dun't know, Mistress. She jes be gone. They looks everywheres fo her. She jes be gone."

"That's impossible," Mary said, "she has to be somewhere." She began moving down the hall towards Colleen's room, mumbling to herself. When she stepped into the room, she found Dora there, standing in the middle of the room, wringing her hands.

"Dora, what's this nonsense about Colleen missing?" she asked the servant girl.

"Yes'm, she be gone."

"Gone where?"

"Don' know, Mistress. When I cames from my cabin dis mornin', she jes not here."

"Well, she could just be out for a walk or over in the quarters, perhaps in the stables."

"No'm, Everbody looks everwheres for her."

Mary had gone to the armoire and opened it, taking inventory of her dresses. "There doesn't seem to be anything missing," she commented almost to herself. "Well, of course she has to be around someplace. Where would she go?" She turned to face Dora. "You tell me right this minute where she is!" she said harshly.

Dora visibly shrank under her mistress' critical glare. It wasn't as if she hadn't lied to white folks before, but keeping Colleen's secret from her mother, was going to be difficult. "I really doesn't knows, Mistress. It be likes I says, she not here when I comes this mornin'."

"You're worthless," Mary told her as she brushed past. She went to her own room where she dressed hurriedly and then went downstairs to inquire of the other servants where Colleen might have gone, but everyone she asked had not seen her.

"Has anyone checked the stables?" she asked.

"Yes'm," Carlton answered, "but she not be there."

"I already know that," she snapped back. Her patience was wearing thin and her apprehension was growing. "I want to know if her horse is missing. Is Princess in her stall? She may have just gone riding and forgot to tell anyone."

"Princess still be there," Matthew told her getting apprehensive himself. He could see his mistress was worried and agitated. "But they is one of the older hosses missin'."

"Well, that must be it then. She just took another horse today and went riding. She'll probably be back soon. I know she's been upset ever since we got the news about Master Steven bein' captured." She's upset with me too, she thought to herself. After the things I said to her about her so-called marriage to Steven. What on earth were the two of them thinking? It was a convenient excuse to go to bed together at any rate.

"Go to the stable and fetch Henry," she told Matthew. "I want to find out what time Colleen went riding."

Matthew hurried off to do her bidding, returning shortly with the groom Henry, who stood nervously fidgeting. He wasn't accustomed to being at the big house, usually working and living exclusively at the stables. When asked about Colleen taking out one of the horses, he became even more agitated. He only knew that Dora had come to make the request of a horse from him and had not told him whom the horse was for. But, he didn't want to get Dora in trouble either.

"One hoss gone, Mistress," Henry told her.

"Did Colleen take the horse?" Mary asked.

"No'm. twernt Miss Colleen."

"Then <u>who</u> was it? Were they getting the horse <u>for</u> Miss Colleen?" Mary asked impatiently. She felt she had been asking a lot of questions, but not receiving many answers.

"I dun know who it be for," he replied. "Some fiel' han' come an' axed for Massa Solomon, I thinks."

"Mr. Solomon……... Now why would he take one of the horses without permission? I swear that man will be the death of me.

But if Mr. Solomon took the horse, then where's Colleen? I guess I'll just have to talk to Mr. Solomon."

Dora and Henry exchanged nervous glances, but said nothing. They knew the way Mr. Solomon was these days with Massa James gone, if they incriminated him in any way, he might just beat them the way he had Jonah.

Even though Ellen had breakfast ready, Mary was too upset over the disappearance of Colleen to eat. She decided to go out to talk with Mr. Solomon right away. When she returned, she was even more distressed, out of breath, her face red.

Anna Bell was waiting for her, having heard of Colleen's disappearance. "Well, someone's lying," she said panting as she came into the parlor where Anna Bell was working on another pair of stockings for their men in gray. "Mr. Solomon claims he never requested a horse; says he knows nothing about it."

"Can you believe what he says? Anna Bell asked her.

"He didn't have the horse with him and it's still missing from the stables. If Mr. Solomon is telling the truth, then Henry lied. I guess I'll have to speak to him again." She had Matthew call Henry back to the house and brought to her where she confronted him.

"Mr. Solomon does not have the horse, nor did he say he ever had the horse. Now, someone is lying to me, Henry. Tell the truth, who took the horse?"

"I'se doesn't know, Misses," Henry replied nervously.

"Why don't you know? You're in charge of the stables, are you not?" Her voice had risen with her impatience.

"All's I knows is, some fiel' han' comes and axed fo' a hoss fo' Mr. Solomon."

"Who was this field hand" Mary demanded.

"I don't know him, Misses."

"So you just hand over one of our horses to someone you didn't know?"

"Yes'm. I tries nots to axed questions."

"I'll deal with you later," she yelled. "Now get out of here!"

"Do you believe Colleen ran away?" Anna Bell asked quietly.

Mary sank into one of the chairs. "I just don't know what to think," she said sadly, "if she has, where would she go and why?"

"I know she was very upset about Steven," Anna Bell offered. "You don't think that had anything to do with it do you?"

Mary paused before answering, debating whether or not she should tell Anna Bell about Steven and Colleen. "Yes she was upset about that, as we all were. But, she was also angry with me."

"Why was she angry with you?" Anna Bell asked. "I thought you were very sympathetic."

"She told me something I'm afraid I wasn't very sympathetic about."

"What would that be, if I might inquire?"

"I should tell you since this affects you as well. Colleen told me that she and Steven were married before he left."

A look of disbelief crossed Anna Bell's face. "But how can that be? Surely Steven would have told me, his mother, about it."

"Apparently, they married themselves one day when we were all gone. No pastor, no real ceremony, no witnesses; they just said their vows to each other."

"Well, then, it's not a real marriage……."

"Except that afterward they had…..you know, that what should be reserved for only husband and wives."

Anna Bell gasped and her hand flew to her mouth. "No! She told you this?"

"Yes, ma'am she did, bold as you please. And I'm afraid I let my displeasure be known."

"I should say so!"

Mary sighed deeply. "She was very angry; stormed out of the room."

"And you're afraid she may have run away because of this incident?" Anna Bell asked.

Mary nodded her head, tears in her eyes. "What if she's gone?" she asked her words a mere whisper.

"For one thing we're not sure yet she has run away; and for another, where would she go?" Anna Bell had put down her knitting and gone over to her friend. "She would most likely go someplace familiar; a relative or friend perhaps."

Mary dabbed at her tears. "You know I believe you may be right. We'll give her a chance to get over her snit, if she's still near home, then I'll contact her friends and relatives. I'm sure she went there, just to worry me."

Later in the evening when Colleen still hadn't shown up, Mary became even more concerned. "It's so late now," she commented to Anna Bell. "If she were anywhere nearby, she would have been home by now. I'll begin at once to notify friends and family of her disappearance."

For day and weeks following, Mary sent messengers to everyone she could think of, even going into Savannah to send telegrams to those further away. She had even had an extensive search done of all the slave quarters and out buildings in case she should be hiding out there. But, it was to no avail; Colleen seemed to have disappeared off the face of the earth.

When Steven awoke he was riding in the back of a horse drawn ambulance with other wounded men; many wearing the blue. The pain in his left leg was horrendous, stabbing, throbbing with every beat of his heart. He raised his head slightly, which only caused dizziness, to see if his leg were still there. He gratefully lowered his head, seeing it was still attached to his body. Someone had applied a tourniquet, but his pant leg was saturated with blood. He had remembered how it looked on the battlefield with pieces of bone and flesh showing through. He briefly wondered where he was, what had happened with the battle, and where he was going. It was only briefly, however, as the jolting of the ambulance caused such sharp pain in his leg, that he passed out again.

The second time he awoke, he found himself in a hospital. Cots were lined up one after the other, row after row, in what appeared to have been a church, judging from the brilliant stained glass windows and the large cross at the front of the building. Other than that, it in no way resembled a house of God. Men lay unconscious or moaning all about him. But, the thing that suddenly struck him was how many of them were wearing the Union uniform, with only a smattering of gray amongst them.

He didn't reflect long on his observation because of the excruciating pain his leg was causing him. The agony was so great; he couldn't help but moan. Bursts of lights flashed in front of his eyes and he thought he was going to pass out again. He fought against it, feeling out of his element, needing to know where he was.

It was then he spotted a woman, a nurse perhaps, she was dressed in a gray dress with a white apron over the top of it. Her yellow hair was piled into a braided bun on the top of her head and her blue eyes looked kind. When she passed near to where he lay, he grabbed the fold of her skirt. He was amazed at how weak he felt, as though that one motion had taken great effort.

She turned to him and smiled. "What is it soldier? Is there something I can get for you?"

"Tell me, please, ma'am, where am I? What is this place?"

"You're in a hospital called Camp Letterman General Hospital. You were severely wounded at Gettysburg, but we'll do all we can to help you get well," she said reassuredly.

"This be a Yankee hospital," a voice from the cot next to him said. When Steven glanced over, he saw a bearded man, lying on his side and raised up on one elbow staring at him angrily. "You're a damn prisoner and just as soon as they chop off that leg a yourn, you'll be kickin' ass off to a regular prison for the likes of Johnny Rebs like you."

"I'm a prisoner?" Steven asked looking at the woman, not sure he was hearing correctly.

"Afraid so, soldier," she said, "you were picked up by Union men off the field at Gettysburg and brought here to this hospital. But, don't worry all soldiers are treated equally here. We have very good doctors who will take care of you."

Steven closed his eyes and moaned. "No, no this can't be happening. I've got to get out here. I can't be a prisoner!" He couldn't imagine anything worse. What would happen to him? How could he get home to Colleen? He had heard horror stories of prison camps. If he didn't die here, he was just as likely to die there.

He heard the man next to him chuckling. " 'Fraid you got nuttin' to say about it, Reb. It don't look like you'll be walkin' outta' here any time soon. 'specially after they take that leg off." He chuckled again as if the thought of it brought him pleasure.

Nausea filled Steven as he thought about them sawing his leg off. He thought he'd rather die than have them do that to him. He remembered the scenes from the field hospitals with the screams and moans predominate and the piles of amputated limbs lying about. He remembered his father in such a hospital, both his legs gone. He almost wished they had left him on the battlefield to die.

When he closed his eyes he saw his beautiful Colleen. What would she think of being married to a one-legged man? How would he provide for her once this war was over? Perhaps he would die here from his wound; let her grieve for a time and then re-marry someone who was whole.

It wasn't long before he saw a man, a doctor he supposed, judging by all the blood on his clothing, going from man to man, directing some to be taken straight off to the surgery room. It wasn't long before he was bending over Steven, looking at the wound on his leg.

"Please sir," Steven whispered, the pain not allowing him to speak any louder. "Please don't take my leg off." He thought the man to look kindly. He was slight with a small salt and pepper beard. But, his dark eyes had a look of anguish, a sadness that told of someone who had been witness to too much death and horror. If the battlefield was a place where men fought, then the hospital was the place where the battle for men's lives was fought.

"I'm sorry son, but that leg's going to have to come off. If it doesn't, you could die," the doctor told him.

"I don't care. Please, sir, leave me with some dignity; don't take my leg," Steven pleaded with him.

"I can't just let you die," the doctor said. "It goes against my oath as a doctor."

"Aw, let Johnny Reb die, iffen that's what the bugger wants," the bearded man next to him called out. "He was out there killin' our'n. I say let 'im die."

"You be quiet, now," the kind nurse told him. "We're all the same here."

The doctor sighed and looked up at the ceiling. "Let me take another look and see if there's anything else that can be done."

“Thank-you sir; I’d appreciate anything you could do,” Steven told him. The doctor began probing his wound causing such excruciating pain that Steven cried out and the tears ran down the sides of his face.

“Well, that bone’s not completely shattered,” he told Steven standing upright. “We could try extracting the bone fragments and sewing it together, but the flesh is so ripped up, I’m not sure there’s enough there to pull together and you’ve already lost a lot of blood.”

“Sir,” Steven gasped through his pain, “I would beg you to try.”

“Alright, soldier, I’m willing to try and save the leg, to sew the pieces of flesh back together, but I won’t guarantee anything. It will be unusually weak and mighty ugly.”

“I ….. don’t….. care….; just save my leg.”

“The doctor put his hand on Steven’s arm. “I only said I’d try. If afterward, the wound starts to fester, I’m still taking it off. And while we’re at it, I’ll sew up your arm as well.”

He had nearly forgotten the arm wound. The pain in his leg was so overwhelming.

Steven nodded, just grateful the doctor was willing to try and save his leg. After he had moved on, the man in the next cot began mocking him.

“Please, sir, leave me with some dignity.” He said it in a high pitched, nasal voice. “I beg you, save my leg!” Then he spat on the floor. “You Rebs is all alike,” he said, his voice returning to its normal pitch. “Bunch of pansy assed southerners who gets their kicks out’a ownin’ slaves, cause they’s too lazy to do their own work.”

Steven was in no condition to argue the politics of the war or their way of life with this angry Union soldier.

"Hey, Johnny Reb," the man said a little louder, as if Steven hadn't heard him all along. "How many Yanks did you kill? Huh? How many?"

Steven closed his eyes and didn't answer, the pain washing over him in waves, so that after awhile he only heard the man as an annoying buzzing in the background.

A little later two men came to bring Steven to the surgery room. Taking him under the arms and legs, which only caused greater pain, they carried him off to another room adjacent to the large sanctuary room. Waiting for him there was the kind doctor he had talked to earlier and one other. He was younger, tall, clean shaven, with a distrustful look about him. Steven thought, perhaps he didn't like Confederates.

" 'Member me, sir?" he addressed the older man. "You promised me you'd try and repair the leg; not take it off." He wanted to make sure they wouldn't just begin sawing off his leg, forgetting he had talked with him previously.

"That leg's too bad to save," the younger doctor said. "We don't have time to do repair work. That takes more effort and we've got others waiting."

"I did promise the boy I'd try to save the leg. I think we can remove the bone fragments, sew those ragged edges together and he might have a chance of having some use of that leg."

"Look Alfred," the younger doctor said to the other man, "we don't have time for this."

"The worst cases have already come through. The ones remaining have minor wounds that can wait. They won't die. We need to take care of this boy now."

"He's a Reb, Alfred," the young doctor said quietly.

The older man said nothing; only looked the younger man in the eyes. "Alright, alright," he relented, "we'll try to save the leg, but I'm not using any of our dwindling supply of morphine. He'll just have to bear it."

"Agreed, as long as we do the repair work," the older man said, "but I've got some whiskey we could give him. Perhaps it could at least dull the pain."

Steven listened to them discussing his fate as if he weren't there. His heart was pounding and he had begun to sweat. He thought he would rather go into battle, than face this surgery.

The older doctor brought in a bottle of golden liquid and pressed it to his lips. "Drink this, son. It'll help," he told him.

Steven gulped, gratefully, the whiskey burning his throat as it went down. He took a couple more large gulps until his head felt woozy. Then the doctor poured the remainder over his wound. Steven screamed with pain as the nurse cut away his pant leg. When the doctors finally began their work, picking out fragments of bone and flesh, the pain was so excruciating; Steven couldn't help but cry out. His leg felt as if it were on fire, and being stabbed over and over. He could feel more blood flowing out onto the table where he lay. Finally, mercifully, he passed out.

When he again awoke, he lay back on the cot next to the surly Union man. This time, however, the man appeared to be sleeping and did not harass him. Steven was also too preoccupied with the intense pain in his leg to worry about the Yankee. He slowly raised his head so as not become dizzy, to glance down at his leg. He saw that it still remained a part of him, had been cleaned and wrapped in bandages. However, the blood had already seeped through the length of his leg from knee bone to foot where they had sewn the wound together. His arm wound had also been treated and bandaged. He laid his head back and clenched his teeth to keep from crying out. The leg throbbed so painfully, he didn't think he would be able to endure it.

The kind nurse was suddenly at his side, holding a bowl and spoon in her hand. "I've got some broth for you, soldier," she told him. "It's been awhile I'm sure since you've eaten and if you're to get well, you need nourishment." She pulled a small stool from another bedside and sat near him; lifting his head, she began to spoon some of the warm liquid into his mouth. He found it difficult to swallow and his stomach felt queasy, but he made the attempt to take the broth, as the nurse was being so kind.

She tried to converse with him, but his mind felt so foggy, he found it difficult to concentrate on what she was saying. Finally, the pain and now having had some nourishment caused Steven to sleep. The nurse quietly slipped away to tend to others.

For the next several days, Steven drifted in and out of consciousness. When he was awake, the pain was nearly unbearable. A nurse would come with broth or stew and attempt to get him to eat. They also gave him as much water as he could drink, which caused another problem. He knew he had wet himself, but had been unable to get up to walk to the latrine. It was humiliating and embarrassing, one more degradation he had to endure because of his wound and capture by the Yankees.

After several days, he remained conscious for longer periods of time. The excruciating pain in his leg was slowly ebbing down to a throbbing. However, if he tried moving it or when the nurses would change his dressings, the stabbing pain would return. It was during these times, he was able to see the results of the surgeon's work. The skin was indented and a long jagged, red wound ran the length of his lower leg, crisscrossed with many laces of thread where they had sewn the ragged pieces of flesh together. It was, as the doctor had predicted, extremely horrible looking.

Nighttimes were the worst. It was then when Steven would awake with dread in his heart, with a surety that he would not live through this. He would listen to the sounds of simultaneous snoring and moaning of the men and feel desperate and lonely; when he would see again the deaths of his father and Gerritt and try to remember the sweet face of his Colleen. It was then he would feel the most despair and the tears would fall from his eyes.

One day when Steven had felt well enough to sit up, the doctor who had performed the surgery, came by to check on him. He was finally able to thank him for saving his leg.

"Don't be too quick yet, son," the doctor told him as he inspected his leg. "The danger isn't past. If it becomes infected, we may still have to remove it. And it's debatable whether or not you'll ever have use of it. The remaining bone may not be sufficient to support your weight. It just may break."

"Regardless sir," Steven told him, "I appreciate all the effort you went through to try and save it."

"Well, you're welcome son, it was quite a challenge. You rest and get your strength back."

"Yeah, so's they kin send you to that prison camp, Reb!" the man in the next bed hollered out. "An' I hope you rot there!"

Soon, with rest and adequate food, Steven was able to sit up more frequently and better observe his surroundings. He noticed the hospital was not as crowded as when he first arrived. Many of the less wounded were moved on to other facilities or sent home and since no battles had occurred in the area after Gettysburg, no new casualties were brought in. There were nearly ten other Confederates that he could see; none close enough for him to speak to. He wondered if he knew any of them. The angry man next to him, he discovered, had lost an arm. He had seen his kind of anger before, too many battles, too much death, too much loss, friends, relatives perhaps and then a loss of a part of his body. It was certainly cause for anger. This man's, right now, happened to be directed at him.

Steven was finally well enough to attempt to get up out of bed. The kind nurse who had been attending him all along brought a pair of crutches. He had discovered her name was Elizabeth.

"Alright now, Steven," she told him, "the first step is to swing your legs over the side of the bed." She helped to pull both his legs together over the side of the cot. A bolt of pain shot down his leg, the sweat breaking out on his forehead, but he was determined not to give up. He knew if he were to ever get back home, he needed to walk, hopefully to run.

"Now take hold of one of the crutches," Elizabeth instructed. "You can use it to pull yourself up. At first, only put weight on your good leg; gradually on, you can try the injured one."

With Elizabeth's help, he pulled himself to a standing position. He felt incredibly weak and light-headed. The sudden rush of blood to his leg caused it to throb unmercifully.

"Just stand still for a moment," Elizabeth told him, seeing how pale he had become.

Gradually, the dizziness faded and he ventured a few steps, leaning heavily on the crutches. He walked down the aisle way and then back, holding up the wounded leg and stepping only on his strong leg. By the time he got back to his cot, he felt exhausted and his leg was hurting terribly.

"Won't be long now, you dirty Reb," the man next to him said smiling, " 'til they send you off to that there prison."

Steven sat carefully on the edge of his cot, waiting to catch his breath. "Sir, I know we fought on opposite sides, but for now, couldn't we put our differences aside?" he asked the man.

"Put our differences aside? Well, now ain't that nicey, nicey. How'm I suppose to just put this aside?" he asked pointing to his empty sleeve. "Or, how do I put aside my best friend lyin' dead at Spotslvannia from a Reb bullet? Huh? How do I just put that 'aside'?"

"War is a terrible thing," he told the man, "men maiming, killing each other. There have been great losses on both sides. I lost my father at Manassas and my boyhood friend at Sharpsburg, but I hold you no malice. Even though I many be a prisoner of the Union Army, in this place, this hospital, I would hope we could at least be civil to one another."

"Bah!" the man exclaimed, but Steven thought his expression had softened somewhat.

The following day after Steven had taken his short walk down the aisle, his cot neighbor was just returning from the latrine. He stood in his path, preventing him from going further. At first he simply glared at him, looking as if he wanted to do him harm.

"Tell me why I shouldn't knock that crutch right out from under you," he said to Steven.

"Because we're both soldiers, but more importantly, because we're both men who have endured much."

The man looked at him for a few moments more and then slowly stepped aside. Steven reached his cot and sat down, looking up at the angry man gratefully.

"What be your name, Reb?" the man asked sitting across from him on his own cot.

"Steven sir, Steven Covington," he answered. "And you are…..?"

"Jack Truman, 61st Massachusetts. Where you from?"

"I live on a farm near Savannah, Georgia," Steven told him.

"A farmer, eh? What you grow on that there farm?" Jack asked him.

"A little of everything, but mostly cotton."

"So, you one of them rich ass plantation owners with about a thousand slaves?" Jack asked with the sarcasm returning to his voice.

"We were well off, yes, and we had slaves to help with the work. But now, I don't know; with my father gone, me here injured, I don't know what's going to be happenin' to our place." Steven had tried not to think about home very often, but with Jack's questions, the pain came back; the death of his father, of Gerritt, of not knowing whether or not he would ever see Colleen again.

"You see, that's what we in the South are fightin' for; our homes, our family, our way of life. You all have been fightin' mainly in the south. Those are our homes, towns and farms that are burnin', that are being destroyed. We just want to protect what's ours, be left alone to live our lives the way we choose.

Jack frowned. "I hadn't really thought about it that way before, but you fellows are the ones who left the Union, didn't want to be part of us anymore."

"Because we felt the government was trying to tell us how we should live our lives, too much regulations."

"You mean like ownin' your slaves?" Jack asked squinting his eyes. "How do it feel anyhow, owning somebody?"

Steven shrugged. "I never thought much about it. It's the way I've always lived; my parents and grandparents before me. Those people are workers. They perform tasks to help with the productivity of our farm."

"Yeah, for free," Jack said disdainfully.

"Well, sir, they are not free. Initially, they can be expensive to purchase and then they must be housed, clothed, fed……."

"But, they'se people ain't they? And even if they do work for you and you takes care of 'em, they ain't free. Don't every man want to be free?"

Steven looked the man in the eyes. "You may be right Mr. Truman. You may be right."

It wasn't long before Steven was able to walk all about the large room, even putting a little of his weight on the injured leg. It still pained him a great deal, but at least the wound had not become infected and the doctor had told him they would be taking out the stitches soon. As he took his exercise, he again noticed the toll taken on the human body by shell and bullet. Many of the injuries consisted of loss of limbs and some with head or face injuries. But, the devastation of flesh he had seen too many times before. Now he also saw the gangrene, the dysentery and cholera he had heard spoken about in the camps. He knew many more would die in spite of the efforts of the doctors.

He was able to speak a few brief words to several of the other Confederates there on his trek around the room. One man had been in his own company, but knew nothing more than he on what their fate might be. Sentries posted there for the sole purpose of watching over the prisoners, discouraged conversation and Steven was ushered back to his cot.

Over the next several weeks, more men left the facility, either to go home or because of death. Even Steven's bedmate Jack, was shipped back to his home in Massachusetts. Upon leaving, he had even been cordial to him; holding out a hand to Steven to shake and wish him good luck after this war was over. Steven had responded in like kind, feeling no ill towards this Yankee who had shown such anger towards him.

Most of the prisoner's health had stabilized to the point where they would be able to be moved. Steven knew it was now only a matter of time before they would transfer them to a Union prison. He kept trying to think of a way he could escape and make his way back to Virginia, but there were as many guards as prisoners and his leg would have never let him get too far. He didn't think a man on crutches would be too difficult to locate if discovered missing. He only hoped, once his leg had healed sufficiently, he would be able to discover a way to escape from the Yankee prison, wherever that might be.

It was a cool day in September when all the Confederate prisoners were gathered together and taken outside to a waiting wagon. Before leaving, Steven looked up at the cross at the front of the room. A bright shaft of sunlight shone through one of the stained glass windows, casting colors of purple, red and yellow onto the cross. He said a silent prayer, asking God to watch over them as they continued on this journey, on this odyssey of war which had begun so long ago. He was also able to thank Elizabeth for the kindness she had shown him during his stay there. As always, she had a ready smile and wished him well.

As they were taken outside, Steven saw how colorful the trees had become, the leaves having started their annual transformation from green to shades of crimson, orange and gold. On their ride to the railway crossing, he also observed lush pastures and burgeoning orchards, neat farmlands and abundant cattle and sheep grazing in the fields.

If nothing else, he thought, the north seemed to have some beautiful countryside. But then, not many battles had been fought in the north. Few of their towns and villages had been devastated, nor had battles scared the fields. He wondered what it must look like in winter. He had never even seen snow until the war when he had had to endure the cold and wet during their winter encampments in Virginia. He hadn't much cared for it then.

By the time they reached the railroad, a large hissing locomotive was waiting on the tracks, carrying several boxcars behind. He was helped up into one of these, along with the others. Inside was a bed of straw where they could sit or lie down on their journey. Where their destination was, they knew not, but as the train pulled away, they knew they were headed east; away from Virginia, from the south and away from their homes. They could no longer see outside unless one peered through the slats in the car. At first, the ten men inside were quiet; each lost in his own thoughts about where they might be taking them and what fate awaited them there. Slowly, as the time past, they began talking. At first telling each other their name and from which regiment and company they were from and who they had served under. Soon, however, they began to speak of the battle, of Gettysburg and the horrors it had evoked, how each had been wounded and where they had been at the time. Again, the names of Little Round Top, Big Round Top and the peach orchard were on their tongues. But, it was Pickett's last charge they spoke of last, for it had been then that most of them had been wounded, and then picked off the field by Yankees before they could be rescued by their own. By the telling of it, it was a catharsis, a beginning of healing.

It took a full day and night to reach their destination near a small town in Maryland. A place called Point Lookout. The large sliding door swung back revealing a line of armed men in blue, directing them out of the car. The men squinted in the bright morning light after the dimness of the boxcar. Steven's first sight of the prison was a tall massive stockade type fence reminiscent of a fortress. At each of the corners was a large guard tower with two or three armed men at each one; an imposing structure, at the least.

The prisoners were herded around to a large gate, which had begun to swing open upon their arrival. Steven limped along on his crutch. The hospital had allowed him to keep one of them or walking without assistance would have been impossible.

Inside they saw ten barracks type buildings, low with flat roofs and nearly as long as the compound itself. They were led to one at the far end passing on the way, more guards and more of the other prisoners, standing or sitting outside in the sunlight. Steven saw the torn and dirty gray uniforms, the bare feet, the unshaven faces and long hair, the sullen unsmiling faces and especially the haunted look in their eyes.

Upon arriving at the last of the long barracks, they were directed to go inside and find a spot where they would now sleep. They were told the latrine was at the far end of the compound and meals were served twice a day. Then they were handed a tin cup, a wooden bowl and a bedroll. More rules were thrown their way, which Steven barely heard. The sights and sounds around him were overwhelming. Thousands of his fellow southerners were milling around. Talking sounded like the din of thousands of swarming insects along with the putrid stench of rotten garbage and body waste.

Once inside the barrack, however, the sight was even more appalling. Bedrolls lined each side of the long building, some with dark shapes of men on them and others empty. It was dark and dank, the only ventilation coming from several small slits in the ceiling, shafts of dusty light from them penetrating the darkness. The smell was nearly overwhelming, putrid and strong. Steven found it difficult to draw a breath the air was so thick with smoke and stench.

They were pushed along by one of the guards and ordered to find a spot on the floor to lay their bedroll. As they walked along the aisle way between beds, Steven looked at the men sitting or lying on the floor; saw the sunken eyes, the emaciated bodies, men with missing limbs or open sores. Some of them were coughing and moaning, lying in their own yellow vomitess and bile. Swarms of flies buzzed around them landing on their eyes and mouths. The smell was so foul, Steven nearly retched, but his heart ached. These were his comrades, men who had fought bravely for their cause and now they had been reduced to this. If battles of war were a living death, then surely this was hell.

CHAPTER FOURTEEN —November 1863

On the long march back to Virginia, after the battle at Chattanooga, Colleen had never felt more exhausted. She had been completely drained, both physically and emotionally. She had even considered revealing her true identity, so she might be sent back home, but then she reconsidered, feeling that everything she had already gone through would have been in vain and she would still not know the fate of Steven. She knew she would not be able to rest until she knew positively what had happened to him; whether he was in some Yankee prison, or wounded in a hospital, or worse, had died. She only knew she needed to find out, so she decided to continue on with the deception. She only hoped she wouldn't have to go to battle again any time soon.

She got her wish, for when they had returned to the large camp, preparations were begun to build winter quarters. Patrick, William and Gordon had invited her and Sam in the erection of an adequate hut to enable them to live through the winter. So with timbers and canvas, gleaned from old Sibley tents, they were able to build a decent size dwelling for the five of them. They were even able to acquire a wood stove, which they installed with a pipe leading up through the timbers to allow for the ventilation of the smoke. Then they chopped, split and stacked wood to heat their little abode throughout the winter. Colleen had done her part and had acquired blistered hands for her efforts. Surely her mother would have never recognized her now, dirty, smelly, callused hands and feet.

When the full force of the winter blasts finally hit the camp in late November, Colleen found the close confinement with four men extremely uncomfortable. It had become even more difficult for her to find privacy to relieve herself and then there was the problem of her monthlies. For the past few times, she had been near streams and rivers where she could take the soiled rags and wash them, hanging them on a bush to dry. She was using the bandage material she had had Dora acquire for her before she left.

But now, in the close quarters with time on their hands, she would repeatedly throughout the day, excuse herself, claiming a weak bladder. The men taunted her about it, but it couldn't be helped. Washing the cloths had also become more arduous as the stream nearby was so cold, her hands would become numb in the water. Trying to dry them was another matter; owing to the bitter cold, they would sometimes freeze stiff and she would have to put them on still wet and half-frozen. She had never before had to attend to this task, as the slaves did the washing of their linens. They were even warmed by the oven before being brought to her. It was nearly enough to cause her to bolt, to run back to her Shannon and warmth.

Lately, her breasts hurt her a great deal from being constantly bound. At night she would loosen them as much as possible and then tighten them again in the morning. She only hoped she wasn't doing any permanent damage. Someday, she would want to nurse her sweet children at her breasts.

The cabin itself was crowded with their bedrolls around the perimeter with a crude table and other utensils near the wood stove. At times it was too hot inside and combined with the men's pipe smoking, made the atmosphere stifling. The others would all strip down to their pants, going about bare-chested. When they had encouraged her to do the same, she told them she was embarrassed at not being very manly, still having a boy's physique. And besides, she wasn't really all that hot; all the while sweat would be running down her back into her pants and beading up on her forehead. But they would tease her regardless, pointing out that Sam still had the skinny body of a boy, and he took his shirt off. Of course she would not relent and so the teasing did not stop; except for Patrick.

Sometimes when she was near tears from their bantering, he would look her in the eyes, a soft compassionate look and tell the others to stop. It was Patrick, however, that she had trouble keeping her eyes from when his shirt was off. On top of being one of the handsomest men she had ever seen, his body, too, was sensual and muscular. Whenever he would move or lift something, she could see the muscles ripple along his back and arms. It made her feel strange, desirous and hungry for something. But, she didn't really understand what it was she was feeling and so tried looking away.

Other times the men would get to arguing as most do when confined to small quarters and Colleen would be afraid it would come to fisticuffs, but so far the worst had only amounted to shoving and shouting in one another's faces. Then Colleen would welcome picket duty just to get out of that small, hot space with all the smell and anger of the men. Drilling and marching still went on during the day, to keep the men in shape and sharp with their skills.

Her first few times on picket duty she had been terrified; was sure the Yankees lurked out in the darkness waiting to stab her with their bayonet and cross their lines. Every twig that snapped, every rustle in the brush or any splash in the river, brought her rifle up to the ready, her heart pounding in her chest. After all, the enemy still lurked somewhere on the opposite bank. But gradually she relaxed, still staying alert, but then recognizing the sounds of skunk, raccoon, and possum in the underbrush or the splash of a beaver into the river.

She began to look forward to these times of solitude, but they were also the times when her mind would wander home, thinking of Shannon. She would think of the days before the war, of the quiet picnics on the river, or the glorious balls at holiday time; when the house would be grandly decorated and all the guests would be dressed in their finest. All the most succulent food would be served; goose, ham, turkey, sweet potato, cakes and sweets of every description. Or sometimes she just thought about a lazy Sunday, when after church they would come home to warm scones and tea, shared with the Covingtons. She remembered how she and Steven would take walks together and laugh. She thought about how it felt to be held in his arms, to kiss his lips, to make love with him.

She thought about how good life had been with nothing more pressing in a day than choosing which dress to wear. She thought about the teas she had with her girlfriends; how they would gossip and talk about the latest fashions or who was planning on taking whom to the cotillion. She missed the companionship of women, the way it had been before, when they would go to Savannah and shop for beautiful clothes, have lunch at the most expensive restaurants and enjoy the flirtations of men. There had been outings to the opera and theater and twice, she had even crossed the Atlantic for a holiday in France and England.

And then the war had come and changed everything. Tears would fill her eyes as she remembered the crushing losses; Mr. Covington, neighbor friends, then Gerritt and now Steven missing. So, on those solitary picket duties, when all was quiet and the stars shone brightly, she cried great deep sobs, silently grieving for what had been.

Back in her bedroll, after everyone had gone to sleep, she began to have nightmares. They terrorized her with flashing scenes of brutal death, blood and mutilations. The sounds in her dreams were those of explosions and screams. Many times she would awaken with tears on her face.

When the snows finally came the troops hunkered down in their shelters. The winds howled outside, flapping the canvas portion of their cabin, but as long as the wood held out, they stayed warm. Patrick taught her to play pinochle and William to sing camp songs.

He enjoyed singing and had a pleasant voice. He would frequently entertain them with different selections such as; “Arkansas Traveler”, “The Goose Hangs High”, or Billy in the Low Grounds”. Sometimes the fare would include theater songs to bawdy whorehouse ballads. It was after one of these rousing songs that the talk would generally turn to women. The men were understandably lonely for female companionship and would, on occasion, retell a particular tryst with some lusty femme fetal.

Colleen usually kept quiet during these discussions, but after having been harassed and subjected to numerous name calling, she finally made up an encounter with her own lusty lady; going into detail about her generous bosom, trim waist, and succulent lips, (those on her face and those between her lily white thighs). She described in detail the slow disrobing, the passionate kisses shared, the caressing of soft skin, the frenzied urgency and then the final penetration and ensuing climax. By the time her tale was told, each man in the room’s eyes were wide, with mouths hanging open. When she looked at Patrick, she saw a slight smile at the corners of his mouth. She wasn’t quite sure how to interpret his reaction, as was many a time with him. At any rate, it had the desired effect in that they no longer harassed her about her love life. They did, however, ask her to repeat the story several times over.

Some of the men in camp enjoyed entertaining visitors if family were close enough to travel there. Women there had definitely brightened the morale. The men in Colleen’s shelter, however, had no family to visit as most were from Georgia and it was prohibitive for them to come see their loved ones. And of course, Colleen's family didn't even know she was there.

During that long winter the men would share stories, mostly of their past, some humorous, some touching. Others, who could read, spent hours in that pastime, sharing with those who could not, the plots of the dime novels. Many men enjoyed outdoor recreation to burn off some of their pent up energies. Almost weekly there would be a foot race or boxing match for them to bet their meager wages on.

For the five of them, it was an opportunity to get to know one another better. Colleen surmised that Gordon was a highly educated man, reading voraciously and trying in vain to teach Sam to play chess. William was rough at times, but had a kind heart and was willing to share anything he owned.

It was also a time when they would talk of past battles they had fought, but seldom did they speak of the horror, the death, and the loss. Then William would sing "Danny Boy" and everyone would feel melancholy, tears even running down Patrick's face. Colleen couldn't help but watch him when this happened, for she had rarely seen a man cry. It endured him to her, although realizing he thought he was in the presence of men and didn't know if he would respond in like if with women. All the same, she felt touched by his emotion.

Their pastimes, the activity, helped to keep their minds off their empty bellies. Rations were meager and frequently the sounds of everyone's stomach rumblings could be heard during quiet times.

Finally spring reached out with its tendrils of warmth, touching the land, the trees and those harbored indoors. The brightness drew them outside more often to listen to bird song and new life. In March, they heard that a fairly unknown man had been named commander of all the Union Armies. His name was General Ulysses Grant. What this meant to of all of them and the war, they did not yet know.

In April the rains came, filling rivers and streams and turning roads into quagmires. Hauling equipment and supplies from one place to another had become an exercise in futility. Some of the bogs were so enormous as to nearly swallow an entire wagon. Colleen felt she would never get the dampness from her skin and feet. No matter how often she took off her boots and socks and attempted to dry them, they continued to feel damp when she put them back on.

But along with the newness of spring, with the warmth of the sun, would also bring a return to the carnage. Already they could see how the Union forces on the other side of the river were growing.

It was about this time that William returned to their shelter after having been out walking the large camp and talking to friends. He had heard news that was tragic indeed. President Davis' five year old son Joe, had fallen from a balcony at his home and was killed. "I heerd the President was inconsolable," William told them. "Joe was his favorite."

Colleen thought about President Davis grieving for his young son. Indeed, it was a terrible thing to have such a young child die. But she wondered, was it anymore tragic than the thousands of deaths that had occurred in this war? Every single person who had already passed on, had someone who cared, someone who had loved them and would grieve too; mothers, daughters, wives. What of their grief?

Then on May 4th, Colleen remembered it was Wednesday, orders came from General Lee himself to break camp and prepare for the march. It was reported that General Grant was sending his troops across the Rapidian on newly floated pontoon bridges near Germanna Ford.

All their winter supplies were abandoned and their haversacks packed with the bare necessities. The three different corps of Lee's army, plus Stuart's cavalry was ready to march by nine o' clock in the morning. They began their advance towards the Federal lines. They were headed towards an area called the Wilderness.

As they walked in formation, led by General A.P. Hill who had been a division commander under Stonewall Jackson and their own 4th Georgia division led by Captain Tinsley and Major Willis, under General Gordon, they felt a sense of dread. No one spoke a great deal, nor did anyone sing or joke as they did on other marches.

They followed the Orange Turnpike, moving towards Germanna Ford where the Yankees were reported to have crossed the Rapidian. The road was clogged with horses, wagons, large guns and men.

Colleen could not shake the feeling of ominous foreboding, more so than she had felt on her trek to Tennessee. She didn't dare voice her fears to the others, for fear they would think her a coward. But isn't that what she was? She was terrified of going into battle again. Everything in her wanted to run, run as far from this place as possible. But where would she run to? It seemed no where in the south had been left untouched. The ruthless Yankees under General Sherman were now invading even her precious Georgia. If he ever made it to Savannah, she might not have a home to go to. And what had her mission been? To find Steven and bring him home, but how had she really thought she was to accomplish that by joining the army? She was still no closer to finding Steven and had only put herself in jeopardy. She couldn't very well rescue Steven if she were dead. She was beginning to think this scheme had not been well thought out.

They finally arrived at the edge of the Wilderness and Colleen could see why it was so aptly named. Ahead of them lay a dense forest of trees, vines and brambles so thick you couldn't see ten feet into its midst. Their dread only increased. Were they expected to go into that thicket and fight?

There they halted for the evening, building fires and laying out their bedrolls only five miles from Union troops. Patrick and Colleen sat near each other, eating hard tack and drinking strong coffee.

"I can tell your nervous laddie," Patrick told her. "You haven't said but two words since we started out."

"I guess I am, aren't you?" she replied.

"Aye, this wilderness doesn't look too friendly, but laddie, we'll give 'em a good fight, eh?"

Colleen shook her head. "I don't know Patrick. I just don't know if I can go through with it."

Patrick touched her arm and she looked into his kind face. "Sure you can, laddie. I saw how twas with the way you fought in Tennessee; you're a real soldier."

"No, no I'm not; if you only knew," she said quietly.

"I do know, laddie," Patrick said.

She looked at him carefully, wondering if he had discovered her secret. "I know you feel you're not, but I know better. When it came down to facin' the enemy, you fought bravely, 'specially seein' it were your first time out. But don't worry, lad, I'll stay by your side. You'll do just fine. Perhaps if you remembered the cause and what it tis we're fightin' for."

"I'm really not sure I do know what that is anymore," she said looking down into the fire. "Do you know, Patrick?"

"Aye, it does become muddled after a bit, doesn't it? But aren't we fightin' for our independence, our way of life, without the government interferrin'?"

"What does that mean, really? Is it so the rich can stay rich; be able to keep their slaves and continue in the lifestyle to which they have become accustomed? Or is it a bunch of politicians in the Southern states who decided they wanted their own union; they were so egotistical to think they were better than the Union as a whole?"

"You make a good point laddie, but you know there are those who already felt separate, that they don't be like those in the north, that our way of life is different, slower, more gentile."

"If it only comes down to keepin' human beings in slavery to maintain a certain lifestyle and allow the rich to stay rich, then I don't think the slaughter of war is worth that," Colleen said perhaps a little too vehemently.

Patrick's eyes narrowed. "I'd hate to think I've been fightin' for all these years just for the rich to stay rich. I'm thinkin' it be more for our own independence, to govern the way we choose."

Colleen shrugged her shoulders. "Then perhaps we disagree, but no matter, we both are here now." Patrick only nodded and took a sip of his coffee.

That night Colleen slept little, disturbed by troubling dreams of Steven, dying in some far away prison.

The following morning, May 5th, broke warm and hazy. Captain Tinsley rousted them up at five o' clock, telling them the Yankees were already on the move into the Wilderness. There was no time to eat as they were advancing down the Orange Plank Road, near a place called Parker's Store, directly into the thick underbrush. Further south from where they marched, was a detachment of Federal troops headed in their direction.

As they began picking their way through the tangle of trees and brush, they began to notice skeletons lying about on top of the ground. Chills went up Colleen's spine when she saw them. Some were only parts, a skull or leg bones, a rib cage, where wild animals had torn them apart.

"Must be what's left from the battle of Chancellorsville last year," Gordon spoke up. "See here, this was a Reb," he pointed out. "You can still see some of his uniform."

Colleen could not shake the dread she felt as she looked at the gleaming skulls lying about, their hallow sockets and exposed teeth, grim testimony to a horror that occurred on this same spot a year before. But then alongside the skeletal remains of these men were the brightly bobbing heads of spring flowers, casting their beauty amongst the devastation.

Captain Tinsley and Major Willis suddenly came down the line, hustling them into position, warning them of approaching Federals. Four more brigades were dispatched to a bramble-covered field, extending their line to head off an attack. Weapons were checked, ammunition passed around and bayonets readied.

Colleen's heart began to pound wildly and her hands were perspiring on her rifle. She had an incredible desire to flee from this death place as quickly as she could. She looked to her left and right; saw the men all along the line, tense, a tight gasp on their rifles. She looked at Sam; saw him trembling, his lips quivering, near tears. When she looked the other way, she saw Patrick watching her. He smiled and winked at her.

"Stay close, lad," he said.

There was no more time for talking as suddenly a spattering of musket fire could be heard. The officers called the charge and they began moving forward towards the sounds of the firing. It wasn't long before bullets were whizzing past their heads, burrowing into the ground and thudding into the bodies of their comrades. Soon they could see blue uniforms darting among the trees and brush. The thickets and brambles were so intertwined; it was difficult to maneuver through them.

Patrick pulled Colleen to the ground as bullets flew over them. Thorns scratched her face, but she barely noticed. "Stay down and shoot," Patrick called out to her. "They have to cross that gully and we'll have the advantage."

Just as he had said, the line of Union soldiers began pouring over the gully. As they lay prone on the ground, they had the advantage of shooting up at them. The effect was devastating and they began pulling back.

The Confederate troops stood and moved forward, calling out as they advanced, pushing the Yankees further into the Wilderness. As they did so, more firing began off to their left. Now they were being attacked on two sides. Colleen continued firing, hiding behind trees as she went. She kept an eye on the men around her, especially Patrick, for fear of being lost in this vast jungle of brambles. The thorns and vines clung and tore at her legs and arms. Several times she fell because of their tenacious hold.

Suddenly a new attack opened up on her left. When she began firing in the other direction, she was surprised to see the men who were making their way through the thicket. Instead of the regular blue uniform, these men were wearing peacock blue with elaborate designs, red sashes, and bright red caps with tassels. They were the elite 140th New York Zouaves and they were fierce fighting men. However, when they crossed the field and began their assault against the confederate forces, they were met with such a barrage of fire, volley after volley of bullets, that they too, were driven back.

Just when Colleen thought they might get a break in the fighting, the shelling began. The balls whistled over head, exploding into the trees, vibrating the ground. With renewed gallantry, the Zouaves surged forward once more. Colleen and the rest of the division began firing back, but the New Yorkers plowed through until they were face to face. Men began fighting hand to hand, being too close to even fire their weapons. Bayonets, rifle butts and fists were used to repel the foe. One man in bright red and blue rushed straight at Colleen, bayonet barred, screaming a war cry. She felt frozen to the spot, as if everything were happening in slow motion. Just as the soldier was about to plunge his bayonet into her, she heard a voice yelling, "Move!"

Quickly she sidestepped and the man lunged inches short of her. She then plunged her own bayonet into the man's back. He cried out and fell to the ground, her knife still in him. "Oh, my god!" she cried out, "oh, my dear god!"

She withdrew the bayonet and stood staring at the fallen man. It was one thing to shoot a man from a distance and another to actually feel the soft flesh of his body, watch the look of terror and pain cross his face and see the life ebb away. She looked up and saw Patrick next to her, out of breath and wide eyed. "Are you safe lad?" he asked. She could only nod; realizing it was he who had called out to her.

Firing began again and they ran towards the line of men advancing further into the wilderness. Suddenly she was aware of a heavy, thick smoke drifting towards her. It was suffocating, causing her to look up from her mad rushing. The wilderness was on fire! It was moving in her direction, scorching flames, reaching towards the mid-afternoon sky. She could feel the heat, the flames blowing her way in waves.

She began to run away from the fire; at first aimlessly and then she realized she might run straight into Federal troops. She stopped, looking around to see if any of her company were nearby. At first she saw no one, could only hear the licking of the flames behind her, the booming of artillery and the volley of gunfire beyond. In spite of her fear of confrontation, she preferred to take her chances with the enemy than be consumed by the fire.

She ran forward cautiously, stopping to hide behind trees, peering around to see where she was headed. How did she get separated from the rest? When had they advanced further into the Wilderness? Where was Patrick?

Finally she saw them, men in gray, with their backs to her, firing into a line of blue. The air was thick with battle smoke and behind her thick smoke from the forest fire. She advanced cautiously, but she still had not seen anyone she recognized. As the bullets began flying past, she too, returned fire. When she had finally joined ranks with the others, she discovered from the men's insignia and battle flag, that she had joined the North Carolinians. She knew she could not leave to try and find her own brigade and simply joined her fellow Confederates to best the Yankees. Some of the men looked at her curiously, but they were much too busy firing, reloading and attempting to maneuver through the thick underbrush.

Men kept falling around her as she attempted to take cover behind trees and brush. She saw men trying to reload so quickly, the muzzles so hot from firing, ignition occurred, sending the ramrods flying. Others forgot to remove the rod before pulling the trigger, jamming the weapon.

She heard the scream of the Rebel cry and saw off to her right, Brigadier General John Gordon, leading his Georgia troops to join with the North Carolinians. Colleen saw William and Sam and then she spotted Patrick, firing into the Yankee line, but she was too far and the fighting too intense for her to reach him.

The volume of fire from the Confederate troops caused the Federals to stagger back, many of them killed or wounded. They kept advancing, pushing back the Yankees to within range of their own artillery.

Colleen tried to maintain sight of Patrick and still avoid being hit. The musket smoke was so intense she could barely see fifty feet in front of her. She could hear men calling out to one another and the cries of the wounded. Then the Yankees would double their efforts, surging forward into their lines, stepping over their own, pushing them back. The Confederates would retaliate, push back and advance to cover the Union line.

Behind them the fire had intensified, consuming everything in its path. The heat could now be felt along the lines, making them all apprehensive. Sweat rolled off Colleen's face and she had an intense craving for water. When would it end, she thought, when they were all dead or burned from the fire?

It was early evening and dusk was coming on, when the Union artillery began firing once more. The shells were landing all around them, blowing holes in the ground, shearing off treetops and maiming men.

Colleen dove into a depression in the ground, trying to escape their devastation. She was trembling, grasping her rifle with both hands. It was then a shell exploded overhead directly into a large pine. The tree cracked and began to fall, directly over where Colleen lay. She only had time to cover her head before the tree crashed over the depression, pinning her legs. She felt an excruciating pain, shoot all the way up to her waist and she feared they were broken. She began to call out for help, but no one seemed to hear her over the noise of the shelling and musket fire.

She tried to pull her legs out from under the tree, to get out of the hole, but she couldn't move them, the weight of the tree holding her fast. She tried harder, laying aside her rifle and pushing with her hands, but the tree wouldn't move. She felt desperate, afraid a Yankee would discover her helpless and shoot or stab her where she lay.

Darkness was enveloping the Wilderness, the only light coming from the still burning fire. The shelling had ceased and the voices were becoming fainter.

"Help!" she cried out, now afraid of being left alone. "Patrick! William! Anyone! Please help me!" And then she heard them; others out there, calling for help, wounded, unable to get away. Chills ran up her spine as she realized so many were helpless and no one was coming. Not only that, but the fire was raging closer and closer. She could now see it licking its way up the tallest trees and then she heard a sound so horrible it chilled her blood. She heard screaming, screaming like she had never heard before; not like those who had been shot or stabbed or even of those hit by artillery. It was the screams of those being burned alive; men wounded who could not get out of the path of the devouring flames. It was horrific having to listen to those suffering, dying and then she realized, she too, was in the path of the inferno.

She felt desperate, pushing on the tree, pulling on her legs, even though it caused her pain, trying to extricate them from under the tree. She began to cry in her frustration, the tears streaking her dirt and soot covered face. She lay back down, the sobs being wrenched from her very soul. She cried for Gerritt, for Steven, for a life she would never share with him. She cried for all the men who had died so brutality in this war, and she cried for herself.

She looked up into the darkness, the fire causing the sky to turn orange, with tendrils of flames shooting from the treetops. The smoke was getting denser, choking her and stinging her eyes. Small animals scurried past her, fleeing the fire.

"I'm going to die," she thought to herself, "just like all those others out there, screaming, no one to save them."

It was then she heard a voice, someone calling out. She sat up as far as she could and turned to her right, leaning on her elbow. She peered into the darkness and smoke. At first she couldn't see him and then he called out again. Finally she saw him, not more than thirty feet away, a young man, perhaps only eighteen years old. The first thing she noticed was his legs, bloody, shattered, and useless. And then she saw he wore the blue, a Yankee, and right behind him, the fire, moving quickly, consuming everything in its path.

"Help me please!" he cried out to her.

"I can't," she yelled over the roar of the blaze. "I'm caught under this tree!" She saw the hope flicker from his eyes. His face was so young, she thought and she was struck by the realization that his eyes were blue.

"Don't let me burn," he said to her. "Please, don't let me burn."

"I told you, I can't help you. She felt so helpless, so frustrated. The fire was coming closer and closer to the young man. He was trying to drag his body away from the flames using his arms, but he didn't get far. Sparks were falling on him, making small holes in his uniform. He lay there and reached out one arm to her, pleading with her. He's only a boy, she thought, he reminds me of Andrew Hunter back home. But he died, too.

"Please, help me!" the boy called out again. "I'm burning!" And indeed, she saw his boots were smoking and his pant leg had ignited.

"There's nothing I can do!" she screamed, the tears filling her eyes.

"Shoot me!" he cried. "For the love of God, shoot me!" His eyes were filled with terror.

She shook her head vehemently. It was one thing to shoot someone when they were shooting at you, a matter of life or death; and quite another to kill a helpless, wounded man. "No, I can't" she said looking away.

"Please!" the boy screamed, causing her to look back. His pants were now entirely engulfed in flames and they were moving up his body. "Shoot me! Shoot me, I beg you! Don't let me die this way!" He was screaming in pain and horror.

Almost calmly Colleen raised her rifle and leveled at the boy's head. A bullet was already in the barrel. She looked down the sights straight into his right eye. Tears were running down his face and he had suddenly become still. She saw his lips form the words, "Thank-you." And then she pulled the trigger. His head snapped back and then he lay still as the fire continued to consume his body.

Colleen's rifle fell to her side inside the depression and she found herself shaking all over, her breaths coming in gasps. She lay down and closed her eyes, tears streaming down the sides of her face. Now all she had to do was wait for the fire to take her as well, but there was no one about to kill her first. She began to wonder what it would be like to burn to death.

Burning brush started falling on the tree that covered her legs, starting some of the smaller branches to ignite. She suddenly cared very much whether she died and again renewed her efforts to extricate her legs from under the tree, pushing with her hands and pulling with her legs. Now she didn't even feel the pain; all she could see was the tree burning and she knew it would only be minutes before it took her. She screamed out with her frustration. "I don't want to burn!"

Suddenly a voice called out, "Colin! Colin lad, where are you?"

"Oh, my god, Patrick, is that you? Here, over here!" she called out to him. And then he was there beside her, his handsome, beautiful face looking down at her.

"Colin, are ye hurt? Can you stand?"

"I don't know. My legs are trapped under this tree," she told him. "Oh please, Patrick, get me out. I don't want to die!" He could hear in her voice she was becoming hysterical. She knew she didn't sound like a man any longer, but she didn't care.

"Hold on laddie," he said jumping down into the depression with her. "I'll have you out in a jiffy." He straddled her, facing the tree, then placing his hands under it, attempted to lift it off her. It didn't move and he tried again, the muscles in his neck and arms, bulging with his effort, but still he wasn't able to lift it. He turned to face her. "Don't worry lad, I'll get you out."

The fire was spreading, moving down the trunk of the tree towards them. "Hurry, Patrick, hurry," she encouraged.

Finally he sat in the depression with her, his back against the tree and his feet drawn up against the dirt wall. "I'm going to try and roll it," he told her, "and if it does, try to pull your legs out."

She nodded as he strained against the tree, pushing with all his strength. Slowly, slowly, the tree began to roll. She pulled and at first nothing, and then suddenly she was free. "I'm out! I'm out!" she yelled.

Patrick stood up and the tree rolled back with a thud. Colleen tried to stand, tried to run from that place in hell, but her legs gave out, wouldn't hold her up. Patrick handed her her own gun and his and then scooped her up in his arms and began carrying her. He made his way through the brambles and underbrush, vines and thorns raking them across the face.

Colleen could feel the strength in Patrick's arms, felt his heart pounding under his uniform, heard his hard breathing as he made his way in the darkness. After they had gone about a mile, he set her down and sat next to her.

"I've got to rest," he told her, breathing hard. "We should be safe here; the fire's going in the other direction."

"Thank-you, Patrick," she told him. "I would have died if it hadn't been for you."

"It's alright, lad. I told you I'd watch out for you, only I lost track of you for awhile, damn Wilderness."

She started shaking again, more so than she had before, her teeth chattering violently. "What's wrong with me?" she asked Patrick. "I can't stop shakin'."

"I think it may be the shock of it all. Do you think your legs are broken?"

"I don't know. They hurt, but not horribly."

He began to feel the long bones in her legs below the knee, gently but firmly. "I don't know if this works with people, but I use to do this to see if the legs on a horse was broken." He smiled and she could see the whiteness of his teeth in the darkness. She smiled back and felt like crying again because of his kindness.

"There's a lot of swellin' but I don't think any bones are broken," he told her. "I think we should stay here for the night. No sense stumblin' about not knowing where we might be. We could run into a Yankee camp."

Speaking of the Yankees reminded Colleen of the Union boy in the woods and the tears came to her eyes. She was glad it was too dark for Patrick to see.

Patrick took off his jacket and laid it on a pile of leaves. "Here, lad, lay yourself down. You've had quite a day and I don't need for you to be goin' into shock."

She lay down gratefully, curled on her side. She wished she could just go to sleep and never wake up.

Perhaps she should have died with the boy. How could she have killed him like that?

She felt movement and discovered Patrick had lain down next to her. He touched her shoulder, felt her trembling and moved closer to her. She welcomed his closeness, needed it. His body was warm, alive. There had been so much death today; she needed to feel life.

"How did you find me?" she asked quietly.

"I told you I'd watch out for you. I felt responsible for you. When we got separated I started lookin' for you. It began to get dark and I was worried about the fire. I just decided to keep lookin' 'til I found you, alive or dead." He said the last word very quietly as if he hadn't wanted to say it at all. "I've become very fond of you Colin."

She began to cry again because he sounded so kind, because he had saved her from dieing and because she had not been able to save the young boy.

"Lad, are you alright?" Patrick asked concerned, touching her shoulder again.

"No, no I'm not. I've done a horrible thing."

"What might that be, lad?"

"I've killed an unarmed man."

"Would that be a Yankee?" Patrick asked.

"Yes, but he shouldn't have died."

"Tell me about it."

So Colleen related the whole horrific tale of the boy in the Wilderness, of the fire and the consequences of her actions.

When she finished, Patrick was silent for a moment. "You did the right thing, laddie," he said finally.

"Burnin' to death is a most horrible and painful way to die. Believe me you did the boy a service."

But Colleen knew that that boy's face would forever haunt her dreams, his pleading, those blue eyes looking at her in pain, his reaching out to her. She suddenly felt overwhelmingly tired, her eyes so heavy and her body ached like she had never felt before. She fell asleep, nestled up against Patrick.

When she awoke slivers of sunlight were filtering through the trees and she could hear a low rumbling in the distance; artillery fire. She sat up slowly, light-headed and aching. She felt damp from lying on the ground. She was covered in small insect bites that itched and were red and swollen. She looked about and noticed they were in a small clearing, scattered about with a bed of dead leaves. Beyond the clearing were the tangled mass of brambles and thickets that Patrick had somehow negotiated last night in the dark.

She glanced over at him lying next to her and saw he still slept, his right arm flung over his eyes. His face was scratched with dried blood where the thorns had torn at his flesh. Strange feelings flooded over her as she watched him sleep. Grateful, yes, but there was something more. He had risked his life to find her. He had always looked out for her since they had met, but this time he had gone beyond duty. If she didn't know she was deeply in love with Steven, married to him, she would have thought her feelings for Patrick came close to love.

She didn't want to think about that, made her feel disloyal and concentrated instead on the condition of her legs. They still pained her a great deal and felt swollen.

Tentatively, she pulled up her pants legs to look at them. They were indeed swollen and had begun to turn black and blue. She hoped Patrick had been right about them not being broken. She bent them at the knee, moving them to see how they felt. There was soreness, but no excruciating pain. Her face stung and as she touched her cheek, discovered she too, had deep scratches from the brambles.

She suddenly heard rifle fire and turned to wake Patrick. When she touched him, he opened his eyes and smiled at her. "How're you feelin', lad?" he asked her sitting up.

"Some better than last night, but I'm powerful hungry and thirsty."

"I'll take that as a good sign."

"Perhaps, but I'm hearin' gun fire and shellin' and if we don't move, we may be in the middle of a battle," she told him, "and I wouldn't want the Yanks to find us first."

"Right you are," he said getting to his feet. "Do you think you can stand?"

"I think so, if you help me," she said holding out her hand.

He took it and slowly pulled her to her feet. She stood unsteadily but she was standing. Patrick came to her, putting her arm over his shoulder and his arm about her waist. "Alright now, Colin, lean on me and let's see if we can find out way back to our own lines."

Colleen knew that was a task easier said than done with everyone's lines in a jumble, fronts askew, regiments and brigades scattered all over the tangled forest, not knowing who was friend or foe.

"Let's head this way," Patrick directed. "I think it's the way to the Orange Plank Road and hopefully we'll run into Hill's division."

So they started off, with Colleen leaning heavily on Patrick. She was just grateful her legs were still working. They walked about a mile and there, just as Patrick predicted, they came across the main road. Once they had walked a way south they were able to find Hill's division, who had recently been joined by Longstreet. Several from the company came to greet them and seeing Colleen was injured, helped Patrick to take her to the hospital tent. It was full of those seriously wounded by the previous day's battle and so they layed her down on the grass outside. The others went back to their company while Patrick stayed with her.

"I'll see if I can find a doctor to look at your legs," he told her.

She grabbed his sleeve, stopping him. "No, I'll be alright for awhile. They've got a lot of very seriously hurt men to care for. I can wait."

"Aye, are you sure?" She nodded. "Then I think I need to get back to General Gordon's company. I'll tell Captain Tinsely where you are. But first, I'll try and find ye somethin' to eat and drink. You're lookin' mighty pale lad and I left my haversack with William."

He left to get her nourishment when she remembered she had lost her haversack in the Wilderness. Fortunately, because of Patrick, she still had her rifle, but there were personal items she needed in that pack. Her main concern was getting more rags for her monthlies. The ones she had she'd been washing and re-using. Now they were gone. It wouldn't be long before she would need them again. She also remembered the small derrgerotype of Steven she had hidden away inside. Tears came to her eyes at the thought of having lost it. It was times such as this when she questioned her quest. How long would she be able to continue fighting, watching men die, suffer injuries? How long could she keep up the deception before someone figured out she was a woman? But then she would think of what Steven might be going through. Had he been seriously injured? Was he in some horrible prison suffering who knew what unspeakable horrors? And then she knew in her heart that she must continue with her search.

Patrick returned with a canteen of water, a large slice of bread and a dripping piece of fat back. "Where did you find that?" she asked incredulous. She knew there was no mess located nearby.

"Don't ask," he told her as he handed her the canteen.

She drank long from the refreshing cool water and then worked on devouring the bread. "Thank-you, Patrick, you don't know how much I appreciate everything you've done for me."

"Don't mention it," he said smiling. "What's a mate for if he can't help out? Someday you may return the favor.

Now I best be getting back, but I'll check on you later."

Crashing artillery volleys could be heard directly across the road from their position, along with a smattering of musket fire. Just as Patrick stood up to leave, they saw General Longstreet himself, riding down the road with Brigadier General Micah Jenkins, a man in his thirties, who had already proved himself a brilliant military soldier, and a few other officers. They were talking among themselves as they rode along. Suddenly, rifle fire opened up on the men from the woods opposite. The assault had come from a brigade of Virginians.

General Jenkins fell from his saddle with a bullet in his brain, along with two other men. Someone yelled, “Friends! Friends!” but by the time the firing ceased, it was too late for the stricken men. It wasn’t until then that everyone saw the blood flowing down Longstreet’s neck and arm.

“My god!” Patrick whispered, “he’s been wounded!” He ran off to help with those who had been hit, leaving Colleen to watch helplessly. It was fortunate indeed, they were so near to a field hospital.

As General Longstreet was carried off, the Virginians in the woods surrounded him, grieving over the fact they had mistaken him for the enemy. Longstreet waved his hat to reassure them he was alive and a great cheer went up from the men. Ironically, it was in this same place where their beloved Stonewall Jackson had fallen in battle.

After this incident, there was a lull in the fighting while Colleen waited for someone to attend to her. She lay there all afternoon listening to the moaning and groaning of the injured men around her. One man, clearly suffering from a wound to his stomach, and near to her father’s age, started calling out for water. He seemed delirious, but she could not ignore his pleas. She moved closer to the man, carrying the canteen Patrick had given her.

"Water! Please, water," he called out.

"Here soldier," she told him, holding the canteen to his lips, "drink, it's water." She poured the liquid into his mouth, but before he could even swallow, the life passed from him. The water ran out from the sides of his mouth, his eyes staring sightless into the sky.

"No, no," she moaned covering her eyes with her hand. "No more, please God, no more." She looked up and saw the man's haversack lying next to him. Cautiously she picked it up and looked inside. There were some personal items such as a straight razor, soap, pipe and tobacco, his tin cup and plate and a Bible. There was also a bit of hardtack biscuit and a sewing kit. Looking further she found a pocket watch and a picture of a woman and young child. These she removed and placed them in the man's jacket pocket. But the pack and the remainder of the items, she decided to keep.

She made her way back to her spot on the grass where Patrick had first left her. She felt guilty about talking the man's pack, but she knew he wouldn't be needing it and she did.

It was growing dark and she could still hear artillery and musket fire across the roads into the Wilderness. She thought about those men she had come to know, Patrick, William, Gordon and young Sam. She wondered if they were again engaged in battle and hoped they were all safe. It was difficult enough watching those she didn't know die, let alone someone she did.

She hadn't realized she had fallen asleep, but suddenly she was being awakened by a weary looking man with smears of blood on his jacket and arms. "Son,

son, can you tell me the extent of your injuries?" the man asked her.

She sat up and began pulling up her pants legs. "I'm sorry to take your time. My injuries are minor compared to the others. Just go to them; I'll be alright," she apologized.

The doctor sighed. "Just show me where you're hurt," he said not unkindly.

"A tree fell on my legs. I don't know if they're broken."

The man began probing her leg bones, squeezing, rubbing. It hurt for him to be examining her, but she clenched her teeth to keep from crying out.

"Well they're pretty swollen and they'll be bruised for sometime, but I don't think they're broken. Rest them for awhile and they should be alright in a few days." He stood up to move towards the man who had died.

"Thank-you, doctor and sir… that man has passed on."

The doctor waved a detail of black men over to where the man lay to be carried off for burial; then moved on to the next man on the ground.

Once it had grown fully dark, the sounds of battle diminished and Colleen once more slept. This time the powerful exhaustion that overtook her body, kept her from disturbing dreams

When the glow of the morning sun broke over the horizon on the third day, Saturday May 7th, Colleen woke chilled from lying on the dew damp ground. She sat up and began moving about, feeling the soreness in her legs. She stood up unsteadily and gathered her rifle and newly acquired haversack and began making her way towards the large tent which had been set up as the hospital. Her stomach lurched as she saw a pile of human arms and legs lying on the ground, blood soaking the grass and flies swarming everywhere. She closed her eyes and turned away.

There was a lot of activity going on; with the wounded being loaded into ambulances for transport to a safer area; the dead gathered up for burial. Colleen felt apprehensive watching the hurried activity. She wondered what would become of her. She certainly didn't want to go to a hospital and take up a bed for some seriously wounded man, and there was always the threat of discovery, but she didn't know how she could make it back to her own division or where they might be.

Doctors and aides were rushing about helping men into the wagons, collecting supplies and paying her no heed. As unobtrusively as possible, she gathered a few bundles of rolled bandages and stuffed them into her haversack. Now she felt she had stolen again, but she now had cloth for her monthlies.

She moved back towards the road, still not decisive about what she should do or where she could go. She wished there was an officer about, who could give her direction, but then again she would hesitate to ask even if there had been someone available. She was afraid he would tell her to go with the ambulances and that was the last thing she wanted to do. What would happen to her there, was anyone's guess. She felt she needed to go forward with her company in order to find Steven.

Her dilemma was suddenly solved when she saw Patrick, William and Gordon coming down the road. She smiled when she saw them, but then it faded as she realized how weary they looked. Their faces and hair were blackened with soot and powder and their clothing was torn in many places. It was obvious they had been involved in heavy fighting in the bramble choked Wilderness amongst the fire.

She limped towards them and when they saw her, stopped and surrounded her. Patrick gave her a wan smile and she so wanted to throw her arms around him, but of course, she refrained. They looked so weary and sad, she did not want to ask what had gone on the previous night.

"We came for you lad, if your able to travel. I see you're walkin' some and that be a good sign," Patrick told her.

"Yes, the doctor finally looked at my legs and told me they weren't broken, to rest them for a few days and they should be fine."

"Well, perhaps then you should go with the ambulances to rest at the hospital for awhile," Gordon said pulling on his beard which had been singed by the fire.

Colleen looked desperately at Patrick. "Please, I don't want to go there. I might not get back and I most want to stay with my company."

"Then you come with us," Patrick said. "I'll not be leavin' you behind if you don't want to."

"Come along then son, or we'll all get left behind," Gordon told her, "Gordon's troops are already movin' out."

She hefted her pack onto her back and shouldered her rifle and began following them down the road, but her legs were still so sore and she limped so badly, that soon she had fallen far behind them. They stopped then and waited for her.

"This won't do," Patrick said with a frown once she had caught up.

Her lip trembled and tears were close to forming in her eyes. She was afraid he would send her back, would tell her she was useless. But instead, he took her gun from her and handed it and his own to William. "Now lad, hop up on my back and I'll carry ye."

She hesitated; for one, she didn't want to cause any further burden for him, but she also was fearful that by carrying her, he might be able to tell she was a woman.

"Come on, lad, you're just a wisp o' a boy. I'll not be burdened," he said turning his back to her.

She hesitated no longer and jumped up onto his back, folding her legs around his waist and holding on to his shoulders. He crooked his arms under her legs to hold her up and they continued on down the road.

With her body pressed close to his, she could smell the soot in his hair, the musky sweat on his body, the hardness of the muscles in his arms as he carried her and she remembered the night he slept close to her in the forest and kept her safe.

"Patrick, is Samuel back with the rest of the company?" she asked suddenly missing the shy young man, from their little group.

Patrick was silent and it was Gordon who suddenly spoke up. "The boy was killed last night in battle," he told her. “It was fierce fighting and he was brave to the end, never backing down from the enemy.”

Colleen felt deeply saddened by the loss of Samuel. She had come to truly care for the gentle, shy young man. He had shared funny stories during their confinement in winter camp, livening up their dreary days.

“Was the fighting very bad?” she asked the men.

“Aye, it got very fierce,” Patrick answered. “I got back to the company just afore six p.m. and the whole brigade was moving out towards the Yanks breastworks. Firin’ was powerful heavy, even the breastworks started on fire. But we kept at ‘em and right soon we had ‘em on the run.”

“Them Yanks weren’t no cowards, though,” William told her as he walked nearby. “They kept turnin’ and firin’, turnin’ and firin’, til we ain’t more’n a few paces apart, shootin’ point blank.”

“It was then just afore dark, that Samuel was hit,” Patrick said. “It was right quick. He didn’t suffer any.”

They were quiet for a time after that and they were finally able to catch up with Gordon’s Georgians. It was calm; an eerie silence hung over the land after the violence of the previous days. The troops were just beginning to move out down the road. The four joined them with Gordon taking a turn carrying Colleen.

All along the way they encountered the smoldering remains of burned men and horses, the stench overwhelmingly horrifying. Many were frozen in grotesque shapes as they had attempted to escape the fire. They saw burial details gathering up the remains and attempting to inter them before leaving. In some places they saw Reb and Yank lying together in a deadly embrace. The details simply buried them together. They had all experienced a new horror, the horror of death by fire and it was the face of hell.

Many times they had to make way for the numerous ambulances passing them by with their load of misery. At times the wagons stretched on for miles and still all the wounded had not been collected.

They marched on through the day, not even stopping for food, there not being much to be had at any rate. Patrick, William and Gordon continued carrying her throughout the day. The march wasn't an easy one; the road being choked with dust and smoke; many fires still burning nearby.

Near towards dark, they finally halted for the night and were told to keep silence as spies had told of Union troops nearby. They rested quietly on the side of the road, no fires, no rattling of canteens, no undo noise.

Suddenly, they heard a great noise go up from the opposite side of the trees, along with the tramping of thousands of feet. "The Yanks are in retreat!" someone called out. "They're on the run!" And then a great cheer went up from the Rebel troops, wave after wave down the line; division after division and then Colleen saw the reason for their exuberance. Riding down the road in the dusk filled night was General Robert E. Lee himself, erect, waving his hat to the troops.

"Three cheers for General Lee!" someone called out and a great roar went up from the men. It sent shivers down Colleen's spine. To hear these men, who had literally gone through hell for what they believed in, to follow this man they admired above all others, was truly inspiring. Perhaps now she understood a little of what their patriotism was all about; to realize the love they carried for home and loved ones and this white bearded man they called General. She knew that is why they were all here and why they were willing to die for it.

CHAPTER FIFTEEN —September 1863

Mary sat alone on the terrace as the orange glow of the sun set over the horizon. Tears wet her face. She felt drained, empty, as if she could no longer go on. Her world was crumbling around her. Colleen had been gone for over a month now. After repeated inquiries and investigation, they had pretty well concluded that she had run off. The why of Colleen's actions could not be answered, nor did she know were she had gone. Mary felt abandoned, alone with no one to help her with the plantation. Things were not good at Shannon. Even though Mr. Solomon ruled with the whip, many of their own slaves had been successful in running away. Soon, she would not be able to pay him and he would probably leave her too.

The crops they had grown had almost entirely been confiscated by the Confederate army. Their own food supplies were dangerously low. She had no idea how she would feed everyone in the months to come. Without the income from the cotton, they couldn't afford the supplies they needed to run the machinery for the gin or the mill. Repairs went unattended, looms stood idle, and since the army had also taken most of their horses, the blacksmith shop too, was barely functioning. Many of her friends had already lost everything. Some, in western Georgia where there had been fighting, had even had their homes burned or taken over by the Yankees. They had no livestock, no food, no home and had been forced to leave their land. For others, those poor to begin with, were literally starving to death, women, and children; left behind by husbands, fathers, who were now dead.

She was terrified of what might come. Gerritt was already gone, Colleen had run off; what if James never came home? What if they too, lost everything to this war? What would happen to her? How would she live?

Fresh tears filled her eyes and she covered her face with her hands, sobbing deep retching sobs. She cried until she could cry no more. When she stood up to go back into the house, the darkness had fallen around her. Tree frogs and crickets had begun their night sounds.

Rose met her at the door with a lamp and helped her to her room. The single light cast eerie shadows onto the walls. They dared not burn more than necessary as they were nearly out of fuel, with no means to get more. So far they still had a fair supply of candles and they hoarded them for the future. The fireplace stood cold. It wasn't needed for warmth yet, but she wasn't sure now they would get enough wood for the winter.

She sat in a chair near the bed and stared at the white sheets and comforter which Rose had already turned down in preparation for her sleeping, but she didn't want to lie beneath the cool sheets. That bed had become a lonely place, a place of troubling dreams. At one time it had been a place of rest and comfort, lying next to James. It was where he would hold her in his arms, kiss and caress her and tell her how much he loved her. They had planned their future in that bed, talked of dreams. Their children had been born and conceived in that bed. Now it was empty and cold and she didn't even know if James would ever share it with her again. There had been no letters for so long, she didn't know if he were alive or dead. His name had not appeared on the death notices in town, but the list was not always accurate.

Finally, exhausted, she crept into her solitary bed and slept fitfully, her dreams of Gerritt and James; alone, dieing in some faraway place and she wept again in her sleep.

Upon awakening, she still did not feel refreshed. It was a rainy, stormy day, which only added to her depression. She went downstairs to breakfast still wearing her nightgown and bed jacket, not even bothering to dress. She sat at the large table alone while Bess put the food in front of her.

"Isn't Miss Anna Bell coming down?" she asked the servant girl.

"No'm, she gots a headache," Bess told her. "She's stayin' in de bed."

Mary sighed and looked over her breakfast. It consisted of biscuits with gravy and eggs. At least they still had a few laying hens and enough flour for bread. But there was no tea, had not been for some time. Instead, there was a strong chicory coffee that could not even be sweetened with sugar, as that too, was scarce.

"Bess, surely we must have some milk for this gruel you call coffee," Mary said to her servant. "The remaining cow has not died, has she?"

"No ma'am," Bess answered hurrying to pour milk into the delicate china cup.

Mary sipped the liquid and made a face. "Not much better," she sighed again. "I do miss the tea."

"Yes'm," Bess said seeing the sadness in her mistresses face.

"There are so many things I miss," she said leaning back in her chair and closing her eyes. "I miss the parties with everyone dressed in their most beautiful dresses, the picnics at the lake. I miss the teas with all the ladies and shopping in Savannah." Her voice became low, choked with emotion. "But most of all I miss my family, James, Gerritt and Colleen. I just don't know if I'll ever see them again." Tears spilled out from under her lids.

She was startled when Matthew came into the room, hands behind his back and head down. "What is it Matthew?" she asked sharply, embarrassed by her tears.

"Dere come a messenger, Ma'am," her told her meekly.

"A messenger," Mary repeated. "What messenger?"

"He brung dis here letter," he said holding out an envelope.

Mary reached out hesitatingly and took the letter. Her heart was racing and her hand shook. She looked for a government seal, something official, but there was only her name. She didn't think she could handle any more bad news. She began to unseal it, a little cry escaping her lips as she did so.

Finally she pulled out the enclosed letter, unfolded it and began to read.

Dora had come into the room behind Matthew and the three servants stood silently watching her. Dora had seen the messenger and had been fearful it could be news of Colleen.

Mary suddenly clasped her free hand to her chest and then her mouth as she cried out. Dora went to her and stood close to her side. "Misses, what does it say?"

"Oh god! It's James!" she said excitedly. "He's alive and he's on his way home!"

" Lordy, that be good news," Dora told her. "When misses, when?"

Mary looked back at the letter and tears filled her eyes. "It says he was wounded at Gettysburg and has been in a hospital, but now he's coming home. He says he'll be arriving on the afternoon train to Savannah on Wednesday. Oh, that's today! He's coming home today!" She jumped up from the table and began running towards the stairs. "I must get ready. Bess, clean up this mess and tell Ellen to prepare a celebration dinner for the Master's return from the war."

"Yes'm, what she gonna cook, Misses?"

"There's some hams left in the smokehouse. Have her fix that; James loves ham and oh, sweet potatoes and snap beans. And have her bake peach pie for dessert."

"Ain't no sugar for no pie," Bess told her.

"Then just tell her to think of something," she said hurriedly. "I have to dress. Matthew, go to the stables and have Henry bring around the carriage at noon." She threw out directives to the servants as she nearly ran down the hall. "Dora, you come with me and help me to dress."

Once back in her room, she threw open the drapes and began looking through her wardrobe. "I want to look extra special for James. I need to find just the right dress and then you can do my hair," Mary told Dora. "Do you know how long it's been since I've seen my beloved husband? Two and a half years," she said without waiting for an answer.

She held up a sweeping blue dress in front of her, looking into the mirror on her dressing table.

"Misses," Dora said quietly, "what that means, Massa James wounded?"

Mary stopped, the smile frozen on her face. She hadn't wanted to think about that aspect of the letter, but she knew it loomed there like something hidden under the bed.

"I'm sure it can't be anything serious. He went to the hospital and he must be fully recovered now."

But Dora wondered why, if he were well, he wouldn't be going back to the fighting.

After Mary had dressed and Dora had brushed and styled her hair, braiding the thick locks and winding them around her head, she was ready to go to Savannah to meet James. Henry had brought the carriage around as she had requested and trying to keep from getting wet, she hurried through the rain to get inside.

As she traveled on to Savannah she thought perhaps she should have informed Mr. Solomon of James's return, but felt he would handle everything once he got home. She couldn't believe how relieved she was to have him coming back to assume the responsibilities. She was so weary of trying to manage everything, to try and find solutions for all their problems, but now James would take care of everything, just as he always had.

The thought struck her that James had been wounded in the same battle as Steven. But Steven had been taken prisoner and James had not. She tried to push the thought of his injuries from her mind. Surely he was all right or he wouldn't be coming home, would he? Or perhaps the opposite was true and his wound had been so severe, he could not return to the army. She shook her head, telling herself she wasn't going to think the worst. She only cared that he was coming home to her and to Shannon.

When she got to the station she discovered the train had not yet arrived. Not many passenger trains came in to Savannah anymore; most were being used by the army to transport troops. While Matthew stayed with the carriage, she paced nervously on the covered platform. A few others waited there as well; a young woman with a child, an elderly couple, a middle-aged man in a suit and top hat.

Finally, in the distance, the whistle of the train could be heard. Everyone walked closer to the edge of the platform watching down the track until the large plume of smoke from the locomotive could be seen. Then as it neared, they moved back again; the wheels squealing, the engine hissing.

Several conductors emerged and placed the wooden steps by the entryways for the passengers. Finally they began to disembark. Men, women, children, climbed down from the train; persons greeting one another with smiles and hugs, but still Mary had not seen James. Had she gotten the message wrong? Was it <u>this</u> Wednesday he was to come home?

Then she saw a man in a Confederate uniform stepping onto the platform. His hair was long and he wore a beard. His clothing was torn and dirty, but it was his left arm that drew Mary's attention, or rather the lack of one. For the man's sleeve hung limp and empty at his side.

She looked closely into his face. His green eyes looked familiar but they were haunted, full of pain. A long red scar ran from his left eye to his jaw. And suddenly she gasped and her knees nearly buckled under her when she realized the soldier was James.

She ran to him and stood in front of him, wanting to embrace him, but afraid. Tears filled her eyes and she found it difficult to speak.

"Mary," he said first and then he put his right arm around her and held on. "Oh, my Mary, my beautiful Mary." And the tears fell from his eyes.

She held him in her arms, rocking gently, the shock of his wounds sweeping over her. She wanted to scream and cry, rage against this horrific war that had taken her son and maimed her husband.

James let her go and touched her face. "It's been so long," he said, his voice husky with emotion. "I've waited so long to see your beautiful face. I would dream of it every night."

She could only nod, the tears still streaming down her face. She put her arm around his waist and began to lead him off the platform. "I'm so glad you've finally come home," she said finally. "Come darling, Matthew is waiting for us. Let's go home to Shannon."

Mary led James to the carriage where Matthew waited. His eyes widened at the shock of seeing his master's wounds, but he said nothing. He held the carriage door open for them to enter.

Once inside, James put his head back on the seat and closed his eyes. He seemed so tired, so worn. Mary thought he looked so much older, his hair grayer, the creases in his face deeper. She wanted to ask him about his arm, the deep wound on his face, but for now, she didn't dare. She was so upset herself over the loss of his arm; she couldn't imagine what he must be going through.

She looked into his dear face, so familiar and yet now, so strange. She had looked forward to the day for over two years, had wanted to tell him so much, but now that it was here, it was a deep sadness she felt and she knew it was not the time to talk of trouble. She reminded herself that the important thing was that he was alive and he had come home to her.

James barely spoke on their ride home, keeping his eyes closed, holding tightly to her hand as if he never wanted to let her go. Her picture of what things would be like when James came home from the war had changed drastically. She had thought the burden of responsibility would once again shift over to him, that she would be able to go back to being the mistress of the house, not concerning herself with matters of running the plantation. But now she saw that was not to be, at least for now.

They finally arrived home to Shannon and as they rode down the tree-lined drive, the rain ceased and the sun began to filter through the glistening leaves.

James leaned forward and looked out the window of the carriage. When he sat back against the seat again, Mary saw the tears in his eyes.

Dora, Rose, Bess and Carlton were waiting on the front porch as they pulled up, anxious to see their master once again. Mary got out first and helped James from the carriage. She could hear the gasps and saw the servants cover their mouths with their hands at the sight of James' wounds. She gave them a sharp, stern look as a warning.

As they climbed to the top of the stairs, she began to give them orders. "Rose, go upstairs and turn down the bed for Master James. Carlton, find him some clean clothing and Bess, tell Ellen to wait on dinner until Master James has rested. Unless of course, you'd rather eat first, darlin'"

"No, no," he said waving them all away. "I'm very weary. It was a long train ride and I need to rest."

The servant women rushed to do as they were bid, as Mary led James to the stairway. There he stopped and looked around at the home he left behind over two years before. "I never thought I'd see this house again," he said almost in a whisper; then he went slowly up the long staircase.

In their room the bedcovers had been drawn back and lying neatly on the chair was a pair of crisp, clean trousers and a clean linen shirt. Mary looked at the clothing with some apprehension. She didn't know if she should help him to dress or not.

He sat on the edge of the bed and looked so weary; he did not seem capable of lying down by himself. She went to him, knelt down and began to pull off his boots.

Then carefully, her hands shaking, she slipped off his jacket. As she was unbuttoning his shirt, he suddenly took her hands and held them in his one.

"It's ugly, my dear. You don't have to do this."

"You are my husband," she told him simply. "I love you." He nodded and allowed her to proceed. When she slipped the shirt from his shoulder, she bit her lip to keep from crying out. Only inches of his arm remained below the shoulder, an angry red scar slicing across the stump. She continued undressing him and then helped to re-dress him in the clean clothes. She knew he needed to bathe, his hair cut and a shave, but for now he only wanted to sleep. She helped him to lie down and for a time he simply looked around the room and at her.

"This is the most wonderful feeling bed," he told her, "so soft, so warm. You just don't know what it's like always sleeping on the ground." And then just like that, he was sleeping soundly.

Mary watched him for awhile and then quietly left the room. She leaned against the closed door, shaking, gathering her strength. Then she went down the back stairs to the pantry and asked Bess to get her a glass of wine. She didn't care if it were the middle of the day. She could see the questions in all their eyes about James and she was glad they hadn't asked. She had no answers right now. James had not told her how it had happened, what he had been through. She was almost glad he hadn't. It had been enough of a shock to see his wounds; she didn't know how she would react to the telling of the awful details. She needed some time to prepare herself.

Once Bess had brought her wine, she took a long drink. Her hands were shaking and her stomach was churning. In all her dreams, she had never imagined the possibility of James coming home so scarred; not only in body, but apparently in mind also. In all the letters he had sent home he had never mentioned the horrors he must have been dealing with. He had only written to ask how she was, what was happening at home. He told her how much he missed her and loved her and wished he were home. He had written about how sad he had been when Clifford died, or how grief stricken he was at Gerritt's death. But there had never been any details. That had probably been for the best. He knew her so well; knew it would have only worried her more to tell her of the horrors, of men maimed and disfigured.

She took her wine into the parlor where she found Anna Bell waiting for her. "I am so happy James has come home," she told Mary. "I heard about his wounds."

Mary nodded and sat in one of the chairs. "His left arm is gone and his face is scarred. I don't know the details. I didn't have the heart to ask; he was so weary."

"But at least, he's alive and home with you."

"Yes, I do have that," she said thinking of Clifford, "and I'm eternally grateful, but he's changed Anna Bell. I could see it in his eyes. He's not the same man who left here in '61."

When she had finished with her wine, she went back to the kitchen to see to the preparations for the special dinner. She wanted to make sure everything was perfect for James' first meal home. The smell of succulent ham, yams, greens and corn, wafted through the kitchen. They seldom had meals such as this anymore; their supplies so meager there were times they only had vegetables from the garden.

James slept for the rest of the afternoon, waking in the early evening. When Mary heard him moving about, she went in to him. It still took her by surprise to see the arm missing.

James was standing by one of the windows looking out onto the grounds. "The gardens need attention," he said to her.

"Yes, it's been difficult keeping up with things," she said going to his side.

"Why hasn't Mr. Solomon had the slaves maintaining them?"

"It's a little complicated and I don't think you need to hear about all of that right now," she said leading him away from the window. "Are you hungry? I've had a wonderful meal prepared for your home coming."

"Yes, of course. That was very nice of you.

Is Colleen downstairs? Is she here? I would so like to see my darlin' daughter."

Mary paused, not sure what she should tell him. "No dear, she's not here."

"Where is she, at friends?"

"No, James," she said quietly, her eyes downcast. "I don't know where she is. She ran off over a month ago."

"A month ago? But why, where did she go?"

Mary shook her head. "I don't know. I had everyone out looking for her. She was just gone, disappeared. She took one of the horses. It happened right after we got word about Steven; that he had been wounded and captured.

James covered his eyes with his hand. "No, no not my little girl. And I didn't know about Steven, either. Where?"

"At Gettysburg," she answered.

They walked downstairs together, James leaning heavily on Mary's arm. She thought he seemed so sad, so frail, so weak. She could see he had lost weight; had heard the stories about how the troops were starving.

When they reached the dining room, James stopped and looked at the elegant table. The best linens were laid out, the best china and silverware, the delicate rose pattern crystal. On the buffet was the ham, studded with cloves, the steaming sweet potatoes and vegetables.

Mary was smiling, sure he would be pleased with the wonderful meal she had had prepared for him. She helped him to be seated while the servants waited to serve them. She sat opposite him and nodded to Bess and Matthew to begin serving them. Soon their plates were full of the steaming flavorful food, blood red wine poured into the crystal.

James put the linen napkin in his lap, picked up the silver fork and took a few bites, when suddenly he began to weep; the tears flowing down his face. The servants looked uncomfortable, not knowing what they should do. They had never seen their master cry before.

"James? What is it?" Mary asked, frightened at his behavior. "Is it the food? Is something wrong with the food?"

He could only shake his head, putting his fork back down on the table. "I can't eat this," he said finally.

"James, I don't understand," Mary said near tears herself. "What's wrong?"

"It's…it's too much. How can I eat all this when our men out there fightin' are starvin'? No one, none of us, has seen this much food in years. The soldiers, the men dieing for our cause are eating rotten apples from the ground, grubs and roots; some days nothing, their bellies shrivelin' and hurtin'. I'm sorry, Mary. I know you went of a lot of trouble, but I just can't." He rose from his chair and began walking from the room.

"But James….what about all this food? What am I to do with all this food?"

He turned back to look at her. "It doesn't matter. Give it to the servants. I'll bet they haven't had a meal like that in a good long while." And he walked from the room, leaving Mary with her mouth hanging open.

She stood and glanced over at the servants standing silent. Waving her hand over the table she said, "Do with it as you will," and she followed James out of the room.

She found him back in their room again, looking out the window. "Are you alright?" she asked him.

"Right now out there, our boys are fightin' and dieing. They're brave men, Mary; brave and gallant men."

"I know they are James and you, Gerritt and Clifford were among them."

He turned and sat on the chair near the window. "To answer your question, no I'm not alright, Mary. I don't think anything will be all right again. Gerritt and Clifford are gone; thousands and thousands of men on both sides, dead or maimed." His voice was low, shaky.

She walked to him and went down on her knees in front of him. "Please darlin' will you tell me about it?"

James was silent for a moment and then looked into his beloved wife's face. How long he had waited to see that face, how many times he had dreamed of her. "So many things were so terrible, I just can't speak of them," he told her. "And how do I adequately tell of the courage, the bravery and strength of the men fightin' their cause?"

"Could you tell me how you lost your arm, got the wound on your face?" She realized it was the first time she had even mentioned his wounds.

He sighed deeply. "I owe that much to you, at least. How could you love with me as disfigured as I am and not explain it to you?"

She was silent, waiting for him to continue.

"It was July 1st," he began. "It was hot, 90o and stifling. We had just come into the town of Gettysburg from the west along a road called Chambersburg Pike. Yankees were all around; artillery fire, shelling from the cannons starting raining down on us. We started charging, firing as we went." He stared straight ahead as he spoke as if he could see the scene he was describing. His voice was calm, even, as though he were talking about cotton prices.

"We came face to face with the Yankees and the fierce fighting began. Minie balls flew everywhere, whizzing past our heads. Men began to fall, wounded and dead. Smoke filled the air so that it was difficult to see the enemy, but suddenly, there they were in front of us. We shot and reloaded as quickly as we could. We began to push them back. We fired so fast the barrels of our guns were hot, but we got them on the run. They pushed back all the way to a place called Seminary Ridge." He paused and looked into Mary's face. "A lot of men were dead, mostly Yanks; more than half their numbers were lying on the field."

"How horrible," Mary said quietly.

James nodded and looked out the window. "It began to get dark and the shelling stopped. We camped for the night, tried to eat a little something, get some rest. We all knew what was coming in the morning, so no one really slept.

When the sun came up we were moved to the edge of a Peach orchard where the Yankees were bivouacked. Our brigade was joined by General Barkdale's Mississippians. There were hundreds and hundreds of us and we were directed to charge across a wide-open field. On the other side were the Yanks. I saw Steven there, one last time before we charged.

So we lined up, the colors in front of us, the Confederate flag alongside, and charged, firing as we went. The Yanks fired back and then their artillery began, landing shells all around us. Men were dropping all around me, but I kept going, shooting every Yankee I saw. Our lines crossed, Rebs and Yanks, all mixed up together. We were fightin' with our bayonets, rifle butts, even our fists.

The cannon fire was increasing, more and more shells exploding around us, hitting men, blue and gray. That's when it happened." He stopped and took a deep breath as if it were difficult for him to go on. Mary put both her hands on his knee, knowing how difficult this must be for him.

"A shell exploded right in front of me," he said. "It knocked me off my feet, deafened me. I was unconscious. When I awoke, the guns sounded further away and it was getting dark. I felt an excruciating pain in my left arm, my face. I tried to move it, but it wouldn't work." His voice had gotten low, strained as though he might break down. "I could feel warm blood seeping down my face, pouring from my arm. I finally forced myself to look. My left arm was shattered below the shoulder, hanging on by just a flap of skin. I touched my face and found it was sliced open to the bone. A large piece of the shell had sliced through my arm and my face. It could have taken off my head."

"Oh god, James," Mary said the tears coming to her eyes.

"I started calling for help. I knew I was getting weaker, losing a lot of blood." He stopped and took a ragged deep breath, looked up at the ceiling. "I didn't… want.. to die. Someone finally found me and took me to the field hospital. It was a large tent set up behind the lines. When they brought me in, I saw lying outside a pile of arms and legs. I knew soon, mine would be among them.

There was no saving my arm. The doctor finished removing it and sewed a flap of skin over the stump. He also sewed closed the wound on my face. For two days, while the battle continued to rage outside, I drifted in and out of consciousness. It was horribly painful and at times I was delirious, but I did realize more and more men were being brought in as the devastation continued. Finally, the battle of Gettysburg was over; so many dead, thousands more wounded and captured." His voice had become so quiet, Mary could barely hear him and tears were streaming down his face unheeded.

"After that they moved me to a hospital in Virginia where I stayed to recover until they let me go home. I thought of trying to contact you, to let you know what happened, but I just didn't know how to do that in writing. I… I wanted to tell you personally. I just didn't know how you would handle it, if you would still be able to… accept me with my disfigurements."

The tears were now streaming down Mary's face as well. She took his good right hand in both of hers, holding it against her cheek. He felt the wetness of her tears. "Oh, my darlin' husband, I love you. I always have and I always will. When we were married I took vows to love, honor and cherish, in sickness and in health, 'til death do us part. I can't begin to tell you how brave I think you are, how much I admire you for going to a war you didn't approve of, but fought nonetheless. My darlin' I love you more."

He leaned over and surrounded her with his good arm while she embraced him. They were both crying, grieving for what had been, for their losses, and for what was still to come. "My beautiful Mary, I love you so."

For the next several weeks James mostly slept, awakening periodically to eat. He had allowed Matthew to bathe and shave him, even though it had been difficult for him to have Matthew see his stump. He at least appeared more like his old self. But he didn't act the same. He went about as if dazed; barely speaking, sitting silently for long periods, staring off at nothing, and suddenly breaking down in tears.

Mary felt he must still be recuperating from his injuries; needed a lot of sleep and was emotional because of it. But when months went by and there was no change, she began to feel extremely frustrated. She tried to be sympathetic to him; always trying to remember the horrific experiences he had been through, but as time went by, it became more and more difficult. At first when James came home Mr. Solomon had shaped up, was out in the fields everyday, making sure the slaves were working. They were only growing food crops now, but because the army took most of those, it was even more important they harvest as much as possible. He had also let up on his harshness towards the slaves, as he knew Mr. McBride didn't allow cruelty. Soon however, he discovered James seemed incapable of making decisions; no longer involving himself in the running of the plantation and soon returned to his harsh and lazy ways.

Mary felt powerless to control him. She also wished James would do something about Mr. Solomon, but whenever she approached him on the matter, he would wave her away telling her to do what she thought best. It was the same with every other matter concerning the plantation. He just couldn't seem to make any decisions and would sit for hours staring outside. Sometimes he would walk down by the river, a sad, solitary figure, seeming to be lost on his own land.

So the responsibilities still fell on Mary's shoulders, making her feel angry and resentful. She knew he had been through much, had seen many horrors and had been wounded, but that was behind him now. He was home where he was safe and was loved. Why couldn't he just go on and take over as he always had? She was weary of it and only wished to be shed of the responsibility. Instead, she was given another body and soul to care for.

She was also beginning to wonder if his mind had been affected as well. He would repeatedly ask for Colleen and when told she was gone, he would nod and say, "Oh yes, that's right, my little girl is gone." And then he would turn around and ask Dora to fetch Colleen for him. Occasionally they would find him in her room, touching her things tenderly, as if doing so he could somehow still feel Colleen's presence. He would do the same in Gerritt's room, sometimes talking out loud to himself. Other times they would discover him missing. After a frantic search of the house, they would find him out at the cemetery, sitting by Gerritt's grave marker they had place there, tears running down his face.

Dora would see him from the upper story windows, sitting out at the family plot, grieving for Gerritt and now for Colleen, too. She had kept her word to her mistress and had told no one where she had gone. Not because she was fearful of being sold, but because of her love and loyalty to Colleen. When she had seen the condition James was in and how much he missed her, she had considered telling him where his daughter had gone. The more she thought on it, the more she thought it a bad idea. What could they do even if they knew? She had joined the army to find Steven. She didn't know what name she had used and she could be anywhere. The thought had crossed her mind that Colleen could have been in the fighting, could have been killed. She also wondered if Colleen had been discovered to be a woman and what would they have done to her if they had? Would they put her in prison? She quickly tried to dismiss those thoughts. She couldn't even think of the possibility of losing her baby.

Another thing Dora had been mulling over since Colleen's departure was the idea of running away. Many of the field hands had already done so, successfully. The thought of freedom was so exciting; being her own person, not belonging to anyone, able to go where ever she wished, not having to do the bidding of any white folks. It was all so wonderfully appealing. But at the same time, it was also frightening. How would she escape, where would she go? She knew she would have to go north to a Union state. She didn't even know where that was; only that it was very far away. So for now she stayed because Mary and James needed her and if Master Steven and Colleen came home, they might need her as well. So she stayed, but she refused to give up her dream.

Steven had nearly traversed the length of the barracks in the Yankee prison camp, when suddenly a bearded, burly form confronted him. "Steven, boy that you?" the man asked clasping his shoulders. Steven squinted, trying to identify the older man standing in front of him.

"It's me, Tom, your ole pal!"

"Tom?" he said incredulous to see his friend. "My god, is it really you?" His friend was dirty, with torn clothing, his beard longer and unkempt, but it was definitely the same kind face under those busy eyebrows he had grown to care so much about these past years.

"That it is," Tom said keeping his hand on Steven's shoulder.

"Move it along!" one of the guards called out.

"Come down here with me," Tom directed, "there's a spot near me you can bunk." They walked a few more yards and then Tom helped Steven lay his blanket down on the dirt floor. "I'll put your bowl an' cup next to mine," he told Steven. "You won't be want 'n to lose it. If you does, you gets no food."

"I'll try to remember that," Steven said sitting painfully on the ground, laying his crutch aside.

Tom sat next to him on his own bedroll. "You wounded at Gettysburg?" Tom asked quietly. "Onest we was chargin' cross'st that field, smoke 'n shells ever'where, I lost track of were you be."

Steven nodded. "I got hit by a shell; busted up my leg pretty bad. Yankee's picked me up, sent me to a Union hospital."

"Were it real bad?"

"Actually, they were very kind. The doctors saved my leg. It was so bad they should have taken it off, but a kind doctor tried repairin' it. Question is, whether I'll ever get full use of it. Then once I was well enough to travel, they shipped me here."

"I'm real sorry 'bout your leg," Tom told him. "I was taken at Gettysburg, too. I made it all the way to the wall, but faced with a bayonet to the gut or surrender, I picked livin'."

"Is it very bad here?" Steven asked, as if the sights and smells weren't enough to give him the answer.

Tom nodded. "Bad 'nough; dirty, diseases, men diein' ever day, not enough ta eat, bad smells, men fightin' with each other who afore had been fightin' together, and I've only been here two months."

"How about escape; any chance of that?" Steven asked.

"Not as far as I can tell. Them fences is too high to go over the top. Even if you could they'se guards on them towers day an' night. Iffen you couldn't tell when you came in, this here prison is on a peninsula next to the Potomac River. Onlys one way out, north or 'cross the river. This here dirt's like rock; no way you could dig under the fence. And they'se got guards walkin' up and down outside; they'd see's you iffen you ever did get out."

"There's got to be a way. I can't just sit in this place and rot," Steven told him. "While my leg gets stronger we need to be alert, keep our eyes open, observe the comings and goings of the Yankees to best figure a way out of here."

Tom nodded. "I'm with you boy. Iffen you can find a way outt'a here, I'm with you."

"How do things run around here?" Steven asked Tom.

"Well, they feeds us twice a day; in the mornin' and in the evenin'. Them Yanks got more grub than the Rebs. Even the prisoners get better food than what we all had. Everyone's to be in their bedrolls at dark.

Anyone caught outside after that, gets shot. Between times, there ain't much to do. Some walk about talkin' with others, relivin' battles, findin' out who was at Fredricksburg or Manassas. Somes plays cards; they'se fellows who's made dice outta wood. Some jes sits and feels sorry for thereselves, talkin' about home, what life was like afore the war. They'se wastin' away."

Steven soon learned the routine of the camp, when meals were served, when they could go outside for exercise, when they were to be quiet in their bedrolls. Tom had been correct about the food, even the paltry stew and bread was better than the occasional fatback and hardtack in the field and it was on a regular basis. He thought if he had to stay for any length of time, he might even gain weight.

During the day Steven walked about the enclosure talking to the men. Again it was as Tom had told him; some only dwelt on life before the war, living in the past. Others talked of the battles they had been in, Spotslyvania, Chancerlorsville, Gettysburg. These were the men who talked of escape, the bold, those with their spirit still intact. Steven sought out these men, finding out what they knew and what yet they still needed to know in order to escape. He traversed the perimeter of the camp with the guise of exercising his leg; checking the walls for weaknesses, the guards' towers and the gates. It was his only distraction.

The remainder of his time was spent with his memories. He thought about the last few years, the places he had been, the conflicts he had fought. He especially remembered the battles where his father had died and Charles at the same place; the bridge where

Gerritt had died in his arms. These memories would come mostly at night, in the dark, when he lay on his bedroll listening to the moans and coughing of the dieing, the snoring of those able to sleep. He would look up at the vents in the ceiling, watching the haze of smoke as it drifted up to swirl in the light from the moon, and the pain would tighten in his chest.

But he would also think of his home and Colleen and sometimes when he closed his eyes and tried to recall her face, it was difficult for him to remember. He saw the color of her eyes, the long beautiful hair. He remembered the softness of her skin and the way she smelled when he kissed her neck. He could recall how sensuous her lips felt against his own and how incredible her naked body felt underneath him. His memories were all he had left as he had lost the small picture he had kept of her. It was gone now; lost in some battle.

Days, weeks and months passed. Many men gave up and died, the bodies taken out on a daily basis. Disease raged unchecked in their close quarters; too many men for the space, allowed for the spread of the dysentery, cholera, and other maladies. As more men had been brought in, tents were set up behind the barracks to accommodate them, as there was no more room. Many of the men had banded together to form alliances, trying to better the living conditions of the prisoners.

Winter had set in and the men spent most of the day walking the perimeter trying to keep warm. Many others stayed inside the barracks, building fires with a meager wood supply causing a build up of smoke, making breathing difficult. Steven preferred the outside and reasonable fresh air to the stifling, choking atmosphere inside. He had rather gotten used to being outside most of the time anyway except for the occasional shelter of a small tent and the crude cabins in winter.

Steven's leg had progressively gotten stronger, although he still walked with a pronounced limp and if he put too much pressure on it, it would give him pain. He tended to favor it, fearing the fragile bone might snap, be unable to heal and thus have to be amputated. But it did not deter him from planning an escape.

The alliance of men, of whom Steven and Tom were a part, were strategizing a way out; had been friendly with several of the guards. They had convinced those Yankees they were in need of more wood for their fires, which was an undeniable truth, but they told them they would be willing to organize a detail of men to cut and chop the wood themselves. They had the guards convinced; now they needed to convince the commander of the camp to allow it.

The commander, Major Allen Brady, a middle-aged angry man, who had had high ideals of someday becoming a general; but politics being what they were and some unfortunate circumstances, led him to command, not a brigade of men, but this desolate prison camp. It was said his anger against the Confederates was so great; he took delight in hurting them whenever possible. He had even galloped his horse through crowds of prisoners, trampling those who could not get out of the way.

Upon hearing of the prisoners desire to acquire their own firewood, he was at first hesitant. He didn't particularly care for the idea of Johnny Rebs being equipped with saws and axes. After consideration and the idea of only having to use three or four men to guard the prisoners as opposed to an entire detail to chop and collect wood themselves, appealed to him. He went even further, visualizing them also chopping the wood for his own men and himself. Why not use the available labor he had at his disposal? So he granted the request with certain rules and stipulations. The detail was to be under guard at all times. They could cut trees on the perimeter of the woods only; no foraging into the trees where they might be tempted to run off; and only those specifically designated would be allowed outside the gates.

After dark, in the relative seclusion of their barracks, the men planned their strategy. It was agreed no escape would be attempted during the first few forays outside the walls. They would try to glean as much information as possible about the terrain, the attitude of the guards, direction and what would be the safest method of escape.

As they huddled around the small fire in the wood stove, they made their plan. "I think we should assign specific duties to each man," Steven told the men. "That way you only concentrate on that one detail and hopefully avoid confusion when reporting back to the group."

Many nodded and expressed affirmation. "Sounds good. What else we needs to know?"

"Under no circumstances does anyone try to run at this point in time. We need to assess every angle, find all the potential hazards and traps; know guard placements and rotations, discover the best direction to run, which way will get us closer to our own troops and yet offer the most cover. We already know we're on a peninsula, but what we don't know is, whether we should run north further into the woods, or go west into the Potomac River. It may be too deep and wide to cross at this point, even for the best swimmers. It's also important to be friendly towards the guards; no matter what they might do, we need to stay passive," Steven said as quietly as possible.

"You tellin' me I gots to kiss them Yankee butts?" one bearded man asked.

"We do whatever we has to," Tom told the man looking him directly in the eyes.

"That's right," Steven agreed. "When you're out there, you can't be thinkin' of them as the enemy, as dirty Yanks. Right now they're our saviors."

"Saviors hell," another said spitting on the floor. "Iffen I had me a gun, I'd blow all their brains out."

"Listen," Steven said looking at each man in turn, all shabbily dressed, dirty, thin, but determined, "each one of us knows what we've been through in this war. We've all lost friends and loved ones to the hands of the Yankees. But the only way we're goin' to get out of this prison is to make friends with those Yankees. If we do that and get them to relax their guard just a little, it could give us those precious minutes we might need to escape."

Everyone finally agreed that what Steven was saying was true. They also realized that for them to get anyone out, they were going to have to co-operate. There was no more time for talking as the bell was sounding. Each man went slowly to his bedroll, huddling under the meager blanket to try and sleep.

It was a cold night, the wind howling outside, rattling the timbers of their barracks, the snow beginning to fly outside, drifting down into the open vent holes. The only heat came from the small fire in the wood stove, not nearly enough to stretch its fingers of warmth into the far reaches of the building where the men lay shivering on the cold earth.

They awoke in the morning to a fresh blanket of snow, not only outside, but also piled up inside the barracks. The men filled their cups and melted it over the hot coals from their fire, drinking it. It was cleaner than what they were given drawn from the trench that ran through the camp. It seemed to be impregnated with some mineral so foul it stank and produced diarrhea in almost everyone who drank it. If one were to let it set for any length of time, a black scum would rise to the surface; consequently the fresh drink was sorely appreciated.

They went outside to walk about in the snow, trying to warm up, get the stiffness out and see who had died during the night. Fortunately, no dead bodies were brought out that morning. Everyone had to congregate at the long ditch behind the barracks, which served as the latrine. It was a filthy, smelly area where no one lingered long.

Many of the men were walking through the snow barefoot, having already been in that condition when they were captured. Some had taken strips of cloth from a ragged shirt or pants and wrapped them around their frozen feet. Steven was fortunate to still have the boots he started with in spite of being wounded in the leg. His had been of high quality leather and he had tried as best he could to take care of them; although they were worn and tattered, they still served their purpose. Those not as fortunate, whose footwear had been cheaply made, thin leather and poor stitching, had literally walked them off. Others had picked up boots off the dead on the battlefield. This was true also of other pieces of clothing; shirts, pants, jackets, even hats, trying not to acquire parts of Union uniforms that would cause his own comrades to think him the enemy. Fortunately, Steven had been given a new pair of trousers in the hospital being as his had been destroyed when he was wounded.

Later in the day, after they had had their meal of gruel and bread, the commander gave orders to have the prisoners form a wood detail of fifteen men and to meet at the entrance gate. Those who had already volunteered to be a part of the escape alliance assembled at the gate. A strange contingency they were indeed, motley, bedraggled, but still loyal to their cause and determined to find a way out of this prison.

Steven and Tom were among them, but Steven was worried about his leg. Even though he seldom used his crutch any longer, his leg was still painful and he walked with a pronounced limp. He hoped they wouldn't think him incapable of doing the difficult labor of cutting and splitting wood and reject him as part of the detail.

Several guards armed with Henry repeating rifles stood before them at the gate. One, an officer, explained the rules to them and that if anyone tried to run or broke the rules, they would be shot and the wood detail suspended. Steven watched the young officer in the blue uniform as he spoke. He was about his own age, clouds of vapor escaping his mouth as he spoke and Steven wondered whether he had a wife at home waiting for him.

The guards on the outside opened the gate; then by twos they were led outside, the guards surrounding them on all sides. Steven looked around the perimeter as they walked down the path from the camp. To the right he observed several log buildings, Union soldiers milling about outside. He assumed these to be housing for the commander and guards. Behind these was a long, low structure surrounded by fencing. Inside, several horses munched on stacks of hay. Next to this was another log building, perhaps where stores were kept. Further on, running past the post and behind the prison, was a river which Steven surmised was the Potomac. Further still, running north from the prison was a rail line where the train had brought them in. Before they reached the rails however, they turned to the left, away from the buildings. In front of them was a large stand of trees going on as far as the eye could see. Tall pines and stately maples reached upward towards the sky. The sun had burst forth after the previous nights' snow, dazzling their eyes with blinding brilliance as it reflected off the whiteness.

Several more guards had come up behind them carrying long bow saws and axes and once they had reached the edge of the trees, distributed them amongst the prisoners.

Steven could look into his fellow comrades's eyes and see their thoughts; now that they were armed with weapons, the desire to attack their captors and run was strong. He cautioned them with a look, knowing it would be suicide to flee at this point, with no plan. They would be shot down like dogs.

They were directed as to which trees to cut and how, making sure they would fall in the right direction. Several took the large tooth, long saws and began working on the designated trees. Once they were down, others took axes and began taking off the branches and then cutting it up into logs. Still others split the logs into more manageable pieces for burning. The remainder of the men stacked the wood into piles.

It was the first hard labor Steven had done in some time and he quickly tired, but he was grateful for the chance to be outside the prison, away from the depressing sights of men dieing, the stench of sickness and garbage. Outside was fresh air, a chance to use his muscles, the sight of the brilliant blue sky and beyond the trees, freedom.

They worked through the afternoon, stacking an abundant supply of wood. The guards changed midway through that they might go inside to warm up. No such luxury for the wood detail however, and though their bodies kept warm from exertion, their extremities were cold to the point of pain, especially when handling the steel blades of the saws and axes.

But the observations went on; how many guards were in attendance at any one time, whether they were attentive to the prisoners' movements, where they placed themselves in regard to the woods and the compound. They checked directions; which way they would need to go in order to reach friendly troops, how heavily wooded the stand of trees was and how the men might traverse it. They listened carefully to the guards' conversations with each other, hoping for some morsel they could use for their own benefit. They even endured the harassing directed their way.

"Hey Reb," the Yankee guards would call out, "hows you likes bein' treated like a nigger? You like being' a slave?"

"Mebbe we should whip you some so's ya know what it done feels like!" another called out.

They did their best to ignore the remarks, but Steven could see how it angered the men. What most Yanks didn't realize was that the majority of all men fighting for the Confederacy never owned a slave in their lives. They were fighting for the greater cause; for the glory of the Confederacy.

As dusk came on casting its long shadow fingers across the white snow, they loaded the wood into long wagons fitted with runners. Once it had all been stacked, the horses pulled the heavy load back to the camp, the prisoners and guards following behind.

Steven was so exhausted and his leg pained him so greatly, he wasn't quite sure he could make it all the way back. But his friend Tom, seeing his agony, slipped his arm behind Steven's back, supporting him. The scar along his shin throbbed so much, he thought he might pass out. He was truly grateful for Tom's help.

Once they reached the gates of the camp, the men were allowed to take half the wood and bring it inside for the use of the prisoners. The men piled wood in front of each of the barracks; the rest of the prisoners grateful for the added fuel.

They were finally served the evening meal of stew and more bread. Steven nearly fell asleep over his bowl. Even though he had endured nearly three years of army life; living outdoors, long marches across hills, valleys, rivers, and engaging in fierce battles, the wound he sustained had sapped him and even now, months later, the hard exertion of labor, exhausted him.

Tom gently took the bowl from Steven's hands as he sat on his bedroll. "You did good today, son," Tom told him, "worked real hard with that bum leg and all. I think we all got lots of information today." The older man laid him gently down, covering him with his blanket. "You rest now son and mebbe next time they lets us go out on wood detail, we'll jes give them Yankees the slip." Steven nodded and Tom smiled.

For the next week, Steven rested his leg and gathered the information the men had been able to acquire while out on wood detail. More of the sickest men died, their bodies carried out and buried behind the walls of the prison. Still others, too weak to even rise from their beds, lingered, no one to care for them. At least the stench from the latrine had lessened with the cold weather and snow. At least with the added supply of wood, they could keep reasonably warm.

A plan for escape began to be formulated, hinging on the privilege of being allowed to again go out and gather firewood. Once they had decided the direction, the path to take and the best way to find their way back to their own troops, the only thing left to accomplish was deciding on <u>how</u> to get away. There was disagreement among those in the alliance. Some felt they should over power the guards, taking their guns and killing them, while others leaned towards slipping away undetected. Of course there was a flaw in the later, as it would be difficult for fifteen men to suddenly disappear into the woods without being noticed by the guards.

But until they could again go outside the walls, they had to endure life inside. Sometimes, especially at night, Steven would look up into the sky and think of being on the outside.

"What do you think our lives will be like after this war is over?" Steven asked Tom as they leaned against the building smoking their pipes. One of the other prisoners had fashioned a few from soapstone and given them away. Tobacco was obtained from one of the guards in exchange for two of the delicately carved pipes.

"I'm thinkin' things will be powerful changed," Tom said inhaling on the sweet tobacco. "Even if we wins this thing, it'll be a whole new country, Confederate States of America."

"Yes, but what about all the repercussions; the loss of life, loss of property, devastation of fields, barns, livestock, what will that mean to the south?"

Tom shook his head. "No tellin' 'bout that. No doubt it'll take some to get back on our feet, but we've always been strong and we'll get our freedom."

"I'd like to get free from this place."

"You think our plan could work?" Tom asked in a hushed voice.

"Only God knows," Steven replied. "I only hope we won't have to rot here the rest of the war."

"How long you think that might be?" Tom asked. "Even the Mexican War twern't this long."

"I just don't know anymore, my friend. It's nearly 1864, almost three years of war. No one thought it would go this long. Everyone thought we'd whip the Yankees in a few weeks. We couldn't have been more wrong."

CHAPTER SIXTEEN
—July 1864

The blistering heat of summer bore down on them, withering everything beneath its scorching rays. Many of the men in camp went about with their shirts off. Colleen envied them, as of course, she always needed to remain covered completely. Even when she bathed, she kept her clothing on, claiming she was, at the same time, cleaning her clothes. Others however, removed theirs before washing them. Colleen attempted to stay far away from the river at these times to avoid seeing the men in their naked state.

She sat by the small cooking fire, her boots off, her jacket on the log next to her and her shirt sleeves rolled up to the elbow. Her mother would be horrified to see how darkened her skin on her arms and face had gotten from her exposure to the sun. Pouring herself a tin cup of coffee, she listened to many of the men as they splashed in the cool river water of the Appomattox, wishing she could also enjoy the refreshment.

They were now south of Richmond in a place called Petersburg. Deep trenches, large wooden breastworks and sharpened logs had been built around the camp, facing the approaching Union Army. She had never seen such massive construction in all her time in the army. She had done her part, suffering aching and sore muscles afterwards and she dreaded what was to come. Likewise, the Union army had also entrenched themselves and put up massive breastworks facing their own. Mortar buildings were also erected with the hopes of some protection during shelling. Life had become one battle after another with little respite in between. She hated this war with its atrocities, maiming and horrific loss of life.

She had begun to think seriously about her method of finding Steven. Even though she had gotten closer geographically, she still hadn't been able to figure out how to get to him. The only information she was able to acquire was the probable location of the prison. She had been told prisoners from Gettysburg were most likely taken to a prison in Maryland called Point Lookout. But where that was exactly, and how to get there, were elusive.

She glanced up as she saw Patrick coming across the camp limping, his muscled, taunt body glistening, his long hair dripping from his swim in the river. Her heart began to beat faster and the thought passed through her mind to wonder what he wold look like naked.

"No, no stop it," she muttered to herself. "I love Steven."

Patrick sat on the log near her, wiping the moisture from his body with his shirt. "Ah, that felt powerful good," he told her. "It's mighty hot. You should go for a swim, lad," he told her.

"I'm fine," she said as the perspiration ran down her back. "I just don't like taking my clothes off in front of others."

"Aye, I know you're modest. It's alright."

"How's your foot?" she asked him skirting the subject.

"It's doing well," he said holding it up for inspection. "It only pains me some walkin' barefoot."

Colleen saw the small indentation scar in Patrick's foot where he had been shot with a minnie ball. She thought back to the last couple of months since the battle in the Wilderness. Things had only gotten worse since that experience and at the time, she would never had thought that possible. When they had left that place of death, with the trees still smoldering, the stench of burning flesh filling their nostrils, they headed towards a place called Spotsylvania Court House, nearer to Richmond in a race with the Yankees to get there first. It was at this juncture that the Confederate supply lines met the Richmond, Fredricks and Potomac and the Virginia Central Railroads. If the Yanks reached Spotsylvania first, Richmond would be vulnerable to attack.

With her leg injured, it had been difficult for her to press on at double quick time. Fearing she would be left behind, Patrick and the others had half carried her most of the way. It had made her feel guilty for them to help her so, as it made them more vulnerable if attacked. Hampering their march had been the scores of ambulances passing by them with their loads of misery, forcing the soldiers off the road, but still more wounded lay uncollected in the woods.

They had marched through the night, further wearying already exhausted troops. Ahead of them was General Sheridan's Union Calvary as well as Jeb

Stuart's, when they had heard musket fire ahead. The enemy had already been engaged. As they had rushed forward, Patrick had left her in the rear with some aides and camp cooks, telling her she could not fight with her injured leg.

The fighting had been fierce with shells exploding all around and the firing almost incessant. Colleen and been able to hear the Rebel cry, the shouts of the officers, and the screams of the dieing. The fighting had gone on nearly all day, Colleen anxiously waiting in the rear. She had begun to wonder if it were more difficult staying behind or being in the thick of it.

They had finally returned, dirty, exhausted, carrying the wounded with them. Colleen had been so relieved to see Patrick come stumbling out of the woods, his face blackened from powder, tears stung her eyes. She had turned quickly away so that he would not see. Gordon and William had also made it back safely, but here was to be no rest for the weary. The men were ordered to dig trenches and put up breastworks. Trees were felled and fences were torn apart in their efforts. It had been far past dark when they finished and fell exhausted into a deep slumber.

When morning had cast its orange rays over the horizon, the men continued with their construction of the breastworks. Colleen was able to help to some extent and insisted she be a part of the fighting that day.

"I'll not have you hurtin' your leg again," Patrick had told her.

"Others fight with more severe wounds," she had tried persuading him. "I only have a badly bruised leg bone."

"Can you run fast?" he had asked her, "for you may have to get quickly away from the Yankees."

She had not been able to answer him for even though her leg was stronger, it had turned black and blue from her knee down to her foot and it still gave her pain.

Patrick had put his hand on her shoulder. "I know you want to fight with the rest of the lads, but you're puttin' yourself in danger."

Everyone is in danger," she had told him. "I'll stay here and fight behind the breastworks."

He had said no more and left to join the regiment who were leaving to reinforce two other regiments defending a bridge on the Po River. It wasn't long before shelling was heard and then musket fire. The smoke began rolling across the landscape, seeping through the trees like the tendrils of an elusive spider web.

For most of the day, their troops had held the Union line at the bridge. Finally the Federals had withdrawn as dusk was settling in. The men returned to the camp behind the breastworks weary from battle. They had just settled in to eat their meager rations when someone called out, "Here come some more of our men!" But, instead of the Confederate gray, it was Union blue, which broke from the trees and began assaulting their breastworks. A volley of musket balls rained through the air, hitting the first of the Yankees as they tried to surmount the barrier. And although they had fired as rapidly as they could, there had been too many of them and they all had been forced to retreat, leaving behind those who had fallen.

Patrick had been by her side the whole way, helping her over rocks and logs until they reached the second line of reinforcement. Federal troops had kept pouring over the breastworks behind them. As soon as they began coming within rifle range of their second line, their twenty-two cannon had begun to fire, killing hundreds and forcing the Yankees back. By this time it had grown dark and the firing had ceased.

No one slept well that night, fearing an evening assault. Then a change in the wind had brought cold winds, rain and hail. It was a miserable time with everyone shivering and soaked through to the bone. When the dawn broke, a thick fog had covered the ground. Men appeared as ghostly apparitions. The ground was thick with mud from the rain.

They hadn't had time to eat even a meager breakfast, when the firing had begun again, the Yankees pouring over the barricade. They had returned fire, shooting as fast as they could, felling Yank after Yank, but still they came. They had run to the woods, the men in blue in constant pursuit. They had scattered, trying to avoid the bullet that would mean death.

Patrick had stumbled, fell, but got up and run again. Colleen remembered how he had limped badly, but he had continued to help her.

The fighting had gone on most of the day; especially in the place they would call the Bloody Angle, where hundreds died a gruesome death. Corpses had piled up eight to ten deep and then finally their own troops being overwhelmed and pushed back were in retreat until they had lost Spotslyvannia. In the end six thousand good Confederate men had died or were wounded. Four thousand more had been captured. Among the dead was Gordon. Colleen had seen how it had grieved Patrick to lose his friend and she had longed to hold him in her arms.

When they had finally gotten to a safe place, she had discovered Patrick had been shot in the foot. His boot had filled with blood and been painful for him to remove. The bullet had entered the top of his foot and gone out the bottom, right through the sole of his boot. The camp doctor had looked at it, cleaned it and bandaged it. She knew why he had stumbled in the woods earlier in the day.

It had been only a few days later when the news had come around that Major General Jeb Stuart had been killed in a skirmish with Federals from the 1st Michigan, led by General George Custer. It had been a major blow to all loyal Confederate men. It had been said that General Lee himself was grief stricken over the loss of his friend.

After the battle at Spotslyvannia, more troops had moved on to a place called Cold Harbor on the north Anna River. It was here another battle ensued in the first days of June. This time, Colleen's regiment had not been a part of the fighting because it had been so decimated by loss and they had been waiting for reinforcements. Seven thousand of Grant's men fell in half an hour. It was a horror of human loss. Many of Colleen's comrades had cheered the death of the Yankee troops, but she had felt only sadness.

From Cold Harbor the army had moved to Petersburg, Colleen's regiment joining them after fresh troops had been enlisted. Petersburg was just twenty miles south of Richmond and was the hub of the last remaining railroad to the capitol. If that last hub were taken and cut, Richmond and the army would be without food.

They had gotten there ahead of the Yankees and began building an elaborate system of trenches and breastworks, some over eight feet high. The Yankees had arrived and built like breastworks on the opposite side of the city. Artillery duels were on a regular basis and the sharp shooting nearly incessant.

Colleen knew another battle was about to ensue. She dreaded it, not with paralyzing fear as she had experienced in her first battle, but with gut wrenching dread, knowing hundreds, perhaps thousands would die; perhaps even she. The fighting, the dieing was wearing on her, as it was on all the men, many having been in this conflict since its beginning three years before. She was sick of the horror; the men who were blown to pieces, those who had lost arms, legs, other body parts. Men were killed or maimed on a daily basis with no rhyme or reason. Others died of dysentery and other diseases; some were driven mad from battle fatigue and still others deserted.

Her own quest at this point seemed futile. Many times she had thought of stealing away in the night and going back home. She wasn't quite sure what kept her here. Perhaps she felt she might still find her way to Steven, or that she continued to live with the thought the war would be over soon and all the prisoners would be released and she could take Steven home. Or maybe it was Patrick and the other men, loyal to the end to the Confederate cause.

News had also come through that the Union General Sherman had invaded Georgia from Tennessee, pushing back Joseph Johnston. By July 17th, they had gotten within ten miles of Atlanta, burning and pillaging as they went. Finally, John Bell Hood had replaced Johnston with the hopes of stopping Sherman, but those troops from Georgia worried about their families back home. Colleen thought if the Yankees could take Atlanta, there would be nothing to stop them from moving on to Savannah. She could only pray her family would be unharmed.

She also prayed her father had remained safe. She worried about him, not knowing what might have happened to him. She had been unable to find him in any company she thus far had fought with and owing to the fact she had a secret identity, had not been able to ask much about him either.

It was the end of July now and ever since they had been in Petersburg, things had been tense. While half the troops were in camp, sleeping, eating, relaxing, the other half would be at the front lines waiting, shooting at anything that moved. Colleen dreaded the twelve-hour guard duty. It felt like being in hell; the sun beating down relentlessly, shells and mortars exploding around them. Several times while she sat behind the breastworks, a large mortar had landed right on top of the men next to her, killing them instantly. When the snipers weren't firing and the shells weren't raining down, they simply sat silent, staring, some fainting from the heat.

It was evening, the darkness had settled in, but the heat had barely abated and now the rains came, filling the trenches with mud. The three remaining friends, Colleen, Patrick and William, slouched through the ankle deep quagmire, sighting over the breastworks for any sign of the enemy.

More and more she kept thinking of the decision she had made to join the army. She was weary; weary of the killing, the maiming, the long marches; the cold and wet, of always pretending to be someone she wasn't. She was tired of hiding her monthies and binding her breasts. She was tired of being a man. She wanted to be treated like a lady again, to have doors opened and waited on. She wanted to bathe in a tub and have her hair brushed. She wanted to eat succulent meals and drink fine wines. She just wanted to be pretty again and have men fawn over her.

Suddenly, in the quiet of the night, they heard a new sound, a clunking, thudding sound. "What is that?" Colleen asked.

"Tis strange," Patrick agreed. "I've not heard that one afore."

"Where is it coming from?" she asked climbing down from the top of the log breastworks.

Others too, were wandering about, trying to discern where the strange sounds were coming from.

"Quiet! Quiet!" William commanded. "Stop movin' around and listen!" Silence fell over the troops and everyone froze where they stood. They could feel a vibration in their feet. Patrick bent down putting his ear close to the ground.

"Diggin'!" he said aloud for everyone to hear. "The Yankees are diggin'"

"Why would the Yankees be digging?" Colleen asked confused. "Is it trenches?"

"Mebbe the blue bellies are diggin' their way inta our camp wif a tunnel," one man said. Laughter followed.

"I'm thinkin' perhaps we should tell the officers," Patrick said getting to his feet.

Someone ran off to report their discovery, bringing back several officers, a captain, a corporal, their best engineers, and a General Porter Alexander, in charge of all the artillery. It was he who commanded where the big guns should be positioned.

They all listened carefully. There was no mistaking the dull thudding sound coming from the ground. The officers ordered a pit to be dug, to probe further down. Picks and shovels were brought over and the hole was dug.

Colleen and the others watched, peering over the rim. "What do you think it is?" she asked Patrick.

"Perhaps General Grant is thinkin' of diggin' through Petersburg and attack from the rear," he answered. Laughter trickled among the men, but the scowl on General Alexander's face showed he was not amused.

"I think it may be a mine," he announced.

"No no, that's impossible," a bewhiskered engineer said. "The Yanks couldn't dig a mine that far. Why, their line is over four hundred feet away."

"I agree," another said. "I think perhaps, the sounds are only magnified by the way the rock formations are, echoing the noise."

The pit had now reached a respectful depth and a man was lowered down into it. Now the faint sound they had heard on the surface was even more distinguishable. General Alexander's face became even grimmer. He looked up at the engineers. "It matters not if you all think it impossible," he said, "the enemy is digging a mine." He walked away and the men only stared at him in silence.

The sun had just started spreading its long shafts of light across the eastern sky, when Colleen and the others traded duties, retiring back to the camp just behind the long line of cannon on the hill, the other half of the men taking their places in the trenches. Colleen was so exhausted, she could barely keep her eyes open and her stomach was growling with hunger.

She could hear the Yankees exchanging fire with their own men. It seemed unusually persistent this morning. The cannons were firing, the smoke drifting over the camp. She watched them fire for a moment; packing the gunpowder, loading the shell into the large barrel, lighting the fuse and waiting for the subsequent explosion.

There was suddenly something different. The earth moved under her feet and then as she watched, the big guns lifted from the ground. It startled her and she looked around frantically for some explanation. Everyone looked as confused as she.

And then the earth rose in one massive mound, a dull roar sounding and then erupting into a deafening thunderous explosion, the large mound bursting forth. Fire and black rolling smoke spewed from the large hole, spraying dirt on everything. The blast had been so violent, it knocked Colleen to the ground. She looked up and saw large timbers from the earthworks, large cannon and other debris flying through the air. She saw pieces of guns, horses and pieces and parts of men. She heard men screaming, officers calling out. Men and horses were running everywhere; everything was in chaos.

She got to her feet wiping the dirt from her eyes. She looked over to where the explosion had come from and saw a great huge gapping crater right through their lines. General Alexander had been correct; the Yankees had dug a mine and they had just blown it up, right under their men, right where she had just been standing guard only a few moments before.

She looked around for her gun. It had been wretched from her hand when the explosion had occurred and found it lying many feet away. She checked to make sure it was loaded and then ran towards the place where many of the men were assembling, officers calling out orders, flag bearers designating companies.

As she joined the others, she heard a new sound; musket fire and wild cheering. She looked beyond the crater and saw through the cloud of dirt and black smoke, a mass of blue, surging forward right towards that horrible crater, the opening through their lines. Colleen's heart began to pound madly, realizing the peril they were in; their defenses gone, the men in disarray.

Officers called out, lining up the troops, telling them to fill the open gap. They began to fire at the approaching enemy on both sides, at the brightly colored flags. Colleen watched as they began running forward into the great crater, pressed on either side by their own troops. One lone gun stood at the top of the crater, swung down, pointing its great barrel into the hole itself. And then the gun began firing straight into that mass of blue who had unwittingly created their own death trap, and still more men in blue surged forward, no place else to go but into the deep crater.

Once the entire regiment of Yankees had poured into the pit, Colleen and the entire Confederate force surrounded that deep hole in the ground. What she saw was absolute confusion and fear. The Yankees were crushed together in one great mass of blue with nowhere to go. The sides of the crater were too steep for them to climb out and their escape was blocked the way they had come in. At first some tried firing up at them, but soon, even that stopped as the press of humanity made reloading impossible.

All of them, Colleen included, had their muskets trained down at the men in blue, as well as the big cannon. She could see the realization cross their faces that they were trapped like rats in a trap; thousands of men, the fear of death in their eyes.

Her fellow troops began calling out hateful slurs at their enemy, shooting down into the masses, the gun sending its deadly shells. Men panicked; began calling out "surrender!" Colleen saw the faces, the horror of death in their eyes. They were reaching up to them, begging to be pulled to safety. Several soldiers in gray took those hands and began pulling them up to become prisoners. She reached out, started to take the hand of a man who was like her brother, a fellow soldier, kindred.

But just as she had grasped his hand, was pulling back with all her strength, someone knocked her arm away, breaking the grip, the man falling back into the crater. She looked quickly to see who it had been and saw William scowling at her. Then she heard the cries, the angry protestations from the Rebels around the perimeter. And she saw why it was they were angry. Among the white Yankees were black faces. The Union had put Negroes into the fight. For the Southerner it was like a slap in the face to have former slaves fighting against them. It was one thing to fight those who were like you, someone you could respect as a soldier, but this for them, was unacceptable.

Some of the Yankees still reached up trying to surrender, as well did some of the Negroes, but they suddenly realized the cause of the anger on the faces of their enemy as they looked about and saw for themselves the black faces among them. They began striking down their own soldiers in blue; those with black faces.

Colleen watched in horror as the anger intensified and the men in gray began shooting down into the crater, over and over, screaming out their rage, the blood spurting, flesh torn. No one stopped them; no officer called out to stem the insanity. The Federals saw the madness, cried out for mercy; some, Colleen saw, had tears flowing down their faces.

Her eyes darted from face to face of her comrades, looking for some way to end the melee. She saw Patrick, staring dumbfounded into the pit; he was not participating in the slaughter, but still the killing went on. It was as if in the horror of war, men had only held on to decency by a thread and now that thread had been broken and the beast within had been released. She looked into the faces of terror, of the unbridled savagery being rained down upon them, and she wept.

After the carnage was over, four thousand men lay dead. Colleen sat by the fire back at camp, her dirty face streaked with her tears. Patrick handed her a cup of coffee, her hands shaking. He squatted in front of her, looking into her eyes.

"Are you alright lad?" he asked her.

She shook her head, afraid to look in his face, afraid she would cry again. "What happened out there today?" she asked quietly.

This time it was Patrick's turn to shake his head. "I dinna know, tis madness. I thinks some men have been at war too long, killed too much."

"I can't do this anymore," she whispered, more to herself than to Patrick.

"Wha'd you say, lad?" he asked.

Now she looked up into his face, her lips trembling. "I said, I can't do this anymore. I have to get out."

"How you plan on doin' that, Colin? You gonna run?" He was looking at her carefully.

"Whatever it takes," she said, "even if it means reveling myself. All I know is, I can't fight anymore; no more killing, no more death. I don't belong here." She didn't care if he thought her a coward.

"None of us belong here, laddie," Patrick said. "But what did you mean by revealin' yourself?"

She stood up, still holding the warm cup of coffee, and walked closer to the river. She was feeling apprehensive about telling him. Would he hate her, be angry? After all, she had been sharing her life with him for the past year, shared a cabin during the winter, eating, drinking, fighting beside him. She had deceived him, lied to him. He might even feel she had put his and others lives in danger.

Patrick rose and followed after her. "Colin, lad what did you mean?"

She turned to face him, determined, the carnage of that morning making up her mind. "I've something I need to tell you, but you must keep my confidence," she said seriously, looking him directly in the eyes.

"You know I will lad," he told her just as seriously.

She sat on a fallen breastworks log and Patrick sat next to her. "Tis serious?"

She nodded. "I'm…. I'm not who I claim to be."

"You'er not Colin Malone?" he asked.

"No…." she paused and took a deep breath. "I'm Colleen McBride. I'm a woman." She glanced over to see Patrick's reaction and was surprised to see him smiling. "Did you hear what I said? I'm a woman. Don't you believe me?"

"Oh, I believe you lass," he said looking her in the eyes with a softness she had not seen before. "I've known for some time now."

It was Colleen's turn to be surprised. How could he have known? She had been so careful. Her mind flashed back. Had there been a time when he might have seen her naked? She had always thought she was alone when she had bathed. Or had there been something she had said, some slip up she had been unaware of?

"You knew?" she asked, "but how?"

"Not at first, I didn't," he told her. "But there was somethin' different about you, a feelin' I had I couldn't put my finger on. I don't reckon the moment I really said aye, Colin is a lass, but once I decided it, the more signs I saw confirmed it."

"What kind of signs? I thought I had been so careful."

"It's a feelin'" he said. "When I was close to you, I would feel differently. At first I was wonderin' about myself, but then I began noticin' small things; the way you combed your hair, how delicate your hands be, how shy you seemed to be, goin' off by yourself, never bathin' in front of others. But then I have to say, I'm quite the ladies man." He said this with a smile, but Colleen had no doubt it was true. "Don't worry lass, none of the others know."

"If you knew, why didn't you report it?" she asked him.

"I felt you had your reasons for doin' it and they must have been powerful for you to endure what you have, the fightin', watchin' men die, livin' in some horrible conditions. And you could have quit long afore this and you haven't. I've also gotten to know you as a friend and I didn't think I should betray you."

She had been looking down at the ground while he spoke but when he finished, she looked up into his beautiful eyes. "That's why you were so protective of me; why you were always looking out for me in the Wilderness?"

"Aye."

"It wasn't because I was just a young inexperienced boy?"

"Perhaps at first, but once I knew, it scared hell out'a me… excuse me."

"You're not going to change on me just because I've confessed now? I think I've heard all the vulgar language ever spoken during my time in the army."

"Jus' tryin' to be gentleman."

"You've always been that," she told him. "I want to say right now, I'm grateful for your protection. I'm sure you saved my life several times."

"I like you lass. I dinna want anything happenin' to you. But it did worry me some, knowin' a woman was in the trenches fightin'. And you fought as well or better than any man, I might say."

This time Colleen smiled. But the smile soon faded and the seriousness returned to her voice. "But today….. what happened out there…..I just can't do it anymore. It was too horrible, beastly."

"Aye, twas," he agreed. "But lass, why did you go through all this? Why pretend to be a man and fight in this way?"

She felt so emotional, so vulnerable that when she tried to speak, her eyes filled with tears and her lip trembled. "My fiancée and I were secretly married before he left for the war in '61. Then last year at Gettysburg he was wounded and taken prisoner. I thought if I dressed like a man and could come here; I might find him. But I found out how ridiculous that was. I haven't gotten any closer to finding him than before I joined, other than to discover where he might have been taken."

"Aye lass, tis a difficult task you have before you." He touched her arm and looked into her eyes. "I admire what you did. Your husband is a lucky man. I only wish I had a fine woman like yourself, who would be so loyal."

"I do love him so," she said, the tears now running down her face. "I'm so afraid for him and now I've wasted a year."

"It wasn't a waste lass, you served your country. You fought well. If you had been at home, could you have done more?"

"No, perhaps not, but I'm not sure what I should do now."

"Will you go home?"

She nodded. "There's nothing more I can do here. I can't continue to be a part of this killing." She knew she was lying to him again, but it couldn't be helped. She had no intention of going back home before finding Steven. She knew if Patrick was aware of her plans to continue her search, only now as a woman, he would object; perhaps even do something to prevent her from going. "My mother knows nothing about my joining the army. I'm sure she was devastated when I disappeared," she continued telling him. "I left her with all the responsibilities of running the plantation. I need to go back and help share the load."

"How will you go back?" Patrick asked her. "Will you tell the Captain who you really are?"

"No, no," she said emphatically. "If the army found out I've been deceiving them all this time, I could be in serious trouble. They might even put me in jail."

"I doubt they would put a woman in jail," he told her. "They'd likely just send you on your way back home."

"I can't risk it. You've got to promise to keep my secret," she said touching his shoulder. "And I'm going to need your help getting away."

"I'll keep your secret, lass. I have all this time and I'll do whatever I can to help you."

Colleen stood and Patrick followed. "I'm going tonight. Will you help me get past the pickets?"

"Aye but, Colleen, I'm fearin' for you. You can't just go out there alone. You could be shot by the Yankees or taken prisoner."

"I'll be very careful, I promise. I'll go to the nearest home, someone loyal to the Confederacy of course, and I'll get help to the railroad to get me back home."

"I don't have another solution for you lass, but if your determined to go, I'll do what I can," he said quietly.

Her stomach lurched at the thought of leaving Patrick. He had been her rock, her protector and also her friend for the past year. It would be difficult to leave and be out there on her own. It was a frightening proposition, but one she was determined to try. She had left home to find Steven and she was determined to see it through.

Once the slaughter of the Federal troops had occurred, Lee decided to move his men. They were to march through the night. It would make Colleen's escape easier as she could slip off into the dark woods and not be observed. In one sense she almost felt guilty about leaving, as if a deserter, leaving the others, the men she had come to know as friends, to continue the fight. On the other hand, she also knew she didn't belong here any longer and never more had that been apparent to her than the madness that had occurred at this Petersburg battle.

As they walked down the back road, the shadows of the dying day reached across their path. Patrick stayed close to her, looking off into the woods for the best place for her to slip off. They slowed their pace until they were the last in the line. Finally they saw what appeared to be a path off into the woods and they slipped off without being seen. After going a few paces they stopped, the path continuing on into the thicket.

The sun was nearly down now, the last rays casting their orange glow across the cool green leaves of the trees. It was quiet here away from the clatter of armaments and the murmurings of men.

Patrick turned to face her, looking into her deep green eyes. "I'm a fearin' for you lass. It's powerful dangerous to be out here alone. Perhaps I should go with you."

"No," she told him touching his chest and looking up into his face. "You can't do that. You could get into trouble and besides, leaving the war now goes against everything you believe in. I won't have it." But inside she desperately wanted to cling to him, to have him continue to watch out for her. She knew that wasn't possible. He would take her home and she knew she needed to continue her search for Steven. "I'll be alright," she told him. "I promise not to take risks. And after all, I'm a good soldier; you told me so yourself."

"But Colleen, lass......"

"Wait," she interrupted, "what if you still believed I was a man? Would you let

me go then?"

"I'm not sure," he responded.

"You know you would. I'm not some naive southern belle. Maybe before the war; I was spoiled, given everything I wanted, waited on by servants. But this war has changed me as it has everyone. I can't take anything for granted any longer. People, relationships, are what is the most important. I want to be home. I want my husband to be home and this war over so that we can get on with our lives."

"Aye lass," Patrick said touching her face. "But I've come to care a great deal for you and now I'll never see you again." His voice was low, full of emotion and it caused the tears to come to her eyes.

She held the hand on her face. "You are a fine man, Patrick," she told him. "One of the finest I have ever known and I will miss you very much, but I can't stay."

He traced the path down her face with his thumb her tears had taken. "I need for you to be safe," he told her. "Stay away from the Yankee patrols and head south."

She nodded and again looked up into his eyes. "You need to go, catch up with the regiment or they'll be lookin' for you. Good-bye Patrick."

"Good-bye sweet Colleen," he said softly. Then taking her face in both his hands, he placed his mouth fully on hers, kissing her gently, tenderly. He released her and turned to go. "Perhaps someday our paths may cross again," he told her. "Look me up if you need me. I love you, Colleen." Then he left, not even looking back.

She watched him go, still feeling the warmth of his lips on her mouth. She had an incredible urge to stop him, to run into his arms, to feel safe. But she resisted and only watched until she could no longer see him. She couldn't know he had felt that way for her. He had been good at hiding things too. But now it was time to move on.

As soon as Patrick was gone, the darkness seemed to envelop her and she suddenly felt frightened. She followed the path for a ways, but soon it became too dark to see and she knew she would have to stop or risk becoming lost. She constructed a bed of fallen leaves and then, wrapping herself in her bedroll, she lay down to try and sleep.

She had been sleeping outside for over a year, but somehow this night seemed more alive, more rustlings, more frogs and crickets. It had been so much more comforting with a fire and the companionship of hundreds of men. Those quiet times in camp she had felt safe. Now the darkness was frightening and she barely slept.

Early morning woke her with a soft rain in her face. She quickly packed up her bedroll and chewed on a piece of hardtack as she continued on down the path. She knew she was headed southeast, but what she didn't know was where it would come out, if at all. She suspected this to be a hunting trail and would hopefully bring her to civilization; a village or house perhaps. Worst case; she would have to turn around and go back to the main road. Only there, she would be more likely to run into Federal troops.

The rain increased to a steady downpour, soaking her, the rivulets running down her neck. She had endured rain before, but somehow it seemed more bearable when the misery was shared with others.

The path continued for most of the morning and she followed it dutifully, trying to be vigilant for any movement in the trees, but she found her mind wandering, forming a plan for her continued search effort.

Her thought to find a home and go there for help, was still her first choice. Her problem would be to explain her attire if she were to revel herself as a woman. What story could she concoct to tell them why she was dressed as a soldier, why her hair was cut short and why she carried a gun and ammunition? Perhaps she thought, she could tell them the Yankees had come and burned her home with all her clothing and some sympathetic soldier had given her his spare uniform. No, she said to herself and shaking her head, that didn't sound at all plausible. Even if Yankees had burned her house, she probably wouldn't be naked and no Confederate solders had extra clothes to share and then give her a good-bye and fare-thee-well.

"What am I going to say?" she said out loud. But before the answer could come upon her, the woods ended abruptly and she found herself at the edge of a wide field. Beyond, she saw a small white clapboard farmhouse and sprawling red barn. A few crops grew in the field; corn, wheat, and soybeans. She wondered who might be there and whether they were loyal to the Confederacy. And then she thought of what she would do. Cautiously she approached the house, wary of who might be living there. As she was in a southern state, she hoped she could count on this family's loyalty.

She slipped through tall stalks of corn, coming up behind the weathered barn. She peered around the corner and saw a man working in the yard unhitching a horse from some sort of farm machinery. He looked to be in his fifties, graying with a long beard and wearing a wide brimmed hat to keep off the rain. Beyond him was the house with its wide porch and brightly colored flowers lining the walk. There were no other out buildings and apparently no slaves. She moved along the side of the barn until she was standing out in the open. Her breathing had become rapid and her heart was pounding. Everything else to come depended on these people; whether they would turn her in to the Federals or help her to continue her search.

The man had come out of the barn from stabling the horse and finally turned around. He was startled to see her standing there; nearly stumbling over the traces he carried. “Ah, young man,” he said to her, “I didn’t see you standing there.”

“I’m sorry I startled you,” she said in her best male voice, “but I need help. Are you sympathetic to the Confederacy, sir?” she asked.

“I am a true Southern patriot, young man,” he said standing a little taller. “How can I help?”

“I’ve become separated from my company; went off on the wrong path, with the rain and all, I got disoriented. I’m afraid I’ve never been very good at directions.”

“ Of course, of course,” the man said advancing towards her holding out his hand. She took it, feeling the hard calluses encircling his palm. “My name’s Jack, Jack Cole.”

“Colin Malone,” she told him.

“Come on in out of the rain,” Jack said putting his hand on her shoulder and directing her toward the house. “If there’s anyway we can get you back to your company, we’ll do it.”

They went up onto the porch and removed their muddy boots and hats before entering a side door into the kitchen area of the house. Colleen saw a small, clean room, dominated by a large wood stove with flat irons for pots and an oven for baking. Shelves lined the walls containing dishes and mason jars filled with preserves. Her nostrils were filled with the sweet smell of baking bread. She had almost forgotten that heavenly aroma; it had been so long.

A short, plump woman, her graying hair piled on her head in tight braids, came into the kitchen from the adjoining room. She wore a full apron over her simple cotton dress and she wiped her right hand on it while her left, brushed back a few stray hairs that had escaped their bonds.

"Look Emily," Jack said, "it's one of our boys, lost from his company. I told him we'd try and help him find his way back."

Colleen reached out to shake her hand. "Colin Malone, Ma'am," she told her.

"Welcome to our home, Colin. We'd be glad to help one of our own," she said smiling. "Here, take off that wet jacket." She began pulling on the sleeves of her uniform and Colleen set aside her rifle, haversack and bedroll and took off her jacket that Emily could hang it by the stove to dry.

"Are you hungry, son?" she asked her. "Of course you are," Emily answered before Colleen could. "Why, we've heard all about how our boys are starvin' out there in the trenches. And look at you, you're so thin. You just come in here and set yourself down. I'll get you somethin' to eat."

"Thank-you, Ma'am. I sure do appreciate it," Colleen said sitting at the table in the dining room. Beyond, she could see the living room and the stairs to the second story. It was a simple home with simple furnishings, but the people seemed like good people; loyal to the cause.

Emily brought her a plate of venison stew with fresh bread still warm from the oven. Colleen thought she had never tasted anything so delicious; it had been so long since she had had a home cooked meal. Jack and Emily sat at the table watching her eat. It made her feel a little uncomfortable, but not enough to stop.

"Where you from, son?" Jack asked her.

"Georgia," she said between bites, "near Savannah."

"What regiment do you belong to?"

"Cobbs Georgians, fightin' with the Army of Northern Virginia."

"Our son is out there," Emily said quietly. "He's with Lee and General Johnston.

Have you been in it since the start? You look mighty young."

"No ma'am, I just joined up last year. I was too young before that. My brother had gone already in '61 and my parents needed me at home then." She had told the lie so many times it just came naturally now.

They both nodded. "Where'd you fight?" Jack asked her.

"Oh, now Papa, he may not want to talk of such things," Emily broke in.

"I just thought he might have run across our Jonathan."

"It's alright, I don't mind," she told them. "My first battle was at Chickamauga. Then I was in the Wilderness, Spotsylvannia and finally Petersburg near here, with many skirmishes in between."

Emily grabbed Jack's arm and looked into his face. "Jonathan was at the Wilderness. He wrote to us about the place; the fires and all." She looked back at Colleen expectantly.

"Jonathan Cole?" Colleen said furrowing her brow as she concentrated. "I don't believe I've ever met him. There are thousands of men in the Army of Virginia."

"He's a tall boy, over six foot, with brown hair, blue eyes and a very engaging smile," Emily told her hopefully.

"I'm sorry," Colleen said. She felt badly that she wasn't able to tell them anything about their son. She could see how desperate they sought information.

Colleen's eye was caught by a moment in the other room and she saw someone coming down the stairs. Long skirts swept down the steps and then she saw a young woman with long blonde curls and a beautiful face. She appeared startled to see a soldier sitting at the table.

"Oh Martha, come in here," Emily said as soon as she spotted the young blonde woman. "This is our daughter, Martha," Emily explained looking at Colleen. "She's nineteen and engaged to be married. Her financee is fightin' in the war as well. Martha, this Colin Malone. He was separated from his company after the battle at Petersburg."

"We could hear it from here," Martha told her in a soft voice. "It was awful; all the explosions and shooting."

"Yes, it was awful," Colleen agreed, remembering the slaughter at the pit.

"Excuse my rudeness," Martha said holding out her hand to Colleen, "it's a pleasure to meet you."

Colleen stood and took the offered hand as a gentleman would. She was struck at how soft it was. Martha sat at the table with them and made polite conversation, but Colleen couldn't help but look at her.

She was a beautiful young woman with golden hair and milky white fair skin. She had a slim figure with a small waist. The simple dress she wore showed the top of her ample bosom, the skirt flowing out at her waist in delicate folds to the floor. It nearly made tears come to her eyes to suddenly realize how much she missed being a woman, how much she longed to once again dress in beautiful gowns, to have men fawn over her as they once did. She wanted to wear her hair long and flowing the way Steven always liked it. She wanted to unbind her breasts and have soft skin again. Her living out doors, sleeping on the ground, the hardships of war, had all taken their toil on her body. Her hands were rough and callused, her arms and face dark and toughened by the elements. And the lack of adequate food and the rigors of marching and fighting, had nearly stopped her monthlies. She only prayed it hadn't hurt her ability to have children. It was time, she thought, time to be a woman again.

She stayed with the Cole's through the day, talking with them of ways she could get back to her regiment.

It was finally decided that Jack would drive her in the buggy to Richmond, where the regiment had supposedly been headed. But Colleen knew that wouldn't happen. She would get what she had come for and leave before they knew she had gone.

That evening she shared a meal with them; beef with potatoes and gravy and warm biscuits. It was a feast for Colleen so long deprived of even simple foods. They invited her to spend the night in their home. She protested, telling them she could sleep in the barn, that she was use to being outside. But they insisted, telling her they hoped if the same happened to their Jonathan, someone would take him in also.

They showed her up stairs to a room at one end of the house. The other room belonged to Martha. The Cole's room was downstairs behind the kitchen.

Colleen thanked them for their hospitality and closed the door to her room. Two candles lit the space, as it was still too warm to burn the fireplace. It was rather small; containing a single bed with a hand stitched quilt and a chest of drawers. Next to the bed was a nightstand with a bowl and pitcher filled with fresh water. A clean towel lay next to it. A rag rug covered the wood floor in front of the bed and lace curtains hung at the window. There were some personal items on the chest of drawers, which drew her attention. She fingered a pocket watch, a set of cuff links, a straight razor and a couple of photographs in frames. One was a picture of Martha and the other a serious looking young man in a Confederate uniform. She picked it up to look at it more closely. She could see tendrils of light colored hair from under the cap and kind looking eyes staring out at her. She knew it must be Jonathan and it made her feel sad. She had seen so many young hopeful men struck down before their time. As she put the photo back, she only hoped Jonathan was still alive. She glanced in the mirror that was hung over the chest at her reflection. She hadn't seen herself in a long while. Tears came to her eyes at what she saw. It was no wonder she hadn't had trouble convincing anyone she was a man in a long while. Her face looked thin and haggard, streaked with grim and dust. Her skin was no longer soft and white, but weathered and brown. Her lips were cracked and dry and her short hair was mussed and dirty.

The Coles had been so kind to her, she felt badly about what she was about to do, but she could see no other way around it. She didn't want to deceive them, but she needed to get on with her search for Steven.

She began to undress, removing the dirty torn uniform and then her underwear underneath, including the wrapping from her breasts. They were stained with perspiration and dirt and had begun to deteriorate. Once they had been removed, she tenderly felt to see if her breasts had been hurt in any way. The bindings had been on for weeks, as she had found no opportunity to remove them.

She began to wash herself with the water and soap in the pitcher. It felt so good. She washed slowly, luxuriating in the feel of being clean again. By the time she had finished, the water in the basin was black. But now she didn't want to put back on the dirty clothes that were lying on the floor. She removed the quilt from the bed and wrapped it about herself. Finally, totally exhausted, she blew out the candles and still wrapped in the quilt, lay on the bed. It was wonderfully soft. She had slept on the hard ground for so long, she had forgotten what a luxury it was to sleep in a bed and it felt so wonderfully free not to be wearing clothing or to be restrictively bound. It wasn't long before she was sleeping soundly.

She awoke just before dawn when she heard movement downstairs. She arose from the bed, the quilt still wrapped around her, and went to the door to listen. The Coles were talking softly, but she wasn't able to distinguish words. She could also hear their daughter Martha moving about in her own room. She heard Martha leave and go down the stairs. Shortly after she heard the kitchen door open and close. She went to the window and saw the three of them leaving the house on their way to the barn; presumably to perform chores. If she were going to follow through on her plan, now was the time.

Quietly she opened her door and stepped out into the hallway. Silence greeted her so she proceeded. She went into Martha's room and quickly looked around. It was similar in size to the other room, but this one was definitely feminine, with lacey pillow covers and bedskirt, a flowered quilt on the bed and combs and brushes on the dresser. There were also framed photographs; one similar to what she had seen in the other room and another young man, also dressed in a Confederate uniform. She presumed this must be her fiancée.

She wasted no more time as she didn't know how long the Coles would be in the barn. She spotted a curtained off area which she suspected to be a closet.

When she drew aside the cloth she saw several dresses hanging inside. She selected one, a flowered, everyday dress with three-quarter length sleeves. At the bottom of the closet were two pair of shoes; a shiny patent pair for dressing up and a pair of high top shoes with good heavy soles. She thought about her own collection of shoes back home, containing more than seventy-five pair. Growing up she had taken all of it for granted, but the war had certainly changed her perceptions. She took the latter and then began checking the dresser. She found a cotton petticoat, bloomers and camisole, some stockings and a shawl. She took all of these things, her heart pounding madly, fearing detection, and took them back to the other room. She dressed quickly, then checking the mirror, she took the brush from the dresser and tried to style her hair to look more feminine. Once again she saw Colleen instead of Colin. The shawl she had put around her shoulders, she now pulled up over her head. A smile crossed her face and she knew she looked like a woman again.

Lastly she left the room, checking the window to make sure the Coles hadn't come back from the barn, then quietly went down the stairs, taking her gun, bedroll, and haversack with her. It might look strange for a woman to be carrying such accouterments, but there were dangers out there and she would be alone.

She stopped in the kitchen and grabbed half a dozen freshly baked biscuits from the top of the stove and some cooked beef from the pantry. These she stuffed into her pack, watching continually for the Coles.

Then she saw them, emerging from the barn and walking towards the house. She gasped and ran towards the front of the house, going out the front door before they could detect her. Fortunately it faced the main road, curving around the woods she had left the day before. She ran towards the road, carrying her heavy gun and pack. She was glad to have gotten use to hard running in the army. Her only impediment was the long skirts, which kept tangling themselves around her legs. She ran and ran until she had rounded the curve in the road. Not until then did she look back to see if she were being followed. She saw no one at present, but she knew she would have to be vigilant as Mr. Cole could ride out to find her.

Now she walked, catching her breath. She felt badly for having deceived the Coles. They had been so kind to her, taking her into their home, feeding her, allowing her to stay in their own son's room. Then she had lied to them and stolen from them. She wanted to remember exactly where they lived with the hope that some day she might be able to explain and repay them. She could just imagine their confusion when they found her gone, along with some of Martha's clothing. And then there would be the dirty, torn uniform left lying on the floor, as well as her boots, jacket and hat on the porch. What would they think? What could they think?

On she walked down the dusty road, heading north towards Maryland and Point Lookout Prison, the morning sun rising in the sky. She knew she must look an odd spectacle, a woman walking on the road, carrying a haversack and rifle, but she cared not. She was on her way to Steven, to the prison to set him free. She just knew if she could convince everyone she were a man and could fight in the war for a year, then somehow she'd be able to convince them to set Steven free.

CHAPTER SEVENTEEN —August 1864

Mary watched James as he sat on the side patio, looking out at the river. A breeze brushed against his hair sending a few tendrils out of place, the empty sleeve of his shirt waved back and forth at his side. There were times when he would do that for hours; just sit and stare. When it happened he would be oblivious to everything around him as if he were in his own world. Who could know what thoughts and images he played over and over in his mind, scenes of war and the deep loss of Gerritt and now Colleen missing, perhaps dead herself.

Other times he seemed to come out of his fog and converse with her and the servants. But he was a changed man and he no longer seemed able to make decisions. When Mr. Solomon had come to him about decisions regarding the slaves, James had merely waved him aside, telling him to handle it however he saw fit. In the past, he had wanted to be involved in every aspect of the running of the plantation, but now he continually deferred to others, herself included.

She did not want the responsibility, didn't really feel competent as she had just begun the massive undertaking three years previous. Now the cotton fields lay fallow, the store houses were half empty, the overseer was beyond her control, delving into the supplies for his own personal use and beating the slaves. As a consequence, many more of the slaves had run away. The books were in a shambles, as she had not known what to do with supplies taken by the army. Money had been spent to plant seeds, feed and clothe the slaves who worked the fields, but none had exchanged hands when confiscated; a loss, but how much? And how much should she calculate for the loss of the slaves, some being worth more than others. She knew she was going to have to talk with James even though she had made the attempt many times before. It was many months since he had come home, but he still had not returned to his old self.

She brought over another chair and placed it directly in front of him and then sat in his field of vision. He neither moved nor acted as if he saw her. "James," she said to him. "James! Listen to me!" she said louder this time touching his hand. "Please talk to me. I know you saw unspeakable things in the war, but darling, I miss you. I need you."

"Mary?" he said finally looking into her eyes. "Did you say something my love?"

"James, we need to discuss our plan for the future of the plantation."

He frowned. "Shannon, what's wrong with Shannon?"

"Well now for instance, what are we to do about all the slaves who keep runnin' away?"

"I'm sure Mr. Solomon can handle it," James said looking past her towards the slave cabins across the river. "He'll have the slave catchers after them."

"But Mr. Solomon is part of the problem. Because of his cruel treatment, even more have run and there are no more slave catchers. Mr. Solomon can't or won't go look for them himself. James, what should we do? We're losing valuable property, not to mention the labor they provide. For example, one of our best weaving girls ran off with one of the men who runs the cotton gin. They were skilled workers; not everyone can perform those jobs."

James just shook his head and looked past her, that vacant look in his eyes.

"Please James," Mary said quietly, "I need your help. I don't know how to do this anymore. If things don't get better we could lose Shannon. The Yankees are gettin' closer all the time. They've nearly taken Atlanta and I hear horror stories all the time; burnin', rapin' and takin' everything they can get their hands on. James, I'm afraid."

He once again looked into her eyes and she saw clarity. He took her hand with his remaining one. "It'll be alright, darlin'. We'll handle whatever comes our way. If we can't keep the slaves from runnin', then we'll have to let them go. We may have to anyway. I am afraid we are losing this war."

"No," she said pulling back. "We can't lose and we can't lose our slaves. How will we manage without them?"

"We will survive," he said simply. "We will find another way."

"There is no other way," she said getting to her feet. "You don't seem to understand the complexity nor the severity of the situation."

"Perhaps not, perhaps not," he said so quietly she barely heard. "Did you know I saw some rivers so full of men's blood that they ran red?"

She knew there would be no further talking to him so she walked away, leaving him still sitting looking out at the river. She went back into the house to see to the many daily chores.

Outside the kitchen house several slave women were washing the laundry in large tubs, linens as well as the family's clothing. Inside the cookhouse, breads were being baked, and preserves put up as the garden supplies were harvested. As Mary went though the house she made sure the dusting was being done, the floors cleaned and the windows shined until they sparkled.

Once she was confident things were being taken care of inside, she went out to the barns. Since no more cotton had been sold in the last couple of years, the reserves were stacked to the ceiling with bales upon bales. No more cotton had been grown, as they had no place else to keep it. She only hoped the war would be over soon and they could sell their cotton again.

She went on to the weaving house, the livestock barn, the smokehouse, the yard where soap and candles were being made and the blacksmith shop, making sure chores were being accomplished and checking to see that things were running smoothly. Lastly, she stood at the edge of the massive fields and watched from a distance as the field slaves worked to bring in the harvest. Mr. Solomon sat astride his horse, riding up and down the rows, his long whip snapping the air over the heads of those he felt to be lax. It was here she felt powerless to control what happened. If James refused to do anything about Mr. Solomon, then she need only worry about whether the crops were in or not.

She picked up her skirts and began the walk back to the house, passing the slave quarters where the little children played in the yards and the elderly watched over them and did household chores. As she walked along the river with its long willow branches dipping into the water, she looked across to see if she could still see James on the patio. The chair where he had sat was now empty.

As she crossed the bridge to the other side of the river, she thought about the massive undertaking of running the large plantation and wondered how James thought they could possibly manage without the slaves. It was ludicrous, impossible.

When she got back to the house, Anna Bell was just getting out of her carriage. She went onto the veranda to meet her.

'What is this all about?" Mary asked her.

"I went back to Briarwood; thought I would move back in now that James is home, but I just can't stay alone in that house," she answered. "I just rattle around there like loose change."

"What has happened with everything that needs overseeing, the harvest, the weaving…."

"I left everything to our overseer and the house to Laura, my personal servant."

"Oh, Anna Bell, you know you're more than welcome to stay here, but I'm afraid those people will rob you blind. They have to be watched every moment."

Anna Bell had reached the top of the stairs and paused to look back at Mary. "I left them all this time while I've stayed here after Clifford died and I found nothing missing. Besides, it's not safe. The Yankees might be here any day. Word is they've nearly taken Atlanta."

Mary looked into her eyes and saw fear mirrored there. She went up to her and put her arm around her friend's shoulder and began leading her into the house. "Of course you can stay here as long as you like. Everything will be alright at Briarwood," she told her. She could physically feel Anna Bell relax with her words.

"Thank-you, Mary. I can't tell you how much this means to me. That Yankee General Sherman is doin' horrible things. They say his army spreads out for sixty miles and he has no control over them. Soldiers are takin' people's livestock, food, burnin' their houses and rapin' the women."

"I know, I heard that too," Mary said. "They say once Sherman takes Atlanta, he'll go for Savannah. We're right in his path."

"It's just all so frightening. What are we supposed to do to protect ourselves? The Confederate Army is being decimated. If they can't keep them out of Atlanta, how can they stop them from runnin' over the whole state?"

"I don't have the answers Anna Bell. We'll just have to prepare the best we can and wait." Mary walked up the broad staircase with her to see her to her room. "It's not that we can arm the slaves or anything like that," she continued. "There would be revolt; so many of them have run away already."

"And I hear that when the Yankees take someone's plantation, they let all the slaves go; some of them even join the Union Army to fight against us."

"At least you've got your husband home," Anna Bell said turning to face her at the top of the stairs.

Mary sighed heavily. "I'm afraid James is not the same man who left here in '61. The war has changed him. It's as if he's a different person, not the man I married and I don't know how to get him back."

Dora had heard part of the women's conversation when they had reached the second floor. She was in Colleen's room with the door open. It was a place she liked to come when her other chores were finished. It somehow made her feel closer to Colleen when she was surrounded by her things. She still missed her terribly; more than she imagined she would. It was as if she had lost her own child. When she had realized Colleen wasn't coming home right away she had grieved, crying, feeling sad all the time. But now a year had passed and she had to face the possibility Colleen might never be coming home.

She alone knew about Colleen's disguising herself and joining the army. After so much time she knew there was a chance she could have been killed and no one would know who she was. She considered telling Mr. McBride what she knew, but had been afraid what the repercussions would be.

She too, had heard through the white folks that the war was going badly for the south. What would happen if they lost, she didn't know. Many of her people had already run, not to be heard from again. She had seriously considered doing the same. Freedom sounded so wonderful; never to be owned, to worry whether you would be sold, never to have to do the bidding of the master and mistress.

She had even dreamed of owning her own house with a little bit of land where she could plant some vegetables. But the actual doing it was another matter. It was frightening to her, to think of leaving the security of the plantation, the only home she'd known since a child, of going out into the unknown. Many of the others felt as she did, not knowing where they would go, afraid of what would happen if they were caught, frightened of the war that was going on somewhere outside their door. They talked about it sometimes in the quarters after hours. Many wanted to run, not caring what lie ahead, freedom worth any cost. Others were willing to stay for the present, with what they knew, the security of a roof over their head and food in their bellies.

So she had put off going, also waiting to see if Colleen would return. As much as she hadn't wanted to admit it, she cared about this family, especially Gerritt and Colleen. It had devastated her when Mr. Gerritt had been killed. She had cried for days; and now poor master with his arm gone and his mind not right. Well someone had to look after him and even Misses, she had so much to do, she needed help. She just couldn't leave now.

A few weeks had passed and it was September. One of their neighbors, the Banyons, who had lost their son Robert, hearing of James' return home, stopped to visit and gave them the news that Yankee General Sherman had taken Atlanta; their own troops retreating and scattering. They told of the looting and destruction and then, how many parts of the magnificent city had been burned. They had received this information from a cousin who had been fighting against Sherman and had witnessed the fall of Atlanta. Now the Union troops were headed towards the sea and Savannah.

Mary remembered better times when she had visited cousins in Atlanta. She had grown up just outside the city on a small plantation and still had relatives there. It was a beautiful city with an Opera House and theater. They had always had wonderful times in the city and it was sad to think of its destruction. She knew her cousins were safe as she had received a letter from them saying they had fled to relatives in Louisiana.

Many plantation owners were talking of how they might protect themselves. Some argued for banning together, arming themselves and attempting to fight off the Yankees themselves. Others were in favor of packing their belongings and taking themselves and their slaves someplace safer. There were those who had already done so, as her cousins had, but no one seemed to have any best solution for all of them.

Mary was at a loss to know what to do and James would not or could not make any decisions. It would have been impossible for them to pack everyone up and leave. They still had over two hundred slaves and there would be nowhere they could take so many. The other option of arming everyone was also out of the question. They, at present, only had six or seven white men on the plantation and there would be no way they could defend all their property against a whole company of seasoned soldiers.

Her only plan for the moment was to do nothing. She could only hope the Yankees would not come to them. But it was not to be. It had only been several weeks in late November, after hearing of the fall of Atlanta, that a messenger came with the news; that the Yankees were only a few miles away. He told of soldiers coming into people's homes, taking their valuables, confiscating livestock and food stores, then torching their homes and barns. He advised them to flee to safety; go to Alabama or Florida.

When Mary heard the news, her heart sank and fear filled her. She began ordering the servants to get the trunks from the attic and begin packing. She told Matthew to bring the buckboard around to the kitchen and smokehouse and load all of their foodstuffs they could carry. She felt panicked and her voice showed it.

"What's gwine to happen to the servants, Misses?" Rose asked her as they stood in the hallway. "Is we goin' wif ya'll?"

Mary paused before answering. "Perhaps just some of the house servants; we can't possibly take everyone."

"But, that ain't right. What be happening to the others, to de fiel' han's?"

"I can't be responsible for everyone," she snapped at her. "They aren't going to hurt your people. It's us they want."

"But Misses, I scairt," the young woman told her mistress.

"We all are Rose! It doesn't help! Now go and do as you are told!"

Rose ran off and Mary put her hand to her heart. How could she get through this? What was to happen to them all?

James came walking down the hall, slowly, calmly, while servants scurried past him. How could he be so calm, she thought, when at any moment the Yankees could come and kill them all?

"Mary dear," James said in a quiet voice, "stop what you're doing."

"Stop? What do you mean stop?"

"I mean, tell the servants not to pack, put everything back, Mary."

She looked at him incredulously. "You can't be serious. We can't just leave all of our things."

"We won't be leaving our things because we're not going anywhere," he told her.

"We're not...... but we can't stay here; we could be killed!"

He went to her and put his arm around her. "Mary, I know you're frightened, but I'm not running off to leave everything to the Yankees. I may not be able to stop them from taking what they want, but I'll be damned if I'll run and just leave it all for them to help themselves freely. No, I looked them in the eye on the battlefield and I'll look them in the eye again."

"James, are you sure about this?" Mary asked. She hadn't heard him speak so lucidly in months, but what he was saying frightened her. "They could kill us; you know that don't you?"

He nodded as he directed her towards the front door. "Yes Mary, they could kill us, but I've faced death many times in these last few years and I'm not afraid of it.

Gerritt is gone and we have had no word for a year from Colleen. It's just the two of us and we can face them together.

This house," he said gesturing about, "is just a house." He then led her outside on the veranda. "Look about Mary. This is the land my grandfather settled on when he came from Ireland. It was lush and green, good for growing things, and he named it Shannon for the river there.

If the Yankees come, if they take our things and burn our home, then we will start over. They can't take the land from us."

"But James, how can we do that if everything is gone?"

"One thing at a time, just as my grandfather did it."

They stood looking out at the land, the river flowing past, the spreading trees, the orchards as the sun cast its last orange glow of the day. James's good arm was around his wife, feeling her tremble and out of the corner of his eye, saw her tears streaming down her face. "Don't be afraid, my dear," he told her. "We'll see this though together. You've been incredibly brave while I was gone."

Mary looked into his eyes and saw how calm he was, how clearly he had spoken.

"I need to tell you how I really lost my arm."

"But you have," she said holding him closer.

"The place, the circumstances are the same, but my heart was gone. It was a long brutal war; Clifford was gone, then Gerritt. I felt as if I didn't want to live any longer. When I went out on the battlefield that day, I took no caution, put myself in harms way. I wanted to die out there that day."

"No James," Mary said, the tears falling from her eyes.

"But I didn't die and now I'm not running from the Yankees. No, Mary we're staying here."

It was two days later; the sun had already cast long shadows across the grass, the air cool, when Mary heard shouting and screams coming from the slave quarters. She went out onto the balcony and looked out over the front lawn and beyond to the river. Everything appeared tranquil; the breeze blowing the soft fronds of the willows across the surface of the water. There were several women gathering fallen twigs for their fires. And then she saw them; bluecoats amongst the slave cabins, moving towards the crossing to the house, scattering the Negroes screaming before them.

Mary gasped, felt her heart race and thought for a moment she would pass out. She turned and went back inside the room where Dora was straightening up. "Dora, go find Master James, tell him the Yankees are here! Hurry! The Yankees are in the slave quarters!"

Dora only paused for a moment and then ran from the room, her eyes wide with fright. What did this mean, the Yankees were here? She had heard such horrible things about the soldiers who wore the blue uniforms. They burned barns and homes and killed innocent people. They had killed Master Gerritt. But she had also heard they were freeing the slaves. She wondered if they would free her.

When she got down to the bottom of the stairs, she saw Master James already standing in the doorway.

Mary and Anna Bell came running down behind her and when they saw James quietly looking out at the advancing troops, Mary called out to him. "James, the Yankees are here! Get your gun! They'll kill us all!"

He turned to her and held out his hand. "Come my darlin'. Stand here with me."

She went to stand beside him, Anna Bell clutching her other arm. Then she saw the Union cavalry riding down the lane. She would have bolted back into the house if James had not held on to her.

"Oh, James, I'm frightened. Shouldn't you get your gun? I could help you load it."

"No dear, I'll not give them an excuse to kill us."

The men on horseback were coming closer and out of the corner of her eye, she could see the soldiers on foot entering their barns. Finally the cavalrymen reined in their horses directly in front of their veranda. The man in the lead wore brass buttons and gold braid on his blue uniform. On his head the broad brimmed hat sported a gold cord, the end tassels draped over the back. On his sleeves were bars of gold braid.

"Captain, I am James McBride and this is my wife Mary McBride and our friend, Anna Bell Covington," James addressed the man.

The Captain touched his hand to his hat. "Ma'am," he said addressing Mary and Anna Bell. Then turning to James, "Sir, did you lose your arm in the war?"

"At Gettysburg," James told him.

"Never been to Gettysburg myself," he said, "fought mostly in Tennessee, til we joined up with Sherman.

Look, I'm afraid we're gonna have to confiscate your property. Need to feed and outfit an army, you know and with all that, the spoils of war. Nothing personal."

"Oh of course not," James replied somewhat sarcastically.

"Please don't hurt us," Anna Bell pleaded.

The Captain ignored her and turned in his saddle to his men. "Alright now, make it quick! We've got to move on."

A loud yell went up from the group as they dismounted and began rushing up the steps, past James, Mary and Anna Bell, into the house. Mary was about to follow them in, but James held her back.

They could hear whooping and yelling coming from the barns and stables and saw their horses being led away by the soldiers; Gerritt's roan and Colleen's spotted filly. Some of them were carrying away chickens and pigs, smoked hams and turkeys from the smokehouse. The Yankee soldiers filled wagons with their booty and hauled it away. They saw Mr. Solomon and his sidekicks standing by watching; watching and not lifting a hand to stop them.

From inside the house they could hear the breaking of dishes, smashing furniture and the screams of the house servants. Mary hid her face in James' shoulder, trying to shut out the horrible sights and sounds. But when they began pouring back from the house carrying her possessions, jewelry that had been in the family for generations, silver edged mirrors, gold jewelry boxes and pearl handled brushes, silverware and even their Confederate dollars she reached out, protesting. The soldiers only laughed at her. They packed Mary's things in their haversacks and tied the larger items onto their saddles.

The Captain called out to the foot soldiers and they began to assemble, still continuing to take what they could. Then taking burning sticks from the slave cooking fires, several of the bluecoats went back inside several of the barns and outbuildings and set fire to them.

James and Mary stood on the veranda of their house and watched them burn. “No!” Mary cried out. “Oh, God no!” She put her hands over her mouth to keep from screaming. When she looked over at James, she saw tears glistening in his eyes. His pain was nearly more than she could bear.

The Captain mounted his horse and sent the infantry on their way. Then lastly, while several of their barns went up in flames, he tipped his hat, rode across the river and went about the slave cabins telling everyone they were free to leave, to go away from this place. And then they were gone.

Many of the slaves gathered their few belongings and began running, running after the soldiers, afraid someone would stop them, calling out that they were free. Others who stayed, were attempting to put out the fires, but it was to no avail.

James and Mary watched silently as their lives went up in flames. “I wonder if they burned Briarwood,” Anna Bell said quietly.

They had nearly forgotten she was there. Mary turned to her and took her into her arms, holding her. There were no words now.

Rose came running from the house, crying hysterically, “Massa, Misses, what we’se gwine to do? Lord! What’s we’se to do?”

James and Mary followed her into the house and what greeted their sight made Mary cry out. Everywhere was destruction. In the parlor furniture was thrown about and broken, the lamps smashed, the piano destroyed. James’s library had all his books pulled from the shelves, pages torn out, his guns gone, his big walnut desk chopped to kindling. In the dining room, the floor was littered in broken china and crystal. Room by room, they surveyed the destruction. Not one room had been spared. Even the grand ballroom had had all the chandeliers smashed to tiny pieces.

Finally in her own room, where the linens had been shredded, the posters on the bed cut down, the mirrors smashed, her clothing ripped to shreds, Mary stood amidst her belongings and wept, deep wracking sobs that would not stop. It was too much to bear; she could take no more. Gerritt was gone, James maimed and Colleen disappeared. Many of their barns were burning with everything inside. And now this, all their things destroyed, gone; what more was there?

James came into the room and put his arm around her. “Don’t cry, it’ll be alright,” he told her.

“No it won’t!” she cried, pulling away. “It won’t be alright. We’ve lost everything!”

“Not everything,” he said, the tears glistening in his own eyes. “We still have each other and we have our home. They didn’t burn our home. That’s more than a lot of people have. I know it seems terrible right now but Mary, we will survive this. As long as we have each other and the land, we can start over."

"I'm too old and too tired to start over," she told him.

"What are to do?" he asked. "Give up and die? Shall we just go out in the grass and lie down to die?"

"I don't know, James," she said crying again. "I'm just too tired to go on."

James took her hand. "I'm tired too, but if we stay together, work together, we can become strong again. We will lean on each other. I love you Mary."

She looked up into his scared face, his lovely dear face and nodded. "There is nothing else is there? Where do we begin?"

"I'm afraid this war is lost. We fought gallantly, but our reserves are gone. It cannot last much longer. Then will come the healing time; a time for rebuilding." He put his arm around her shoulder and began to lead her from the room. "First, we need to find out who among the slaves will remain loyal."

"How will we know?"

"Set them free."

"What? What do you mean set them free? How can we build again if we free the slaves? They are valuable."

"Soon when this war is over, they will be free anyway. The time has come to let those go that want to and see who will stay."

They went back downstairs into the kitchen where they found their cook Ellen and Matthew trying to clean the mess there; flour spilled everywhere, jars of preserves smashed on the floor, cooking pots overturned.

"Matthew," James said to the tall black man.

"Yes sir, Massa," Matthew answered.

"I need to have you go to the slave quarters and tell everyone still there to gather on the front lawn. Ellen you will do the same for the house servants. I have something important I need to tell all of you." Matthew and Ellen went to do as they were bid.

Finally, after some period of time, all the servants, whether they be field hands, skilled workers, stable hands or house servants were gathered on the front lawn. James and Mary went out onto the veranda to face them. The air was still thick with black smoke from the burning barns. Remnants of the contents were spilled around the entire area. The day had grown dark, the light from the fires illuminating the sky.

Persons of all ages stood before them; old folks, young people, small children and babies in arms. Mary remembered helping to deliver some of those babies. Everyone was silent, waiting to see what their Master and Mistress would say. There were perhaps nearly one hundred of them still there, milling about, wondering what would become of them. Were they really free as the Yankee soldier had told them? Could they just leave, or would they be whipped? Dora was among them and the same questions were going through her mind.

Everyone turned towards the house when James appeared on the top step of the veranda; this man who had bought them, had directed them as how to live their lives, for whom they had toiled for nearly all of their lives.

"I'm grateful to see all of you who still remain," he told them. "A great tragedy has occurred today with the loss of some of our barns, but we will rebuild and be strong again. What I need from all of you, is your help. For those who wish to go, I will not stop you. I will give you your freedom papers. But for those who wish to stay, I welcome you. You also will be given your papers, but if you choose to stay, you will be given a fair wage and can keep your home.

If you leave, you will need to think of where you will go, how you will support your families….. However, if you remain and work for me, I promise you security, a home and a wage that you can spend as you like. You could even save enough perhaps to buy your own piece of land someday.

That is my offer. Think it over, but no matter what you decide, you will be free. No one can sell or buy you again, nor will there be any harsh treatment. I am firing Mr. Solomon. One of you will be my new foreman.

That is all I have to say, you are dismissed." And he and Mary walked back into the house.

They began talking amongst themselves; wandering back to their cabins, not believing they were really free.

Dora stood looking up at the spot where Massa James had been standing. Free. She was free. He had said so. It was something she had been dreaming of her entire life.

"Free," she said it aloud, just to hear the sound of it. "I'se free!" she said it again. "Them's the sweetest words I ever did hear." Tears blurred her vision as she thought of the possibilities. She could go and find her family. Perhaps her Mama and Papa and little brother and sister were still on the same plantation they had been when she was sold to Mr. McBride. But how to find her way there was another matter.

She turned to watch many of her people going to their cabins and bundling their meager possessions in preparation for leaving. But Dora knew this war between the white folks was not over and even though they might have their freedom papers, there would be no guarantees of their safety. Rogue Confederate defectors had been hanging blacks whenever they found them. To be out there on the road was risky at best.

Then she looked back at the house and saw Misses Mary carrying outside, an album which had contained photographs of her wedding day and of Mr. Gerritt and Miss Colleen. She could see the book had been ruined, the photos torn. Mary sat on the top step, the shredded book in her lap. She touched the pieces of the pictures, trying to put them back together. Great tears filled her eyes and spilled onto the book.

Quietly, Dora reached into her apron pocket and pulled something out. Opening her fist she saw the beautiful emerald ring lying in the palm of her hand. It was the ring Massa Steven had given Colleen, the one she had left behind. Dora had gone to the place where she had hidden it when she saw the Yankees coming and had put it in her pocket, hoping they wouldn't find it.

Dora looked back up at Mary, her face in her hands, sobbing for the losses she had endured and she thought to herself; how can I leave her now?

September 1864

When Steven awoke, he was disoriented, had forgotten where he was. He blinked his eyes feeling groggy. He looked around trying to remember where he might be. He appeared to be in a dilapidated barn. Shafts of light stabbed through holes in the roof, showing the dancing dust in the air. He was lying on a bed of straw in what had once been a horse stall. Boards were missing from the walls allowing the breeze to drift through. Except for a few pieces of rusty, broken farm equipment, the barn was empty. It appeared as though no one had used it for many years.

It reminded Steven of the day back in '61 when he had raced his stallion against Gerritt's roan and he and Colleen had met in the old barn on their plantation. How he had wanted her that day, how he had loved her.

He still loved her so much, but more than three years had past since that day he had kissed her good-bye. It had been so long since he had touched her and looked into those beautiful green eyes. He had long since lost the photo he had brought with him of her. Her image had become blurred in his mind. But one thing time hadn't erased was how much he missed her. If anything, he missed her more intensely the longer he was away from her. Sometimes he wondered if he would ever see her again. Had she waited for him or had she tired of his lengthy absence and found someone else? After all, their marriage hadn't really been legal. He had had no correspondence with her since before Gettysburg. Perhaps she thought he was dead. Perhaps she thought he was rotting in a Yankee prison camp.

He stood up from his bed of straw and walked to the middle of the barn, standing in a shaft of light. He was dirty and his clothes torn from his months on the run. His hair and beard had grown long and unkempt. "She probably wouldn't know me if she walked in here right now," he said aloud.

He heard coughing coming from another one of the stalls and looked over to see Tom curled up, still sleeping. That cough of his had been progressively getting worse; a result of living within the prison with the sick and dying. He went to him and touched his shoulder, waking him. As Tom sat up, the coughing increased.

"Old friend," Steven said to him, "it's daylight and we should keep moving. Hopefully, we'll find us some breakfast."

Tom nodded, still coughing and got to his feet. "Sure hope we kin find them friends of your'n soon," he finally said. "I'm afraid I ain't getting' no better."

"I hope so too, Tom."

They left their resting place for the night and went out into the bright sunlight, following the road south while watching at all times for Union scouting troops. It had been three months since their escape from the Union prison camp. They had at first thought they might find a Confederate regiment and rejoin the army, but because Tom was so ill and Steven's leg was still painful, they knew they would not be able to fight again. But then, their objective was to find their way home to Georgia. They had periodically come across a Confederate patriot, civilians who had been kind enough to give them a meal or a bed for a few days. This was how they had learned of the terrible battle in the Wilderness and the horrible losses incurred by their troops.

After months of traveling and hiding from Union troops, they realized they would need help to accomplish their task of getting home. Steven had remembered friends of his family who lived in Virginia on a large plantation and who they had frequently done business with, including the buying and selling of slaves. Colleen's family as well, were friendly with them and had on occasion, traveled there to visit.

They hoped to be able to find these friends and obtain shelter and perhaps safe passage back to Georgia. It had been many years since Steven had visited this family with his father. He remembered that their name was Jeffries and their plantation was near Richmond. Virginia had suffered so much of the ravages of the war, homes destroyed, fields burned, livestock lost and property stolen, Steven didn't know if this place still existed. But, except for walking all the way back to Georgia, he felt there weren't other options.

After they had walked for two hours, Tom's breathing became more labored and the coughing had increased. In spite of the fact they had found nothing to eat, they had to stop and rest. They found a shady spot under a tree and along the banks of a small stream. It was far enough from the road that they would not be seen from passing troops.

Steven took a tin cup from the haversack he carried, filled it from the clear, cool stream and brought it to Tom. "Thankee son," Tom said sipping on the water. "I'm jes plain tuckered out."

"I wish we could have found something to eat; give you some strength."

"Jes give me a few minutes and I'll be ready to go again."

Steven lay back on the long grass looking up through the branches of the tree. He wasn't sure how much longer Tom could go on. His condition seemed to worsen every day. At least they were out of that disease infested prison. Tom would probably already be dead by now if they hadn't escaped.

He thought back to that day last spring when they had finally freed themselves from that hellhole. They had gone out twice more on wood detail, gathering valuable information as well as fuel to warm them during the winter months. They had experimented with separating to range further into the forest. The guards had seemed relaxed; a few of them following each group, thereby reducing their power and effectiveness. Times back inside the walls, they attempted to befriend certain guards who seemed receptive. From them they subtly learned of their location, which way certain Union troops were headed and the outcome of battles. Even though they knew the guards were only relating wins by their own troops, they could see the war for the South was in a downward spiral it could probably never recover from.

The winter spent in the prison had been miserable. Even though they had a supply of firewood, it was limited. Therefore, they kept the barracks fire to a minimum, only feeling its heat when standing directly next to the stove. There had been no extra warm clothing, only what they had been brought in with. The one meager blanket issued to them was multi-functional. They wrapped themselves in it at night; it was worn around the shoulders during the day like a coat as they walked about the compound and they huddled beneath it as they sat around their small fire.

Many of the men had arrived barefoot, their boots gone long since. They had marched and fought with no protection for their feet, but then the cold and snows had come and many walked about with pieces of their blanket, torn and wrapped about their feet. Some received such severe frostbite, their toes blackened and some even broke off.

Steven had been grateful for the boots he still wore, such as they were. The soles were nearly worn through and the leather tops were torn, but at least they provided some protection and warmth.

Consumption, dysentery, and typhus ran rampant among the men. There was a prison doctor who had done what he could, but without many supplies or medicines, there wasn't much he could do. Men became weak and died, daily. It was only pure luck that Steven felt he had not succumbed to the diseases. Just before their escape, Tom had come down with consumption and croup. It had only gotten worse.

On their last trek into the forest, the wood detail had decided it would be now to make their escape. It was spring; the weather had warmed. The snow was gone and the leaves had returned to the trees. Tracking the escapees would prove to be more difficult.

The detail was led out by a company of Yankee guards, working their way further and further into the darkness of the trees. Most of the men had separated into pairs, Steven and Tom being together. They worked into the morning, cutting and felling trees. The two guards who had followed them had gotten relaxed, talking, sipping coffee from their tin cups. It was late afternoon when they, as well as the guards, were tired and not as alert, that they suddenly heard the signal; a shrill whistle. Before the guards could re-act, they had bolted. They ran off into separate parts of the forest, confusing the Yankees. They could hear shouts and rifle fire, but they didn't stop. They had gotten away clean. They had zigzagged through the trees, keeping the sun in sight as their guide. That evening they had slept in the shelter of a low depression filled with fallen leaves.

The following morning they had found their way out of the trees and onto a road going north along the peninsula, looking for a place to cross the Potomac into Virginia. They had walked nearly forty-five miles, taking over a week to travel. They feared coming too close to Washington which would be heavily fortified. They stayed along the riverbank, hiding from patrols when they had finally discovered a small village, the sign over the general store reading, Popes Creek. Skirting around it they saw a raft, tied up close to a shack; the owner obviously used to cross over. Waiting until dark, they had crept silently into the river, untied the raft and used it to float themselves across the wide expanse. They remembered another time when they had crossed this river together, when Gerritt had still been with them. Once across they had made their way southwest, always on the lookout for patrols. Many times they had had to hide in the underbrush when a carriage or horseback riders would pass by. They could never trust anyone at this point.

Steven looked over at Tom who had fallen asleep. He hated to wake him, but they needed to move on. He touched his friend on the shoulder and shook him gently. "We need to go, Tom," he told him.

"I'm up. I'm up," Tom said stiffly getting to his feet.

Steven thought how old he looked, so much more so than when they had first met. They had called him the old man, and he was several years older than his own father; but the war had taken its toll. Deep creases lined his face, his hair and beard had become even grayer and his joints were stiff and sore. Now this disease ravaged his lungs. They had been through a great deal together, were good friends and he didn't want to see him die as well.

Steven picked up the haversack and rifle lying nearby and began walking through the long grass towards the road. He thought about how they had acquired the pack and gun. They had been free from the prison for several weeks, hiding and scavenging food wherever they could find it. Sometimes they ate from farmer's fields and orchards and other times they had been fortunate to find patriotic Confederates who fed them and even allowed them to sleep for a few days in their barns.

They had been near Spotslvannia and had seen a lot of troop activity on the part of the Yankees. They had kept hidden and watched carefully, afraid if they attempted to go around they would be detected by roving scouts. Then they heard familiar sounds; the booming and explosions of artillery, the firing of muskets and the yells and screams of men in battle. It wasn't long before wagons came lumbering past their hiding place, filled with the wounded. They could hear their moans and cries as they lurched over the rough road. Blood seeped through the floorboards and trailed along behind. Several hours later, darkness had settled over the landscape, the remainder of the Union troops followed, the battle obviously ended for the moment.

Once each side had withdrawn to their own camps, Steven and Tom had cautiously stepped out of hiding and walked to where the battle had taken place. Except for a few medical personnel still gathering the wounded, the area was deserted. Ghostly shapes littered the ground; dead men and horses, broken caissons.

The moon shone as a crescent in the night sky, only affording them a modicum of light. They walked among the dead being careful not to step on anyone. Uniforms of gray mingled with blue and the red blood of both saturated the ground.

They began looking for supplies in the discarded haversacks. They took two and filled them with hardtack, biscuits, fat back, even ammunition. Then they had also taken two muskets which were lying about. They slipped away just as the burial details began collecting the bodies from both sides. It was a time of truce, a time when blue and gray came together to gather their dead without fear of harm; a shared sadness, a common reality of war. They had thought of going to the Confederate medical unit, but they knew not what might become of them if they did so. Not being wounded, they might be returned to the fighting, especially with the South desperate for men. They might have been considered deserters, being on the run. So for now, they preferred to stay on their own; attempt to get back to Georgia.

They had been wandering over the countryside now for over three months, trying to find the plantation Steven remembered from his youth. He recalled its name was Paradise and the family name was Jeffries. At times when sheltered by a Virginia family, they would ask if they knew of such a plantation. Occasionally they had received leads as to their whereabouts, but no one seemed to know if the family had been spared the destruction of the war.

Tom seemed to be in even more pain after their rest by the stream and his coughing was incessant. Not only did Steven worry about his friend's health, but he was also concerned about their safety. It was becoming increasingly difficult to hide from roving troops when he couldn't stop the coughing. Steven himself, still walked with a limp and after traveling all day, it would pain him a great deal. He worried it would give out or worse, the fragile bone would break and he would be helpless.

"You know Steven, lad," Tom said between coughs, "I think you might do well to leave me. I'm afeared I'm slowin' you down."

"I'm not leaving you Tom," Steven told his friend. "We've been together since the beginning and we'll stay 'til the end. If we can get to Paradise Plantation we can get you a doctor."

"Maybe….. too late for that. This consumption's got the better of me." Speaking those few sentences caused another fit of coughing. Steven could see blood on Tom's sleeve where he had covered his mouth.

"Don't try talking any longer," Steven told him. "Reserve your strength for walking." He knew if they didn't find the Jeffries soon, Tom would die.

Their travels that day led them past cornfields and orchards where they helped themselves to the bounty, stuffing as much as they could in their knapsacks. That evening as they scouted for a place to rest, they ventured further into the woods. Darkness had settled around them, making it difficult to see the path. It was then they saw a soft glow shinning through the trees. Cautiously they crept closer, their rifles at the ready. They could see the flames of a fire and several men sitting around it. Tom stayed back so as not to alert them with his coughing, while Steven got close enough to see who they were.

Hiding in the underbrush, he peered out at the men by the fire. They were laughing and eating meat that was roasting over the fire. Just watching them made Steven salivate. He also saw they wore Confederate uniforms, but he knew of no troops in the area. His stomach was growling and his body weary; he decided to make a bold move.

"Hello!" he cried out, slowly standing with his hands in the air, his gun over his head, "friendly Reb here."

The men jumped up, grabbing the weapons and pointing them in his direction. "Show yerself," one of them called out.

"Coming out," he warned them and then stepped out into the small clearing.

"Where you come from soldier?" another asked when he saw Steven's uniform.

"My friend and I escaped from Point Lookout prison a while back. Before that we were with Toombs Georgians."

"Where's your friend at?" the man asked.

"He's back there a ways," Steven said motioning to where he had left Tom. "We've been wandering the countryside ever since, keepin' away from the Yankees."

"You'se lookin' mighty poorly," the third said. "Why don't ya git yer friend and set yourself for a spell."

"I'd be much obliged," Steven told them. "We've been walkin' a good long spell today and we're mighty tired. My friend is ill and could use a rest.

I'll just leave my rifle here so you'll know I have no ill intent." Steven laid his gun on the ground and stepped back into the trees to find Tom. Shortly, he was back with Tom leaning on his shoulder, the coughing still evident.

"Set yerself 'ole man," one of them said, hurrying up to help Tom sit near the fire. "Help yerself to this here water," he said giving Tom his canteen.

Tom readily accepted and sat down wearily. "It's been a long road, boys. Sure do appreciate yer lettin' us share your fire."

"You fellas hongrey?" one of them asked. "We got plenty to share." And using a large hunting knife, sliced off a hunk of meat and handed it to them.

"Much obliged," Steven told them as he began eating. He discovered it to be pork and wondered where they might have gotten it. Then looking around further, discovered there to be many other possessions a poor Confederate soldier had not known for some time;

things such as this meat, bottles of wine, new boots on their feet. On one man's hand he saw an expensive ring and on another a gold neck chain, the third wore a bejeweled watch fob with an elaborate timepiece. Near their knapsacks were thick, warm blankets and piles of food stuffs. They also carried a large supply of weapons. It was then he realized who these men were; they were deserters, renegades, perhaps even part of the feared guerrillas who went about the countryside seeking their own vengeance; at times even killing innocent citizens. They followed a man by the name of John Mosley. They were known for the hanging of prisoners. They also went about pillaging, stealing, and plundering those less fortunate, their own countrymen at times, who had been left vulnerable because of the war. They were the lowest of the low and Steven felt disdain for them but, he dared not show it as they wouldn't hesitate to kill one of their own if they felt threatened. He decided they would rest a spell, get something to eat and drink and then be on their way.

"So what was that there prison like?" one of them asked.

"Purty much what'd you think…..hell," Tom told him.

"A lot of men died there," Steven said. "And it's where my friend here, came down with consumption."

"Ya see," one younger man said looking at another of his companions, "that there's another good reason to desert."

The man gave the young man a hard jab with his elbow and gave a nervous laugh. "We all jes sorta got separated from our company," he said.

Steven only nodded, knowing he was lieing. "Where'd ya'll fight?" he asked instead.

"We were in the thick of it, we was," the oldest of the group told them. "Meself, I started at Bull Run. I jinned up with these others at Cold Harbor. That fightin' was bad; lots'a good men a diein'."

Steven nodded again. He thought for a moment of asking where their loyalties lay, but then thought better of it. He glanced over at Tom who gave him a look that said he should be careful.

"You fella's goin' back to your company?" one asked.

"We can't do that," Tom told them. "We don't know where they'se at and both of us can't fight no more." He started coughing again and had to stop talking.

"Tom here caught consumption and I've got a bad leg; wounded at Gettysburg," Steven continued. "I've friends here in Virginia. It's been a long time since I visited them and I don't really remember where they live. If we could find them, I could get help for Tom. Then perhaps they might be able to help us get back to our families in Georgia."

"What be their name?" the younger man asked. "I'm from around these parts and I might a heerd of 'em."

Jeffries," Steven told him, "from the Paradise Plantation."

"Jeffries. I think I have heerd of 'em," he told Steven, "at least afore the war there be Jeffries near about to White House landin' on the Pamunkey River. It be about three days walk from here."

"You know of them?" Steven asked nearly incredulous. It was difficult to believe after all these months of searching, he might finally find the people he was looking for; and from a deserter as well.

"Yep, yep, I believe that be their name," the young man continued. "We'uns had a farm not fer from their place. Our'n were further south near Mechanicsville. Maybe you all heered of the fightin' that went on there back in '62. Anyways, I believe my Paw even did business a few times with ole man Jeffries. "Course I can'st say iffen it be them there you all are lookin' fer."

"I'm much obliged for the information," Steven told him. He began to feel hopeful that this young man might truly be correct. He had remembered the name Pamunkey River once the young man had mentioned it. If they could find Paradise Plantation, they would be closer to finding their way back home.

"Don't know iffen you heerd," the older man said, "but Sherman jes took Atlanta, burnt it to the ground. Word is, they'se headed for Savannah. Thought you jes might want hearin' that piece, you all being from Georgia."

Steven's stomach lurched at the thought of his precious Colleen and family being in peril. Now more than ever, he needed to get home.

The men all settled down for the night, Steven and Tom being given blankets by their evening companions. They really felt no fear from them as they had nothing much for them to steal. Even the weapons they carried were older models and not desirable compared to what they already obtained.

When Steven awoke, the dawn was just beginning to filter through the branches of the trees. Birds were calling out their morning songs and the pungent smell of coffee filled his nostrils. He sat up and saw the eldest of the three men pouring a cup of coffee from a pot on the fire. He realized none of them had given their names and didn't know what to call this man. It was probably for the best, he thought.

"Coffee?" the man asked offering him the cup.

"Thank-you," Steven said reaching for it. He sipped the hot liquid and thought how wonderful it tasted. He hadn't had coffee since before he had been captured. He knew it had probably been stolen, but at the moment, he didn't care.

Tom woke with a coughing fit so severe he could barely catch his breath. Steven went to him and gave him the coffee to drink, but he couldn't even swallow the soothing drink. Steven noticed there was even more blood that Tom had coughed up than before. He felt even greater urgency to find the Jeffries and medical help for Tom. He prayed the young man had actually known what he was talking about.

After sharing a breakfast with the men who had been their hosts, they took their leave, their haversacks filled with biscuits and hardtack. Even though Steven's views on the rightness of what these men were doing had not changed, his feelings towards them had softened. They were fellow southerners, soldiers of the Confederacy and they had been kind to them. He knew men did unusual things in unusual times and people did what they needed to survive.

He and Tom traveled all day, having to stop frequently to allow Tom to rest. When evening came and they had not yet reached the river, Steven knew the three-day walk the young man had spoke of was turning into a much longer trek. He couldn't help but think of the news they had received that Georgia had been invaded and Atlanta taken; burned. He had been to that glorious city many times and the image of its destruction was saddening. He also worried about his mother and Colleen. What would happen to them if Sherman swept across their path on his way to Savannah?

Finally after three days of travel, they reached the Pamunkey River. From there they went south following it downstream towards White House Landing. They met up with more of the locals who were kind to them, giving them food and drink in spite of the fact it was a war ravaged place. Everywhere they had gone they had found homes burned, dead livestock and devastated fields. Fences had been torn down and used for firewood, orchards had been cut down and the land scarred by shells. Even the people themselves were suffering. Goods were hard to come by. A barrel of flour now cost $425 and a single stick of firewood was $5.00. Some of the citizens had taken to eating rats, but no matter where they went, they were given praise for being soldiers of the Confederacy and they shared what they had.

Some knew of the Jeffries and told them they believed their plantation had been spared the ravages of the torch, but beyond that, they didn't know if the Jeffries were still there.

After two more days of travel, they came upon a large plantation, vast fields surrounded by hundreds of slaves cabins, but the vast tobacco fields lay fallow and the cabins were empty. They went a little further and there on the banks of the river they spotted a large brick Federal style mansion surrounded by spreading lawns, now overgrown and full of weeds.

"That's it," Steven told Tom. "This is the Paradise plantation. I remember."

"Don't look much like Paradise no more," Tom commented.

"At least it's still standing," Steven said stopping to look up at the impressive structure. "I only hope Briarwood and Shannon survived."

They walked up the long drive to the double doors at the front of the house, Tom leaning heavily on Steven, his breathing coming in gasps. They knocked and waited for someone to answer. What if the Jeffries had abandoned their home as so many others had when the nearby fighting had become intense? Some of the homes had even become headquarters for one general or another. What would they do then? For months they had been searching for this very place and now that they had finally found it, it would be devastating for the Jeffries to be gone. Steven knew Tom could go no further.

As they waited, Steven noticed the barns out back of the house. A few were burned down but the others looked liked ragged skeletons with its parts picked at by the bone collectors. Large exposed holes revealed the empty interiors.

A gray-haired, elderly black man, his back stooped over and his eyes hazy finally opened the door. "Tell me, is this the Paradise Plantation?" Steven asked the man.

"Yes sir, marse," he answered.

"And is your master, Mr. Jeffries?"

"Yes marse."

"Then go fetch him and tell him Steven Covington is at his door."

"Yes sir," the black man said, turning around.

"Who is it, Roland?" a voice from behind him said. And then Steven saw a rather short man in his mid fifties, his graying hair combed to the side to help disguise a balding head. His dark eyes were bright and clear. It had been many years, but Steven recognized Mr. Jeffries.

"Sir, it's Steven Covington," he told the man, "Clifford's son. You last saw me as a boy." He knew he was horrible looking, his clothing torn and dirty, his hair and beard long and unkempt. His own mother probably wouldn't recognize him.

Recognition flared in Mr. Jeffries eyes and he come forward to greet them. "Steven? Oh, my Lord. Is it really you, boy? My yes, you have your father's eyes."

A stab of pain went through him at the mention of his father. "Yes sir. We've traveled a long way trying to find you."

"Pardon me, of course, please come in, come in and rest yourself.

Roland," he said to his servant behind him, "tell cook to prepare a meal for our guests. We don't have much, but what we have we are happy to share." He directed them down a central hallway and into a room across from a large staircase leading to the upper floor.

Inside was a small parlor with chairs, sofas and oil lamps set about on small tables; a simple assemblage for a man so wealthy.

"Mr. Jeffries, I would like you to meet my friend Tom Hunter. We have been together since the beginning of the war. He is ill and I was hoping you might be able to arrange some medical care."

Mr. Jeffries put out his hand to Tom. "I am pleased to meet you Mr. Hunter. I will try to get you the help you need, but nearly all the doctors are either out in the field tending to the wounded or at the hospitals doing the same. I'm sorry I'm not able to offer you more assurances than that. We haven't had any medical care in these parts for some time."

"That's quite all right Mr. Jeffries, we understand. We're just grateful for your hospitality."

"Please call me Stewart," he told them. Then he sighed. "Everything's different now. We lost nearly everything; our equipment is gone, the fields haven't been worked for several years, most of the slaves are gone except for a few loyal house workers and we've been burning the furniture for firewood. It nearly killed Grace, my wife, when we had to chop up the piano. And there's been other things; items that were in the family for generations. We've started scavenging from the remaining barns. If the slave quarters weren't made from block, I would have burned them. But at least we still have the house, that's more than many others can say.

But enough whining from me, tell me how it is you were looking for me?"

"Tom and I were both captured after the battle of Gettysburg," Steven told Stewart. "I had a bad leg injury and was in a Yankee hospital until I was sufficiently recovered. Then they sent me to prison in Maryland; Point Lookout. Tom was there as well."

"Oh my Lord, Steven, that's awful," Stewart broke in. "How did you get out?"

"We created an escape plan with several other men to work on a wood detail outside the prison. When the time was right, we made our escape. That was last spring. We've been trying to get home to Georgia ever since, when I remembered your plantation here in Virginia. I couldn't quite remember exactly where you were located. It took us some time to find you."

"You did the right thing, son. You and your friend shall have shelter for as long as you need it. We have plenty of room. We have closed off a large part of the house, but there is still far more space than Grace, Patti and myself can use. Do you remember Patti, Steven? She's our daughter." Stewart stopped to light a pipe sitting on the side table.

"I'm afraid I don't, sir," Steven told him.

"She was married two years ago. Her husband went off to fight like everyone else. He was killed at Sharpsburg in '62, not far from here. That was two years ago and after that she moved back in here with us."

"I'm sorry to hear that," Steven told him.

"Yep, ain't narry a family done gone untouched by this here war," Tom said which started him coughing again.

"You must have seen a lot of action if you've been in it since the start," Stewart said to them. "Did your father sign up as well or did he stay at home to run the plantation?"

"He signed up to fight," Steven said. "He was a good soldier, but he was killed at Manassas."

"Oh my Lord, no," Stewart said putting his hand to his forehead. "I'm so sorry Steven. He was a good man, a good friend. We may not have been able to see each other often, living so far apart, but we corresponded regularly. We were old school chums you know; Clifford and James McBride as well. I believe you all are still good friends?"

Steven nodded. "James was there with my father when he died. He was at Gettysburg with us. I have heard nothing of him since then. As far as I know, he's still alive. Before we left, I married his daughter Colleen."

"Ah, sweet Colleen," Stewart said smiling. "The last time I saw her she was a small girl but already so beautiful."

"She's a beautiful woman, too," Steven said. "I've been away from her for over three years and I desperately want to get home."

"I understand; I'll see if there's anything at all I can do. The trains aren't reliable what with the Yankees tearin' up the tracks all the time and most of the passenger trains being used for the soldiers. But I'll do what I can. In the meantime ya'll are welcome here."

"Thank-you Mr. Jeffries, ah Stewart."

"Come now," Stewart directed getting to his feet, "let's see what cook has made up."

"They were served a delicious meal of beef vegetable soup, yams and fresh bread. Stewart's wife Grace joined them. She was a small plump woman with gentle mannerisms and kind eyes. She spoke little, but smiled as they ate and talked. Afterward Stewart took them up stairs to the bedrooms. These too, were sparsely furnished, many of the accoutrements having been removed, but the beds were still there and had been freshly made up.

"I've arranged for the two of you to have baths if you like," Stewart told them. "Roland is heating the water over the fire as we speak."

"By cracky, I can't even 'member the last time I had a hot bath in a real tub," Tom said sitting on the edge of the bed. "But I'm afreared I got a few critters livin' here abouts in my uniform."

"Don't worry Tom, I'll see to it both of you get clean clothes," Stewart told them. "My servant Gideon will bring in the tub and towels. And Tom, I'll see what I can do about getting that doctor."

"I'm much obliged, Mr. Jeffries," Tom told him between coughing.

Stewart waved his hand towards the door. "Come Steven, I'll show you to your room next door."

After Stewart had left him alone in the room and Steven sat waiting for his bath, he looked about at the spare furnishings. The bed, a massive four-poster, was the only piece of furniture left in the room. A large ornate rug covered the floor and heavy drapes hung on the windows. But there was no dresser, no armoire, no chairs, no paintings on the walls. It made him wonder what Briarwood looked like now. They had left his mother alone to run the plantation by herself. How could she have managed? When they left, they thought they would only be gone a few months. How could they know it would go on so long? Was his home still standing? Were the slaves still there; so many had run now. And what had happened to Mary and Colleen. How were they able to cope? He felt even more desperate to get home to find out.

As he lay in the warm tub of water, scrubbing the dirt and grime of weeks past from his body, he felt the stress and tension washing away as well. He thought about how much the little things meant so much now, things he had taken for granted in the past; like a warm bath, clean sheets on the bed, the smell of fresh bread baking and just having a roof over his head. He didn't think he could take anything for granted again. Life was so precious, so very precious.

After the bath, with clean nightclothes and having shaved, Steven felt an overwhelming exhaustion weighing heavily upon him. He crawled between the cool white linens, laying his head on a down pillow. He realized he hadn't been in a real bed for over three years. It felt incredible and it wasn't long before he fell into a deep sleep.

Disturbing images intruded on his sleep. He dreamed he was in the middle of battle with shells exploding all around him, bullets flying past his head, screams of men hit. It was cloudy, smoke from the firing filling the air. He couldn't see well, peering across the pasture to spot the enemy, looking for flashes of blue in order to aim. He could feel his heart pounding, his breath coming rapidly. Then he saw them, Yankees pouring towards him, their weapons all pointed in his direction. He attempted to fire at them, but his gun was jammed and was useless. Suddenly he saw her, Colleen standing in the line of fire, wearing a long white gown, fear showing starkly in her eyes. She said nothing, but held out her arms to him, beseeching him to help her. He called out to her, telling her to go back, to run! But she appeared not to hear him, only holding out her arms.

The blue mass of Union soldiers was coming closer, beginning to fire their weapons. Now he was screaming, "Colleen! Run! Run!" Then he saw a look of horror cross her face and her hands went to her stomach. Beneath her fingers a red stain began seeping across the white gown. She pulled her hands away and the blood dripped from her fingers. He screamed her name again, over and over.

He sat straight up in bed, trembling, Colleen's name still on his lips. He looked around and was disoriented, forgotten where he was. He realized he was alone and at first it frightened him. He hadn't been alone for a very long time; there had always been others with him; in the Yankee hospital, in the prison, even on the road with Tom. Then he remembered the Jeffries; he was safe in their home.

He couldn't get back to sleep and got up to check on Tom. Walking down the hall to his room, he could hear Tom coughing. He slipped inside, the darkness enveloping him. He made his way to the side of the bed and lit the lamp. Tom was half sitting, propped up with pillows and there was blood on the front of his nightshirt. He felt alarmed and touched his arm. Tom opened his eyes and smiled.

"Jes can't seem to sleep," he told Steven. "Lyin' down makes it worse. Sure does feel good ta be in real bed again though, don't it?"

"It sure does, Tom," Steven told him. "I'm going to go downstairs and see if I can find something to help you sleep."

Tom only nodded as the coughing overtook him again. Steven left him and went down the wide staircase to the first floor. A light was shinning in the parlor where they had first talked with Stewart. Steven stepped inside and found Stewart there in a dressing gown and holding a glass in his hand.

"Steven," he greeted when he saw him, "come in my boy. Couldn't sleep? I have that problem myself. Sometimes a drink helps. Would you care for one?"

"No thank you sir, but I would like to take one to Tom. His coughing is much worse and I thought perhaps a drink of something might help quiet it."

"Splendid idea," he agreed going to the sideboard to pour the liquid. "I'm afraid all I have is whiskey. The Yankees took all my good wine and brandy; and of course you can't get more now. Use to get most of mine from France and Germany," he said turning around and holding out the glass. "Maybe when this war is over, the blockade will be lifted and once again we can trade with Europe."

"Yes sir," Steven agreed. "I think I'll take this drink to Tom now. His cough seems to be worse. I'm really quite concerned about him."

"I've gotten a message to a doctor I know in Richmond. Hopefully he will be able to come out soon and see your friend."

But it was not to be. After several more days the doctor sent back a message saying he was far too busy to take time away from his patients. He was sorry for the man suffering from the consumption, but one man did not merit his time away from hundreds of suffering. Tom held on for two weeks longer and then he died. Steven wept when they buried him out in the family plot. He had been a good friend, a companion for nearly four years. They had lived together, eaten together, slept alongside one another and fought together. They would have given their lives for one another. He was the only one left now; of the four friends who had been together at the start of the war, only he remained. Steven felt sad he was not able to bring Tom home to Georgia; just one more casualty of the war.

The temporary stay at the Jeffries turned into months. The logistics of getting Steven back home across state lines proved to more complicated than anticipated. Steven felt comfortable with his hosts, but still felt troubled that he could not get home. He longed to be with Colleen and to see his mother again. He had written several letters and sent them to both Briarwood and Shannon, hoping a least one would reach its destination. But with the war and everything in chaos, he wasn't sure if any of them would reach their intended.

Steven became like a member of the family to the Jeffries, taking him under their loving wings and helping him in his time of need. Grace Jeffries was warm and compassionate, treating him like a son. He knew she had been through a great deal and yet she remained cheerful and loving.

And there was their daughter Patti, who still grieved for her husband. She was Steven's age, a striking beauty with porcelain skin, long blonde hair, and blue eyes. Even though Steven attempted to engage her in conversation, she always seemed so sad. When Christmas arrived he thought perhaps she would cheer from the holidays, but instead she became even more remorse, missing her husband more desperately. Steven too, felt sad at being away yet another year. This was the fourth Christmas he was not able to spend with Colleen.

Steven did what he could to help out, cutting and stacking firewood, stripping more boards from the barns until only the supports remained. He hauled water and even swept floors and cleaned barn stalls, whatever chores were required; things that had always been done by slaves in the past. But not much of anything was as it had been any longer.

Later in January they heard the news that on Christmas Eve past, Sherman had taken Savannah. There hadn't been much resistance and the mass destruction that had ravaged Atlanta, did not occur in Savannah.

Steven felt an even greater urgency to get home. He still had heard nothing from his mother nor from Colleen. With Sherman in Georgia, he knew not what might have happened to them.

He wondered how much longer this war would go on; how many more people had to die. He knew the people of the South were proud, but he also knew the Confederacy was a lost cause. All he wanted to do now was get home to Colleen and make her his bride, legally so that they might live happily ever after. Where was his dear sweet Colleen?

CHAPTER EIGHTEEN —March 1865

Colleen's trek had been halted dead in its tracks by the cold winter weather. She had traveled along the road from the Coles for a good part of the day until a wagon with a man, a woman, five children and all their worldly possessions stacked perilously high and tied on with rope. When they had seen her walking alone, carrying a rifle and a dirty, worn haversack over her shoulder, they had stopped.

"Ma'am, what you be doin' walkin' out here by yourself?" the man had inquired of her.

"Well sir, I'm tryin' to git to my kin north of here," she told him in her best back woods accent. "Them Yankees done burned down my place, kilt my ma and pa and stol' all our'n horses. I escaped into the woods with jes this here gun. I found this soldier pack along the way. It done had some food and ammunition in it."

"Well missy, you can't be walkin' all alone on this here road. No tellin' who'se you'se bound ta run into," the man said scowling. "They'se all kinds of rabble out here; deserters, refugees hongry for anythin' they kin gets their hands on, not to mention dirty Yanks who'd likely kills ya as looks at ya."

"Yes sir," she told him, "but I've gots no place else to go. I got kin north of here and I was hopin' to go there."

"You jes git yourself up on this wagon," the woman had said. "We'se headed that way ourselfs. Yankees done burned us out too. We're headed to Richmond. We'll all be safe there. President Davis will protect us. You kin ride along a spell."

"Thank'ee," she had told her. "I'm mighty grateful." She had wondered where she would sit on the vastly over loaded wagon, but walking to the back she had seen two boys sitting on the rear with their legs dangling over the edge. They had scooted over to make room for her. She sat next to them, her legs hanging off as well, her rifle across her lap.

"Howdy," she greeted them.

"Howdy ma'am," they said politely. They looked to her to be about nine and twelve years of age. Besides the two of them were two younger girls sitting a top of their belongings, the fifth child, a baby boy, sitting on his mother's lap.

They had started up with a lurch, the pair of horses straining against the heavy load, the small girls on top holding on for dear life.

"You runnin' from them Yankees too?" the younger of the two boys asked.

She nodded. "They burned down my house," she told them. She had hated lieing to them. It was one thing to tell falsehoods to adults, but somehow it was worse with children.

"Us too," the older boy had told her. "We got some of our stuff out afore they lit the torch and put it on this here wagon. Now we'se goin' to Richmond. President Davis is gonna keep us safe."

She had said nothing, but doubted President Davis would be able to protect anyone.

"Why's your hair so short?" the younger one asked.

"Um, I had lice and had to cut it off to get rid of 'em."

Both boys had nodded. "Yep, we gots them critters too," they had said and then mentioned it no longer.

She stayed with the Russels for several days, camping with them in the evening hours, they being kind enough to share their meager provisions with her. Around the fire, it seemed all they could speak of was the war and what it had been before the war had come.

During the daylight hours as they had traveled towards Richmond, they had come across more and more refugees; some headed the same direction as they, others south, to what they hoped would be safety from the Yankees. Some, like the Russels, had wagonloads of their possessions. Others simply walked, carrying what they could on their backs. They saw Confederate men still in uniform, dirty, shoeless, vacant looks in their eyes from the horror they had witnessed. There were women sitting alongside the road, weeping, wringing their hands and calling out for lost children or husbands. It struck her how many poor there were, made even poorer by the war. Her world had been so different, with wealth, servants, anything she had desired.

It was so sad, these last remnants of the Confederacy. So much had been lost and what had been gained? Would they be able to maintain their own Union? She doubted it. The South had not the resources to continue the war much longer. She knew of the hunger, of the lack of ammunition and supplies. She had personally seen the hallow look of hunger in men's eyes, the desperate loyalty they had shown to the Confederacy and General Lee, but to no avail. The vast army of the Union was seemingly endless, no matter how many they might kill.

Colleen had parted with the Russells a few miles before Richmond, telling them her relatives were nearby. She thanked them profusely for their kindness. From the Richmond area she planned on heading northwest towards Maryland. She also knew Grant and his army, were not far away, trying to advance on Richmond and keeping themselves between the city and Petersburg where Lee still battled.

Again she found herself walking along the road, but this time she was not alone. Many others walked there as well, trying to find a place where they would be safe. Most were headed south towards Richmond. No one paid her much attention. They cared not if her hair was short or that she carried a haversack and rifle. She continued for several days, camping alongside the road at night with others nearby for safety. The scariest people on the road were the transient men wearing the Confederate uniform. They were deserters or mercenaries or just those who had witnessed too much horror and had lost their senses.

She found it unsettling to be alone after spending so much time with vast numbers in the army. She would build herself a fire, mostly for comfort as she had nothing much to cook, roll up in her bedroll, and fall into a fitful sleep. Her dreams were troubled, images of dieing men, severed limbs, blood pouring over the ground like a river and fires consuming everything in its path. She also dreamed of Steven, dieing a horrible death in a Yankee prison camp and other times Patrick haunted her memories.

At times during her walk towards Maryland, she would try to engage people in conversation, asking anyone she could if they had heard of Point Lookout prison, but no one seemed able to help her.

She had finally gone as far as Fredricksburg, the scene of one of the first horrific battles of the war. She remembered Steven writing her that he had been in this place. It still bore the scars of battle with homes shelled and burned, broken caissons and the bones of horses lying about on top of the ground. It made her feel strange, melancholy, to think of Steven being here, fighting for his life. She had moved on and here when she had reached the Maryland border, the Potomac River, she had stopped. There were several dilemmas she had to consider before crossing. She knew on the other side was Union territory and if caught, might be imprisoned or hung as a spy. She didn't know if her northern accent would be good enough for her to pass as a Yankee. She had never heard too many of them speak to know if she pronounced things correctly. And the crossing itself would be difficult. It wasn't that she didn't know how to swim and she certainly had forded streams and rivers in her time in the army, but this river was much too wide and deep to simply swim it and of course there was the problem with the long skirts. No, she knew she must find a boat to get her across.

She had spent a day traveling back south along the Potomac until she had discovered a large home on the Virginia side of the river, the family being sympathetic and had given her shelter. The name of their home was Stratford Hall and the family name was Potter. They had already taken in twenty other unfortunate refugees from time to time, but had no one else at the moment and were willing to put her up as well. They at least, had been spared the looting of the Yankees and their barns and storehouses were full. Colleen couldn't help but wonder how many others had such bounty and what difference it might have made if a portion had been shared with the loyal soldiers who fought so hard for the cause.

She had told the Potters of her need to get into Maryland and this time she had told the truth; that she was looking for her husband and believed him to be there. They had at first tried to talk her out of going, describing the dangers she might encounter, but when they realized she was not to be dissuaded, they arranged for a friend to take her across on his boat.

But winter had come on and she ended up staying at Stratford Hall during the coldest months. It had been an extremely severe winter with sub-zero temperatures and deep snows, unusual for Virginia.

Colleen felt frustrated and depressed. If it was possible that Steven could be so close, she was anxious to go find him, to finally be in his arms again. It had been nearly four years since she last saw him, touched him, kissed him and now more than ever, she seemed to miss him greater than she had when he first left. But what if he weren't there? What if he had never made it to

Point Lookout? At those times she would wander about the Potter's large house, looking out the windows at the blowing, swirling snow and think about Steven. The Potters were kind and she had everything she needed, a warm house, food, clothing and servants, but she felt helpless, unable to pursue her quest.

When the warm winds of March finally came again, she was anxious to begin her journey. Mr. Potter, a tall stately looking man, insisted on going with her, explaining that he was a man of some consequence and might be able to influence the commander at the prison to allow her to search for Steven. And besides, he had argued, she should never be alone in Yankee territory.

The boat turned out to be a flatbed barge that the man used to ferry supplies back and forth across the lines; mostly hard to obtain luxuries such as fine wines, caviar, and oysters. Colleen discovered that many of the wealthy Virginians were willing to pay a high price, in Yankee dollars, to maintain their high quality of life. It disgusted her to know these landowners were living in luxury while their own soldiers were starving in the fields, but she needed Mr. Potter's assistance to cross the river.

The barge owner Mr. Baldwin, was a large, hairy man with long red hair and beard. He smelled terribly and when he smiled, showed blackened, rotted teeth. He chewed tobacco and would spit every few minutes, not caring where the disgusting wad would happen to land. She felt apprehensive about going with this man, but her desire to find Steven was even greater and after all, Mr. Potter would be with her.

It was a chilly day near the first week of March when she stepped onto the barge to cross the Potomac. She pulled the shawl she had been given tightly around her and sat on one of the many crates scattered around. She still carried her rifle, not wanting to leave it behind. Mr. Potter led two of his saddle horses onto the boat for them to ride once they were on the other side. Then holding the reins, he sat on the crates as well.

Mr. Baldwin stepped onto the barge, pushing with his long pole to move them away from shore. He kept pushing against the bottom of the river, walking the length of the barge as he did so, to move them out into the current of the river. Once the large raft had begun to move along on its own, Mr. Baldwin went to the rear where the tiller was fastened and where he could steer the boat. Once there however, he turned and smiled at her; at least that was what Colleen assumed it was, but it actually looked more like a leer. It made her feel uncomfortable and the thought crossed her mind that she had lived with hundreds of men for a year and had never felt as uncomfortable as with this man. Of course, it may have been different if the soldiers she fought with had known she was a woman.

"Yer a real purty gal," he had said to her and then spit into the water, "but what 'cha got all yer hair cut off for?"

She ran her hand over her head. Now that she had resumed her identity as a woman, her short hair embarrassed her. It had grown out some since she had left the army, but not enough to equal the luxurious tresses she had had previous. "I had to cut it off….lice," she told him.

Mr. Baldwin spat again before answering, this time the glob landing on the deck at his feet. "I get them critters all the time. I ain't gonna cuts off my hair fer no lice."

She had pulled the shawl tighter around her and tried to ignore him by looking out over the water. On the other side, somewhere over there in Maryland, could be Steven. Sometimes the thought crossed her mind that he may have died in the prison. During her time in the army, some of the men had told stories of the horrors of prison camps, of the diseases and lack of food, of the hundreds dieing there. When these thoughts threatened to panic her, she would push them aside. Steven <u>had</u> to be alive.

"Iffen yer cold little lady, I kin warm ya jes fine," Mr. Baldwin said breaking into her thoughts. When she looked over he was leering at her again.

"I'm fine think-you," she told him. "I'm going to look for my husband."

"Yer married? That don't make no never mind to me," he said. "I've had my share of married womens."

"I said, no thank-you," she said more firmly. "Don't kid yourself Mr. Baldwin, I know how to use this gun."

He laughed aloud, throwing his head back. "That's what I likes; a feisty womans."

"Mr. Baldwin, I'll ask you to hold your tongue in the presence of a lady," Mr. Potter finally spoke up. "If you value your pay, you will not speak that way to Miss Colleen again."

His conversation ended when Mr. Baldwin needed to turn the barge towards the opposite shore. When he had gotten to the shallows, he began to pole again as he had before, walking the length of the boat. Everytime he passed in front of her she could get a whiff of his stench.

They finally docked at a deserted wharf. Mr. Baldwin threw a rope over one of the docks' pillions and then turned to her. "We be here, Ma'am."

Mr. Potter went ahead of her to lead off the horses, then turned to give her a hand. Before taking it, she looked up at the large man who had taken them across. "Thank-you Mr. Baldwin, I appreciate your efforts to get me across the river," she told him. When she stepped up on the dock, Mr. Baldwin lifted her by placing his hand under her bottom. She turned abruptly and glared at him, but this time said nothing.

Mr. Potter helped her to mount up sidesaddle on the little filly he had brought for her. Then he mounted his own horse, giving directions to Mr. Baldwin. "I expect you to be back here in two days time," he told him. "If we're not here, you wait for us, you understand?"

"Yes sir, Mr. Potter."

"If you're not here, I'll be sending my men after you and that'll be the end of your little business here."

"Two days, I'll be here," he told the tall imposing man.

They started out on a trail that led along the river and then veered off into a dark wooded area. "That wharf is mostly deserted," Mr. Potter told her. "It's called Colton's Point, but about the only time it's used is when traders come down with their mules with goods for Mr. Baldwin to ferry across. Of course now and then a Yankee patrol will scout through here to make sure no Rebs try to sneak through. Washington isn't that far away, you know. It would be a grand feather in some chaps hat if he could get close enough to President Lincoln to do him harm."

When she had looked over at him, he added, "We'll not have to worry about them. Most of them know me and they're well paid."

Colleen studied his handsome chiseled features, the expensive clothing he wore, the fine silk top hat on his head and thought him to be an arrogant bastard. It made her wonder if others had looked on her and her family the same way during their days of luxury. She supposed they had. She knew now she had been terribly spoiled.

"The nearest town is about eight miles from here,' Mr. Potter told her. "When we arrive, we can inquire about the prisons exact whereabouts and go from there."

After they had traveled into the woods, the trail allowed for them to travel in single file only. As it was more difficult to converse, they lapsed into silence. The trees here were very dense, the brambles and thickets surrounding and covering everything in their path. Small shafts of light would penetrate through the canopy of leaves here and there, while rustling could be heard in the underbrush from some small animals. If it weren't for the trodden down trail, passage through would be extremely difficult. It reminded her of the Wilderness battle where so many horrible tragedies had occurred. She closed her eyes against the sights and sounds that crowded into her mind; the sounds of gunfire and shells exploding, of men calling out, of their screams, the sight of severed limbs, blood soaking into the ground, the fire consuming everything in its path including human flesh. Once again she saw the boy in the woods who had pleaded with her to kill him and the look in his eyes when she finally pulled the trigger. And she remembered that smell, that horrific smell of burning bodies.

She shuddered and opened her eyes trying to dispel the imagines that threatened to overwhelm her. She understood those whose minds had found the burden too great and turned inward. It was only through sheer willpower that she could push the terror away and the knowledge that she needed to find Steven.

Finally they had found their way out of the woods and onto a main road leading into the town Mr. Potter had spoken of. Colleen noticed immediately the difference on this side of the river. People traveling along the road in carriages or on horseback were dressed in fine clothing, traveling with purpose, many with smiles, greeting one another with pleasantries. She saw no homeless families traveling with all their worldly goods or crying women by the side of the road. There were no ragged soldiers, their clothing in tatters and barefoot. It was obvious Mr. Potter was known on this side of the river as well, as several times he was greeted by name.

The city was of medium size with the name of Leonard Town. It contained an imposing courthouse, a theater, an emporium, several boutiques, a barber, general store, amongst others, as well as a large hotel. It was here that Mr. Potter stopped, dismounted, and gave the reins to a black doorman, giving the man a few pennies.

Colleen did the same and followed him inside, leaving her rifle with a porter. The lobby was not furnished as ornately as the one in Savannah, but it was till impressive, with gilded cornices and marble floors. Ornate chandeliers hung from the ceiling and a large carpeted staircase wound its way to the upper floors. It had been a long while since she had been in such luxury. But this time she was in a simple dress which had grown dirty during her travel and her hair was short. Many people stared, but for once she didn't care. They didn't know what she had been through.

She also saw a few Union soldiers about, which made her nervous. The only time in the past she looked upon the men in blue was when they were shooting at her. But now they gave her no heed and she relaxed.

Mr. Potter had gone to the main desk and was recognized immediately. "Mr. Potter sir," the desk clerk greeted, "how might we serve you?"

"I need two rooms," he said taking off his riding gloves, "one for myself and the other for the lady."

"Certainly sir. We have the usual accommodations you require available," the uniformed man told him. "Would you be so kind as to sign the register?"

As he bent over the book to add his signature, Mr. Potter continued speaking to the clerk. "Tell me my man, have you heard of a place called Point Lookout; a prison camp for Confederate soldiers?"

"Indeed I have," he told Mr. Potter. "It's south of here along the peninsula, near where the Potomac joins with the ocean; about half a days ride."

Mr. Potter nodded as he looked up. "Thank-you for the information," he said as he handed the man several bills and as Colleen noticed, they were Union bills, not Confederate. "I have one more request."

"Anything sir," the clerk said smiling, obviously anxious to please if it meant more money in his pocket.

"I want you to send a message to Senator Danforth, he lives just outside of town, between here and Lexington Park and tell him Mr. Potter would like to meet with him this evening in this hotel. Say, dinner time?"

"Yes sir. I'll send someone directly," the clerk said accepting the added money Mr. Potter held out to him. He then rang the little bell on the desk, bringing a small Negro boy to guide them to their rooms.

"I didn't know we'd be stayin' in a hotel, Mr. Potter," she said as they ascended the stairs. "I feel badly that I have no money to contribute towards our expenses and I am not dressed appropriately."

"Well, I'm not about to sleep along the road somewhere and I knew it might take some time to find your husband. We might as well be comfortable in the process. And please, don't worry about the money, it looks as though you haven't enjoyed many luxuries for some time."

"That's true. My journey has taken me a long way from home. I've been absent for a year."

"That is a long time. I admire your dedication to your husband. I don't know too many women who would go to such lengths as you have for their mates."

He hadn't known the half of it, she thought, not having told him of her foray into the war disguised as a man.

They paused in front of the door where she was to stay. "Please draw a bath in Mrs. Covington's room," he told the young boy.

"Yes sir," he answered, scurrying off to do as he was bid.

"You have a nice bath, rest for a spell and then come downstairs to the hotel restaurant about 8:00 for dinner."

"I can't thank you enough for everything you're doing," she told him.

He waved her aside. "Don't worry about it. It gives me pleasure to help whenever I can." And then he was off down the hall to his own room.

Colleen went inside the room, closing the door behind her and sighed. Before her was a large four poster bed hung with lace with matching lace curtains on the windows. A settee and small table sat near the spacious windows and ornate bedside tables held blown glass lamps. Elaborate stencils had been painted on the walls and expensive oriental rugs covered the wood floors. On another wall opposite the bed, was a large fireplace with a carved oak mantle. On it was a beautiful timepiece carefully ticking out the minutes. Over in another corner stood her rifle.

Separate from the bedroom was a private bath with a large porcelain tub and even a commode. A wash basin filled with fresh water stood on a stand with a large mirror above it.

"Oh my," Colleen said aloud. "How long it's been since I've had such sumptuous accommodations." She went to the mirror and looked at her reflection. It grieved her to see the sunburned faced and short hair. If Steven saw her now, he probably wouldn't even recognize her.

She splashed water on her face and using the sweet scented soap and soft towel, washed her face and hands. "I guess that will have to do for now," she thought and since no one had yet arrived to fill the tub, she lay down on the bed still fully clothed and fell immediately to sleep.

She was so tired and slept so soundly, she didn't recall dreaming and didn't wake until there was a knock at the door. She answered groggily and discovered it was the porters with the hot water for her bath. Finally after many buckets had been poured into the large tub and everyone had gone, she undressed and slipped into the depths of its warmth.

At first she simply reclined, her eyes closed, enjoying the incredible feeling the bath gave her. The water had been perfumed with scented oils and she felt she could stay there forever; warm, secure, floating, as though she had no cares in the world. Soon she took the soap and began washing herself, feeling every bump and bruise. She was also painfully thin from her difficult months of fighting. Finally and only when the water had begun to grow cold, did she get out and dry herself.

Going into the bedroom area she discovered, lying on the bed, beautiful new clothing; a dress, petticoat, stockings and shoes. There were also new under garments and a creamy colored satin nightgown. There was a note from Mr. Potter telling her he thought she might like something nice to wear to their dinner with the senator and of course, something pretty to sleep in as well. She had been given simple, clean clothing to wear during her stay at the Potter's, but nothing this elegant.

She fingered the folds of the skirt, feeling the softness of the fabric, a beautiful pale blue, silk. It had a gathered neckline which could be pulled down low off the shoulders. Tears sprang to her eyes as she looked at the beautiful things. "How can I wear these nice things when Patrick and the others are still out there in the mud and the trenches fighting and dieing? Oh god, Patrick, where are you now?" Her last statement was said in a whisper and then she quickly wiped at her tears. "How can I speak another man's name when Steven may be suffering as well? What's the matter with me? I'll do whatever Mr. Potter wants me to do to get Steven back."

She dressed in the new things, discovering to her surprise they fit perfectly, even the shoes. But she felt she had not exposed so much skin in a long while. Parts of her arms remained white, while the lower portion was brown. Then she sat at the dressing table with the large oval mirror and attempted to do something with her hair. She combed and brushed it with the items she found on the dresser and then sighed at the results. Even though her hair was shinny and clean, it still did not seem very feminine. Using her fingers, she created a few curls that fell forward on her forehead and a few more around her ears. She wished she had a few pretty combs to put in. It had only reached a length where it touched her shoulders.

She remembered most of the men she had fought with had had longer hair than she, including Patrick. They found it too burdensome under the circumstances to maintain. She however, would hack away at it with her bayonet every couple of weeks, afraid if it grew too long, she would look like a woman again. She remembered how it seemed to amuse Patrick every time he discovered her barbaric haircutting method.

"No wonder he thought it funny if he knew I was a woman," she said aloud to herself and looked up to see herself smiling in the mirror at the memory of Patrick.

"Well Mr. Potter, I guess this will have to do," she said standing and going to the door. "And now, time to meet the senator."

As she descended the wide staircase, she saw Mr. Potter waiting in the lobby. He looked as dapper as usual, this time carrying a walking stick with a gold leaf knob on top. He smiled when he saw her and extended his hand. She took it and he kissed her fingers.

"Such worn hands for a lady," he commented. "I'll bet they could tell some tales of where you've been since departing from your home."

She pulled her hand away, embarrassed by their condition. "You do look lovely, my dear," he said, "a real transformation."

"I want to thank you so much for the clothing. It's beautiful, but I wonder how you knew my size?"

"I have a keen eye is all," he said taking her arm and leading her towards the restaurant. "And after all, you've been with us for several months now." They were seated at a pre-appointed table and Mr. Potter had a bottle of vintage wine brought over. He poured them each a glass and then held his up in a toast. "Here's to finding your husband, safe and well," he said clinking his glass on hers.

Colleen sipped at her wine, a taste she hadn't experienced for some time and then looked him directly in the eye. "Mr. Potter, I can't thank you enough for everything you're doing to help me find my husband. I mean how you took me in, this hotel, the clothes and a senator. How will I ever be able to repay you?"

He put his hand over hers and patted it as if she were a child. "You needn't worry about that now. I've investigated your family, the McBrides of Shannon Plantation, Georgia as well as your husband's family, the Clifford Covingtons of Briarwood, and I find that your father is a very influential man; knows a senator or two himself. I'm sure your father and father-in-law will be more than grateful I have taken such good care of you. Not to mention Mr. Covington's relief should we find his son. I'm sure I will be more than repaid for my efforts."

Her eyes narrowed at what he had just told her. Now she understood; he expected her father and Clifford to reward him monetarily for being kind to her. She should have known he wouldn't do something just out of the kindness of his heart. He used people for his own advantage, just as he had used the war to become even wealthier while others starved and died. She was sure the others he had taken in must have rewarded him as well. He did nothing without some pay off in the end.

She also wondered how he had been able to find out about her family and Steven's. Surely he wouldn't have sent a messenger all the way to Georgia and the Confederate postal system had broken down to the point of being nearly non-existent. Apparently all the telegraph wires had not been destroyed. If she hadn't so desperately needed his help, she would have told him to go to hell.

It was then she saw an elderly gentleman walking towards their table. He wore an expensive suit and shoes. His hair and neatly trimmed beard were snow white and she could see an expensive diamond ring on his finger.

Mr. Potter stood up as he approached and shook his hand before introducing her to him. "Senator Danforth, this is Mrs. Colleen Covington. She is the reason I called for you this evening."

He took her hand lightly and nodded his head. "My pleasure," he said in a deep voice. "What can I do to be of service to you?"

"Why don't we sit down and order and I will explain everything to you," Mr. Potter said.

After they had told the waiter what they desired, Mr. Potter told the senator about Colleen's quest. "What I would need from you sir," Mr. Potter said leaning in to speak, "would be a signed paper saying we have permission to go inside the prison to search for her husband."

"I'm not sure," Senator Danforth began, "we're still at war and Point Lookout is for Confederate prisoners. I don't know if I have the leverage to grant such a request, especially since it's under the jurisdiction of the army."

"I understand the situation," Colleen told him. "I just want to see him, to make sure he's alright. I'm not asking for his release. I just want to see him."

"Mrs. Covington is the daughter of James McBride, a very influential man in Georgia, who I am sure will be very grateful for any help we can give his daughter," Mr. Potter said. "As you know, the Union is bound to win this war and with the prisoners soon to be released, I'm sure Mr. McBride as well as her father-in-law, Mr. Covington would show their appreciation to you for the kindness you might show Mrs. Covington."

It sickened Colleen to hear Mr. Potter bargaining for Steven with what monetary rewards he might gain for his efforts. And he must think that would be something substantial or he would not be expending his time and money. But Colleen knew he just might not be able to collect on his investment. For one thing, Clifford Covington was dead and she knew Anna Bell no longer had the large resources to pay some kind of ransom. And when she had left home over a year before, her own plantations reserves were dangerously low, not being able to sell their cotton. The painful thought that they had not heard from her father in some time, not even knowing if he were dead or alive, weighed heavily upon her. These were things she would not share with Mr. Potter or Senator Danforth. Let them continue to think she was fabulously wealthy and that her family would reward them; as if they would give money to some Yankee senator and a Confederate traitor.

"Well I guess it wouldn't hurt for me to write a note to the commander of the prison requesting that you be allowed to search for your husband," Senator Danforth said looking at Colleen.

"I would greatly appreciate your efforts," Colleen told him, "and I will be sure my father knows how helpful you have been."

Their meal arrived and Senator Danforth nodded. "I will pen my request as soon as we finish our dinner."

The senator was good to his word, writing a letter to the commander of Point Lookout before leaving for his estate. Then Colleen and Mr. Potter retired for the evening, planning to leave for the prison in the morning.

But in spite of having a warm, soft bed and wearing a beautiful negligee, Colleen couldn't sleep. The thought that she could be seeing Steven the next day was almost more than she could bear. It had been nearly four long years since he had gone away to war. She had been only seventeen then and now she was an adult, twenty-one and Steven twenty-three. When had her birthdays come and gone? It hadn't seemed to matter if Steven wasn't there with her. But now it was possible she would finally see him. She wanted to so desperately and yet she was terrified as well. She was afraid the separation, the horrors of war and being a prisoner would have changed him. He couldn't help but be. But she was changed as well, had seen and been a part of things she should never have been part of.

And then she worried that Steven might not be there. Even though she had been given the information that prisoners from the Gettysburg battle had been taken to Point Lookout, what if he were somewhere else? There were numerous Union prisons scattered about the north and it was possible he could be in any one of them.

The most frightening thought of all was that Steven might already be dead. The message they had received about his capture, also stated he had been wounded. If the wound had been too severe, he might not have survived it. She knew all too well the devastation taken on the human body by rifle or shells. And if he had made it alive to the prison, he could have died there. Among the troops there had been the horror stories of life in some of those camps. Every soldier in the field knew he did not want to be captured by the enemy.

As badly as she hoped Steven was alive and well, she also wondered how, after searching for a year and a half, could she just see him and then walk away. She would want to get him out and she didn't know how that could possibly happen. She knew she couldn't just break him out and she wasn't at all sure Mr. Potter would be willing to loan her enough money to bribe the commander with only the hope of being doubly repaid by her father.

It seemed she had only just fallen into a restless sleep when a porter was knocking on her door to wake her. She dressed quickly in the new dress Mr. Potter had gotten for her, wanting to make an impression on the camp commander as well as looking her best if she were to find Steven.

Mr. Potter was waiting for her in the restaurant. He insisted on having breakfast before they left, but she was too nervous to eat. She felt full of nervous energy and wanted to be on their way. She could hardly stand watching Mr. Potter eat. It seemed as if every bite were in slow motion. She wanted to scream, "Hurry up!" He finally had the horses brought around and they started out for Point Lookout.

It took them nearly the entire morning to get to their destination. Coming out of dense woods, the imposing camp loomed before them. Colleen had never seen anything like it before; the massive walls with its guard towers, the complex outbuildings and the entire company of guards. Beyond the prison was the river and between, a cemetery.

Colleen's heart began to pound frantically and her palms were sweaty on the reins as several horsemen rode out to meet them. Mr. Potter explained they were there on business and asked to be directed to the commander. After checking to make sure they carried no weapons, they escorted them to a log building next to the largest gate Colleen had ever seen. It was the entrance into the interior of the prison and high above it, flew the stars and strips of the American flag.

They tied their horses to a post outside and were led inside where they saw a man sitting behind a desk, working on some papers. He looked up when they came in and then stood when he realized there was a woman present. He was a stockily built man whose uniform appeared rather tight. His black hair was thinning at the temples and he sported a long handlebar mustache. He extended his hand to her and it felt oily to the touch. It made her feel as though she wanted to wash afterward.

He introduced himself as Major Allen Brady and then Mr. Potter introduced them both and began to explain the reason for their visit. "We would be very grateful if you could let Mrs. Covington know if her husband is here and well. She has been searching for him for over a year."

"I'm not sure about that," the Major told them, "we can't just let every wife or mother come in here looking for a loved one. After all, this is a prisoner of war camp."

"I understand your situation," Mr. Potter said reaching into his breast pocket. "But this is a special situation. As you can see, Mrs. Covington has the expressed permission of Senator Danforth." He handed the note over to the commander and paused while he read it. "As you might well surmise, it is a unique case. I'm sure the Senator would greatly appreciate your co-operation. Perhaps there might even be a promotion."

Colleen looked over at Mr. Potter surprised. The senator had said nothing about a promotion for the Major. But then, Mr. Potter had only mentioned the possibility of one. He was certainly wily with words, she thought.

"I see," Major Brady said scratching his chin. "I suppose it would be alright if a Senator has given his permission. The problem is, we don't have records of the men who are or have been here. We don't take names; we just collect Reb prisoners and put them in here."

Mr. Potter looked over at Colleen as if he weren't quite sure how to proceed.

"Is it true sir, that the men who were captured at Gettysburg are here?"

"That's right. Most of 'em were transported here; this being the closest camp to the battle."

"My husband was captured at Gettysburg."

"It's like I said Ma'am, we don't keep records of the men here."

"I would like to search inside for myself," Colleen told him.

The commander began shaking his head. "I don't think I can allow that. There are hundreds of men in there. It would take much too long and I couldn't guarantee your safety. It could cause a riot."

"Major Brady, I would hate to report to the Senator that you didn't do everything possible to help Mrs. Covington when he expressly wrote asking you to do so."

The Major looked first to Mr. Potter, then to Colleen, obviously displeased with having his authority questioned. There was a long silence while he weighed his dilemma. "I'll permit you inside only with a detail of soldiers," he finally told them, "and then only for a limited time. I tell you to get out, I will have you removed. You must understand; there have been hundreds of men inside those walls. Many have come and gone. The cemetery behind camp will attest to that. Even if your husband were here at one time, it doesn't mean he is now."

"I understand and thank-you, sir. I do appreciate your co-operation," Colleen told him.

Major Brady called for a detail of soldiers to escort them into the prison and they proceeded through the large gates. Above in the guard towers, men with loaded weapons looked down upon them.

Upon entering Colleen saw row after row of the long, low buildings with hundreds of thin, dirty, emaciated men sitting or standing about. The stench that assaulted her nostrils was horrific. Mr. Potter coughed and quickly covered his nose and mouth with his handkerchief, but she blinked hard and continued on. She had smelled some of those odors before; sweaty, dirty bodies, rotting garbage and decayed flesh, only not to such a degree. She was appalled at the conditions these men were living in.

The men looked at her strangely, staring as if they couldn't believe what they were seeing. They acted as if she were sort of an apparition. Some called out to her, asking if she were an angel. Others, obviously not in their right minds, mistook her for a beloved sister or wife, pleading to take them out of this terrible place. She knew it had probably been a long time since any of them had seen a woman.

She began questioning every man she saw, beginning at the first building. She even ventured inside to talk with those who were too weak to walk about and was continually followed by the armed soldiers. The conditions and smells inside were even worse than outside, but she continued on. What if Steven were one of those who were too ill to get up from his blanket? What if she passed him by simply because she allowed herself to be revolted by what she saw? Mr. Potter chose not to enter the buildings himself, staying outside, shuffling his feet, trying to keep his expensive shoes out of the mud.

She went from building to building, asking everyone she saw, "Do you know Steven Covington? He was with Cobbs Georgians, wounded at Gettysburg." She was having no success and her time was running out. The detail of soldiers were rushing her, telling her to hurry and even Mr. Potter seemed irritated as though he couldn't wait to get out of there. But she was determined to check every building and ask every man she saw. She was beginning to feel slightly panicked when she had gotten to the next to the last building and still no one had any word of Steven. What if she were too late? What if her beloved Steven lay out back, already dead?

"It's time to go ma'am," one of the soldiers told her.

"Just a few minutes more," she pleaded. "I've nearly finished."

"Finished or not, the Major says you gotta go."

"Please! A few minutes!"

"Ma'am? You be Mrs. Covington, ma'am?" A thin man with a deep scar across his face had approached her. His Rebel uniform was so torn and dirty it was indistinguishable as being Confederate.

"Yes soldier, I'm Mrs. Covington," she answered him. He was no taller than she and could look him directly in the eyes.

"You be jes as purty as he said," the man told her smiling and showing a mouthful of missing teeth.

"You know Steven? You know where he is?" she asked excitedly. "Tell me where he is, please!"

"I knowed Steven," he said in a half whisper, "but he ain't here no more. He been gone fer a long time."

"What do you mean he's gone?" she asked anxiously, her heart pounding and the tears threatening to come. "Did he….did he die?" She could barely ask the words that stuck in her throat.

"Hell, no. Steven, he be too smart fer that. He done escaped."

"Escaped?" Colleen asked incredulously. It was a possibility she had not thought of; that he would be able to get out of this hellhole. "Are you sure, Steven Covington escaped from here?"

"Sure I'm sure and I helped," the man said chuckling.

"Twer Steven's idea to form a wood detail, get some of us prisoners to go outside the camp fer firewood. He even gots the commander to agree. I wuz part of the detail. We went outside the walls ever so offen to cut and gets wood. We did it for months. Steven had a plan. When the time wuz right and the signal was gived, we'd all make a run fer it. So when them stupid guards….." He looked quickly over at the soldiers who were glaring at him. "So when they all wuz not payin' no 'ttention, no how, the signal was gived and we all lit out. 'Course I twern't so lucky and got couch't agin, but ten men got away, Steven one of 'em." With this he slapped his knee and laughed.

"You're sure, you're sure Steven got away?" she asked nearly breathless.

"Sure as I'm standin' here a 'fore ya. I'll swear on the good name of President Davis. They even had dogs, a whole company of men out lookin' fer 'im, but they didn't gets 'em."

"When did this happen?" she asked. "When did he get away?"

"Um, twas last year May. Like I says, it be a while back."

Colleen took his hand, not caring that it was dirty and crusty. "Thank-you, sir. You have helped more than you could know. I am so grateful to you. Thank-you."

"It's alright. I'se jes glad I could help. I sure hope you finds 'im."

Colleen turned and walked out, leaving the compound, her head spinning. He had been out for nearly a year, a year ago while she was fighting in the Wilderness. Where was he? Had he gone home, been captured again and gone to another prison, or had he rejoined his company or was he out there on the road somewhere? She knew it was possible she might never find the answers. There were families north and south whose loved one would never come home, whose body was never identified and buried in some of those vast graves she had seen, or lost and wounded in the woods, only to die there alone.

She and Mr. Potter mounted their horses upon returning to Major Brady's headquarters, the commander himself standing in the open doorway, smiling as though he were pleased she had not found Steven. They rode out and headed back towards Leonard Town where they had started.

Once they had lost sight of the camp and were again in the trees, Colleen began to cry. And once she had started, she couldn't seem to stop; great wrenching sobs that shook her body and tore her soul. She had not allowed herself to cry for a long time and now it was as if the floodgates had burst open. She felt as though all her efforts had been for nothing, the disguise, the fighting she had done, the horrors she had witnessed, all to find Steven and now he was gone and she knew not where to look.

Mr. Potter handed her his handkerchief and patted her hand as they rode along. "I'm so sorry, my dear," he told her. "I know you've been searching for him for a long time and were hoping to finally find him. But my dear, at least he's not suffering in that hellhole. My god, what an awful place!"

She nodded, unable to answer him. The tears flowed for many more minutes. She cried for Steven, for the insanity of this war, for all the men, women and children who had died and for herself. "I just don't know where to go from here," she said finally, wiping her eyes and blowing her nose.

"You'll come on home with me," he told her, "back to Stratford Hall in Virginia. Perhaps your husband has made it back home to Georgia. We'll try to contact someone down there by wire. There might be someone who could find out for you."

She nodded and a thread of hope remained. Perhaps he had made it home. "Thank-you," she told him.

Once they had crossed back over the river and gotten back to Mr. Potter's estate in Virginia, they had gone to the telegraph office and tried to wire for information. But of course, the nearest telegraph office to Shannon was in Savannah and the only information they could obtain was what Mr. Potter had already found out; her family's assets, how much land they owned, the number of slaves, etc. But there seemed to be no way to get a message all the way to Shannon. Atlanta had fallen; Savannah was now occupied; Union troops were everywhere in the state. Rebel soldiers were desperately trying to defend remaining territory and everywhere there was chaos.

Mr. Potter did ask for a messenger to be sent with the information that Colleen was at Stratford Hall and asking if Steven had returned home, but they knew not if messengers were available to perform such a task with all the telegraph offices now occupied by Federal troops.

When it became apparent that it would be impossible to find out if Steven had returned to Georgia, Colleen wanted to leave immediately to go home. But Mr. Potter would not allow her to leave on such a journey across several states in the middle of warfare, alone. It was true there had been increased activity in the Richmond area. Grant was moving closer to try and take the Confederate capitol, while Lee was on the defensive protecting it near Petersburg.

The roads leading out of Virginia were not safe for anyone, let alone a woman. Mr. Potter had also argued that spring could bring severe weather with hard rains, causing some roads to become impassable with flooded streams and rivers. The cold had also been a factor to be reckoned with. He insisted she stay with them until they could be assured that travel would be safe enough for her to attempt a trip back to her home. He had even suggested that she shouldn't go unless someone in her family came to Virginia to assure her safe passage. She suspected he did not want her to leave until he had been compensated for his expenses and troubles in caring for her and searching for Steven. She wondered if he would resort to keeping her captive in order to assure himself of his reward.

Colleen felt frustrated and depressed. If it was possible that Steven could be home, she was anxious to continue on with her journey, but she still hadn't come up with a plan as how to get back to Georgia. It was now 1865, four long years and still the war went on with more death and destruction. But she wasn't ready to give up. If nothing else, she felt even more determined.

Steven watched the winter of 64-65 from the relative comfort of the Jeffries home. It was colder than any he could remember, even when he had been holed up with the army. At times it would rain steadily and then shift over to snow, freezing everything solid. He thought about the soldiers still out in the field with their clothes in tatters and many barefoot. He knew of men who had slept in trees to stay up off the frozen ground. How many more would die because of the severe weather conditions?

It was late February and as Steven peered through the frost-encrusted pane of glass, he felt despondent. The South was losing the war. That he knew. Hundreds of Confederates were deserting every day, cold, hungry and desperate to go home to their families. Lee's army was shrinking while Grants was growing, ever pushing against their weary troops still fighting at Petersburg.

President Lincoln had just been re-elected to office and to help further destroy the Union of the Confederacy, Washington's congress had passed the Thirteenth Amendment, to abolish slavery. The thing the big plantation owners had feared, was becoming a reality; the loss of their labor.

Besides the mass of deserters from the army, there had also been a huge increase in Confederate refugees, families fleeing further south, hoping to find safety and a new start, while others were flocking to Richmond, hoping the government and President Davis could protect them. It was happening before their eyes; the Confederacy was falling apart. After the invasion of Georgia and the rampage of Sherman and his troops, the governor of that state was threatening to secede from the Confederacy.

"Tea?" a voice said behind him. He turned to see Mr. Jeffries holding out a cup of steaming liquid.

"Yes, thank-you," he told him taking the cup. It felt warm on his chilled hand.

"Do you think this cold weather will break soon?" Stewart asked as they began walking towards the dining room. Most of the house had been closed off to keep from heating such a large area. Only the fireplaces in the parlor, dining room and kitchen were kept going and then at night, in the bedrooms. Most of the servants who had not already run away or been freed by the Yankees, were sleeping on beds in the large kitchen as there was no extra wood to heat their cabins.

"I hope so," Steven responded to his question. "I want to get back to Georgia as soon as possible and I can't do that until the roads are at least passable. Of course, when I was fighting in the war, we would trod though mud nearly knee deep, through swamps and bogs with mosquitoes big as birds. Even horses got mired down. But I wouldn't recommend those conditions for travel."

"I can imagine you must desperately want to get back to your wife," Stewart said as they joined Grace at the table. "Four years is a very long time."

"Yes it is and I do want to go back to Colleen, more now than ever before. While I was fighting, there was a cause, a reason to stay. I had my friends and comrades around me and we believed in what we were doing, because if we didn't, who would? Then of course when I was a prisoner, I couldn't go home, but now that I am free and not fighting any longer, it seems that all these other external circumstances conspire to keep me from home. It's very frustrating."

Stewart nodded sympathetically. "My understanding is that the railroad from Richmond to Petersburg is still open, but of course that whole area is surrounded by Federal and Confederate troops. There is still fighting going on."

"I'm not afraid of going into an area of battle, but past Petersburg there are no more rails and it's still hundreds of miles to Savannah across two states. With my weak leg, I don't know how long it would take me."

"Oh, Steven, you wouldn't have to walk," Grace told him. "You could take one of our horses."

"You have already been so kind to put me up for this long, I couldn't take one of your three remaining horses."

"When winter passes and the roads are fit for travel, we will discuss this again. Now let's eat," Stewart said with finality.

At night when Steven slept, he frequently dreamed of being in battle, of the rush of troops across a wide field, the thud of bullets hitting flesh, the stench of burned powder in the air. Again he would feel the hot flare of a shell, the ground rumbling beneath his feet, the fear that always threatened to overpower him. He would see men blown to pieces, piles of amputated arms and legs and rivers of blood. He heard the screaming of dieing men and the cries of those who loved them. He would wake in a sweat, shaking, breathless.

At other times he dreamed of Colleen, seeing her as an apparition that always seemed to be out of reach. He would call to her, but she would not answer, disappearing before his eyes. He felt his heart aching for her, reaching for her, wanting to hold her in his arms, to kiss her beautiful mouth and make love to her.

March 31st 1865

The entire month of March had been one day after another of steady rain. As Colleen watched the downpour from the veranda of the Potter's house, she knew she could wait no longer to go home. She had felt like a prisoner here, being cared for only for the reward that would result. Mr. Potter had given her excuse after excuse why she shouldn't go and even though some of them were legitimate, she didn't care anymore. Even if there were dangers, even if she had to walk all the way back to Georgia, she knew she had to go. She had been thinking of it for some weeks now, formulating a plan. She knew she could expect no help from Mr. Potter; he didn't want her to go. It was as if he were holding her hostage. He wouldn't allow her to leave until he had collected his money from her father.

She would have to slip out unaware. She seemed to be good at it. It meant leaving under cover of darkness when the residents of the house were asleep. She would begin gathering supplies for her journey; fortunately she still had her rifle and haversack. Mr. Potter had at one time, suggested she rid herself of them, claiming she no longer needed them, but she had been insistent on keeping them. Once she was as prepared as she could be, she would slip out and head south.

She knew the heaviest fighting was still around the Petersburg area so she would attempt to go around that town. She wondered sometimes if Patrick were still there, still fighting with General Lee. She didn't want to think about anything happening to him. When those thoughts broke into her mind, she would quickly push them away.

She didn't relish the idea of walking all the way back to Georgia, but if it was what she had to do, she would do it. Steven could already be there and she was determined to get home to him.

She had suddenly thought of a family in Virginia her father knew, someone he had done business with, had bought slaves from and even been school chums with. She thought she remembered where they were, not far from where she was now. She wished she had thought of them sooner. Perhaps she could have been home by now. She thought if she could find them, they might be able to help her, perhaps lend her a horse for her journey. Their name was Jeffries.

March 31st 1865

Steven was nearly ready to go. The Jeffries had helped to supply him with food and clothing for his trip. They were also giving him the loan of one of their horses. He could wait no longer; his desire to get home to Colleen was becoming more than he could bear.

He was in his room checking his knapsack, making sure he had everything he needed. It wouldn't be long before he would see his sweet Colleen again. He calculated it would take him several weeks of steady travel to reach Georgia, but at least this time he was able to ride. There had been so much walking all those years in the war. He reflected on how it seemed everything reminded him of something of the war.

There was a knock at the door and Stewart Jeffries entered the room, carrying a rifle and a box. “Steven, I kept the rifle you brought with you and I thought you might need some more ammunition.” He handed them over to Steven.

Steven took the rifle, feeling the weight of it, the coldness on his palm. He would never again hold a rifle without thinking of the men he had killed; of firing the weapon over and over until the barrel was hot and smoke filled the air, until everyone of the enemy in front of him was dead.

“Thank-you,” he told Stewart. “You have been so kind to put me up all these months. I will try to repay you somehow.”

“It’s been a pleasure having you here. It’s the least I could do for your father. He was a good friend. I only wish you would stay a bit longer. This damn war is bound to be over soon.”

Steven shook his head. “No, Lee will keep on fighting. Too many southerners still believe in the cause and as long as there are those who will still fight, I’m afraid this war will go on. If I were able, I think I too would go back and fight.”

Stewart saw the sadness in his eyes, the pain of the things experienced and he could only nod. “Well, you will do what you must and I don't blame you for wanting to get home to your wife.

Do you know when you will leave?"

"In a few days. I hope the rain will stop by then and the roads will dry up, but I'm going regardless."

The following day they began to hear cannon fire from the direction of Richmond and then word came that Lee's lines had been broken, their numbers depleted and stretched beyond their limits and the Yankees were headed for the capital. The citizens there had been told to evacuate and it wasn't long before they began to see every means of conveyance; wagons, buckboard, carriage, dray and mules, carrying people and their possessions, passing by the Jeffries Plantation, all on their way to someplace else. All those who had fled there for safety, were now on the move again, headed south, trying to get away from the Union troops.

Steven wondered what Lee would do now. Would he regroup, call in more troops from General Gordon's regiment? Would he be able to retake Richmond?

The rain had stopped for now and the sun had come out, helping to dry the muddy roads. It would be only a matter of days now before he would leave on his journey back home.

April 6th 1865

Colleen's haversack was filled. She had extra ammunition and her gun were all under her bed, ready to go. It had been fairly easy to obtain the supplies. She had wandered into the kitchen on occasions where rolls and loaves of bread would be cooling. She simply slipped one or two into the folds of her skirt and took it back to her room, wrapping them in clean linens. Sometimes it was an apple she confiscated or a few raw vegetables. To find the ammunition, she had gone into Mr. Potter's library when he had gone off on one of his dealmakers; another scheme to swindle someone out of their money and found a gun cabinet stocked with rifles and ammunition. There she had found her own, the one she had carried through her time in the war. This she took, along with some ammunition for it.

She had everything she needed and was anxious to get started. She would leave that evening after everyone had gone to sleep. She was nervous that night at dinner, but she tried not to show it, smiling, talking amicably with the Potters. After eating as they were drinking their tea, Mr. Potter told her he had heard Richmond had fallen. The Yankees were now in the city.

At first she didn't know how to respond, her mouth hanging open. Finally she composed herself and said something appropriate such as, "How awful," but she knew she could wait no longer.

She lay in her bed that night waiting for the house to grow quiet. She judged it to be around 2:00 A.M. when she finally slipped out of bed and dressed quickly. She pulled the haversack out from under the bed and slung it over her shoulder. Then she wrapped a bedroll across this and lastly grasped her rifle. She tiptoed from the room, carrying her shoes so they would not make a sound on the wood floors; going down the wide staircase near the railing. Once a loud squeak issued forth from one of the steps and her heart nearly stopped beating. She stood still and listened. She heard nothing and continued on. Painfully slow, she opened the heavy front door, praying the hinges had been oiled recently. She slipped outside, closing the door behind her. Then, only stopping to put on her shoes, she went down the path to the road heading south. She was on her way to find the Jeffries.

She traveled all day, stopping to rest and eat on the way. She had even gotten a ride for a short time by a couple fleeing south. This time no one questioned a woman alone or that she carried a gun. Things were in chaos; there were Yankees about.

By the second day she felt she was nearing the Jeffries plantation and began asking those she met on the road if they knew of it. Finally she met someone who had delivered supplies to the Jeffries at one time. He gave her the directions to Paradise. She was only a few miles away.

April 8th 1865

Steven had been delayed again by the invasion of Richmond by the Yankees. Even though he now wore civilian clothes, he did not want to be mistaken for a Confederate spy and sent back to prison. He didn't think he could bear that. They had heard horror stories from some who had passed by their door, of their own soldiers blowing up the arsenal before abandoning the town, of shells exploding, setting buildings on fire. And then company after company of the blue coats converging on them, tearing down the Stars and Bars and running up their own flag, the stars and stripes of the Union. Some told how they wept when they witnessed their flag being torn down. They also heard that President Davis had fled some days before, fleeing further south, fearing if caught he would be imprisoned and executed.

But now Steven was ready. He was to leave the following morning. There was to be no more delays, no more excuses. It was time to go home.

Just as he was about to climb the stairs to his room, there was a knock at the door. Stewart called out to Steven from the back of the house to answer it, as he was busy. Steven walked to the entrance thinking it was another refugee looking for help. He opened the door and saw a woman standing there. She had a haversack slung over one shoulder and carried a musket. He looked into her face and staggered back, grabbing the door jam for support; before him stood his beloved Colleen.

When the door opened, she had expected to see an older man or perhaps a Negro servant, but instead a young man answered her knock. Her eyes widened, her heart pounded and a scream escaped her lips when she realized it was Steven standing there only a foot away. She dropped her gun and threw herself into his arms.

He embraced her, holding her tighter than he had ever held her before. He finally had her in his arms and he never wanted to let her go. "Oh, my god Colleen," his voice was a whisper, the tears coming to his eyes. "Colleen, Colleen my darling."

She began to cry as well, holding on, realizing how long she had been waiting for this moment. Her knees felt weak and if Steven hadn't been holding her so tightly, she would have collapsed.

Finally he released her, holding her face in his hands. The face he had dreamed of so many times for the last four years. "My god, Colleen." He didn't seem able to say anything else; he was so overwhelmed. And then he kissed her finally, at last, tasting her tears, the sweetness of her mouth.

"How? What are you doing here?" he finally stammered.

"Steven, you're alive!" Colleen cried. "You're really alive! I wasn't sure. I went to the prison where you'd been and they told me you'd escaped, but that was nearly a year ago and I didn't know if you'd gone home or back to the army, or if you were dead." She knew she was babbling but she couldn't seem to stop. She was so excited she was trembling. She couldn't believe he was actually here.

"You went to the prison? How did you manage that?"

"It's a long story and I will tell you all of it. But please, right now just hold me and kiss me."

Steven placed his mouth on hers, tenderly, sensuously, longingly and she kissed him back as if she would never stop.

"Steven? Who is at the door?" They heard Stewart's voice behind them. They broke away from each other reluctantly and turned to face him.

"It's Colleen, Stewart, my wife. She's here," Steven told him smiling.

"But how my dear?" he asked. "How did you find your way to Virginia and how did you know Steven was here?"

"I didn't know. It was just a coincidence. I happened to remember my father doing business with you and I thought I would stop for help back to Georgia. I was hoping Steven had gone home," she said looking into his eyes.

"Oh, my lord," Stewart exclaimed. "It's providence, that's what it is. It's providence! Well, don't stand there on the doorstep. Come in, come in."

She stepped on into the house and Steven bent to pick up her haversack and rifle that had fallen there. "When did you start carrying a gun?" he asked her. "Is it for protection? I didn't even know you knew how to use one."

She smiled. "Oh yes, better than you know. It comes in handy when you're fightin' Yanks."

"Yanks? What do you mean fightin'? You ran into soldiers on your way here?"

She nodded as they walked towards the parlor. Steven had his arm around her, not wanting to let her go. They sat down and she continued with her story. "I fought Yankees at Cickamauga, the Wilderness, Petersburg….."

"Wait, wait," Steven said. "I don't understand. How did you fight in all those places? Those were battles fought by the Army of Virginia."

"I was there, dressed as a man. In September of '63, I cut off my hair, dressed in men's clothing and joined the army. I fought with Lee's army for over a year."

"My god!" Steven looked completely stunned and Stewart was laughing. "Why, why would you do such a thing?"

"To find you. We got word you had been wounded and taken prisoner. I thought at the time, it was the right thing to do."

Stewart was still chuckling, shaking his head. "And you pulled it off! What a woman!"

Steven put his hand on her cheek. "Yes, what a woman. But why would you take such a risk? You could have been killed!"

"Because I love you so and I couldn't just go on not knowing where you were."

Steven wiped at the tears that ran down his cheeks. "You went through all that, fighting as a man, seeing all those horrors of war, because of me?"

Colleen nodded. "It was horrible, but I'm not hurt and we're together again and I'm never going to let you go again." She took his hands in her own and squeezed them hard.

"It looks to me like the two of you have a lot of catching up to do," Stewart said standing. "It's wonderful to have you here, Colleen. I'm so happy the two of you have finally found each other again." He walked out of the room talking to himself, "fought in the war. My god, a woman soldier!"

For the rest of the evening, they talked and talked, telling each other what they could of what had happened to them since the war began four years before. There was so much to catch up on, so much time lost. Steven told her a little of what he had experienced inside the prison and of his and Tom's escape.

"I know one thing," Steven told her, "I don't think I could ever own slaves again. I know now what it feels like to be held against your will; not to be free." He paused for a moment and then looked down at his hands. "I was with Gerritt when he died," he told her as they sat on the bed in Steven's room. "I held him in my arms. I promise you, he didn't suffer. I'm just sorry I wasn't able to bring his body home." His voice choked on the words.

Colleen only nodded, the tears coming to her eyes thinking of her dear brother. "You don't have to apologize to me. I know what it was like out there."

"I guess you would. I still have to get use to that; you fighting in the war. How were you able to fool everyone? You certainly look like a woman to me."

"Well, as I said, I cut my hair, I bound my breasts and wore men's clothing and of course I never took them off in front of anyone." He could only shake his head.

"I'm so sorry about your father," she said. "We had a funeral for him. Your mother came to stay with us after that. She was well when I left.

Tell me how you were wounded. Was it very bad?"

So he explained the circumstances surrounding his wounding at Gettysburg, showing her his leg with the deep scaring and deformity of the skin.

She tentatively reached out and gently touched the scars, tracing the lines down the length of his leg. Tears filled her eyes. "You might have died," she whispered. "And I certainly seem to be crying a lot for being so happy. I guess it's just because I have all these emotions inside of me I don't know what to do with. I'm so happy to be here with you and I'm sad too, for all the horrible things that have happened."

"From now on we'll be together. We'll go home and start our lives over. We'll put all of this behind us and be happy." He kissed her then, gently, tenderly, then more passionately, his lips trailing down to her throat and then the top of her breasts.

She felt the gooseflesh stand out on her skin as Steven's kisses continued down between her breasts. She began to unbutton his shirt, pulling it off his shoulders. She ran her hands over his chest, his shoulders and muscular arms. It felt so good to touch him again.

He pulled her dress down to her waist, caressing her breasts, her arms, then taking her hands in his, he turned them palms up and kissed them, felt the roughness, the calluses there. Again he was reminded of what she had gone through to find him. It only made his love for her stronger.

Soon they had removed the remainder of their clothing and were lying together beneath the cool linens. They stroked and kissed one another, their passions rising.

"Oh god, Colleen, I can't tell you how long I've dreamed of this day when I could hold you in my arms again and make love to you."

Colleen could feel his excitement, his hardness and she wanted to feel him inside of her. She stroked his hair and kissed his mouth, pulling him over her. His breathing was rapid and he was trembling. When he entered her she cried out; not from pain but from joy. Their ecstasy peaked until they were both fulfilled. Afterward, they lay entwined in one another's arms, their heart rates slowing.

Steven stroked her arm, noticing the darkness of her skin on her forearms, while the upper portion remained soft and white. He kissed the top of her head, smelling the scent of her. He thought of her fighting in that cruel war with its horrendous loss of life, the maiming and brutality and he didn't know how she could have endured it. She was so much stronger that he ever had imagined.

"I'll never be separated from you again," he told her. "I don't care if the whole world goes to war, I'll never leave you."

"I love you so much, Steven," she told him. "If you did go, I would follow you to the ends of the earth." They made love again and then fell asleep in each other's arms

During the night Steven's dreams were disturbed by visions of horror and he awoke with a cry, but Colleen was there to hold him, to comfort him with understanding.

The following day April 9th, word came that General Lee had surrendered to General Grant at a place south and west of Richmond called Appomattox. The war was over.

Steven put his face in his hands as he sat in the parlor after hearing the news. So many feelings swept over him. In one sense he felt a huge relief; now the killing would end. But on the other hand, the cause they were fighting for had also come to an end. There was no more Confederacy, no President Davis, no slavery, no more life as they had once known it. They had lost. It was as if everything had been for nothing; the fighting, the killing, the soldiers starving and freezing. Four long years and they had accomplished nothing.

Colleen stroked his hair and then got on her knees in front of him, taking his hands from his face. "I know this is difficult, but let's just go home, like you said it, start over. The Confederacy fought long and hard. There is honor in that, but we couldn't win. We don't have the resources and to continue would only cause more to die, to suffer. Now it's time for us to begin our lives together."

"Yes, yes, you're right. We'll go home."

"Two days later, they finally set out for home. Stewart gave them the loan of a buggy and horse. He stood on the veranda as they prepared to leave. "I can't thank-you enough for your kindness," Steven told him. "Even when supplies were short, you still took me in. I will always be in your debt."

"Just get yourself and this beautiful young woman home safely," Stewart said, his hand on Steven's shoulder.

"Thank-you sir," Colleen said waving. "We'll try to wire you when we get back."

Steven snapped the reins and clucked to the horse as they began their journey home. They took the main road and later they had to pass through Richmond. Yankees were all over the city, making them uncomfortable. These were the men that not long ago, they had faced across the battlefield. They saw the American flag flying over the courthouse just as they had been told. On the other side of the city they were shocked at the devastation. Whole buildings had been bombed out, burned down, small fires still burning. They barely spoke to each other as they drove slowly through the former Confederate capitol, the symbol of their cause, now in ruins.

Steven and Colleen spent the night outside of town, alongside the road with other refugees. Everyone was on their way back to their homes, not even knowing if they were still there. All the talk around the campfire was of Lee's surrender and the end of the war. Some were relieved that the fighting was over. Others were sad at the loss of their newly acquired union, of the horrific losses, only to fail.

As Colleen and Steven sat on the ground, wrapped together in the same blanket, the horse munching grass nearby, Colleen saw Steven smiling. "What are you smiling about?" she asked him.

"I was just trying to imagine you dressed as a man, living out of doors, bathing in rivers and sleeping on the ground." He touched her face. "My beautiful, spoiled, southern belle."

"I was a good soldier," she told him seriously. "I did my share."

"I have no doubt. If you could do everything you have to find me, you are a mighty strong woman. I believe you could do anything you set your mind to."

In the morning they continued their journey south, the sun shinning brightly in the sky. Not a cloud was in sight, the sky an azure blue. They neared Petersburg, the scene of many months of battle, the place where it had all come to an end, that horrible place of death where Colleen had finally left the army and the last place she had seen Patrick. She wondered where he was now, if he had survived to see the end.

They came upon a large Union camp just outside the city. Colleen and Steven pulled to the side of the road as they watched the men tearing down tents, filling wagons and packing supplies. Over a rise in the road came an entire regiment in gray, Confederate soldiers, being led by an officer on horseback. The officer wore a clean, but faded uniform, sitting straight in the saddle. He had a neatly trimmed beard, short with a small point below his chin.

"That's General Gordon," Steven told Colleen as more and more of the Rebel soldiers poured over the road, marching straight, eyes forward carrying the stars and bars, their regimental and company flags. There were even cavalry on horseback; the horses gaunt, their bones showing through the flesh. A drummer and a man playing the fife led them, the men singing "Dixie".

"I know," she said quietly. "I served under him as well."

He could only look at her in wonder, knowing it would take time to get use to this idea of her fighting.

General Gordon reined in his horse before the Union General, also on horseback. He had not known his face, only his reputation. He was General Chamberlain.

General Chamberlain signaled for the bugler to call out formation. The Union soldiers lined up, facing their former enemy. They stared at each other, everyone noticing the differences; the blue uniforms clean, with shinny brass buttons. Their guns were held at attention, the bayonets fixed and glinting in the sunlight.

The Confederates stood tall, looking their victors in the eyes, but their uniforms were torn, dirty, some not completely covering their thin bodies. Most were not recognizable as uniforms and most of the men were barefoot. Their faces were drawn with sunken eyes and dark circles under them. Their hair and beards were long and unkempt. But they stood proud, the strength still in their eyes.

An order was given and the men in gray began to stack their arms, pyramid shaped with bayonets skyward. Next came the ammunition boxes, stacked next to the rifles. Lastly, the man holding their flag, the red and blue stars and bars came forward, allowing it to flutter in the wind one last time before draping it over the pointed bayonets.

Colleen and Steven were close enough to see the tears running down the man's face. Then others came forward, each one touching the flag, sobbing, kneeling before it. Then again they all took their place in line. No one had said a word; the men in blue standing across from them with agonized looks on their faces, some with tears shinning in their own eyes.

"We've lost," Steven said next to her. And when she looked over at him she saw the tears on his face, felt the trembling of his body. "It was all for nothing."

She placed her hand on his arm. "We are one again," she told him, "joined under one flag."

"Their flag," he said almost angrily.

"There is no 'their' or 'they' any longer," she told him. "They and we are one. That flag," she said pointing at the Stars and Stripes, "has always stood for bravery, for men and women willing to fight and die for what they believed in. When we were together and settled this country, when we fought for our freedom in the Revolutionary War. It still does, for all of us."

Steven nodded finally. He knew what she said was true. Then they heard another command and all the men in blue held their muskets to their chests, a salute of respect to their brothers.

"It's time for us to go," she told Steven and he nodded. He clucked to the horse and he started off down the road, past the soldiers, the victors and the defeated, back to Georgia and their home, back to start over, to mend what the war had torn apart.

The war was over and the beast was gone.

About the Author

Linda Penninga lives with her family in Grand Rapids, Michigan. Her formal education was in the medical field, but has always been a voracious writer. This is her fourth book and the first of her published work.

Printed in the United States
41016LVS00001B/3